Nerve Damage

Nerve Damage

Peter Abrahams

HARPER LUXE

An Imprint of HarperCollinsPublishers

FOR MOLLY FRIEDRICH

This book is a work of fiction. The characters, incidents, and dialogue are drawn from the author's imagination and are not to be construed as real. Any resemblance to actual events or persons, living or dead, is entirely coincidental.

FIRST HARPERLUXE EDITION

Library of Congress Cataloging-in-Publication Data
Abrahams, Peter, 1947–
    Nerve damage : a novel / Peter Abrahams.—1st ed.
        p.   cm.
    ISBN: 978-0-06-113797-6
    ISBN-10: 0-06-113797-9
    1. Terminally ill—Fiction.   2. Spouses—Fiction.   I. Title.
PS3551.B64N47 2007
813'.54—DC22

                                        2006047092

ISBN: 978-0-06-123318-0 (Luxe)
ISBN-10: 0-06-123318-8

07 08 09 10 11   ID/RRD   10 9 8 7 6 5 4 3 2 1

What comes out in the end is the result
of discarded finds.

—PICASSO

Many thanks to
JEFF ABRAHAMS, DAVID CHAPMAN,
NIKI COHEN, NICK FOTIU
AND JEFF MACKILLIGAN

One

Sometimes the dead live on in your dreams. Delia was very much alive now, sitting on a terrace wall high above a tropical bay, bare legs dangling. She'd never looked better—her tanned skin firm and glowing; her eyes, light brown with flecks of gold, narrowing in the way they did when she was about to say something funny. Her mouth opened—sunlight glinting on her lip gloss—and Delia did speak, but too soft to hear. That was maddening. Then came the realization from a nondreaming brain region that this glittering bay lay somewhere on the Venezuelan coast, and all that tropical sunshine went dim. Venezuela: the word alone was still destabilizing.

A vein throbbed just under the skin of Delia's temple, a prominent blue vein shaped like a bolt of lightning. The weather changed at once, a cold breeze springing up and ruffling her hair. Things were going bad. Roy reached over to smooth out the ruffles, but the hair he felt was not Delia's; finer, and straight instead of curly.

He opened his eyes. Wintry light, frost on the window, posters of ski racers on the walls: Jen's room.

"I always hated when men did that," Jen said, her voice still husky with sleep.

Roy turned his head. The eyes that watched him— pale blue, not brown—were very pretty in their own way. "Did what?" he said.

"Touched my hair."

He withdrew his hand. Blond hair, not brown; that special brown, also flecked with gold.

"But with you it's okay." Jen waited, maybe for him to say or do something. Roy couldn't think of anything. Their faces were a foot apart. Jen was very good-looking, her skin a little roughened from the weather, but that only made Roy like it more. What was left of the dream broke into tiny pieces and vanished.

"You feeling all right?" Jen said.

"Fine."

Under the covers she moved her leg against his. "I had some news yesterday. Out of the blue."

"Good news?" said Roy.

"I think so—it's a job offer."

"What job?"

"Like what I'm doing now," Jen said. She ran the ski school at Mount Ethan, twenty minutes from her condo. "But on a much bigger scale, and it pays twice the money."

"Where?" Roy said, thinking Stowe, close by, or maybe Killington, a little farther.

Jen looked away. "Keystone," she said.

"That's in Colorado?"

She nodded. Then her eyes were meeting his again, maybe trying to see inside, to read him.

"Well," Roy said. And came very close to following that with *Why don't we get married?* Why not? They'd been like this for two years, somewhere between dating and living together. Was there a reason not to take the next step? No lack of comfort between them, no lack of affection, sexual heat. An age difference, yes—he was almost forty-seven, Jen was thirty-four—plus she wanted kids and he no longer did, but so what? Roy found himself smiling at her.

"Well what?" she said.

And was just about to speak the words—*why don't we get married?*—when the thought came that blurting it out right now might not be the way to go. He could do better than that. And wouldn't a more formal presentation—at Pescatore, say, Friday night—be better? So, for now, he just said, "Congratulations."

"Congratulations?"

"On this job offer."

"Oh," Jen said. "Thanks. I'll have to think about it, of course. Colorado's far away."

"I understand," Roy said, realizing from that last remark about the distance that on Friday she was going to say yes. Two days away. He felt pretty crafty.

Jen got up and went into the bathroom. The moment he heard the shower, Roy picked up the phone and reserved Pescatore's best table for seven-thirty Friday night. As he hung up, a memory dropped into place: his only other proposal of marriage. Nighttime, in the tiny bedroom of the Foggy Bottom apartment, the first place that had ever been his own, a blue light from a passing squad car down on H Street flashing on Delia's face. That time he'd just blurted it out.

Roy lived in a converted barn halfway up the east side of the Ethan Valley, originally a vacation place he and Delia bought cheap. No money back then—Delia was still new at the Hobbes Institute, a think tank specializing in third-world economic problems, and Roy's work hadn't started to sell. A falling-down barn, complete with bat colony and a hippie squatter: Delia's face lit up at first sight. They fixed it up themselves, meaning Roy did the fixing while Delia made impossible suggestions, kind of like a princess in a fairy tale. That side of her—this was not long after Delia got her PhD in economics from Georgetown—was something she showed only to him. As for the actual renovation, Roy didn't need any help. He'd always been good with his hands. Other sculptors he knew had learned welding for their art; he was the only one who'd gone the other way, working every summer through high school and college at King's Machining and Metal Work up in the little Maine town he came from.

Right now—a few hours after leaving Jen's—he was stuck in the middle of a kind of broken arch made mostly of old car radiators welded at the corners, each one turned at a slightly different angle in a way that was reminding him of stop-motion photography, an effect he hadn't intended and wasn't sure he liked. Also, he was eighteen feet off the ground—near the top of the ladder, getting close to the roof of the barn, oxygen and acetylene tanks strapped to his back in a converted scuba pack contraption—and the arching part had barely begun. Roy stood there, one hand on the ladder, one on the torch, waiting for an idea. He could feel shapes forming here and there in his mind, but they refused to come out of the shadows, be visible, let him get his hands on them. Way down below, the phone began to ring.

The answering machine picked up. "Hey," said Murph, owner of Murph's Salvage and Wrecking, and Roy's biggest supplier, "Murph here. Maybe got something for you." *Click.*

Roy climbed down the ladder. A very strange thing happened on the last step: he lost his breath. Roy was in such good shape, had been in such good shape for so long, that he almost couldn't put a name to it: just a common everyday thing, losing your breath. Had he been easing up on his routine? The day before he'd run from the barn to the cross-country ski parking lot and back, seven miles, and on Sunday he'd snowshoed all morning on the lower ridge loop, passing a whole group of college-age snowshoers in some race he hadn't known about. So—was he nervous about Friday night? Had to be it. A man was never too old to get nervous: annoying in a counterintuitive way, but true, at least in his case.

Late in the afternoon, Roy drove down the valley to Murph's. That meant passing the green in Ethan Center. *Neanderthal Number Nineteen,* last in the series that had made his name, stood at one end. He'd given it to the town not long after Delia's death. Roy liked seeing it in winter, when snow rounded the flat surfaces, somehow bringing out all the Neanderthal characteristics. Characteristics he hadn't intended, not consciously: the series title—and the very notion of seeing something Neanderthaly in those huge forms— had been Delia's; the main reason, Roy had always thought, that the series, and his whole career, took off.

"Little snort?" said Murph. They sat in his office, overlooking the yard. Without waiting for an answer, Murph splashed Jack Daniel's into two mismatched mugs, slid the one with the Valvoline logo across the desk to Roy. "You, Skippy?" Murph called over his shoulder.

"Me what?" said Skippy, hunched over a computer in the corner. Skippy was Murph's nephew, a pimply-faced kid who'd dropped out of Valley High School a few weeks before.

"Little snort," said Murph.

"Uh, take a pass," said Skippy, tapping at the oil-stained keys.

Murph raised his mug. "Here's to salvage."

"Salvage," said Roy. *Clink.*

"Just wait'll you see," Murph said.

"What is it?" said Roy. He peered through the grimy windows. A light snow was falling on the acres of junk and wrecks in Murph's yard, everything tinged orange by the sun just going down behind the mountains on the west side.

"You're not gonna believe it," Murph said.

"Try me," said Roy.

"Skippy," said Murph. "G'wan out to the yard, bring back that thing."

"Thing?" said Skippy.

"For Mr. Valois. What we were talking about before, for Christ sake."

Skippy rolled back his chair and clomped out the door, boots untied, greasy hair in his eyes.

"My sister's kid," Murph said.

"I know."

"Dropped out."

"I heard."

"What am I gonna do with him?"

The door opened and Skippy came back, snowflakes in his hair and a twisted hunk of steel in his hands. He laid it on the desk: a crown-shaped hunk of steel, almost a perfect circle, but much too big to fit a human head, formed from two braided and blackened . . . what?

"Recognize 'em?" said Murph.

"No."

"Coupla rotor blades," said Murph. "Off that chopper that went down over Mount Washington last month."

Roy picked it up: heavier than he'd imagined, and cold from lying in the yard. A strange combination of beauty and ugliness—*crown of thorns* was what he thought first, and then *wedding ring.*

"Just imagine the forces must of done this," said Murph. "Like here where it's all stretched." Murph made a cartoon noise like metal stretching.

Roy knew something about the forces unleashed in helicopter crashes. He put the thing down, hands not quite steady. "What's the price?" he said.

"Hey, Skippy," said Murph. "Didn't I tell you?"

Skippy, back at the computer, muttered, "Tell me what?"

"That he'd want it." Murph poured more Jack Daniel's. "I'm gettin' to be one of them art . . . what's the word?"

"Connoisseurs," said Skippy, not looking up.

Murph glanced at him, his bushy eyebrows rising. "Yeah, connoisseurs." He tapped the thing with the edge of a dirty fingernail. "How does twenty bucks sound?"

"Ten," said Roy.

They settled on fifteen.

Roy put the thing in the bed of his pickup, started to drive out of Murph's yard. But he hadn't even reached the gate before he found himself braking, as though his foot were doing the thinking. Roy got out and brought the thing inside the cab, laying it on the passenger seat. Not a thing, but a piece—the most important piece, he knew that already—in the broken-arch form that was rising in his barn. This crown, this ring, had a presence of its own. He could feel it, on the seat beside him.

A wild storm blew through the valley that night. Snow, sleet, back to snow, and enough wind to rattle the windows of the barn; but Roy, up on the ladder, was unaware. A broken arch of old radiators, a mangled ring of helicopter wreckage, even that stop-motion effect—everything worked, although the meaning came to him only gradually during the night. The challenge was to fight the tempting idea that those twisted rotor blades were the keystone to the arch, the missing piece that the broken arch was waiting for to make it whole. The arch was broken, would always be broken. The ring was nothing more than failed potential, just a dream. Therefore it couldn't fill the empty space in any symmetrical way, couldn't fit there comfortably. It had to not fit, to look fragile, like the whole structure could fall apart at any moment. How to make that happen was the problem.

Dawn, unnoticed by Roy, behind the dark visor, was glazing the windows in a milky light by the time he thought he'd solved it. The welds—he ended up using only three—were as crude, sloppy and obvious as he could make them, and the neatest he went at with a blowtorch, half severing the connection, going a little crazy with the heat, rescarring what was already so defaced. Then he did some more random blowtorching, just for the hell of it. A violent urge rose inside him, like he wanted to punch somebody in the face.

Sweat was dripping off Roy's face when he climbed down the ladder. He raised the visor, circled the base of this new work, studying it from all angles, especially the worst ones. He thought: *yes.* And then: *maybe.* Roy was still going back and forth when he finally glanced outside, saw the high drifts, trees down, big branches stuck in the snow like spears flung down by giants. That was when the title hit him: *Delia.* Not *Delia Number One:* this was beginning, middle and end. He began to understand what the piece was about: culmination. And therefore, at the same time he began to look forward to Friday night at Pescatore's, very much.

Roy shrugged off his backpack. He took a deep breath, one of those little physical expressions of satisfaction, completion, knowledge of earned rest in the offing. Letting out that breath, Roy felt a tiny tickle at the back of his throat. He coughed—just a little cough at first—and it made the tickle go away, but for some reason Roy couldn't stop coughing. He moved toward the kitchen, coughing and coughing, opened the tap and gulped down cold water.

That stopped the cough, but for only a second or two. Then came a deep, rending sound that tore through his throat, too powerful and urgent to be called a cough, and the water spewed back out. It thickened in the sink and turned red—pink at first, then crimson—running slowly down the drain.

The next breath Roy drew was normal; and the next, and the one after that. He tried to remember the last time he'd stayed up all night and couldn't. *Never again, old-timer.* A chain saw started up somewhere outside.

Two

"Wow," said Krishna Madapan, Roy's dealer, walking around *Delia*. Friday morning: the roads were clear again and Krishna had stopped in on his way from New York to Stowe for the weekend. He was dressed all in cosmopolitan black, as usual, although today he looked half country, half city, in ski pants and a mink coat. "May I venture an opinion, Roy?"

"What if I said no?" Roy said.

Krishna blinked—his only reaction whenever anything tried to knock him off the rails—and continued. "This is your best," he said. "No disparagement or denigration of any of your other works, you understand, but—simply your best."

"I don't know," Roy said, looking up at the piece; he was seeing nothing but flaws today.

"Of course you don't," said Krishna. "That is why you are what you are. And why I am what I am, I might add."

Roy didn't quite get that, but before he could ask for clarification, Krishna had pulled out his cell phone. "Who are you calling?" Roy said.

"My driver," said Krishna.

Roy glanced out the window, saw that Krishna was traveling by limo. The driver was just putting his newspaper aside and flipping open his own phone.

"Be a good fellow," Krishna told him, "and bring me my camera."

The driver made a face that only Roy saw. A few seconds later, he was coming up the path, camera in hand, slipping and sliding in his leather-soled city shoes. Krishna took pictures of *Delia* from many angles.

"This objet trouvé at the top," he said, "I cannot for the life of me identify."

Roy told him what it was.

"Ah," said Krishna, and gave Roy a quick sideways look. He'd known Delia; in fact, she'd brought the two of them together. "Your very best," Krishna said again, quietly now, possibly to himself, perhaps even moved. He pulled up the collar of the mink, as though the temperature had fallen. Then he noticed that the driver was gazing up at the sculpture, too, his mouth a little open. "What is your name, please?" he said.

"Luis," said the driver, turning quickly, as though caught doing something bad.

"And what do you think of this work of art, Luis?" Krishna said.

"Me?" said Luis.

"You."

Luis licked his lips. "Those are radiators, right?"

Krishna nodded. "Common automotive radiators."

"That's what I thought," said Luis. "But it's art anyway, huh?" He studied it for a moment. "Weird," he said.

"Weird how?" said Krishna.

"Weird how?" said Luis. He thought. "It kind of reminds me . . ." He lapsed into silence.

"Of?" said Krishna.

"This one rush hour on the L.I.E."

"The L.I.E.?" said Krishna.

"You know how it gets," said Luis. "But this was a few years ago, freezing rain. Everyone was going real slow, but it didn't do no good 'cause there was a big crack-up anyway—happened right in front of me—like in slow motion."

"A slow-motion crackup?" said Krishna. He gave Roy a significant look, as though he'd proved something.

A significant look misinterpreted by Luis. "I don't mean nothin' by it," he said. "Nothin' bad." He glanced at Roy. "You the artist?"

Roy nodded.

"No offense," Luis said.

"None taken," said Roy.

A good review, in fact. And coming from the limo driver, instead of some New York critic with God-knew-what agenda, maybe one to be treasured. Roy suddenly felt great, even better at that moment than when, on his way out the door a few minutes later, Krishna shook his hand and said: "This one will be in the first paragraph of your obituary, my friend. More important, I have some buyers in mind already. The fattest kind of fat-cat buyers." He laughed. Roy laughed, too: not from the prospect of a big sale—his needs were simple and he already had more than enough—but just because of how Krishna got so much fun out of life.

He walked them outside. Luis opened the rear door for Krishna. Krishna got in, carefully hiking up his mink coat. The door closed on a corner of it anyway, no one noticing except Roy.

He headed back up the path. Sections of *Delia* appeared in three windows, an effect that brought him to a stop. He was still standing there when a rusted-out sedan drove up, burning oil. Skippy got out.

"Mr. Valois?" he said, a breath cloud rising over his head.

"Yes?"

"Um." More breath clouds rose, like smoke signals.

"What's up, Skippy?"

Skippy cleared his throat. "The thing is, more or less, I had a look at your, you know, sculpture thing, the one over at the green." Pause. " 'Course I've seen it like a million times, going by. But yesterday I went and had a look, if you know what I mean."

"And?"

"And, um, Uncle Murph said you don't bite."

"I don't bite?"

" 'So why'nt you just go over and ask him? The worst that can happen he says no.' "

"Ask me what?"

"Yeah," said Skippy. "So which is why I'm here. Hope it's not a bad, um . . ."

This was getting a little unbearable, especially at three below. And Skippy—like most of the local boys and unlike all the skiers, antiques hunters and second-homers—didn't dress for the cold. Today he had on jeans, a light jacket, unzipped, and sneakers; no gloves, no hat, a runny nose.

"Come inside," Roy said.

"Yeah?" said Skippy. "Well, okay."

Skippy entered. He looked around. His gaze landed on *Delia,* and stayed there. "Hey," he said. "That's why you wanted all those rads."

"Yeah."

"And the rotor thing—it's way up there." Skippy moved around the base, head tilted way back, one or two teeth rotting already. "How high, anyway?"

"Twenty-four feet, two inches at the top of that bent blade," Roy said.

"Is this Number Twenty?" Skippy said. "In the *Neanderthals?*"

"No."

"Doesn't look like a *Neanderthal,*" Skippy said. "They were cavemen, right?"

Roy nodded.

"So what's the story behind this one?"

Roy smiled. "Hard to put in words."

"Sorry," said Skippy. His eyes, even behind that droopy screen of greasy hair, had trouble meeting Roy's.

"Nothing to be sorry about," Roy said. He touched the nearest column of the arch. "It's called *Delia.*"

Skippy took another look. "So it's meant to be, you know, a real person?"

"Not exactly."

"An imaginary one?"

"No. It's about a real person, I guess you'd say, but not a representation of her."

"So there's a Delia?"

"My first—my wife," Roy said. "She died about fifteen years ago." Fourteen years, eight months, two weeks, to be exact.

"Oh."

A silence fell over them, not uncomfortable. Thirty seconds went by, maybe more. It felt to Roy like there were three people in the room, getting along fine. "A helicopter crash," he said. "Off Venezuela."

Skippy's eyes went quickly to those twisted blades up above.

"Delia was trying to get them to grow pineapples," Roy said. "She had it all worked out—acreage, marketing, irrigation, everything."

Skippy said, "Does Uncle Murph, um, know how she . . ."

Roy shook his head. "Hadn't met your uncle at that point." And Roy didn't talk much about Delia, in any case; if her death came up, he usually just said *plane crash*. Which was how Tom Parish, Delia's boss, had referred to it in that first phone call. *I'm afraid I've got bad news, Roy.* The details—thunderstorm, mechanical failure, helicopter—had come later, along with the body.

"Oh," said Skippy.

Two bodies, in a way, since Delia had been three months pregnant at the time.

"How old are you, Skippy?"

"Sixteen," Skippy said. "But I'm reliable—ask Uncle Murph."

"I don't doubt it," said Roy. His gaze was drawn to three pimples on Skippy's cheek, forming an inflamed little triangle.

"So," said Skippy. He cleared his throat, and then again. "Is that a yes?"

"What's the question?"

Skippy's face reddened, somehow turning all his pimples white. "Assistant," he said. "A job. Part-time, lifting heavy stuff, cleaning up, that kind of thing."

"You want to be my assistant?" said Roy.

Skippy nodded.

"What about the job with your uncle?"

"There's nothing for me to do at Uncle Murph's. He's just trying to, you know, take the pressure off of my mom."

"What does she do?"

"Cleans condos on the mountain. Plus some wait-ressing." There was a long pause. "I'm not bad on the computer," Skippy said.

Roy had never had an assistant, didn't need one. He named a date. "Why don't you come in for a couple hours? We'll try to figure something out."

"Yeah?" said Skippy. "Hey. Thanks." His right hand twitched like it knew handshaking might be appropriate. But no handshaking happened. Skippy backed toward the door. "Thanks a lot." He opened the door, went out, closed it. Then came a knock.

"Come in," said Roy. He never locked the door. The knob turned but the door didn't open. Somehow Skippy had locked it. Roy opened the door.

"Like what time?" said Skippy.

"How's two?" Roy said.

"Cool," said Skippy.

Jen walked into Pescatore, looking great. Roy got up, pulled out a chair for her, helped push her to the table. She shot him a quick glance over her shoulder. "What's with you?"

"Just my normal self," said Roy.

"Right."

The mountain rose outside the window, some of the lower runs lit for night skiing. The moguls on Wipe Out cast rounded shadows, like hundreds of little black holes. A skier in white landed a perfect daffy, veered right and vanished behind a grove of spruces.

"How does champagne sound?" Roy said.

Jen made a little bubbling noise.

Roy laughed and ordered a bottle of Pommery. He didn't know anything about champagne, but Pommery was what Krishna served at openings where he really believed in the artist.

"This is nice," Jen said, taking a sip. "Did your ship come in or something?"

Roy tasted the champagne; really nice, but it went down the wrong way, tickling his throat just a little. This was the moment for saying, *Maybe it's just about to;* and Jen would ask what he meant by that; and he'd pop the question. And it probably would have happened just like that, except for the tickle in Roy's throat. He coughed, a delicate, quiet cough at first, setting down his champagne flute and covering his mouth with his napkin. But the cough was just getting started, like a powerful engine revving up. It dipped into a deep, ragged register and kept going, on and on.

"Drink some water," Jen said, passing him a glass, her eyes widening.

But by that time, Roy had noticed the tiny red drops on the white linen. He made an excusing-himself-from-the-table gesture and went to the bathroom.

No one there. He hurried into a stall, bent over the toilet, surrendered to the cough. The cough got to work, this time really showing him what it could do. Blood filled the toilet bowl, in splatters, strings, gobbets.

"Hey, buddy," said someone outside. "You all right in there?"

The cough died at once, as though it preferred privacy. Roy gasped in some air. "No problem," he said, but in a voice that sounded much older than his own.

Silence. Then came slow footsteps on the tiles— footsteps he'd missed on their way in—followed by urinal sounds, sink sounds, door sounds. Roy left the stall, just a little wobbly. He had the bathroom to himself again, himself and his image in the mirror: a pale image with a dark glimmering dawning in its eyes. Roy splashed water on his face, drank from the tap—cool water soothing on his raw throat—and went back to the table.

"You all right?" Jen said.

"Fine," said Roy.

"You're sure?"

"Fine," he said again, and picked up as though nothing had happened. Jen ate salmon, Roy lamb; they drank champagne; split a piece of a cake called chocolate sin; and had a good time. Roy told a pretty funny story about a collector he'd met, her pet cheetah and a pizza delivery boy. But he didn't pop the question.

Three

It wasn't that Roy was a particularly acute reader of facial expressions. But he knew that people liked delivering good news; their eyes lit up with it. Therefore a lack of lighting up was a bad sign. No light in Dr. Bronstein's eyes: they were dark, thoughtful, maybe a bit puzzled.

"Sorry to keep you waiting, Mr. Valois."

"That's all right."

Dr. Bronstein opened a folder, peered down at a sheet of MRI film; then his gaze rose slowly back up to Roy. Roy stood a little straighter, just to show Dr. Bronstein how fit he was. *I went to U Maine on a hockey scholarship, doc, full ride.* Roy came close to saying it.

"May I ask a question?" said Dr. Bronstein.

"Shoot."

"Of course, we'll need a biopsy," said Dr. Bronstein. "And nothing's definite at this point. Not definitively. But have you had much contact with asbestos—in your work, for example?"

"Asbestos?" said Roy. "No."

"I understand you're a sculptor," said Dr. Bronstein.

"Yes, but I work with metals."

"What kind of metals?"

"Recently it's been mostly junked car parts," Roy said. "Before that I did some pieces with I-beams I bought from a demolition company in Worcester."

Dr. Bronstein's eyebrows, white and overhanging like snowy cornices, rose. "Did you spend much time at the actual demolition sites?"

"None," Roy said. "They e-mailed me pictures and I chose from that."

Dr. Bronstein's eyes slid back to the MRI film. "And before the I-beams?"

"Spring steel rods," said Roy. "And before spring steel rods, car parts again, which was where I started."

"Brake linings?" said Dr. Bronstein.

"No," said Roy. "Mostly radiators, sometimes engine blocks, a few axles."

"Were you ever in the military?"

"No."

"Work in a mine?"

"No."

"How about construction? Plastering? Pipe fitting?"

"No," Roy said. "What's this all about?"

"Those are all nexus points for asbestos exposure," Dr. Bronstein said.

Roy raised his hands, palms up.

"This could be a long time ago," said Dr. Bronstein, "a teenage summer job, for example."

"I worked in a machine shop," Roy said.

"Doing what?"

"Metalwork," Roy said. "Welding, mostly."

"Did that involve insulation? Fire retardant? Boiler construction?"

"We built assembly-line parts for a chemical company," Roy said. "Mostly outdoor work."

"That wouldn't do it," said Dr. Bronstein, ticking off boxes on a page in the folder.

"Do what?"

"Are you familiar with the term *mesothelioma,* Mr. Valois?"

A very complicated word; Roy wasn't sure he'd heard it right. "Say it again."

"Mesothelioma." Dr. Bronstein enunciated every syllable. Roy didn't miss it this time: the word brought to mind those cheesy Japanese monster flicks.

He shook his head. "Never heard of it."

Dr. Bronstein's gaze again rose from the film, fastening on Roy's face, just below the eyes. "Mesothelioma—malignant mesothelioma—is a disease caused by asbestos exposure, invariably."

"What kind of disease?" said Roy.

"A serious one."

"But what's the name of it?"

Dr. Bronstein looked confused. "I told you—mesothelioma."

Roy's voice rose a little; that aroused the tickle in his throat. "What's another name?"

"Another name?" said Dr. Bronstein, backing up. Dr. Bronstein was a little guy; Roy could have ripped him apart. "Oh, I see," he said. "Cancer. Mesothelioma is a form of cancer usually affecting the lungs but sometimes the peritoneum or heart as well."

"And I have it?"

"Can't say for sure without a biopsy. An open biopsy, that's the gold standard. I'll have to send you down to Dr. Honey in Boston for that. May be the world's leading mesothelioma expert—I trained under him, as it happens, which is why—" Dr. Bronstein broke off, and it grew very still in the examining room, no sound but Dr. Bronstein's pale finger tap-tapping at Roy's MRI film.

"You can only get this from asbestos?" Roy said.

Dr. Bronstein nodded.

"But I've never been exposed," Roy said. "So I couldn't have it."

Dr. Bronstein gazed at the lower half of Roy's face.

Roy's voice rose again. "How could I? You said 'invariably.' That was your very word. So if I've never been exposed, then how could I have it?" The tickle grew stronger in his throat.

Dr. Bronstein licked his lips. "You couldn't."

"Exactly," said Roy. "And I feel normal. Stronger than ever, in fact." Roy thought of telling Dr. Bronstein about all those collegiate snowshoers he'd blown by on the lower loop.

"There is the matter of the cough," said Dr. Bronstein.

"Except for the cough," Roy said. With an effort of will, he overcame the tickle, made it go away. "But a cough could be anything."

Dr. Bronstein's gaze rose a little more, and now met Roy's. "That's why we need the biopsy," he said. "Then we won't have to speculate."

Tuesday nights in winter meant Kegger-league hockey in the valley, all players thirty-five plus, no checking, no slapshots, no uniforms, helmets optional; beers after at Waldo's with losers buying, not optional.

All the teams had women's-clothing names, a practice long preceding Roy's arrival. He was on the Thongs. Tonight they were taking on the first-place D-Cups. Most of the players had high school or college hockey experience, a few had made it to the minor pros, and one, Normie Sawchuck, first-line center for the D-Cups, had skated two seasons with the Bruins. Normie, twenty or thirty pounds overweight now—he ate and drank for free at Normie's Burger Paradise— was still the fastest player in the league, especially on his first few rushes.

And Normie was leading a three-on-two now, bearing down on Roy, gliding backward on right defense, the position he'd played all his life. Roy could actually skate backward faster than he could forward but that didn't put him in Normie's class, nowhere near. Normie cut across the blue line, ice chips flying off his blades, faked a pass to his left-winger, a fake that Roy ignored—Normie never passed this early in a game— and deked right. Roy went with him, keeping both shoulders turned up ice, ready for anything. But not that: suddenly the puck came loose off Normie's stick. Or seemed to, because when Roy reached for it, it was gone, now tucked back between Normie's skates. The Kharmalov move: Normie giggled as he blew by Roy. But not quite by. Miracle One: Roy, whirling, flailing with his stick, somehow managed to nick the puck. It came loose, bounced against the boards, and Roy, sweeping it up saw—Miracle Two: nothing but open ice between him and the goal. He wheeled away—could actually feel his jersey billowing in the wind, as though some hockey god had suddenly turned him into Bobby Hull—and angled in alone on the goalie. Roy didn't even bother with a move, just went high on the stick side. Flick of the wrists and—*ding*. The puck banged in off the post, rippling the net.

"Fuckin' A," said the goalie.

The whole game was like that. Final score: Thongs 6, D-Cups 1. Roy had a hat trick, zoomed around all night, wasn't even sweating at the end. When had he last played like this? Years and years ago, or maybe never.

"Christ, Roy," said Normie, bringing a couple of foaming pitchers to Roy's table at Waldo's, "whatever you been smoking, I want some."

Roy felt so good he almost skipped the biopsy.

An open biopsy, the gold standard, meant a general anesthetic. Roy had never had one before. He lay on a gurney under bright lights. The anesthetist—or maybe a nurse, Roy wasn't sure about all the personnel—approached with an IV and said, "Nice veins."

"Thanks," said Roy.

"What's that bruise?" she said, inserting the needle.

"Puck."

"I'm sorry?"

"From hockey."

"It flew into the stands?"

"No," said Roy. He started to feel a little funny. "I play hockey." *Been skating since I was three.* Roy was wondering about adding that little fact when Dr. Honey, his face masked, loomed into his line of sight. Dr. Honey had bright blue eyes, ceramic eyes, if that made sense, that all at once seemed scary.

But his voice was gentle. "We're going to take good care of you, Roy," he said. "Your job is to count backward from ten."

"What's yours?" said Roy.

Everybody laughed.

"Ten," said Dr. Honey.

"Nine," said Roy. "Eight, seven, six—that's my favorite number—fi . . ." He began to feel light, lighter and lighter, as though he could float into the air, drift out of the room, out the front door of Mass General, out of Boston, home. Not home to Ethan Valley, or the old home in Foggy Bottom, but the very oldest home, way up in the woods of Maine. Dr. Honey's ceramic eyes closed in. "Bobby Greelish," Roy said.

"What was that?" said Dr. Honey.

"Missed it," said someone behind him.

"Bobby," said Roy. "Where's Bobby?"

"See the size of that rat?" said Bobby.

"Where'd it go? said Roy.

Roy and Bobby worked out in the open, welding steel basins for the assembly line at the chemical plant in Bath, one of Mr. King's biggest customers. They were in plain sight of Mr. King's office window, and he kept an eye on them so there was no fooling around. Except when it rained: then they moved under a corrugated roof that blocked Mr. King's view. There Roy and Bobby got away with all sorts of things, like building a go-kart, customizing Bobby's motorcycle, melting random meltables, vaporizing spiders and other bugs with their torches. They were searching for the giant rat, torches in hand, when Mr. King came up undetected behind them.

"You boys stealin' from me?" he said.

They whipped around, shutting off the nozzles. "Stealing from you, Mr. King?"

Mr. King's hair, what little he had, was plastered down on his skull from the rain. It dripped off his bony nose and pointy chin. "I pay you to work, don't I?

Goddamn good money. So when youse not workin' I call that dippin' your dirty hands straight in my pocket."

"We were just testing the mixture," Roy said. "We weren't—"

"Takin' food right off of my fuckin' table's what it is." Mr. King looked from one to the other, his little eyes darting around in fury. "I oughta can both your sorry asses."

"But, Mr. King," they said. That would be bad: the money they brought home—both boys raised by single moms—was important.

"Sure," said Mr. King, mimicking them. "Now it's 'but, Mr. King.' " He glanced across the yard, seemed to get an idea. "Tell you what," he said, calming down. "Mebbe I can see my way clear to givin' one more chance."

"Thanks, Mr. King."

"I'm a softie, always been my problem," said Mr. King. "But fact is, could be I got a special job."

"Yeah?" said the boys. They were getting pretty bored making those steel basins day after day.

"Ayuh," said Mr. King. He crooked a finger at them.

The special job lasted till it was time to go back to school and turned out to be kind of fun.

"This here, boys," said Mr. King, leading them to the farthest corner of the yard, dark forest just the other side of the barbed-wire perimeter fence, "is where it all begun."

They gazed at an old tumbledown building, paint mostly peeled off, windows broken.

"Where what all begun?" said Bobby.

"King Machining and Metals, for fuck sake," said Mr. King. "But my granddad started out in cement. You're lookin' at the old warehouse. Thing is, now I need the space, so you boys is gonna knock it down fer me."

"Knock down the building?" said Roy.

"Whole shootin' match," said Mr. King. "Bust it into itty bitty pieces. Dump 'em in the Dumpster."

Mr. King's old cement warehouse was timber-framed, probably not very well built in the first place, now pretty frail. Roy and Bobby busted it into itty bitty pieces, mostly using ten-pound sledgehammers, but sometimes chain saws, and when things got a little crazy, their own bodies as battering rams, testing whether they could actually run through walls. Lots of old supplies lay around the warehouse, including rotting bags of this and that. Heavy work to carry all those bags to the Dumpster, so usually the boys just went at them with chain saws. When the bags split, the stuff inside came boiling out, like a blizzard was blowing through what was left of the warehouse, coating them from head to foot, like two snowmen in August. The boys got a kick out of that, plus it saved them work because the white stuff vanished in the next rainstorm, or even in a strong breeze. Mr. King peeled off a twenty-dollar bonus for each of them on their last day.

Four

C hest sewn back up—only four stitches needed— and still a little groggy, but feeling no pain, Roy waited for the biopsy results, no one else in the outer room. Dr. Honey had lots of old *National Geographics*. Roy found himself staring at a beautiful photograph of a forest cabin with bright red wildflowers growing by the front door and a fast-running brook in the background. For a while, he could hear the water and almost smell those flowers. The loveliness of nature and how sweet just being alive could be overwhelmed him. Then the grogginess began to dissipate, and the weaknesses of the photograph became apparent: it was like an all-dessert meal, too rich, too superficial, too eager to please. But just before Roy closed the magazine, the picture made a connection with something deep in his mind, hooking onto a bit of residue not yet swept away with the ebbing drugs inside him.

Roy took out his cell phone, called information for North Grafton, Maine, asked for Bobby Greelish's number. No listing for a Bobby or Robert Greelish. The only Greelish in the directory was Alma: Bobby's mother. Roy called her.

"Mrs. Greelish?" he said. "Roy Valois."

"Roy?" An old woman; he didn't recognize her voice at all. "This is a surprise. How's your mom these days?"

"Fine," said Roy. His mother had left North Grafton long ago for an apartment he'd bought her in Sarasota. "I'm looking for Bobby, actually."

"My Bobby?" said Mrs. Greelish.

"Yes," said Roy. "Bobby."

"You mean you never heard?"

"Heard what?"

"Bobby . . ." Her voice thickened. There was a muffled pause, as though Mrs. Greelish had covered the mouthpiece with her hand. Then, her voice under control, she came back on the line and said: "Bobby passed away, two years this Christmas."

"Bobby's dead?" Roy thought: *motorcycle accident.* That was his hopeful side piping up.

"Passed," said Mrs. Greelish. "He caught this horrible rare disease."

"Called?"

"Excuse me?"

"The name," said Roy. "The name of the disease."

"Oh, sorry, Roy," said Mrs. Greelish. "It's a big long word—I never did learn to say it properly. Bobby'd get a little impatient about that."

So Roy wasn't totally unprepared for the biopsy results, could even be said to have taken it well: he could read that on the faces of Dr. Honey and his staff.

"You've got someone to do the driving?" said one of the nurses on Roy's way out.

"Waiting in the car," Roy said.

He drove himself back up north, alone. Clear blue sky with silver overtones, small golden sun, glaring but somehow cold, snow that grew whiter and whiter the farther north he got: a lovely winter day, and winter was Roy's favorite season. He especially liked when ice sheets coated the granite outcrops where the road builders had blasted through, and there was lots of that today, those hard rocks shining bright. It brought tears to his eyes, and Roy, no crier but here in complete private he couldn't come up with a good reason not to, let them flow. Not for long, though—one exit, maybe two. By the time he'd crossed the Connecticut River and entered Vermont, he'd pulled himself together.

Diagnosis: sarcomatous unresectable malignant pleural mesothelioma, stage three in the Brigham staging system.

How many stages?

Four.

So it could be worse.

True.

Good. So where do we go from here?

From here?

In terms of treatment.

Ah.

Sarcomatous unresectable malignant pleural mesothelioma: there turned out to be a lot of meaning crammed into that little phrase. The word *unresectable* alone packed a tremendous punch.

Treatment: palliative care.

Palliative?

It means—

I know what it means. Is that all you've got?

There are clinical trials, but you don't qualify.

Why not?

The diagnosis.

Isn't that a little circular?

Dr. Honey had seen some justice in that remark. Then he mentioned that his wife knew all about Roy's work, was amazed at her husband's ignorance. After that he brought up an experimental program a friend of his was about to start at Hopkins.

Can you get me into it?

I'll try.

Try hard?

Prognosis: four months to a year.

Roy went cold all over when he heard that. And Dr. Honey seemed to shrink in size, as though Roy was suddenly seeing him from a distance, already going or gone.

How certain are you?

Nothing is certain in this profession, not certain in the absolute sense.

So it could be thirteen months?

It could.

Fourteen?

Possibly.

Eighteen?

Nothing is certain.

That means there's hope.

Always.

I had a hat trick the other night.

Hat trick?

An unfamiliar term to Dr. Honey. Roy, wishing he hadn't said it, didn't explain. *Hat trick* sounded pretty frivolous next to a word like *unresectable*.

Roy drove up to the barn. A kid in a sweatshirt and unlaced boots was shoveling the path. Roy did his own shoveling. He got out of the car and said, "Hey."

The kid swung around. "Hi, Mr. Valois. Figured you must be, you know, delayed, so I thought I'd just, um . . ."

Skippy. Was this his tryout day? Roy had forgotten all about it. What had he told him? Show up at two? Roy checked his watch—three-thirty—then noticed a new path shoveled all the way across the yard to the shed, and another, completely unnecessary, that seemed to be following the entire perimeter of the barn.

"I really don't need . . ." Roy began. Skippy waited, a full load of snow poised on the blade. "Come on inside," Roy said.

Skippy flung the snow up and over the high bank and they went inside.

"So cool," said Skippy, his gaze right away on *Delia*.

"In what way?" Roy said.

"In what way?" said Skippy. "It's awesome, Mr. Valois, all those rads. Got something in mind for the next one?"

Next one. That coldness came over Roy, but not as intense this time. "How about coffee?" he said.

"I'm good," said Skippy.

"I'm having some," Roy said. He went into the kitchen, reheated coffee, poured two cups. Back in the big room, Skippy was near the computer.

"Frozen, huh?" he said.

"Happens all the time," said Roy. "I just unplug and replug."

"Um," said Skippy. "Mind if I see if maybe I can . . ."

"All yours," said Roy.

Roy pulled up a chair near *Delia*. Skippy tapped away at the keyboard. The room darkened. It was peaceful, just the three of them, a family by no one's definition, but that kind of peaceful just the same.

"All set, Mr. Valois."

Roy got up, his chest a little sore now, and went to the computer.

"Shouldn't happen again," Skippy said. "And I've cleaned up your desktop."

"Thanks."

"Want free phone service?"

"Free phone service?"

"I could write a little program, hook you up."

"Would it be legal?" Roy said.

Skippy turned to him, greasy hair in his eyes. "Like how do you mean, Mr. Valois?"

"You can call me Roy," Roy said.

"Okay, Mr. . . . um," said Skippy.

Turk McKenny was the goalie for the Thongs, and also Roy's lawyer. He had an office on the top floor of a white house overlooking the green. Roy could see part of *Neanderthal Number Nineteen* through the window.

"Hell of a game, Roy," Turk said.

"Thanks."

"Shoulda seen the look on Normie's face when you stole the puck."

"A fluke."

"I don't know," Turk said. "Raised your game a notch or two lately. What's up with that?"

"That will you've been bugging me about," Roy said.

"Huh?"

"I'd like to get it drawn up."

Turk took his feet—he wore Shetland-lined suede slippers—off the desk.

"Now," said Roy, "if possible."

Turk slid a notepad closer, put on half-glasses. "We can certainly get started," he said. His head tilted, eyes peering over the rims. "Anything special get you motivated?"

"The usual," Roy said. Which was pretty funny—so funny, in fact, that Roy started laughing. For a moment or two he wondered if he'd be able to stop. Then out of nowhere the cough erupted, swallowing the laughter, taking over completely. Roy lurched from the room, hand over his mouth, and hurried down the hall to the bathroom. He coughed over the sink. No blood this time, only a little yellowish liquid, the consistency of raw egg white. Egg white instead of blood: Good sign or bad? How could it be bad? Was there hope? *Always.*

Roy went back to Turk's office. Turk was hovering by the door.

"What is it, Roy? What's going on?"

"Nothing."

"Come on."

Roy shook his head.

"It's me," Turk said.

Roy was silent.

"And if that's not enough," Turk said, "at least let me do my job."

"What does that mean?" Roy said; the sound of his voice was rough and ragged.

"I'm your lawyer," Turk said. "Don't keep me in the dark."

They were friends, went back a long way: had played against each other in college—Turk a four-year starter in net for Dartmouth—and even before that in a high school tournament final in the old Boston Garden. Delia had liked him, too: Turk had been a pallbearer at her funeral. And Turk *was* his lawyer, the only lawyer he'd ever had, looking over everything—taxes, investments, contracts, including the one with Krishna. Roy took a deep breath, aware at the same time that it wasn't as deep as his normal deep breaths, not nearly.

"Totally confidential?" he said.

"Goes without saying," Turk said. "But I'll say it anyway."

Someone had to know. Otherwise: potential chaos. So, standing right there by the door—both of them on their feet—Roy told Turk everything. That turned out to be hard, speaking it aloud, somehow making it more real. Roy couldn't imagine doing it again.

Turk didn't interrupt, didn't make a sound, just went a little pale around his lips. When Roy was done, he said, "God help us." Turk put his hand on Roy's shoulder. Roy didn't really want that, certainly didn't want hugging or anything of the kind, and none happened.

"What's this Hopkins thing?" Turk said.

"Waiting to hear," said Roy.

"Meaning there's some hope."

Always.

They sat down. Out on the green, a little kid was throwing snowballs at *Neanderthal Number Nineteen.*

"Anything in the bottom drawer?" Roy said.

"Read my mind," said Turk. He opened the bottom drawer, took out a bottle of single malt and two glasses, poured an inch or so in each one. That was gone right away. He poured more. An expensive single malt, but for some reason it had no taste, not to Roy.

"What I want is pretty simple," he said. "Jen gets one half, the rest goes to my mom."

Turk wrote on the pad; he had neat, small writing, kind of strange given those fingers, twisted and thick. "The house?" he said, not looking up.

"Sell it."

"And your inventory?"

"Sell that, too."

"What about the effect on prices?"

Roy didn't care. But why not maximize what Jen and his mother ended up with? "Krishna will know what to do."

"Have you talked to him?"

"No."

"Jen?"

"No."

Turk opened his mouth to say something, closed it. Roy slid his glass across the desk. Turk poured more, paused, and poured more for himself. He put down his pen, drank, leaned back in his chair. Silence fell over the room, thick, as though it had a physical dimension, seeming to block the passage of time.

"Remember that goal you scored against Harvard?" Turk said. "I was thinking of it the other night at Waldo's."

Roy hadn't scored enough in college to forget any of them, but that had been the biggest, maybe the only big one, an overtime gamewinner in the national semifinal; they'd lost to Minnesota in the championship game. He had a crazy thought: *I wonder if it'll be in my obituary?* Not so crazy—he understood at once where it must have come from: Krishna's remark about Delia. *This one will be in the first paragraph of your obituary, my friend.* The cold feeling came again.

"What was that thought?" Turk said.

"Nothing."

"Totally confidential."

Roy laughed, a normal laugh this time. "It's stupid," he said. But with all the blurting he'd been doing in this office, why stop now? "I was just wondering whether that goal would make it into my obituary."

"They'll probably just stick to the art, don't you think?" Turk said.

That struck Roy as funny, too. He drank more, made himself really taste it this time and found he could; it tasted great. His head buzzed a little. Why the hell not?

"Maybe we could find out," Turk said.

"Find out what?" Roy said.

"What's in your obituary. Aren't they written way ahead of time, all set to go except for the last little . . . ?" Turk abandoned the rest of the sentence.

Roy hadn't known that, hadn't thought much about obituaries, didn't spend any time on that page of the paper. But some reporter, or maybe more than one, had already gone over his life, got all the pluses and minuses in black-and-white. How did it add up?

"Didn't Mark Twain get to see his own obituary?" Turk said.

"How did that happen?"

"His death was falsely reported," Turk said. "He wrote something funny about it. But in this case I was thinking along the lines of one of those kids."

"What kids?" Roy said, struggling all of a sudden with a complex thought based on the notion that only the living read obituaries and therefore reading your own was somehow cheating death.

"The kind that knows how to get past all that Internet security," Turk said, "root around behind the scenes at some big newspaper. Aren't kids like that a dime a dozen these days?"

Roy knew of one. Cheating death: that sounded pretty good.

Five

Roy awoke with a new shape in his mind. He didn't have a crisp image of this new shape, just knew it was attenuated, thin, delicate, more delicate than anything he'd ever done—although that wouldn't be hard; delicate, and related somehow to silence. The shape—or one of the shapes—of silence. His hand was moving toward the sketch pad he kept on the bedside table when the phone rang.

He picked it up. "Hello."

"Oh, sorry, Roy, didn't mean to wake you," Jen said.

"You didn't."

"Can't fool me," she said. "I know that sleepyhead voice."

Roy lay back on the pillow. "Guilty as charged," he said.

"Good thing," she said. "Because I happen to be in the neighborhood."

Roy glanced at the clock. "Not working today?"

"It's Thursday, Roy. My day off."

"Oh."

"You all right?"

"Yeah, fine."

A long pause.

"Aren't you going to ask me over?" she said. "I've got muffins."

Roy laughed, and asked her over.

There'd been other day-off muffin deliveries like this, Roy always staying in bed, waiting for the sound of the opening front door. But now he rose, brushed his teeth, washed his face, threw on clothes; had coffee brewing by the time Jen came in, snow on her knitted hat, a bag from Muffins Etc. in her hand.

"You're up," she said.

"Thought you might want coffee."

She came over, put her arm around him. "After," she said, and gave his ear a little lick. At that moment the sun came out and bright light shone through the tall windows of the barn, casting a long shadow of *Delia* across the floor and up the far wall. Roy and Jen went into the bedroom.

Dark in the bedroom, the blinds still drawn. They got into bed, undressing; except for Roy's T-shirt—he left that on.

"Come here, stranger," she said.

"Stranger?" he said.

"I hardly see you anymore."

"That's not true."

He pulled her close. A little later, she rolled on top, took hold of him, stuck him inside and sat up—something they both loved; Roy because he liked watching her face from down there, Jen for reasons he didn't know, only felt grateful for. Jen leaned forward, sliding her hands under his T-shirt, up his chest. She paused.

"What's that?" she said.

"Nothing," Roy said, taking her hand, guiding it away from the bandages.

"Did you hurt yourself?" she said.

"A little nick," said Roy. "Nothing."

"You're sure? I—"

He reached up for her, drew her head down, quieted her with a kiss. Then he rubbed the underside of one of her breasts in a way she liked. That made her twist down on him in a way he liked—only this time, for the first time, he started to go soft inside her. *Oh, no.*

He knew the meaning, the implication, almost before he was aware of what was going on. A whole cascade of black thoughts got released in his mind, came pouring in and overwhelmed him. He thrust harder, moved faster, tried to drive out the black thoughts with others—sexy, pornographic, dirty—forcing up memories of wild nights from his past, crazy-over-the-top things, some with Jen.

No good. He and Jen finished in a haphazard way.

After, they lay together, not touching. Roy could feel her thinking, but his mind was going blank and sleep was coming fast. He welcomed it; *so tired.* He was almost there, almost gone, when Jen said, "I can't compete with a dead woman, Roy."

Roy tried to open his eyes, but the lids were so heavy. "It's not that," he said.

"I think it is."

"No."

"Then what?"

"Nothing."

Jen sat up. Roy got his eyes open. Jen was looking down at him, sheet pulled up over her chest, eyes angry.

"Just be honest about it," she said. "I understand. She was this great lady and you can't let her go."

"That's not it."

"No? Then what about that thing out there?"

"Thing?"

"Sculpture. Art. Whatever. You're telling me that's letting go?"

Whatever: he couldn't help getting annoyed at that, heard the annoyance in his response. "You're reading too much into it."

"Am I?" Jen said. "Did you know you sometimes say her name in your sleep?"

"That's not true."

"Believe what you want," she said. "And look at you now—you can hardly get up the energy to have this conversation. Am I that boring?"

Roy reached for her. She moved away, to the edge of the bed. "You never bore me," he said.

She shook her head. "You don't care that much, Roy. That's what I'm starting to see. To see and feel."

"It's not true."

She didn't seem to hear. "Take that job offer I told you about—what was your reaction? You didn't say stay. You didn't say go. Then you kiss me like that, like . . . like nothing matters more. What is it you want from me?"

Roy forced himself to meet her gaze. What did he want? That was easy: to marry her and live happily ever after; or maybe in the other order. Roy said—made himself say, and tried to say it gently, although that harsh raggedness got into his throat again, at the worst possible moment, nothing he could do about it—he said: "Go."

She was shocked. He could see it. But he didn't say another word. Once he started, there'd be no control, and what ended up being said would cause a lot more pain in the long run, the kind of loss-pain that never goes away completely. Roy knew something about it. *Delia* was the proof. And therefore: Jen wasn't all wrong when it came to what made him tick.

Her expression changed. The shock wore off, replaced by anger, a cold anger he wouldn't have thought her capable of. "I wondered about this once or twice," she said. "Now I know."

"Know what?" said Roy.

"That you got damaged, too," she said. "In the crash."

Roy shook his head.

"Like it deadened some nerves," she said. "Deep inside."

He stopped shaking his head, said nothing.

Her anger faded. She patted his arm when she said good-bye.

"Some weird stuff turned up in the yard the other day," Skippy said. "Mr. . . . um, Roy?"

Roy glanced up. He was working on a pencil sketch of the new idea, this attenuated silent thing, and getting nowhere. "Sorry," he said. "Missed that."

"Weird stuff," said Skippy, hooking up a new tank of acetylene. "In the yard. Uncle Murph says it's from a nuclear power plant."

"What does it look like?"

"Hard to describe," said Skippy. "All bent up. Shiny. Wanna see it?"

"Yes," said Roy. "But later. Right now, I'm hoping you can help me with something on the computer."

"The free phone service?"

Roy shook his head. How to make this sound sensible? "It's one of those places where you're not supposed to go."

Skippy perked up. "Oh, yeah?"

"But I'm not planning to do any harm," Roy said. "Just looking for a piece of information, to . . . to settle a bet."

"What kind of information?" said Skippy, already moving toward the computer.

"It's a little complicated," Roy said, launching into a long and disorganized story about college hockey, the satisfaction of beating—and beating up on—the Harvard boys, the preparation of obituaries, the eminence of the *New York Times*. Skippy had all sorts of questions—why the teams in the Kegger league had the names they did, how much the bet was for, whether college was fun—but none about the legality or difficulty of hacking the *New York Times*. It took him ten minutes.

"Here you go, Mr. . . . uh." The printer made its chugging sound. Skippy handed Roy his obituary.

ROY VALOIS, SCULPTOR, DIES AT [INSERT]
by Richard Gold

ROY VALOIS, a sculptor whose large works are displayed in many public spaces around the United States and at several prominent museums, died yesterday at [INSERT]. He was [INSERT].

The cause was [INSERT], according to [INSERT].

The self-taught Mr. Valois worked almost exclusively with recovered materials, usually scrap metal, but he was "no primitive," according to Kurt Palmateer, former head of the Mass MoCA Museum in North Adams, Mass., where the first sculpture in what became Mr. Valois's *Neanderthal* series is part of the permanent collection. "There is a sense of refinement and a deep formal concern that, if anything, connects him to Henry Moore and even to neoclassicists of the nineteenth century," said Mr. Palmateer.

Roy Valois was born in the western Maine town of North Grafton on [TO COME]. He went to local schools, where he excelled at sports, eventually entering the University of Maine on a hockey scholarship. But it was while working at a summer job that involved welding and other metalwork that Mr. Valois found his true calling. His first piece, now standing in front of the public library in North Grafton, was built in his off-hours during the summer of his junior year in college. Made from brass fixtures salvaged from a sunken freighter and titled *Finback,* the piece attracted the attention of Professor Anna Cohen of the University of Maine art department, and led eventually to a two-year fellowship at Georgetown University.

It was there that Mr. Valois began to attract the attention of collectors. Prices for several works in the *Neanderthal* series—"a tragic epic in scrap steel," in the words of the critic Hilton Kramer—have topped $100,000. It was also at Georgetown that Mr. Valois met his wife, Delia Stern, an economist later employed by the United Nations. She died in an airplane crash off Venezuela in [TO COME]. They had no children and Mr. Valois never remarried [VERIFY]. He is survived by his mother [VERIFY], Edna Valois, of Sarasota, Florida.

Roy read his obituary twice, his hands a little shaky the first time, steady the second. *A tragic epic in scrap steel*—he could live with that. That crazy juxtaposition made Roy laugh out loud; looking up, he saw Skippy staring at him.

"They have humor in obituaries?" Skippy said.

"Maybe not intentionally," said Roy.

Skippy nodded as though that made sense. "Win your bet?" he said.

Roy didn't answer. His attention was suddenly drawn back to the last part of that last paragraph: *his wife, Delia Stern, an economist later employed by the United Nations.* That was a mistake. Delia had worked for the Hobbes Institute, not the United Nations. Not a big mistake, in no way central to the story, but Roy didn't like the idea of a mistake appearing in his obituary. Plus he remembered that Delia had written a very negative analysis of UN budgetary practices, an analysis that had provoked a condescending letter from some bureaucrat in New York. Letting the mistake go seemed disloyal.

He grew aware of Skippy, still watching him, a funny look on his face. "Something wrong, Skippy?"

"Your nose is, like, bleeding, Roy."

A drop of red fell and blotted the obituary. "It's nothing," Roy said. He went over to the kitchen area, held paper towel to his face.

"You okay?" said Skippy from the other side of the counter.

Roy nodded. He removed the paper towel. Another red drop fell, this one landing on the pine floor.

"That'll do it for today, Skippy," he said. "Thanks for the help."

"Hey, you're welcome," said Skippy. "But what about the nuclear thing I was telling you about?"

"I'll come over tomorrow," Roy said. "And let's keep this little computer adventure to ourselves."

"Adventure, yeah, sure," said Skippy. "I already forgot."

When Roy got the bleeding stopped, he called the *New York Times*, asked for Richard Gold, was put through.

"Mr. Gold? It's Roy Valois."

"How can I help you?"

Had he not recognized the name? "I believe you wrote a piece about me," Roy said.

"Your name again?"

Roy repeated it.

"Doesn't ring a bell," said Gold. "When was this?"

"I'm not sure when you wrote it," Roy said. "It hasn't been published yet."

Pause, a long one. Roy thought he heard soft tapping at a keyboard. When Gold spoke again, his tone was harder. "You're the sculptor?"

"Yes."

"And you're referring to your obituary?"

"I am."

"Did Palmateer tell you?"

"Palmateer?"

"The museum guy I got quotes from," said Gold. "They're supposed to keep those interviews confidential."

"I haven't spoken to him in years," Roy said. Then he had a sudden thought: *This could end with Skippy in trouble.* "I found out by accident."

"What kind of accident?"

"It's not important," Roy said.

"I disagree," said Gold. "If it involved any—"

Roy talked over him. "The reason I'm calling is that there's an error in your story."

Gold swallowed what he'd been saying. "Error?"

"Have you got it on your screen right now?"

"Of course."

"The third last sentence, about my wife," Roy said. "She didn't work for the UN. The only job she ever had was with the Hobbes Institute."

"Spelling?"

Roy spelled *Hobbes.*

Long pause. "No mention of that in my notes," Gold said.

"But I'm telling you now that—"

"And the UN reference came from a reliable source."

"Reliable source?" said Roy. "Who would that be?"

"Can't reveal that," said Gold. "I'll recheck and get back to you."

"But there's nothing to recheck," Roy said. "She was my wife. Who'd know better than I?"

Gold ignored that. "What really concerns me," he said, "is this supposed accident of yours."

"Accident?"

"How you came upon the text of this piece. I'd appreciate some elaboration."

Roy had been interviewed by reporters a few times, had liked every one. But hanging up now—banging down the phone, actually—without another word, he decided he didn't like Richard Gold at all. He felt a tickle coming in his throat and moved toward the sink.

Six

"Lookin' good, Roy," said Freddy Boudreau, Ethan Valley police sergeant and first-line center for the Thongs.

Tuesday night in the locker room at the rink. Roy, lacing up his skates on the bench, fumbled with the knot. "Oh?"

"Lost a few pounds," said Freddy. "Been workin' out?"

Before Roy could answer, Turk spoke up from the other side of the room. "Not everybody lives on cheeseburgers, Freddy." A remark that could have sounded light, but did not. There was anger in Turk's tone, and Freddy caught it. He shot Turk a puzzled glance.

Roy didn't want any of this. "I gave up fries," he said. "That's the secret."

Freddy turned to him. A little pause, and then he laughed. "Can't do that myself," he said. "Where'd I get my carbs?"

The horn sounded.

"Let's play hockey," Roy said, reaching for his stick and standing up. Freddy ground his cigarette butt under his skate blade and led them out of the locker room and onto the ice, smoke coming out of his nostrils.

The Zamboni was just gliding off, leaving the surface slick and smooth. Roy had long ago stopped noticing little rink details like that, but he was noticing now, the kind of fresh take that sometimes follows a rainstorm, or waking up in a new place. Little details like a Mars wrapper, frozen under the ice; a twist of Christmas tinsel hanging from a strap on Turk's mask; black puck streaks all over the white boards, like an abstract painting of speed and violence. Roy loved hockey, loved its rituals, too, like the way at the end of the warm-up every player circled back to the goal and tapped the goalie's pads with his stick blade. Roy always tried to be the last one doing that, a superstition inside a superstition, and now he made an extra turn up ice before skating in alone. He raised his stick, gave Turk's right pad a whack as he glided by.

"Don't let anybody get by you," Turk said through his mask. "Got a hangover like you wouldn't believe."

Just a little whack, not hard, but Roy felt a twinge in his left forearm. A twinge, nothing at all, easy to ignore, and getting nicked up was part of the game. But this twinge didn't end up being easy to ignore; in fact, got worse as the game went along. It took away his shooting, his passing, even slowed down his skating. Lots of guys got by him. The Thongs lost by six or seven goals, pretty much all of them his fault. Had he ever played worse?

Roy stayed on the ice after it was over, skating around by himself. Turk, clomping out last from the locker room, the huge goalie bag tugging him sideways, called over the boards, "You okay?"

Roy nodded.

"Coming to Waldo's?"

"Later."

But Roy went home instead. He had a good look at his arm: seemed fine, not even a bruise. He iced it, poured himself a drink, stared at the TV. After a while, he noticed that his answering machine was flashing.

Roy checked it. "Richard Gold speaking. We've got conflicting stories here, Mr. Valois. I'll need some documentation connecting your deceased wife to the institute you mentioned." He left his home number.

Documentation? Like what? Roy thought he remembered seeing Delia's photo-ID card, and maybe some pay stubs as well, but all that was long gone, along with her clothes, favorite coffee mug, other things he'd held on to for a year or two, finally realizing they kept reminding him of death, not her.

Roy called Gold, went into his voice mail. "What kind of documentation are you talking about? Delia worked for the Hobbes Institute, not the UN. That's a fact. Not telling you how to do your job, but why not just call them? Her boss at the time was Tom Parish. Maybe he's still there."

Roy took some Advil and went to bed. So tired, and wanting only to put his mind to sleep, to be without it for a few hours, but the ache in his arm kept him awake all night. In the morning he drove to the clinic at the base of the mountain. From the waiting room, he could see the tiny shapes of the first skiers of the day zigzagging down, trailing clouds of overnight powder. Tiny, distant shapes, but one was zigzagging in a way he thought he knew.

He filled in forms, checking *no* to all those questions about past or current illnesses, as he'd always done in doctors' offices. They X-rayed his forearm, front, back, sideways. Not long after, the doctor appeared and told Roy he'd broken his ulna.

"Common nightstick fracture," the doctor said, holding up the film. "See?"

Roy said he saw.

"Snowboarding?" said the doctor.

"Hockey," Roy said.

"Rough game. Slashing? High-sticking?"

"It wasn't intentional," Roy said.

"Just above the glove," the doctor said. "See it all the time." He led Roy to the casting room. "Any special color?"

Red, Roy thought: Delia's favorite color. Where did that come from? He said: "No."

The doctor chose blue, wound Roy's arm in a plaster cast that ended an inch below the elbow. "Clean break," he said. "That's the good news."

"And the bad news?" said Roy.

The doctor blinked. "No bad news," he said, "other than the fracture itself, which should heal nicely in six weeks. Come see me then." The doctor saw some look on Roy's face. "Don't worry," he said. "You'll be back on the ice by spring." He held out a vial. "These are for pain."

"No thanks," said Roy.

He stopped by the yard on his way home.

"Hey," said Murph. "What's with the cast?"

"Hockey," Roy said. "Out six weeks."

"You puckheads," said Murph. "Never know when to quit."

"Is that bad?" Roy said.

"Huh?" said Murph.

Roy glanced around the office. "Skippy here? He said something came in from a nuclear plant."

"That's just my theory, the nuclear angle," said Murph, pushing himself up from the desk. "But you can see for yourself."

"Skippy's off today?"

Murph snorted. "Fuckin' moron. He's off all right."

"What do you mean?"

"They got the little wiseass down at the station," Murph said. "Picked him up last night on a DUI."

"Is he okay?"

"Hell, no. He's driving his ma nuts. And then she drives me nuts." They left the office, walked down the outside stairs, crossed the yard, frozen mud cracking under their boots. "She's leaving him in the tank for a couple days," Murph said, "maybe teach him a lesson."

"Is that a good idea?" Roy said.

"You got a better one? The kid's a loser."

Roy followed Murph past a mound of rusty barbecue kettles, a wrecked Escalade lying on its side, headhigh rows of brass cloth. Murph pointed. "Whaddya think?"

"No idea," said Roy, gazing down at the thing: a highly polished silvery cone, about twenty feet long, topped by a much thinner cone, even shinier, that very gradually narrowed to a point. Roy read the word *Candu*, stenciled in red at the bottom. "How much for just that top part?" he said.

Murph shrugged. "I don't even know what the fuck it's made of," he said, running a horseshoe magnet over the metal.

"A hundred bucks," Roy said.

"For a hundred bucks I'll throw in Betty Lou," Murph said; Betty Lou was his wife.

Roy crouched down, touched the tip of the upper cone: very sharp, icy cold.

He went home, the narrow cone in the bed of his pickup, his casted arm resting in his lap, still aching. Three messages on his machine, the first from Turk:

"Didn't see you at Waldo's last night. Give me a call."

The second from Jen: "Hi, Roy. I dropped into the clinic today, just saying my good-byes. And I heard about your arm. You okay?"

The third from Richard Gold: "Trying to confirm that name you cited, Delia's—your former wife's boss. Tom Parish? One *r* or two?"

Roy listened to Jen's message once more, maybe twice, but he didn't return her call or any of the others. Instead he dragged the shiny cone to the center of the floor, not far from *Delia,* and just looked at it for a while. Sometimes he got ideas that way.

Not now. The blurry image of a delicate, attenuated silence that had been in his mind refused to grow clearer. He pulled up a stool, got out his sketch pad and a soft pencil. Nothing happened at first. Roy was used to that, had learned patience in his work. *No hurry:* that was what he always told himself.

The pencil began to move in that way it sometimes did, Roy following more than leading. The first few lines might have had something to do with the cone, attenuation, silence, but then they turned into a fluted pilaster, and another, four in all, with a double door between them and a pediment above. Roy was just finishing a set of broad, shallow stairs, when he realized what he had: the facade of the Hobbes Institute on Constitution Avenue.

No more sketching happened after that. *Silence* withdrew completely.

He went to the phone, called Richard Gold, again ended up in voice mail. Roy was one of those people not bothered by little frustrations, but now he heard his voice rising. "Tom Parish with one *r.* How hard can this be?"

After that, he lay on the couch. Snow began to fall; he could see it through the skylights, the flakes appearing dark from that angle, dark and plummeting fast, as though propelled by tiny motors. He got his arm in a comfortable position, almost painless. His eyes closed.

"This is fun!" Delia said.

"Didn't I tell you?" said Tom Parish. "Any more of that champagne, Roy?"

Plenty, in the cooler on the deck of *Bellissima,* Tom's thirty-two-foot powerboat, maybe thirty-five—Roy, an inlander, didn't know much about boats. He grabbed a couple of cold bottles and went forward. Tom stood at the control console, the breeze ruffling his blond hair; Delia sat on the gunwale, an empty flute glass dangling in her hand. The boat wallowed in the swell, engines idling. Night, Chesapeake Bay, Fourth of July, fireworks erupting every few seconds from many points on the coastline. Roy popped a cork, poured champagne.

"*Salut,*" said Tom.

They drank. Delia gazed at the spectacle, all that blooming light reflected in her eyes. "It's like—what's it like, Roy?"

Fireworks went off, *pow pow pow,* red white blue green, the whole blazing show bobbing on every wave in the water. Roy shook his head; too hard to describe.

"I'll tell you what it's like," said Tom, gazing into his glass for a moment, then draining it: "War at play."

Delia glanced over at Tom and laughed. Roy didn't quite get it, but Tom was a brilliant guy.

The phone was ringing. It sent an electric pulse across the room, a pulse aimed directly at the break in Roy's arm. He got off the couch—the little action making him breathless for some reason—and answered it.

"Roy? Freddy Boudreau here, down at the station. I wake you or something?"

"Just watching TV," Roy said.

"Anyways," said Freddy, "this kid here in the tank, says he works for you, and we don't want to hold him or nothin' but no one's come to get him."

"Skippy?"

"You got it."

Roy drove to the police station. Freddy stood at the counter in his blue uniform, Skippy on a chair behind him, staring at his knees.

"What's with the arm?" Freddy said.

"Nicked it last night."

"In the game?"

"Yeah."

"When did that happen?"

Roy shrugged. "Didn't notice at the time."

"You stud," said Freddy. He jabbed his thumb back at Skippy. "True this numbnuts works for you?"

"Skippy helps out sometimes," Roy said.

"He blew point-one-eight last night. Plus no insurance, and he had both taillights out, which was how come we pulled him over in the first place. Meaning he's got a court date next month."

Skippy stared at his knees.

"How much to bail him out?"

"Nothin'," said Freddy. "Just have to turn him over to a responsible adult."

"I'll see who's around," Roy said.

Freddy laughed. Roy walked Skippy out of the station.

"Drop you off at your mom's?" he said as they got in the pickup.

Skippy shook his head.

"Murph's?"

"He hates me."

"No, he doesn't."

"Right," said Skippy. He let out his breath, a long, resigned exhale, like a groan but softer. "Maybe just take me to Junior's."

"Who's Junior?"

"This friend of mine. Lives near the bridge."

"What's his last name?"

"Cordero."

"Tell you what," Roy said. "Stay in my spare room tonight. In the morning, you'll have to work things out with your mom." Roy knew some of the Corderos.

Skippy nodded, a very slight movement. He smelled pretty bad.

The phone woke Roy in the morning.

"This is Dr. Honey." So many doctors recently, Roy had trouble placing him at first. "Dr. Chu, the colleague at Hopkins I mentioned, has agreed to see you. No absolute guarantee he'll include you in his study, but I urge you to get to Baltimore as soon as possible."

"I, uh . . ." Roy, for some reason suddenly wanting to tell Dr. Honey all about his broken arm, barely stopped himself.

"Any questions?"

"No," said Roy. "Just—thanks."

"I'll transfer you to my assistant," said Dr. Honey. "She'll fill you in on the details."

Dr. Honey's assistant filled Roy in. He took notes. Then he went down the hall, looked in the guest room. Skippy was sleeping on the bare mattress, still fully dressed, boots and all; the sheets Roy had given him lay folded on the bedside table.

"Time to get up," Roy said.

No reaction.

"Your mom's probably—"

The phone rang again. Roy went into the big room. The early-morning sun, bright and silvery, made sparkles on *Delia,* nudging the Fourth of July dream into Roy's conscious mind. He picked up the phone.

"Mr. Valois? Richard Gold. I'll need information on Tom Parish."

"One *r*," said Roy. "Don't you check your messages?"

"I got that," Gold said. "But I was hoping for a little more."

"For Christ sake," Roy said. "Is this the way your paper handles everything? Delia worked for the Hobbes Institute. Tom Parish was her boss. He recruited her, in fact."

"From where?"

"The State Department," Roy said. "But she hadn't been there more than a few months and I don't see how—"

"Did she have any military training?" Gold said.

"Military training?" Roy said. "Of course not. She was an economist—with a PhD from Georgetown and a job at the Hobbes Institute. Period."

"It's not that simple," Gold said. "The problem is—"
Roy heard commotion in the background. "Hang on a
second," Gold said.

Roy hung on. He heard soft muffled sounds, then
a little crash, as though a glass had fallen. After that,
nothing. "Mr. Gold?" Fifteen or twenty seconds went
by. Then came a click, followed by the dial tone. "What
the hell?" he said.

Roy called back. Voice mail. "Forget the whole
thing," he said. "Write whatever you want." What
difference did it make?

Seven

R oy and Skippy met Skippy's mom in the parking
lot at Dunkin' Donuts. Skippy's mom sat in the
passenger seat of a van with painted-over lettering on
the side. The man behind the wheel was eating a pink
glazed doughnut, the only color on a dark day.

"Who's that?" Roy said.

"The boyfriend," said Skippy. "The new one."

The new boyfriend had a bushy white mustache. Roy
parked beside the van. Everybody looked at everybody
but no one made a move. The new boyfriend also had
strong jaw muscles. They bulged as he chewed on the
doughnut. Roy got out of the pickup, walked over to
Skippy's mom's door.

Her window slid down, about halfway. Roy could see
nothing of Skippy in her face. "Hi," he said. "I'm Roy."

"Uh-huh," said Skippy's mom.

"I'll be away on business for a few days," Roy said. "It'll be a big help if Skippy could stay at my place, take care of things."

Skippy's mom glanced at the boyfriend. Some sort of silent communication passed between them. Skippy's mom turned back to Roy. "You payin' him?" she said.

"Yes."

She thought about that. The boyfriend's jaw muscles bulged. "How much?" Skippy's mom said.

"That's up to Skippy to tell you," Roy said.

"Huh?" said the boyfriend.

Skippy's mom looked past Roy at Skippy, sitting in the pickup. He had earphones on, was gazing straight ahead, eyes blank.

"Yeah, okay," said Skippy's mom. She gave Roy a hard stare. "But when he screws up don't come cryin' to me."

The boyfriend polished off the rest of the doughnut.

"Like damages and so forth," Skippy's mom added, but Roy was already walking away.

She raised her voice. "It's on you."

Skippy heard that and slumped a little more.

Delia lay in the cemetery behind the Congregational church. It was a place Roy never went, but he did before setting out for Baltimore. Some of the grave-stones, closest to the church, dated from the 1600s. The newer ones stood on a slope rising toward the forest, Delia in the last row, next to the trees. She had a plain granite stone, dark gray, with nothing on it but her name and dates.

Roy found the stone covered with snow almost to the top. He remembered one winter as a kid in Maine when a snow fort had collapsed on him, and the buried-alive feeling that followed. Roy cleared the snow away—one-handed—down to the frozen turf. Some people in his position might have thought about being back together in the not-too-distant future. *Four months to a year.* But Roy just didn't believe it; not only that, he didn't think anyone else believed it either, not in their deepest parts. If you really believed a rosy afterlife with lovers and families back together was in the offing, believed it as fact, then what would be the point of getting so worked up about death? But everybody did, the fear of death somewhere in their minds from the moment they first found out about it, and the death of someone close was the worst thing that could ever happen.

"Or am I missing something?" Roy said aloud.

Had he and Delia ever discussed this? Not really. He tried to imagine what she'd say now, and couldn't.

"I looked up Dr. Chu on the Internet," Roy said. A brilliant guy, with degrees from the best schools and scientific prizes from three countries.

Brilliant guys are a dime a dozen. The question is— can he do it?

That thought came to him in Delia's voice, so clear she might have said it aloud. In fact, he couldn't swear she hadn't said it aloud, not on any sensory basis. It stunned him. Roy crouched in front of the gravestone, a wind rising in the trees.

He got through the funeral all right: hearing the news—everything about that call from Tom Parish still completely unfaded in his mind—had been the big blow. The Institute flew the body back from Venezuela, in an ornate white coffin she would have hated. Lots of people came to the service—old college friends, art-world people, hockey people, Washington people, including Tom Parish—none of whom Roy saw anymore, except for Krishna and the hockey guys. Tom told a funny story about Delia squeezing a donation out of some tinpot dictator. A guitarist sitting on a stool by the grave site played "For All We Know"—one of Delia's favorites, especially the Billie Holiday version. Not long after came that first spadeful of earth, landing with a soft thump on the coffin. Roy had flinched at the sound. No one said anything about the baby inside her: still a secret between Roy, Delia and the obstetrician.

The wind picked up. Snow started to fall, hard little pellets that stung Roy's face. He rose, walked out of the graveyard, her voice still fresh. *The question is— can he do it?*

Roy drove his pickup to the gas station at the southern edge of town, pulled up at the pumps. He filled the tank, was replacing the nozzle when he noticed the car on the other side: a Subaru wagon, packed top to bottom, with two big ski carriers on the roof. Roy looked up, and their eyes met, his and Jen's.

She looked great, the kind of woman who, unknown, he would have wanted to know—in some former period of his life, of course. A snowflake clung to one of her eyelashes; her skin glowed like it was a sunny day.

"Hi, Roy."

"Hi."

"I'm off," she said.

What if Dr. Chu really could do it? Roy's heart started beating very fast; he thought of saying *Don't forget about me, don't even sign a lease, everything may change,* but got a grip and simply nodded.

Jen glanced over at the pickup, saw the suitcase sitting on the front seat. Some over-the-top romantic thought ran through her mind—he could see it—like *Is he coming with me?*

"Business trip," Roy said quickly, heading off any meeting between those unspoken thoughts, his and hers.

Jen smiled. "You're a businessman now?"

Roy felt his face redden. "Taking a quick tour of scrap yards," he said.

"Working on something new?"

"Just an idea."

"You always have good ideas."

"I don't know about that."

They looked at each other.

"Feeling all right, Roy?"

"Great."

"Arm okay?"

He waved it in the air to show just how okay; that hurt.

Cars pulled in behind them. She came forward, kissed him on the cheek.

"Drive safe."

"You too."

Roy followed her as far as the interstate. Jen tapped her brakes good-bye as she took the ramp. He kept going.

Before we get started," said Dr. Chu, "I have something to show you."

Dr. Chu came around his desk, opening a folder. His office had rice-paper blinds and simple wood furniture, reminded Roy of a yoga retreat he'd tried a year or so after Delia's death, lasting less than a day. Dr. Chu took a photograph from the folder, showed it to Roy: a picture of Dr. Chu, wearing shorts, a T-shirt and flip-flops, standing next to one of the *Neanderthal* sculptures with a big grin on his face. Roy noticed a palm tree in the background: Number Twelve, on the campus of the University of Miami.

"Two years ago," said Dr. Chu. "The annual conference."

"What annual conference?" said Roy.

"The International Association for Mesothelioma Research," said Dr. Chu. "Of which I am the founder, in fact. But my point was how our paths seem to have crossed previously in this way."

Roy had thought of that already: it gave him a bad feeling. "Dr. Honey says four months to a year," he said.

Dr. Chu slid the photo back into the folder, moved around the desk, sat in his chair. "I know Dr. Honey," he said. He gazed at Roy, his eyes not so friendly now; almost a different man from the tourist in the photo. *You want this guy on your side, you dope:* Delia's voice again, this time so clear she might have been in the room. Roy decided he preferred this unsmiling version of the man anyway and kept his mouth shut, waited for Dr. Chu to say more about Dr. Honey.

But Dr. Chu did not. Instead, he thought for a moment or two and then said, "I will outline my approach in the area of unresectable pleural mesothelioma. The common weakness of all current chemical and radiation treatments is their lack of curative result, a result that will almost certainly persist notwithstanding current work with pemetrexed/cisplatin, pemetrexed/gemcitibane, gemcitibane/carboplatin with or without bevacizumab, flavopiridol with or without FR901228, or other compounds presently in trial phase. The reasons for this are various—as the biology of cancer is even more various. My current phase one study in nonsurgical stage two and three is predicated on a neoadjuvant combination of tumor antigen and an angiogenesis inhibitor cocktail developed in my lab."

Pemetrexed, gemcitibane, flavopiridol, neoadjuvant— all these strange words, so unconnected to the language as he knew it: Roy began to lose the thread. Even ones he thought he knew, like *antigen*, now eluded him. The only one that stuck was *cocktail*, a very optimistic word. Sound flowed by, logical, persuasive, egotistical, but his mind turned to other things. *Can he do it?* Through the window Roy could see a distant scrap of blue, maybe Chesapeake Bay.

He grew aware of a change in Dr. Chu's tone, saw that the doctor was leaning forward. ". . . both to starve the cancer cells and turn them against each other at the same time, do you see?" he was saying. "To put it in the simplest terms, I am not interested in three extra months, four extra months, even a year or two." His voice fell, as though he were imparting a secret. "I want more, much, much more."

Roy nodded. He did, too.

Dr. Chu sat back.

"Questions?"

"How's the study going so far?" Roy said.

"Since it is a phase one study, very early, there are only five participants at this moment, four if we restrict the definition to only those still actually living," Dr. Chu said. "I would categorize the current status of the study as promising."

"Then I want in," Roy said.

"We have not discussed potential side effects." Dr. Chu went over potential side effects—rashes, nausea, hair loss, confusion, other things, none near as bad as death in four months to a year. "Questions?"

"No."

Dr. Chu rose, picked up a stethoscope. "I will now listen to your chest."

Roy raised his shirt, fumbling a little. Dr. Chu glanced at the cast on Roy's arm, said nothing. Dr. Chu placed the end of the stethoscope on Roy's bare chest. His touch was light and gentle. He listened. Their faces were very close. Dr. Chu's eyes had an inward look; he might have been in a trance. Intelligence radiated off him; Roy could feel it. At that moment, he believed his insides were being examined by something more probing than any scanning machine.

Dr. Chu stepped back. "We begin first with a vitamin infusion, mostly B12 and folic acid."

"When?" said Roy.

"If you'll go to the waiting room, the nurse will call you soon."

"So I'm in?"

"You are in."

He was in. Was this a moment for handshaking? None ensued. He went to the waiting room.

Roy had the waiting room to himself. He filled in forms. He drank from the watercooler. He studied a framed aerial photograph of the Great Wall of China. An hour went by. What did *soon* mean? He spent a few minutes on some magazines, all of the celebrity type, of no interest to him. Then he noticed a section of the *New York Times* in the wastebasket beside him. Roy fished it out.

Section D of a days-old paper, business and sports, with a coffee stain in the bottom right corner. Roy leafed through the business section—where sometimes there were stories from the art world, but not in this one—and moved on to the sports. But just before the sports came a page of obituaries. He scanned it, looking for Richard Gold's byline. And Richard Gold's name was there, although not as a byline, instead in a context that made him feel very strange.

RICHARD GOLD, TIMES REPORTER, 41

by Myra Burns

RICHARD GOLD, who won several important awards during a fifteen-year tenure at the *New York Times*, died yesterday at the age of forty-one. He was killed during a robbery at his house in northwest Washington, according to Sergeant Irwin Bettis of the violent crime unit of the Metropolitan D.C. police. "This is a terrible loss for the *Times* family," said managing editor—

"Roy?"

Roy looked up. A nurse stood before him.

"All set to go," she said.

Eight

"I'm Netty," said the nurse. "No sense asking which arm—what happened?"

"Hockey," Roy said.

"My, my."

He rolled up his right sleeve.

"What a nice vein," Netty said.

"Thanks."

"Might feel a little sting." She stuck in the IV needle. Roy felt nothing. Vitamins flowed into him. She watched the IV bag. "Where you from, Roy?"

"Vermont."

"Supposed to be beautiful."

"Yeah."

Their eyes met. The nurse was middle-aged, heavy, with a soft, tired face. "Dr. Chu's a brilliant man," she said.

It took ten minutes. Roy went back to the waiting room, feeling pretty good. Was it possible that the vitamins were doing their work already? He breathed, deep breaths, the first real breaths he'd taken in a while.

Roy put on his coat, moved toward the chair where he'd left Section D of the *Times*. But at that moment the door to the hall opened and a man in a wheelchair came through, pushed by another nurse. The man had an oxygen tube in his nose. Judging from his hair, slightly gray at the temples, he might have been Roy's age, but the rest of him was skeletal. Skin the color of cold ashes, except for raw unhealed sores here and there; eyes dull; neck scrawny: and shivering, although he was covered with a blanket.

Was he in the study? Roy didn't want to be anywhere near the man in the wheelchair. He left Section D of the *Times* where it was and hurried out of Dr. Chu's office.

Roy checked into a hotel, went down to the bar and ordered dinner: chowder, T-bone steak, roast potatoes, Caesar salad, a glass of heavy ale, and then another, plus pecan pie with ice cream for dessert. A big dinner: but Roy had always had a big appetite, had often polished off meals like this, after a day on snowshoes, for example. This time the chowder would have been enough. Roy forced the rest down.

"I like to see a man eat," the bartender said. "Here on business?"

Roy nodded.

"What do you do, don't mind my asking?" she said.

Roy gave his usual answer for situations like this. "I'm in metals," he said.

"Like gold?" said the bartender.

He got that a lot. "Scrap," he said.

"Oh." She moved away; the usual reaction, except for the odd man who asked if there was any money in it. Roy kept eating. After a while, she said, "Mind the TV?"

Roy didn't mind. The bartender turned on the TV.

Local news. A reporter stood in front of a small white house on a tree-lined street, Georgetown, maybe, or Chevy Chase.

". . . still no suspects in the murder of D.C.-based *New York Times* reporter Richard Gold, who died of blunt force trauma to the head."

A photo of Gold appeared: bald, fine features, thin lips. He was reaching for a phone.

"Robbery is the probable motive, according to investigators. Mr. Gold's wallet is missing, as well as a flat-screen TV and other valuables. Anyone with information is urged to call the number on your screen."

The bartender watched, hand on hip. "They never learn," she said. "Soon as they start using the credit cards they're toast. Happens every time."

Roy had a good sleep. In the morning he showered, shaved, checked himself in the mirror. He looked all right, except for the broken arm and those four stitches in his chest, maybe a little redder than they should have been by now. He went to the hospital for his first treatment with Dr. Chu.

Roy didn't actually see Dr. Chu. First Netty took his pulse and blood pressure.

"Numbers okay?" said Roy.

"Normal."

Then she collected three test tubes of blood, putting different colored stickers on each. After that, she had Roy strip down to his boxers and stand on the scale.

"One seventy-two," she said. "Is that your usual weight?"

"More or less," Roy said, although less was the true answer: he hadn't been under one ninety since junior year in high school, and had topped two hundred several times since. He stepped off the footpad, felt sweat popping out suddenly on his upper lip. Netty was slipping the test tubes into envelopes, her back to him. Roy slid the two scale weights leftward to the neutral position, expecting the right end of the arm to bob up, meaning the calibration was too light, probably way off, and he weighed one eighty at least, or more likely a few pounds more, seven or eight, say. But the arm didn't move, just hovered there in perfect balance, a picture of harmony. At that moment, not a good one, came a foreshadowing of a new idea for *Silence*. What about that part of him—could it keep going all by itself?

"Roy? Roy?"

He heard her, turned from the scale.

"You can put your clothes back on. Just leave that sleeve rolled up."

Fully dressed, sleeve rolled up, Roy followed the nurse out of the examining room, along a corridor and into another room in Dr. Chu's suite. An unmedical kind of room—soft lighting, a fountain playing on a descending series of honey-colored stones, a suede couch—the only medical touch being one of those rolling IV-bag racks.

"The treatment room," said Netty. "Dr. Chu had it designed by a feng shui master. He came all the way from Beijing."

"That doesn't sound very scientific," Roy said.

Netty smiled a wise smile. "If you'll just lie down on the couch."

He lay on the couch.

"Get comfortable."

He shifted around like someone getting comfortable. Netty wheeled over the IV rack. "Might feel a little sting."

This time he did, and not just a little. It hurt so much that Roy almost let out a sound. Had she done something wrong? He glanced down at his arm, saw the needle neatly in place, not a drop of blood anywhere. So: no clue. But his skin seemed so white, like someone else's. Colorless liquid flowed from the bag, down the tube, into his arm. It could have been water.

"All you have to do now is relax," she said. "Think you can do that?"

"Sure."

"I'll be back in twenty minutes."

Roy lay on the couch like a relaxing man. He watched the surface level slowly falling in the IV bag. Invisible chemicals swam in that liquid. Were some of them already reaching the cancer cells, arrayed in some potent molecular formation, all set to unleash their sophisticated attack, cutting off blood supply, turning tumor against tumor, and whatever else Dr. Chu had in mind?

Fight like bastards. Delia's voice.

"There's a war inside me," he said.

After that, he was quiet. He listened to the fountain, water falling on rocks. So many different sounds, actually, gurgling, trickling, bubbling, and others for which he had no words. He'd never even thought of working with water. To shape water: How would he begin?

A fountain stood in the lobby of the Hobbes Institute. He saw it once, at a reception, not long before the Venezuela trip, a fountain with Neptune, cherubs and coins winking on the bottom. All the women wore black, except for Delia, in red. Delia was a great one for circulating at parties, but on this night she didn't leave Roy's side, her hand on his arm almost the whole time.

"This is my husband, Roy. Roy, I'd like you to meet Paul Habib."

"Hi."

"Hi, Roy," said Habib. "Heard so much about you."

"Likewise. Looking forward to Venezuela?"

"Venezuela?"

"My mistake," Roy said. "I thought you were part of this pineapple caper."

Paul Habib smacked himself on the head. He was a big guy with closely trimmed hair and a full beard, a consultant to the Hobbes Institute, on loan from somewhere Roy couldn't remember at the moment, or maybe hadn't been told in the first place. "The pineapple caper, of course, of course," he said. "A little jet-lagged right now, but, yes, I'm on the trip. Looking forward to it, in fact. Delia's work on this has been brilliant."

"Think they'll buy it?" Roy said.

"Who?"

"The Venezuelans," Roy said. "Growing pineapples."

"Right, the Venezuelans," Habib said. "The numbers work, no doubt about that, thanks to your wife. So it's a matter of getting them comfortable with the idea. Never easy, though, is it, Delia?"

Delia's hand tightened a little on Roy's arm. "What isn't?" she said.

"Rewiring people's heads," Habib said.

"I wouldn't know," Delia said. "Isn't that your job?" She turned to Roy. "I'd love a glass of champagne."

"And one for you, Paul?" Roy said.

"Thanks," Habib said.

But when Roy returned with the drinks, Habib was gone.

"Some problem between you and Paul?" he said.

"No," Delia said. "He gets on my nerves sometimes, that's all."

"In what way?"

"The usual workplace way," Delia said. "It's nothing. Let's have fun tonight."

"I'm your man," Roy said. "Here's to Venezuela."

"No," said Delia. "To us."

They drank to themselves, Delia downing her glass in one gulp. "Got a penny?" she said.

Roy fished one from his pocket, handed it to her. Delia made a wish, her lips moving silently—he saw how she'd looked as a little girl—and tossed it in the fountain. The penny spun in coppery slow motion to the bottom.

"Let's go home," she said.

"Now?"

They went home. In bed, she said, "You can do anything you want to me tonight."

"Time's up."

Roy found he was staring at the water flowing over those honey-colored rocks in Dr. Chu's fountain. He turned his head, saw Netty standing beside him. It was almost like waking up.

"That wasn't so bad, now, was it?" she said.

"No," Roy said. He glanced up at the IV bag, now empty except for a few last drops clinging to the plastic. Roy resisted the impulse to ask her to squeeze them into the tube, to coax every last microscopic warrior into his body. "It was good."

She nodded as though she'd heard that before. "We'll need you back at the same time tomorrow," she said. "Here's an after-hours number to call, just in case."

"Just in case what?" Roy said.

"You have some sort of bad reaction," she said. "But you won't—it's never happened."

"Not with this cocktail, you mean?"

"No, not with this cocktail."

Roy took the card she handed him, saw her name was really Annette. "Netty," he said. "I've got a question."

"Shoot."

"The man in the waiting room yesterday, the one on oxygen—is he in the study?"

Netty took in a deep breath through her nose. "He was."

It took Roy a few seconds to get that. "He died?"

"Late last night. Dr. Chu is with the family."

"So the study's down to three."

"Four, with you," Netty said. "And there'll be more, many more. Dr. Chu is a brilliant man." She patted Roy's knee. "Don't think of any of the others. Don't think about anybody. Concentrate on you." She slid out the IV needle, swabbed the spot with alcohol.

Roy rose, dizzy for a moment, but he mastered it.

"And, Roy?" Netty said. "He was never a big strong man like you."

She was looking up at him in a way that reminded him of an encouraging parent or coach. Roy gave his chest a thump. Netty laughed. He left the building, walked across the parking lot. Yes, there was a huge gap between the man in the wheelchair and him. Roy took a few running steps, just to show he could do it, and he could, hardly breathless at all. A big strong man.

Fight like bastards.

When had he last drunk a milk shake? Roy couldn't remember; probably in high school. He found an ice-cream place, ordered the biggest milk shake they sold, mocha fudge swirl with marshmallow topping, and took it with him in the pickup. Kind of sickening, but he made himself keep sipping. He was almost done as he drove into D.C.

Roy hadn't been there in years, not since Delia's death, but it hadn't changed much and he still knew his way. The sun came out as he turned onto Constitution Avenue, shining on the Capitol dome to the east, turning it lemony. Roy went by some Senate office buildings and there it was, with those four fluted pilasters: the Hobbes Institute. He found a meter on a side street, stuck in a few quarters and walked back. Winter, but there was real warmth in the sunshine this far south. It felt good.

Roy climbed the broad stone steps of the Hobbes Institute—they looked lemony, too—and moved toward the double doors. Brass doors, although he remembered them as dark wood. And one other change—two security guards, standing on either side. No guards back then, but why should that be a surprise, with how the world had changed?

"Hi," Roy said, reaching for the handle. The security guards stepped in front of him.

"Do you have an appointment, sir?" one said.

"No," said Roy. "But my wife used to work here."

"Her name?"

Roy told them. The other guard consulted a clipboard, shook his head.

"Her name wouldn't be there now," Roy explained. "This was a long time ago. Tom Parish was her boss."

They gazed at him.

"Is he still here?" Roy said. "Parish with one *r*. His title was director of research, something like that."

The guard checked his clipboard, shook his head again.

"What about Paul Habib?" His title? Roy wasn't sure he'd ever known it.

Another head shake.

Roy tried to remember other Hobbes Institute names, couldn't at the moment. "Look," he said, "I'd just like to talk to someone from the Institute. They'll understand right away. It'll only take a few minutes."

All he needed was a two-sentence note over some official signature confirming Delia's employment.

"The Institute, sir?" said the first guard.

Roy's voice rose a little; he couldn't help it. "The Hobbes Institute," he said. "This building you're guarding."

"Sir?"

That was when Roy noticed the flag on a pole to one side, a flag he'd maybe seen before but couldn't identify. Then he noticed a plaque on one of the doors: CONSULATE OF GREECE.

He stepped back, down a few steps so he could see up to the pediment where the words *Hobbes Institute* were carved into the stone. No words there of any kind, and no sign that there ever had been, the facing smooth.

"Where did they go?" Roy said.

"Who, sir?"

"The Hobbes Institute, of course," Roy said. "The people who own this place. Or did."

"Never heard of it," said the first guard, turning to the other one. "You?"

The head-shaking guard shook his head once more.

Nine

Roy backed away from the Consulate of Greece, just stood on the sidewalk for a few moments. He looked around. Was it possible he'd made a mistake? Maybe there was more than one building with four fluted pilasters and a triangular pediment. Twin buildings: the concept was not unknown. Roy scanned the long line of facades, and there, just a few doors down, saw— but no. Moving closer, he took in the details of a much bigger structure: six pilasters, not fluted, a pediment, but rectangular, and on it the engraved words *Washington Historical Society.* Long engraved: the shapes of the letters were softened by erosion.

Roy walked on, spotted no other possibilities on either side of the street for several blocks. He returned to his original thought: they'd moved somewhere else.

He backtracked, reexamined all the buildings, this time looking for *Hobbes Institute* on a sign, on a brass plaque, anywhere, but not finding it.

A little group of tourists came starting-and-stopping down the block—somewhat like walking birds—following a guide.

"Excuse me," Roy said.

The guide turned.

"I'm looking for the Hobbes Institute."

"Sorry."

He pointed. "It used to be right there."

"Isn't that the Greek consulate?" she said.

"I'm talking about years ago," Roy said.

"It's been the Greek consulate as long as I can remember," the guide said. The tourists rocked back and forth behind her, a crowded flock brought up short. The guide gave Roy a quick second look, as though there might be something not quite right about him. "Maybe this will help," she said, handing Roy a map and moving on.

A tourist map, with all the famous sights well marked, but what was the chance a small private think tank like the Hobbes Institute would be included? None. Roy checked carefully anyway, reading every bit of print on the map. It wasn't there.

The security guards were watching him. Roy walked away, in no particular direction, but soon found himself on the side street where he'd parked. He got into the pickup, sat there. He gazed at the crumpled milk-shake container on the floor. The bent shapes, the balloon-style lettering, the picture of a happy cow all mesmerized him. A long time passed before he was struck by the obvious idea.

Roy opened the glove box, took out his cell phone. He didn't like cell phones, secretly believed that the technology sometime in the midtwentieth century had been good enough, but Krishna, tired of not being able to reach him instantly, had added Roy to his friends-and-family plan. An obvious idea: he called information, asked for the number of the Hobbes Institute, first in D.C., then expanding to Maryland and Virginia, after that New York, and finally the whole country. There was no listing.

Roy bought a PowerBar and ate it on the way to Baltimore. Back at the hotel he changed into sweats and went to the gym on the top floor. Roy didn't spend much time in gyms—hockey, hiking, snowshoeing, skiing were enough to keep him fit. But now—now was different.

StairMaster: thirty minutes. At first, a little breathless, but that could happen to anybody. He pushed past it. Then came free weights. Roy squatted four sets of ten at two hundred and fifty pounds, then, despite the cast, benched three sets of one forty-five. He followed that with one hundred sit-ups on the slant board. Not bad. Not bad for just about anybody. Could it all be a mistake? Or was it a dream? Had he fallen off the ladder, working with those twisted helicopter blades, say, and was he now in a coma, a coma he might soon emerge from, good as new? He checked himself in the mirror. Could that action, checking himself in the mirror, be part of a coma dream? Why not? A woman on a stationary bike was checking him out, too, a woman he'd never seen before. That pushed the coma-dream concept a little too far. Her image gave his a quick smile.

Roy went back to his room, showered, started getting dressed to go down to the bar, order exactly what he'd had last night, maybe even seconds on dessert. Outside the sun was setting, leaving streaks of gold on the highest windows of the tallest buildings. He sat on the bed to put his shoes on.

Roy opened his eyes. For a moment or two, he didn't know where he was. Then reality hit, a series of blows like a combination from a clever boxer: hotel room; daytime; fully dressed except for shoes; his lungs.

He checked the time: forty-five minutes until his appointment at Dr. Chu's. He'd been out for fourteen hours. Roy put on his shoes, brushed his teeth, splashed water on his face, went down to the coffee shop.

"Three-egg omelet with hash browns, plus toast, orange juice, coffee. Oh, and bacon on the side. And fruit cup."

No dinner. He should have been ravenous. But when the food came—taking up all the space on the serving tray—Roy found that he was not. In fact, not hungry at all. He made himself eat every morsel.

The man at the next table signed his check and walked out, leaving a newspaper behind. Roy reached across and took it. The *Washington Post*. He leafed through. Page eight, right-hand column at the top: still no leads in murder of times reporter.

Roy scanned the story. Richard Gold's credit cards hadn't been used. His flat-screen TV and other valuables hadn't turned up anywhere. Repeated neighborhood canvasses had led nowhere. The last paragraph was about a memorial service to be held that afternoon at a synagogue in Georgetown. Roy tore that part out and put it in his pocket.

Netty took his pulse and blood pressure.

"Numbers okay?"

"Normal."

"Any change?"

"Change?"

"Since yesterday."

Netty checked the chart. "Slightly lower," she said. "But that kind of fluc—"

"Lower being better."

"In this range, yes." She looked at him for a moment. "Do you want the actual numbers?"

"I do."

"Pulse sixty-eight. Blood pressure one eighteen over eighty-one."

"That's pretty good, right?"

She looked at him again. "Yes," she said, and seemed about to say more, but did not. Instead she came over with a needle, filled three more test tubes with his blood.

"Where does the blood go?"

"The lab."

"Did yesterday's results come back?"

"Not yet. But it's too early for any changes to show up."

"Then why bother taking the blood?"

"Roy. Can I say something?"

"Sure."

"Let Dr. Chu take care of the science. You just take care of you."

One part of Roy knew that made sense; another part flared in anger. Netty looked away. She busied herself with the different colored stickers. Roy got a grip.

"Did you want to weigh me today?" he said.

"Please," said Netty.

Roy stripped down to his boxers, stepped on the scale. Netty came closer, balanced the weights.

"One seventy-three," she said.

"And a half," said Roy.

She peered at the numbers. "And a half," she said.

"And yesterday?" said Roy, although he knew full well.

Netty checked. "One seventy-two."

And he hadn't even eaten dinner! Roy kept that little fact to himself, an ace in the hole. He got dressed, followed Netty to the feng shui room, lay on the suede couch. Netty hooked him up to the cocktail, said, "Twenty minutes," and left him alone.

Roy closed his eyes, listened to Dr. Chu's fountain. His body was a battlefield for this very quiet battle. Much too early to tell how it was going, of course, but: yesterday had been good—isn't that what the numbers were saying? And now, when all those cancer cells were still off balance—like so many teams when the opposition skates down for a quick opening goal—now here they came again, microscopic warriors by the million. Had to feel good about that. *Fight like bastards.*

Delia's voice again, so clear she might have been in the feng shui room with him. Fifteen years of silence and now he was hearing her again: What was that about? Roy didn't know, but found it comforting. He tried an experiment. "Where's the Hobbes Institute?" he said aloud. He heard nothing but the fountain.

Roy opened his eyes. The IV bag was empty, except for those last few stubborn drops, clinging to the plastic. Roy rose and squeezed the IV bag, forcing the remaining drops into the tube, on their way to the front. Netty entered.

"Roy? Everything all right?"

"Yup."

She unhooked him. "See you tomorrow."

"Yup."

"Still got the card?"

"Card?"

"With the emergency number. In case you have a reaction."

Roy shrugged; he knew perfectly well where the card was—in his wallet—but he wasn't going to need it. He bought a Hershey bar from a lobby vending machine on his way out of the hospital.

Roy had never been in a synagogue before. He had a notion that men and women didn't sit together, but it wasn't like that at all; in fact, the rabbi was a woman, plus only a few men wore skullcaps—including Roy, who'd taken his from a box by the door, thinking it was expected—and just about everything was in English. But there was Hebrew writing carved on the walls; the shapes of the letters kept catching Roy's eye.

From a seat at the back, he listened to stories from the life of Richard Gold. First came someone high up at the *New York Times,* who talked about Gold's passion for getting it right. Then a woman from a gay rights organization talked about the importance of Gold's support and what a stand-up guy he was. Finally, a man named Jerry, tears streaming down his face, said that Gold was the sweetest man that ever lived and how empty the house would be without him.

After, in the parking lot, Roy waited while people said good-bye. Little clusters here and there broke up and cars drove off, one by one. A light rain began to fall, the drops much colder than the air, and the last cluster, around Jerry, broke up, too. Jerry walked alone to his car, slowly, like every step involved an act of will. Roy followed him, caught up as Jerry reached his car, an old but pristine Volvo. Jerry fumbled with the keys.

"Excuse me," Roy said.

Jerry looked up, his eyes wet and silvery.

"Sorry for your loss," Roy said.

"Thank you," Jerry said. He blinked. "I'm afraid I can't quite place—"

"We haven't met," Roy said.

"You're a friend of Richard's?"

"Not exactly," Roy said. "We talked on the phone a few times. My name's Roy Valois."

A little pause. Raindrops trembled on Jerry's bald head. "The sculptor?" he said.

Roy nodded.

"Richard mentioned you." The expression on Jerry's face changed.

"Not favorably," Roy said.

"No, maybe not," Jerry said. "I'm not sure why. I'm not sure about anything today." He folded his arms across his chest, hugging himself. The keys fell to the wet pavement.

Roy picked them up. "I contacted him about a story he was working on."

"He always had so many stories on the go," Jerry said. He gazed into the distance. "What happens to them now?"

"I don't know." Roy held out the keys. Jerry looked confused for a moment; then he took them. "The story was my obituary," Roy said.

The word itself made Jerry wince, as though he'd felt a sudden pain inside. "He hated obituary assignments. The future—that's what interested Richard. He always had to know what was around the corner."

Jerry bent closer to the door lock, tried to stick in a key that was much too big. Roy pointed out the right one; Delia had had a car just like this when they first met.

"Thanks," Jerry said. He tried with the right key, but couldn't get it to work either.

"I know this is the wrong time," Roy said. "But Richard was looking into a mistake in his research on my background. I wonder if he mentioned anything about it."

Jerry straightened, glanced up at Roy. He was a very small man. "Now I remember. He said you must be a megalomaniac."

"Why?"

"Didn't you break into the morgue? Still young—already so hooked on how posterity was going to rate you. That's what he said."

"The mistake's not about me," Roy said. "It's about my wife."

"I don't understand."

"She died. I just want the facts to be right."

"Oh, God," Jerry said. "Recently?"

"No."

Jerry covered his face with his hands for a moment, composed himself. "What do you want from me?"

"I'd like to know if he was making any progress on the correction," Roy said.

"Not that he told me," Jerry said. He gazed down at the keys. Roy took them from him and unlocked the door. Jerry sighed, a racking sound that sank deeper and deeper inside him. "Maybe there's something in his notes."

Roy waited. He knew he should feel bad about what he was doing, but did not.

Jerry opened the door. "You can follow me if you want."

"Thanks."

"Don't thank me," Jerry said. "It's what Richard would have done." His voice rose in anger. "He cared about the facts."

The house—two stories, white with black shutters and trim, immaculate—stood on a side street off Connecticut, not far from where Roy and Delia had lived after the apartment in Foggy Bottom. Jerry parked in the driveway, Roy on the street. A locksmith was at work on the front door.

"Just about done," the locksmith said.

Jerry led Roy inside. "I don't know why I'm bothering," he said.

"Bothering with what?" said Roy.

"Changing the locks." They stood in the kitchen. Tidy, except for wreckage of a wooden chair, piled in a corner.

"Wasn't it a break-in?" Roy said.

"No, as a matter of fact," Jerry said. "They either had a key or Richard let them in, according to the police. But the point I was making is how am I supposed to live here?" He gestured to the floor, a spot between the counter and the broken chair. "That's where I found him. What was left of him, the bastards." He hurried from the room.

Roy moved to the corner, poked at one of the splintered bits with his toe. That last conversation with Gold came back to him: *hang on a second;* a little crash, as though a glass had fallen; dial tone. An idea rose in his mind, crazy, impossible: How about gluing all the pieces back together, but roughly, clumsily, emphasizing rather than disguising the repair?

Jerry returned, necktie gone, eyes red. "The study's upstairs. I don't think you're going to find much—they stole his laptop, too. But you can try his daybook."

"It happened last Thursday?" Roy said.

"Somewhere between seven-thirty when I left for work and nine when the car service came for him," Jerry said. "Normally, I don't go in that early on Thursdays. Normally."

"What do you do?"

Jerry waved that question away and led Roy upstairs. Roy knew he might have overheard the killing of Richard Gold, or at least the beginning of the attack.

Had the killers let themselves in? Or had Gold gone phone in hand to the door? Were there good reasons for sharing any of this with Jerry? None that Roy could think of.

They went into the study. "That's his desk," Jerry said. It stood by a window, overlooking a backyard with a big stone barbecue and two chaise longues. A bluebird glided down, snatched a white scrap of something in its beak and flew away. Jerry opened a desk drawer. A cell phone and a leather-bound daybook lay inside. Jerry handed Roy the daybook.

He leafed through. Gold had neat, small handwriting, never crossed out anything. When had Roy first called Gold? He tried to reconstruct events, basing his calendar on Kegger-league games. And there, at the bottom of a left-hand page with notes like *NAFTA invu,* and *mining indictments?—check 2:30,* he saw: *obit—.* Last entry on the page. Roy looked at the top of the next one, read, *notwithstanding three more expected indictments—Edwards,* which didn't seem to follow, and then came more about the mining story. A few moments went by before Roy noticed the rough edges along inside of the binding and realized a page had been torn out.

He turned to the end—last notation: *J—re dinner—* and found the rough-edged evidence of another missing page. There wasn't a word about him, Delia, the Hobbes Institute, the UN.

"Anything?" said Jerry.

"No." Less than nothing. "But thanks for the help." Roy held out his hand.

Jerry shook it, his own hand cold and trembling. "That megalomaniac remark," he said. "I wouldn't want to leave you with a false impression."

"About what?"

"About what Richard thought of you. After you contacted him, he looked up images of your work and was quite impressed." Jerry took the cell phone out of the drawer. "In fact, he went out to Georgetown and took a picture of one of those *Neanderthals* of yours."

Jerry pressed buttons on the cell phone. "I'm not too good at this," he said. "Richard was the—" He clamped down on the rest of it.

Richard Gold's cell-phone photos: first, Jerry himself, wearing a Redskins cap and smiling a goofy smile; then a big man with blond hair fading to white, standing under an umbrella on the far side of a busy street; after that *Neanderthal Number Three*, donated by Roy to the university.

"Here we are," said Jerry.

"Go back," Roy said.

"Go back?"

"To the one before."

"But—"

"Just do it."

Jerry went back to the photo before *Neanderthal Number Three,* the fair-haired man.

"Who's that?" Roy said.

"No idea," said Jerry.

Roy took a close look. Not a very clear image, the man's face shaded by the umbrella; and almost fifteen years had passed. But: Tom Parish. Time had been good to him.

"Did Richard say anything about this picture?" Roy said.

"No. He just showed me the sculpture." Jerry had a sudden thought; it made him look sick. "Why? What are you suggesting?"

"Nothing," Roy said. "Nothing to do with you. Can you tell where it was taken?"

But Jerry was unnerved now, shook his head quickly from side to side, not really looking. Roy scanned the photo for details, noticed a newspaper box next to a Starbucks, and next to that what looked like wine bottles in a display window.

"All set," called the locksmith from downstairs.

Jerry jumped at the sound.

Roy turned to go, paused. He gestured at the smashed-up chair. "Want me to take care of that?" He couldn't help himself.

Jerry gazed at the pieces for a moment, then shrugged. Roy, stooping to pick them up, realized he was still wearing the skullcap. He folded it neatly and put it in his pocket.

Ten

Rain fell harder. Roy set his armful of wood on the passenger seat. As he drove off, a police cruiser pulled over, took the spot he'd had. Roy circled the block. The cruiser was still parked outside Jerry's house but no one was in it. Roy did a U-turn, found a space on the other side of the street, a space with an unblocked view of Jerry's front door and the cruiser. He waited. Rain pelted down on the pickup, light drumming waves of sound that washed over him.

"I've never been there," Roy said.

"Where?" said Delia.

"Venezuela," Roy said. "What we've just been talking about. Your trip."

"It's not my favorite place."

"What's wrong with Venezuela?"

"Nothing."

"That doesn't sound convincing."

She rolled over, laid her head on his chest. Her lips moved against his skin. "Do I have to convince you, Roy?"

"What do you mean?"

"Nothing. Maybe I just don't feel like going."

He tangled his fingers in the curls of her hair. "Why not?"

"The whole thing's just so . . ."

"What?"

She sighed; her breath flowed, warm and soft against his chest. "It's not worth talking about. I have to go. That's that."

"But I thought you were excited about this project. What about the pineapples?"

"Fuck the pineapples," Delia said. Then she laughed to herself, a low, throaty laugh Roy loved. She reached down, took his balls in her hand, hefted them like a produce manager sizing up the goods. "Fuck the pineapples," she said.

Roy opened his eyes.

"What the hell?" he said.

No rain. No rain and late in the day, tree limbs, chimneys and roofs all in black silhouette against an orange sky. Across the street, the police cruiser was gone and Jerry's house dark. A woman walked up to the front door, laid a bouquet on the front step and moved off, entering a house down the street.

"What the hell?" Roy said. He'd wanted to talk to that cop. "What's wrong with me?" He drove back to Baltimore.

The same bartender was working the hotel bar. Roy ordered what he'd had last time—chowder, T-bone steak, roast potatoes, Caesar salad, heavy ale, pecan pie with ice cream. Tonight he actually felt hungry. All at once, with no warning, he found himself rising into a good mood, as though some internal helium pump had clicked on. He hadn't been in a good mood in a while, had almost forgotten the power of its lift.

"How'd the scrap business treat you today?" the bartender said.

"Not bad."

"I was talking to this cousin of mine," she said. "He says with commodity prices like they are, there's real money in scrap."

What would Murph say to something like that? *Not from where I'm sitting.* Roy said it.

"You're just the modest type," she said. "I can tell." She leaned forward a little, was wearing a low-cut top to begin with. "There aren't many modest guys around these days," she said. "But there sure as hell should be."

Roy laughed.

She gave him a quick look. Roy read a lot into it, maybe too much. "What's your name?" she said.

"Roy."

"Nice name—I've never known a Roy," she said, topping up his glass. "I'm off in an hour, just dropping in that little fact."

No, he hadn't read too much into it. The bartender was nice-looking, smart, a little on the plump side, even matronly—but that felt right at the moment, perfect, in fact. Roy was about to smile, take the next step, when she added:

"I'm Jennifer, but friends call me Jen."

That ended it right there. The rest was awkwardness, confusion, distance.

Up in his room, Roy scrolled through the numbers on his cell phone until he came to Jen's. She'd be in Keystone now—maybe, with the time difference, still on the mountain, getting in one last run; she loved being the last one down. Sometimes in the moguls she made a whooping sound. Roy gazed at her number, came close to dialing it, so close that he knew one night he would. He deleted it instead.

Roy awoke in the night, very hot, the sheets soaked with sweat. He took a cold shower and remade the bed with fresh sheets. Outside his window, a full moon hung in the sky, seemingly very near, its surface details sharp. A huge rock, forever circling overhead: there was something unsettling about it, at least tonight. Roy got back in bed and just lay there, eyes open, mind full of black thoughts, refusing to come to order, the good mood long gone. Then, out of nowhere, came the memory of an image he'd sometimes used as a little boy to get himself to sleep, a practice he'd totally forgotten. The image: an igloo in a wild blizzard, and inside Roy, sitting calm and cross-legged before a cozy fire. He could see it now, all the component parts at once—blizzard, igloo inside and out, the fire from little Roy's point of view, little Roy himself from an external point of view—in a way no person ever sees anything, whole and complete. And a perfect peace slowly enfolded him. Roy slept.

He felt good in the morning, opened the drawer of the bedside table even before getting up, took out the phone books—Baltimore, D.C., metropolitan counties in Maryland and Virginia. He found many Parishes, including fifteen Thomases, two Toms and eleven T's. There were also four Paul Habibs and eight P's.

He began with a Thomas Parish on Crestview Lane in Silver Spring.

"Hello," he said. "I'm looking for a Tom Parish who used to work the Hobbes Institute, and maybe still does."

"Huh?" said a woman; she sounded very old.

"Tom Parish," Roy said. "Who worked for the Hobbes Institute."

"You'll have to speak up."

Roy tried again, louder.

"My husband Tom?" she said. "But he's been dead for three years."

"I'm sorry," Roy said.

"What was that?"

He raised his voice again. "I'm sorry. But did he ever work for the Hobbes Institute?"

"Why, Tom worked at GE for thirty years. Is this about the pension?"

Roy refined his technique as he ran through the Thomas Parishes and into the Toms. He got two disconnected numbers, one endless ring, three answering machines, and the answer no expressed in different ways. By the time he reached the T's he was on the road, headed for the hospital, a list of the remaining possibilities in his hand. He finished up in the waiting room, made a sublist of callbacks—the

four nonresponding Thomases plus three nonresponding T's.

"And how's Roy today?" Netty said, taking three
more vials of blood.

"Good. Any lab results yet?"

"Dr. Chu will see you before you go," Netty said.
"Then you're not due back for twenty-one days."

"How come?"

"Three days on, three weeks off—that's the routine," Netty said. "I'm sure Dr. Chu told you."

"Not that I remember."

"So much to take in all at once," Netty said, fastening on the blood pressure cuff.

Pulse: seventy-three.

Blood pressure: one twenty-five over ninety.

"Those are up," Roy said.

Netty checked the chart. "Always higher in a doctor's office."

"But I was in a doctor's office yesterday."

"Let's get you weighed," Netty said.

Roy stripped down to his boxers, stood on the scale.
Netty tapped at the weights.

"One seventy . . ." She peered at the numbers.
"Is that a four or a five?"

"Five," said Roy. "One seventy-five on the nose."

Netty wrote the number on the chart, in a box next to yesterday's box—173 and a half—and the box from the day before that—172. Roy waited for her to make some comment, but she did not.

Roy had squeezed the last drops from the IV bag and was sitting back down, watching the water pulse and shine in the fountain, when Dr. Chu entered.

"Ah," he said. "Seeing with artist's eyes."

"I don't know about that," Roy said. "Have you got the lab report?"

"Lab report?"

"On the blood Netty's been drawing."

Dr. Chu opened a folder. "Two days' results," he said.

"And?"

"The numbers are within the expected range."

"What does that mean?"

"Mean?" said Dr. Chu. "It means that the statistical norms have not been exceeded."

"Norms?" Roy said, thinking if his blood was normal, then maybe he was already on the way back to his old self.

"Typical results for stage three disease of sarcomatous cell type," said Dr. Chu.

"Are you saying that the treatment is working or not?" Roy said.

"Oh, the treatment," said Dr. Chu. "Much too early to see any effects of the treatment. We are now only trying to establish a baseline."

"But I feel better," Roy said. "The cough, the breathing, everything."

"Excellent," said Dr. Chu.

"I've put on weight."

"Excellent."

"Take a look at the chart."

Dr. Chu looked at the chart. "Four pounds!" he said. "And that's with the cast probably getting lighter as it dries out and starts crumbling away."

Roy had forgotten to factor in the cast, meaning his real weight was less than he'd thought. He almost asked Dr. Chu for an estimate of the cast's weight, but stopped himself.

"Any other questions?" said Dr. Chu.

"Yes," Roy said. "Can I have one more treatment?"

"Certainly," said Dr. Chu. "Several more cycles, the next one in twenty-one days."

"I meant tomorrow," Roy said. "One more hit before I go."

"One more hit?"

"Of the cocktail," Roy said. "The antigens and the angio thing."

"Oh, we couldn't do that," said Dr. Chu.

"But I'm sure I can tolerate it," Roy said. He sat up straighter.

"I have little doubt," said Dr. Chu. "But think what would happen."

"What would happen?" Roy said.

"The statistical integrity of the whole study." Dr. Chu made an explosive sound, spread his hands like a bomb going off.

"What if a fourth treatment made all the difference?" Roy said.

"I have no reason to suspect that is the case," said Dr. Chu.

"But what if it was?"

Dr. Chu nodded, as though Roy had made a good point. "That would come under the purview of another study," he said.

The fountain gurgled in the background.

"Maybe I could drop out of the study," Roy said.

"Drop out?"

"And just continue with the treatment," Roy said. "A kind of study of one."

"I am sorry," said Dr. Chu.

Roy didn't want to leave the room—had the strong feeling that nothing could kill him as long as he was connected to that IV bag—but what more could he say?

He sat outside in the pickup, the list of the remaining Thomas and T. Parishes and all the Paul and P. Habibs in his hand. So hard, to make this little correction. And when he found the Hobbes Institute and had his piece of paper proving Delia's employment there, what then? Back to square one with some new reporter, starting with the admission that he'd been rooting around in their computers, almost certainly a crime, a crime that implicated Skippy. All that, for a few words that he would never see in print, no matter how long he lived.

But Delia hadn't worked for the UN. She'd worked for the Hobbes Institute, even given her life for the Hobbes Institute, if you wanted to put it that way.

He got out his phone, dialed the first Thomas Parish still on the list: Thomas and Carol, 94 Elder Road, Falls Church.

"I'm looking for a Thomas Parish who used to work for the Hobbes Institute."

"And I'm getting sick of this," said the man on the other end. "I'll tell you what I told the others—I never even heard of the Hobbes Institute. Got that? Now stop bothering me."

"What others?" Roy said.

"Some reporter. And the guy from the embassy or whatever it was."

"Embassy?"

"Morocco? Mauritania? Something like that. The jerk wouldn't believe me."

"That you weren't the Tom Parish he was looking for?"

"Exactly. Kept saying I sounded just like him. The nerve. Plus he never identified himself, not by name. Just like you, by the way."

"Sorry, Mr. Parish," Roy said. "I didn't mean to trouble you. But can I ask you one more question?"

"What?"

"What color is your hair?"

"No color," said the wrong Tom Parish. "I was bald at twenty-two."

"Thanks, I—"

Click.

Roy went back to the list. An hour later, he'd crossed off every Parish except for one T in Annandale still unreached, and had also worked his way through the Habibs, eliminating all of the Pauls and all but two of the P's. Three chances left, probably slim; and what if Tom Parish had an unlisted number, or lived in Delaware, say? So: Time to go home, was it not?

Roy turned the key. At that moment, he thought of the photo on Richard Gold's cell phone: Tom Parish, with his full head of fading blond hair, standing under an umbrella in front of a Starbucks, part of a wine-store display window on one side, a newspaper box on the other. Roy had a good memory for visual things, could call up the image pretty clearly. The newspaper box was green with yellow writing, the kind used by the *Washington Post*. He drove out of the parking lot, headed south for D.C.

Eleven

Were there systematic ways of going about this? Probably, but Roy wasn't systematic, had always been more of an experimenter; and besides the sun was shining brightly, the air warm enough for cracking the window open a few inches—the softness of that air, even in winter, reminding him of how it had been to live here, he and Delia. He confined his research to a quick listing of Starbucks addresses in upscale commercial parts of Washington and drove by them, waiting for the right one to pop into view. It took an hour or so, and then, on the other side of the street, the triptych he was looking for rolled into place like a strip of film: newspaper box, Starbucks, wineshop. Now he could see the whole display window, read the lettering on the glass: wine, inc. Roy pulled into a parking space.

Where was he? Roy spotted a street sign: Twenty-second Street NW, probably a block or two from George Washington University—in fact, not far from that first apartment in Foggy Bottom. He got out of the pickup, crossed the street, and as he did saw his image reflected in the Wine, Inc. window; an image that didn't look exactly like him, more like a slightly older, more slender brother. Roy went into Starbucks.

No one inside who resembled Tom Parish: two workers behind the counter, some college kids at a back table, a smartly dressed woman checking the CDs on the rack. Roy ordered coffee and the biggest chocolate chip cookie they had; cookie for calories, coffee to prevent any of that crazy nodding off.

He sat in the pickup and waited. A woman came out of Wine, Inc., set up an easel beside the door, placed a sign on it: Tasting Today, 5:00—killer pinots from oregon and central coast. She was tall, with smooth café au lait–colored skin and straight hair, glossy black. The angle of the easel didn't seem right to her. She changed it three times, then saw that the sign itself was tilting a few degrees from straight and fixed that, too. She glanced up and down the street, her movements a little too quick to be graceful. Her gaze fell on Roy, stayed on him for a moment, then slid past. She turned and went back in the shop.

Two hours later, coffee and cookie long gone, Roy was still there. Any point in continuing? All he knew was that Richard Gold had taken a picture of Tom Parish from just about this same spot. Was Tom a regular customer of this Starbucks? Possible, but also possible that he seldom came this way, or had been waiting for a cab, or—

Tom Parish appeared, walking into Roy's line of sight from the left. He wore a dark suit and a plaid bow tie; Roy remembered those bow ties of his. Tom wasn't moving quickly. Roy got a good look at him in profile—prominent nose and chin, that blond hair not only fading to white but receding, too—had no doubt about his identity. Tom passed the newspaper box and Starbucks and went into Wine, Inc.

Roy got out of the truck, crossed the street. All at once he felt a little breathless. No reason to be nervous, he told himself—he was about to wrap this up. He calmed down, or maybe hadn't been nervous to begin with, but still couldn't get enough air. Roy took a deep breath, or tried to, and opened the door to Wine, Inc.

Wine, Inc. was a long, narrow shop with a sales counter on the left and rows of wooden wine bins on the right. There was no one inside except the tall woman, behind the counter, and Tom Parish on the other side, talking to her. Roy caught the phrase "not in writing, of course, Lenore."

"Funny man," she said; but she didn't laugh. Up close, Roy saw she was older than he'd thought, maybe his own age. They both noticed Roy.

Roy looked at Tom Parish: Tom Parish, for absolute sure. His character—worldly, assured, rooted deep in privilege, prep schools and the Ivy League going back for generations—was still written on his face, even more so.

"Hello, Tom," he said.

Tom and Lenore exchanged a quick glance, perhaps puzzled.

"Excuse me?" said Tom, turning back to Roy.

"Tom," Roy said. "Hi. It's been a long time."

Tom's brow furrowed. "I'm afraid you're making a mistake," he said. "My name's not Tom."

"Thomas," Roy said, taking a step closer. "Thomas Parish. It's me, Roy Valois."

No recognition on Tom's face. "Sorry, friend. Mistaken identity."

And the voice: cultured, detached, distinctive—a voice easily remembered. "Oh, come on," Roy said. "Roy Valois—Delia Stern's husband."

Tom spread his hands. "I'm afraid we're no further ahead." Lenore, eyebrows raised, looked from one to the other.

"Delia worked for you at the Hobbes Institute," Roy said. "We used to go out on your boat." He remembered the name. *"Bellissima."*

"I've never heard of the Hobbes Institute," Tom said. He looked at Lenore. She shrugged. "Or owned a boat, for that matter," Tom went on, "although God knows I wish I could afford to, and *Bellissima* sounds like an excellent name."

Lenore nodded.

"She died in Venezuela—you called with the news," Roy said.

"You're not making much sense," Tom said.

"Tom?" Roy said, taking another step. "What the hell's going on?"

"Now, please," Tom said, backing away. "This is starting to get a little tedious."

Roy felt himself turning red, although he didn't feel embarrassed or even angry, just confused. "For God's sake, Tom," he said. "You spoke at the funeral. It's not funny."

"We're in agreement on that," Tom said. "But for the last time, my name's not Tom. Now if you'll excuse me." He turned and walked toward the rear of the store, to a door marked employees only.

Roy followed.

"Sir?" said Lenore.

Tom pushed open the door and went out.

Roy started running, but all at once felt very hot, his skin on fire.

"Sir?" Lenore ran after him, caught up in an instant. "You can't go in there. It says employees only."

But Roy kept going; normally a pretty fast runner, but not today—so hard to run with no air, and his skin burning up like this. He tore off his jacket, tore off his shirt, banged through the employees-only door.

A storage room: a bank of floor-to-ceiling coolers, cases of wine, a portable display of plastic grapes wound around a trellis. Tom was reaching for the knob of a door—this one unmarked—in the far wall, a rough wooden wall, unfinished.

"Sir."

Lenore grabbed Roy's shoulder from behind. The strength of her grip shocked him, or maybe she'd simply found some delicate nerve by chance. He cried out at the pain and shook her off.

"Tom!"

Tom heard him, glanced back, then banged open the unmarked door. Roy glimpsed a room on the other side, a room divided into cubicles, with workers in headsets at their screens, monitors hanging from the ceiling, big maps on the walls—the Balkans, Middle East, North Africa. The door closed.

Roy got to it, grasped the knob, felt Lenore's grip again, even harder this time. Pain maddened him. Tom was maddening him, too; and his whole life right now. He whirled around, lashed out with his fist, something he would never do to a woman; Lenore backed away, avoiding him with ease. She pulled a cell phone from her pocket.

Roy swung back to the door, tried the knob. Locked? Locked. He tugged at it, shook it, put his shoulder to the door, kicked at it, barely aware of Lenore's voice, a low murmur into the cell phone. At that moment, in midfury, he felt a slight tickle in his throat, almost imperceptible. He coughed a gentle cough, a voluntary cough, just to get rid of that tickle. A gentle cough, but it caved in his chest for some reason, as though he'd been hit by a battering ram, and he tasted blood, and then it was trickling from his mouth, at first a thin pink trickle dripping onto his bare chest, then thicker and redder, and finally crimson. Roy sank to the floor.

Lenore gazed down, eyes narrowed, face puzzled. From the door to the shop came a woman's voice: "Hello? Anyone got information on those killer Pinots from— hey! What's going on in here?"

Roy saw two women in the doorway, one holding a bottle of red wine. He couldn't answer because answering required air in the lungs, and he had none.

"I said what's going on," said the woman with the bottle.

Roy shook his head, or tried to.

"This gentleman," said Lenore, "appears to be unwell."

"Stand back," said the woman with the bottle. "I'm a doctor."

"Then fuck you," Roy said. But no sound came out. In fact, he couldn't even keep his eyes open. A fog rolled in, very cold, putting out the fire in his body, cooling him down. It felt good. "This is better," he said.

"Did he say something?" said the other woman.

"Not unexpected," someone said; a voice Roy recognized but couldn't place right away. A man's voice, highly intelligent, a little stiff with the language, as though learned from books. "Reaction rates approach thirty percent, in theory." Dr. Chu. Roy thought about opening his eyes.

"Reaction to what?" said someone else.

"The current study," said Dr. Chu. Paper crinkled. "Here, with my compliments, an abstract. When he stabilizes, send him to us by ambulance."

"What if he doesn't?"

"He will," said Dr. Chu. "This is actually quite mild."

Roy heard gurgling water. Very pleasant. He could visualize its pulsing, shining surface, a flowing complexity of bumpy shapes, all governed in the end by gravity. He realized he hadn't paid nearly enough attention to gravity in his work, a shocking oversight that scared him. He opened his eyes.

"Hi, Roy." Netty gazed down at him. He was in the feng shui room, on a gurney or rolling bed instead of the couch. "How do you feel?"

"Fine," Roy said. He sat up, not in one easy motion, but he did it.

"Easy, Roy."

Tubes were twisted around his arm. "What's this?" he said. "The cocktail?"

Netty shook her head. "Just some fluids to balance your electrolytes," she said. "You had a reaction to the treatment."

"Meaning I can't have more?"

"More?"

"More treatment."

"No, no, nothing like that," Netty said. "You're still scheduled for the twenty-fourth. These things happen. Dr. Chu is not particularly concerned."

Roy looked around. No windows in the feng shui room, no way to tell day from night. Netty must have read something on his face.

"You spent the night at the G. W. University Hospital," she said. "But you're stabilized now, and as soon as you feel up to it—"

"What day is it?"

Netty told him. "Don't worry," she said, snapping on surgical gloves. "All perfectly normal for a reaction like this." She took out his IV.

"I was in D.C.?"

Netty nodded.

Memories stirred in his mind, the details strange, abnormal, dreamlike. "Where's my truck?"

"Your truck?"

Roy stood up. He felt taller than usual, an inch or two maybe.

"You all right, Roy?"

"Fine. Can I go now?"

"No rush," she said. "Whenever you're ready."

Roy was ready. Half an hour later he was on a train to Washington. A slow train, much too slow. He tried to take deep breaths, testing himself on how deep he could make them. Pretty deep, he thought. Rain streaked the windows, the world outside reduced to two colors, brown and gray.

The pickup was where he'd left it; five wet and ink-smeared tickets on the windshield, but it hadn't been towed. Late afternoon: the rain falling harder, a warm glow in the window of Wine, Inc., people moving around in the shop. The easel again stood outside: TASTE THE WINES OF SUNNY SPAIN! Roy crossed the street and went in.

"Hi," said a man standing at a table near the front door. He had a round friendly face and a powerful build, a little soft in the middle, as though he was a decade removed from college football. A button on his jacket read: *I'm Westie. Ask me about wine.* "Like to try some Rioja?" he said.

"Rioja?" Roy said, taking a quick look around: ten or twelve customers in the store and two other clerks, one at a second table farther back in the store, the other ringing up a sale. No sign of Tom or Lenore.

"I've also got this really nice Priorat," Westie said. "Earthier than the Riojas, but a lot of up-front fruit as well."

"Okay," Roy said. "I'll try that."

Westie poured about an inch of wine in a small plastic glass—tiny in his big thick hand—then watched Roy take a sip.

"Nice," Roy said.

"See what I mean about the fruit?" Westie said.

"I do," said Roy. He took another sip.

"What happened to your arm?"

"Hockey."

"My favorite sport," Westie said.

"You play?"

"When I was a kid. Then I switched to football. But I missed it for a long time. The speed, you know?" He opened a new bottle. "Also a Priorat, but from old vines," he said. He lowered his voice. "We're not really tasting it today—but for a hockey player." He poured some in a fresh glass, handed it to Roy.

Roy tried a Priorat from old vines.

"Feel those tannins?" Westie said.

"I think so," Roy said.

"I always say 'feel' instead of 'taste' when it comes to tannins," Westie said. "Does that make sense?"

"You'd have to ask them," Roy said.

A little pause; then Westie laughed. He reached for a clipboard. "Care to join our mailing list?"

"Maybe later," Roy said. "Is Lenore around tonight?"

"Lenore?"

"Another salesclerk," Roy said. "Or maybe she's the manager."

Westie looked puzzled. "We've got no one named Lenore here."

"A tall black woman," Roy said. "Very striking."

Westie screwed up his face. "Are you maybe thinking of the Wine Emporium in Washington Circle?"

Roy took a good look at Westie: smooth, unlined skin; shaving cut under his chin; so young. "That must be it," he said. "Thanks for the wine."

"My pleasure."

Roy took his glass of Priorat from old vines and wandered toward the back of Wine, Inc., just like any customer at a tasting. A man at the second table swirled his wine around and gave it a hard look, like it was trying to fool him. Roy kept going, past a bin of South African Sauvignon Blanc, toward the door marked EMPLOYEES ONLY.

He glanced around—no one watching—and pushed the door. One of those doors with an insulation strip on one side and no knob, the kind that just swung open, designed for lots of burden-bearing traffic, and also a door he'd pushed through three days ago: but this time it didn't budge. Roy leaned into it. No result.

"Excuse me?"

Roy turned. Westie.

"Looking for the rest room?" he said. "It's over there." He pointed to a door in the corner. "Unisex," Westie added with a smile. "Just knock."

Roy knocked and went in, an ordinary little bathroom with no way out but the way he'd entered. He
stood there, not knowing what to think. The face in
the mirror—so thin?—had a new line on it, a shallow
vertical groove between the eyes: a marred and frailer
version of himself, like a bad copy.

Roy must have lost track of time. After a while,
there was a knock on the door and Westie called, "Everything all right, sir?"

There was an intensity, too, about the face in the
mirror, as though something enormously complex and
demanding was going on beneath the surface.

A second knock, much heavier. "Sir?"

"I'm fine," Roy said.

Twelve

Roy stood behind a very fat man at a fast-food place, ordered what he ordered. Reaching into his pocket for money, he felt something silky. Roy pulled it out: the skullcap from Gold's funeral. Not silk, but nylon—a cheap little scrap with prominent seams and stitching, and as a hat, completely useless. He folded it into a neat triangle and transferred it to the chest pocket of his shirt.

Roy ate his greasy meal as he drove, chewing up the burgers, fries and wings, swallowing every morsel, packing it in. For drink, he had another huge milk shake—this one strawberry vanilla—which he finished downing as he turned off Connecticut and parked in front of Jerry's house. The lights were on and Jerry's Volvo sat in the driveway.

Roy went to the door, a black door with a silver knocker. He raised it, could tell from the look, feel, heft, that it really was silver, or mostly. Also a pretty object, shaped like a sunflower. Roy hesitated. He'd never felt like trouble for anyone before; and for his own good, wouldn't it be better to go home, rest, eat, exercise, get back to work—if not on *Silence,* then on something else—so he could be in top shape for his next treatment? Roy banged the lovely knocker against the door, hard.

Five or ten seconds later came the sound of footsteps on the other side. And Jerry's voice: "Who is it?"

"Roy Valois."

"What do you want?"

"To talk."

The door opened. Jerry didn't look good—red-eyed and unshaven, somehow even smaller than before. "About what? That obituary of yours?"

"That's part of it," Roy said.

"Why do you care so much?"

"There's more to it than the obituary."

"Such as?" said Jerry.

"It will take a few minutes," Roy said.

Jerry closed his eyes, as though composing himself, and stepped back. Roy went in. The house was filled with the smell of flowers; they were everywhere—in vases, glasses, bottles, even a tennis-ball can—and at the base of every vessel lay the signed accompanying card. All those flowers gave Roy a bad feeling. He remembered the flow of bouquets after Delia's funeral, their gaudy oppression weighing on him till he'd tossed them all in the trash.

"Aren't they beautiful?" Jerry said. "People keep sending and sending them."

Jerry led him into the kitchen. A big sheet of poster board lay on the table, and on it dozens of photographs—Gold with Jerry, Gold alone, the two of them with others. "I'm making a collage," Jerry said. "For permanent framing." He shifted the photos around. "It's not easy, placing them right." He glanced at Roy. "You're probably good at things like that."

Roy had never been interested in collages, didn't like the implication—if it was one—that they bore any relationship to what he did. But he said, "I can give it a try."

He sat down with Jerry at the kitchen table arranging photos. There actually did turn out to be an art to it, an art Jerry lacked, despite a lot of effort, and that Roy understood, without a second thought.

"Try cutting these into ovals," Roy said.

Jerry picked up the scissors.

"No," Roy said. "Sideways ovals."

Jerry cut some photos into sideways ovals. Roy arranged them on the poster board. "Hey, that's kind of witty," said Jerry. "But you don't even know these people."

Roy said nothing.

Jerry started gluing the photos on the board. The expression on his face grew less miserable: not happy, but at least absorbed.

"How's the investigation going?" Roy said.

Jerry's hand paused, just for an instant. "They called this morning," he said. "No progress." Jerry dabbed glue on the back of a photo of Gold standing beside a cactus.

"The credit cards . . ."

"Haven't been used," Jerry said. He laid the photo on the board, pressed the corners down. "The laptop, BlackBerry, none of that's turned up. The fingerprints they took ended up matching an electrician who did some work last month."

"But they still think it was a robbery?" Roy said.

"Of course, with all the missing stuff," Jerry said. "What else could it be?" His hand, holding another photo by the edge—Richard and Jerry in straw hats— began to shake.

"I don't know," Roy said, taking the photo from him and sliding it in place. "Something's going on."

Jerry turned to him. "Something about Richard?"

"I don't know that either," Roy said. "Who's in charge of the case?"

"I'm not sure," said Jerry. "The person I talk to is Sergeant Bettis. Did he say his first name? I can't remember."

"I'd like to talk to him."

"Why?"

Where to begin? "It's—" Roy felt a sudden sharp pain in the right hand side of his chest, up high.

Jerry was watching him. "What?"

The pain vanished, just like that, leaving behind nothing but a few drops of sweat on his forehead; almost not an event at all. "Nothing," Roy said. He took a deep breath, felt like the lower parts of his lungs had been tied off. "It's about Tom Parish—the guy on Richard's phone. He used to be my wife's boss. But when I tracked him down he claimed to be someone else and didn't seem to know me."

"I don't get it," Jerry said.

Roy tried again from a different angle, bringing in the Hobbes Institute, Consulate of Greece, Venezuela.

"So what are you saying?" Jerry said.

"That picture on Richard's phone," Roy said. "Suppose it's a connection."

"A connection to what?" Jerry said, his voice rising in pitch, growing querulous. "What could all this Hobbes business have to do with Richard?"

Roy had no idea, but he also had no other place to go. "I'd like to see what Sergeant Bettis thinks."

Jerry gazed down at the collage, touched a sailboat in the background of one of the photos. "I'll call him," he said.

Sergeant Bettis arrived in twenty minutes: a man of Roy's height, but broader, broader even than the way Roy had been before . . . before all this. He wore jeans and a windbreaker; his face sagged a little, as though he needed sleep. The kitchen chair creaked under him when he sat down.

Roy told his story, didn't organize it any better than he'd done with Jerry. Sergeant Bettis took notes and said nothing till Roy finished, not really coming to an end, more just falling silent.

Sergeant Bettis leafed back through his notebook. A minute went by, maybe more. He looked at Roy, his eyes dark, intelligent, impartial. "How old are you?" he said.

Roy told him.

"What got you interested in your obituary?"

Roy hadn't expected that. "A buddy of mine and I were talking," he said.

"Yeah?" said Sergeant Bettis. " 'Bout what?"

"Hockey."

"Ice hockey?"

"Yes, but—"

Sergeant Bettis wrote something in his notebook. A brief entry, brief enough to have been *ice hockey.* "Go on," he said.

"We were just wondering whether . . ."

"Yes?"

This was going to sound a little lame. "Whether a goal I once scored would make it into my obituary," Roy said.

"Must have been a big goal," said Sergeant Bettis.

"Not really."

"Was this in the pros?"

Roy was conscious of Jerry's eyes going back and forth, and the look in them: trying to follow some game he didn't know. "College," Roy said.

"Where?"

"University of Maine," Roy said.

Sergeant Bettis wrote it down. "And this buddy of yours," he said. "Would he have a name?"

"I don't think that matters," Roy said. "The important thing is this . . ." Other than a few speeding tickets, Roy had no experience with cops. He searched for the right cop word, maybe not finding it. ". . . this discrepancy between my wife's—"

Sergeant Bettis interrupted. "Curiosity, then," he said. "Fair to say that was the motive?"

"Motive?" said Roy. "Motive for what?"

"Breaking into the files of the *New York Times*," said Sergeant Bettis.

Roy sat back. "I'm not sure where you're going with this."

Sergeant Bettis spread his hands, surprisingly small hands for a man his size. Roy had a crazy thought—more than that, abnormal, at least for him, almost disturbed—that he, or more accurately the Roy before all this, not long ago and maybe again, please, Dr. Chu, could take Sergeant Bettis in a fight. "Just collecting facts at this stage," Sergeant Bettis said. "How did you go about it?"

"Go about what?"

"Hacking into the paper."

"Sergeant Bettis? I think you're missing—"

"Study some programming up at the University of Maine?"

"Programming?"

"Writing code, that kind of thing," said Sergeant Bettis.

"No," Roy said.

"So you had some help?"

"Help?"

"In breaking into the site."

"No," Roy said. "I had no help. But—"

"How did you do it?" said Sergeant Bettis.

Roy held up his hand. "Whoa."

"Whoa?"

"I think you've gone off on a tangent," Roy said.

Sergeant Bettis smiled, as though he'd had an amusing thought. "What do you do for a living?" he said.

"He's a sculptor," said Jerry.

"Sculptor," said Sergeant Bettis.

"Famous," Jerry said.

Roy shook his head.

"How would you react"—Sergeant Bettis glanced at his notes—"Roy, if I tried to tell you how to mold your clay?"

All at once Roy remembered what third grade had been like, specifically the day Mrs. LeClaire caught him with matches, and the scene that had followed. Now, as then, he said nothing.

"You wouldn't like it, would you?" said Sergeant Bettis. "Same with me, when someone tells me how to do my job."

Roy said: "If it helped with the final result, I'd want to know." Proving he'd learned at least something since third grade.

NERVE DAMAGE • 153

Sergeant Bettis gazed at him. He nodded. "Fair enough."

"I'm just saying there might be some connection," Roy said.

"And I'm just saying fair enough," said Sergeant Bettis. He went back through his notes. "Let's see this guy's picture on the cell phone," he said.

Jerry went upstairs.

"Vermont," said Sergeant Bettis.

"Yes."

"Never been myself. Cold."

"Can be," Roy said.

Jerry came back down. "It's not there."

They turned to him. "What's not there?" said Sergeant Bettis.

"Richard's phone," Jerry said. "The one with the pictures. I'm sure I left it on his desk. Now it's gone."

"Did you look in the drawer?" Roy said.

"Of course I looked in the drawer," Jerry said. "I looked everywhere."

"Maybe you took it someplace, to another room," Roy said.

"*I* didn't take it anywhere," Jerry said.

Sergeant Bettis's eyebrows rose. "I hear a suggestion of some nature," he said.

Jerry darted a quick glance at Roy.

"So do I," Roy said.

Jerry said, "The last time I saw Richard's phone it was in your hand." He couldn't meet Roy's gaze.

"I left it on the desk," Roy said.

Sergeant Bettis had no trouble meeting Roy's gaze; in fact, his eyes had brightened up and he didn't look so tired anymore.

"I'd like to look myself," Roy said.

"You don't trust me," Jerry said.

Sergeant Bettis rose. "Let's all take a look," he said.

They went up the stairs—Jerry, Roy, Sergeant Bettis—and into the study. Sergeant Bettis looked around. A photo of Michelangelo's *David* hung on the far wall. "It was your wife," he said, "who worked for this institute?"

"Correct," said Roy. "Delia."

Sergeant Bettis rubbed his face. "Let's see about this phone."

Jerry gestured toward the desk. Sergeant Bettis went over. "This is where they got the laptop?"

"Yes," Jerry said.

Sergeant Bettis shifted some cables aside. A dust ball drifted off the desk. "And the phone?"

"Jerry took it out of the top drawer," Roy said. "I left it right there." He pointed to the blotter.

Sergeant Bettis opened the top drawer. Empty.

"Where's the daybook?" Roy said.

"Daybook?" said Sergeant Bettis.

"Where Gold took notes for his stories," Roy said. "There were pages torn out. Pages that had to do with me."

"You saw them?" said Sergeant Bettis.

"Saw what?" Roy said.

"The missing pages."

"No," said Roy. "How could I?"

"Then how do you know they were about you?" Sergeant Bettis said. "These missing pages."

"I"—what was the word?—"deduced it."

"You deduced it."

"Not that pages were missing," Roy said. "That was obvious. But the entries before—"

"Did he show you?" said Sergeant Bettis, turning to Jerry.

"Show me what?" said Jerry.

"Where the pages got torn out," said Sergeant Bettis. "From this daybook or notebook or whatever."

"I don't think so," Jerry said. "What's going on, anyway? I don't want to be doing this right now."

"Did he mention them?" said Sergeant Bettis. "The missing pages?"

"I just don't understand," Jerry said.

"No," Roy said, his voice rising. "I didn't mention them—that's when Jerry brought out the cell phone. But all we have to do is find the goddamn thing and I'll show you." He faced Jerry. "You must have taken them somewhere, the phone and the daybook."

"I didn't."

"Think, Jerry."

"I'm trying," Jerry said. He scrunched up his eyes for a moment, then opened them. "It's no use. You had them. That's all I remember."

Roy bent down, peered under the desk.

"Search the whole house if you want," Jerry said. "I don't care."

Sergeant Bettis turned toward the door. "Call me if you happen to find anything."

"Wait," Roy said.

Sergeant Bettis paused in the doorway.

"One other thing," Roy said. "When Tom Parish left—ran away from me, really—he vanished into this strange room behind the wineshop."

"What kind of strange room?" said Sergeant Bettis.

Roy described it: cubicles, workers in headsets, monitors everywhere, big maps on the walls.

"Yeah?" said Sergeant Bettis.

Roy rode to Wine, Inc. in Sergeant Bettis's unmarked car. They went inside. No one was there except

Westie, coming toward the door. "I was just closing up," he said. He noticed Roy. "Oh, hi—did you want one of those Priorats after all?"

Sergeant Bettis showed his badge. "This won't take a minute."

Westie's eyes widened. "What won't? Is there some problem?"

"Not involving you," said Sergeant Bettis. "I'd just like a peek at your storage room."

Westie glanced at Roy. "But why?"

"Part of an ongoing investigation," Sergeant Bettis said.

"Gee," said Westie, "I don't know. Maybe I should call the owner?"

"Is that Lenore?" said Roy.

"I told you, sir," said Westie, sounding a little aggrieved. "There's no one here by that name."

Sergeant Bettis gave Roy a quick glance, then turned to Westie. "No need to go to any trouble," he said, now moving toward the rear of the store. Westie trailed after him, biting his lip; Roy followed.

Sergeant Bettis put his hand on the employees-only door and gave a slight push. Now it swung smoothly open. They went into the storage room.

The storage room: floor-to-ceiling coolers, cases of wine, display trellis with plastic grapes, unmarked door in the unfinished wooden wall—

But no. There was no unfinished wall at the rear of the storage room. A solid brick wall stood there instead, no door in it. Brick wall? No door? Roy approached slowly, ran his hand over the bricks. They felt like bricks. He tapped at them. The gazes of Sergeant Bettis and Westie pressed on his back, physical pressure he could feel. Roy struck the wall with the side of his fist, as though it might come tumbling down. But it did not.

He rounded on Westie. "When did this happen?" he said.

"When did what happen, sir?"

"This brick wall. There was an unfinished wall here just yester—" For a moment, he couldn't remember how much time he'd lost in the hospital. "There was an unfinished wall. I saw it with my own eyes. When did these bricks get laid?"

Westie looked astonished. "But it's been like this as long as I've been here, sir, almost two years."

"That's a lie," Roy said. He pounded on the wall with the flat of his hand, then shouted, "Tom! I know you're over there."

Westie stepped back, palms up. "What's going on?" he said, confused, even frightened.

"Nothing," said Sergeant Bettis. He put a hand on Roy's arm. "We're done here. Sorry to trouble you."

Roy shook free. "We're not done."

Sergeant Bettis took hold of him again, much harder this time. "We are," he said, drawing Roy back toward the employees-only door. Roy gazed at the brick wall. It seemed so real.

Thirteen

"What happened to your arm?" said Sergeant Bettis.

They stood on the street, outside Wine, Inc. The display window went dark.

"Hockey," Roy said.

"Still playing?"

Roy nodded.

"You like the fighting?"

"What fighting?"

"Thought there was lots of dukin' it out in hockey." Sergeant Bettis threw a quick combination in the air. That crazy notion of taking Sergeant Bettis in a fight, at any time in their respective lives? It vanished from Roy's mind at once.

"On TV, maybe," he said. "We don't even body-check in our league."

"What about off the ice?" said Sergeant Bettis. "Get into fist fights from time to time, a little brawling?"

"What kind of question is that?" Roy said.

"Just trying to paint a picture," Sergeant Bettis said. Westie came out of Wine, Inc., buttoning his coat. He took one glance at them, then hurried away in the direction of Washington Circle. "The boyfriend—Jerry?—says you're a famous sculptor."

Down the block, brake lights reddened on a car. It pulled to the side, stopped under a streetlight: a silver sports car, maybe a Porsche. Westie got in. The car drove off.

"I said," said Sergeant Bettis, "that Jerry makes you out to be a famous sculptor."

Roy turned to him. "Not that famous," he said. "But so what?"

"Famous people tend to be concerned about their reputations," Sergeant Bettis said. "Stands to reason."

"Does it?" Roy said. "What are you driving at?"

"An obituary is all about reputation, right?" said Sergeant Bettis. "No surprise that you'd want a little look-see."

"I told you," Roy said. "It was all about that stupid goal."

"I know what you told me," said Sergeant Bettis. "But suppose a famous person, for whatever reason, sneaks that look-see and doesn't like it, maybe even feels a bit insulted, like how his reputation adds up. Maybe he gets pissed off at the guy who wrote it."

Silence. Sergeant Bettis's eyes—dark, intelligent, impartial—met Roy's. Roy laughed. "You're saying I killed Richard Gold?"

Sergeant Bettis didn't see the joke. "Anything you want to tell me?"

"Sure," said Roy. "For starters, I'll remind you that I was at home in Vermont when he was attacked, quite possibly, as I mentioned, on the phone with him."

Sergeant Bettis nodded. "I had one like that," he said. "A guy of means, not from art sales, something else. But my point—he made sure to give this enemy of his a call just before the car bomb went off. Rubbing it in and establishing an alibi at the same time, if you follow."

Roy took a deep breath; tried to—but again found the bottoms of his lungs tied off, unavailable. "So I paid someone else to do it?" Roy said. Breathless, almost panting, like a guilty man.

Sergeant Bettis's voice softened, came close to striking a gentle note. "If you did, we can probably work something out. But it would have to start now, like right here."

"You're wasting your time," Roy said. He paused to catch his breath, got only some of it. "And mine."

Sergeant Bettis's eyes lost their impartiality. "Maybe," he said. "I've been wrong before." He opened the door of his unmarked car. "Who wouldn't be, twenty-two years on the job?" He stepped into the car, looked at Roy over the roof. "One thing that's changed in those twenty-two years—there's nowhere to hide in this country, not anymore." He got in the car, drove slowly away.

Roy took a few steps along the sidewalk, toward the Starbucks. A narrow alley separated it from Wine, Inc. Roy followed the alley, past some trash cans and a wheelless bicycle frame chained to a pipe, around to the back of Wine, Inc.

Another alley, this one wider, ran behind the buildings. Nighttime, but Roy could see pretty well by the city's luminance. There were two reserved parking spaces behind Wine, Inc. A sign on the wall—a wall of solid brick—read: RESERVED FOR EMPLOYEES OF WINE, INC. ALL OTHERS WILL BE TOWED. Solid brick. He tried to resist the urge to run his hand over it and didn't succeed.

Roy moved back to the narrow side alley. The side wall? Also brick. But up high, near the corner where the two walls met, he saw a small slatted square, the kind that indicated the presence of a ventilation fan.

One of the trash cans was empty except for an inch or two of water sloshing around at the bottom. Roy dumped the trash can out—stinking water, as though fish had gone bad in there—and stood it upside down under the ventilation fan. He'd never actually climbed onto a trash can before, but how could that possibly be a problem given his sense of balance, his strength, his agility? Shouldn't have been, but it took three tries, and on the last the trash can wobbled and almost toppled him over.

Roy stood on the trash can, just breathing for a minute or two. *Come on, boy.* He rose up on his toes and peered through the slats of the ventilation fan. A dark space on the other side, but not completely dark: a glow spread from . . . from what? Wine coolers—those floor-to-ceiling wine coolers. Roy could make out cases of wine, the trellis with the plastic grapes, dusty bottles on a table, the glint of a corkscrew beside them. This was the storage room behind the employees-only door; no other room—with cubicle workers, monitors, wall maps—existed behind it, no other room where Tom Parish had disappeared from sight. And nothing beyond the storage room except the alley, with its two parking spaces. Roy closed his eyes tight, opened them, and saw again what he'd just seen. This was no hallucination. So, by logical necessity, was that office or call center or map room or whatever the hell it was in fact the hallucination? Roy couldn't make himself believe it. He thought of a line Delia had quoted once when he'd asked how her work was going: something about holding two contradictory thoughts in your mind at once. The exact words? The source? He couldn't remember, but he had the obscure sensation that Delia had been this way already, was farther up the trail. Kind of crazy—Delia hadn't been a great one for trails and hiking, and two or three runs on the mountain was usually enough skiing—but it calmed him a little. What she liked about winter was sitting by the fire in the barn and watching the snow fall; *the reflected flames flickering in her eyes, lighting up those golden flecks.* That memory calmed him more. He climbed off the trash can.

Roy caught a cab to Jerry's. One light shone in an upstairs window. He got into his truck and started on the long drive home, the pieces of the broken chair beside him. As the miles went by, those pieces began pulling at him, demanding his attention, rebuilding themselves in his mind. Roy found a Home Depot off the Garden State Parkway, bought a sixteen-ounce bottle of Elmer's Super Wood Glue, and in the parking lot, put the chair back together, carefully making every joint wrong. A series of wrongs, all slightly different, that added up to . . . what? He didn't know.

A man passing by with a brand-new plunger in his hand took a long look and said, "Buddy? They got ones just like that inside. Thirty-five ninety-nine."

Rain in Hartford, sleet at the Massachusetts line, snow in Vermont, first heavy wet flakes, then small and hard, flying through the yellow cone of the headlights: Roy passed a wreck, then a second, and a third, all of them bad. People died on the highway every day, passing from normal life, through terror, to nothing. *Slow-motion crack-up:* Krishna's driver's take on *Delia.* But real crack-ups on the road happened fast, the terror part, act two, probably lasting no more than a few seconds; in contrast to the long second acts people dying from some other causes went through. Those people, the ones who got sick, who really did die in slow motion, had too much goddamn time to think. Not nearly enough time to live, way too much to think: Therefore? Roy blew by a snow-plow, glanced down at the speedometer: eighty-five. *The question is—can he do it?* He eased off the pedal.

Roy drove up to the barn. The wind rose, hitting high notes in the trees. The driveway was unshoveled, Skippy's old sedan not there. Roy got stuck halfway up and waded on foot through the snow to the front door. Lights shone, but only in the big room. He could see *Delia* in the tall windows.

Roy unlocked the door, went in. He heard music, the thumping, repetitive bass that rappers liked.

"Skippy?"

No answer.

He put down his bag. Everything looked fine.

"Skippy?"

Roy walked through the house, checked the spare bedroom upstairs. No sheets on the mattress, but there was a blanket, clothes were scattered here and there and the bedside radio played. No sneakers, though. Roy shut off the radio. He left the porch lights on and went to bed.

In his own bed. Ah. He took a deep breath, almost a real one. His eyelids—so heavy, as though they'd gained weight, gained with no effort while he had to struggle to hold on to every ounce of the rest of his body—fell shut. Roy hadn't eaten in hours, knew he should go down to the kitchen, fix himself a meal. But he wasn't hungry, and in any case couldn't force his eyelids back up. Outside those notes the wind made rose higher and higher. Snowflakes thumped on the windows, soft and fast, like drumming fingers.

"This," said Delia, "will be the bedroom."

"Isn't it a bit small?"

"We'll just have to take that wall down."

"We?"

"And the window needs to be bigger. That's east, isn't it, Roy?"

"Yes."

"We'll have sun in the morning. And the bed goes right there."

"Maybe we should have one in every room," Roy said.

Delia tried everywhere for the right bed. She hit antiques stores from the Eastern Townships to the Berkshires, but nothing was quite right. They were still sleeping on a mattress on the floor when Delia left for Venezuela. And Roy still slept on it now.

Sun in the morning. Roy opened his eyes. He felt pretty good. He rose, went to the window. Snow covered the valley, pure white everywhere. It was like seeing the clouds from above. He thought of all those cartoons that take place in heaven; one of his favorite cartoon subgroups.

The phone rang. "Roy? Freddy Boudreau. Saw your truck in the driveway on my way in. How was the trip?"

"Good."

"How's the arm?"

"Healing fine."

"Good news—gettin' torched without you on the blue line, need you back soon," Freddy said. "Reason I'm calling, that kid you had taking care of the place—"

"Skippy?"

"Locked him up yesterday, in case you been wondering where he was."

"Not another DUI?"

"Nope," said Freddy. "But that would be preferable, all around."

"What do you mean?"

"Illegal gun possession," Freddy said.

"I don't believe it."

"Smith & Wesson thirty-eight," Freddy said. "One of those sneaky little models with the real short barrel. Serial number filed off, by the way—that's a separate crime, tacked on. Bail's set at ten grand."

"Oh, God," Roy said. "Is his mom—"

"Uh-unh."

"Murph?"

"Murph at the salvage?"

"That's his uncle."

"Haven't heard from him."

Roy got dressed, went outside: everything soft, round, white, including his truck. Roy took the shovel off the peg by the door. He'd always liked shoveling snow—the full-body rhythm, the squeak the blade sometimes made digging in, the shovel loads holding their shapes for brief moments in the air. Some guys did a sloppy job of it, moving just enough snow to free their cars, but not Roy—he always made sure there was no loose snow, left the ground hardpacked, the banks squared at their bases, all angles right angles. Just not today: today he was sloppier than the sloppiest, and even that pitiful effort wiped him out. He leaned on the truck, sweating a cold sweat, breathing fast shallow breaths. Long trip, aftereffects of Dr. Chu's cocktail, maybe just an off day—weren't there lots of possible reasons? A passing car tooted at him. Roy made himself straighten up and smile and wave at whoever it was.

"Hey, Roy," said Freddy, behind the desk at the station, "good to see you." He took a second look. "You okay?"

"Fine. Is a check okay?"

"From you, yeah," Freddy said. "We don't cash it or nothin'. And if you sign this surety here, you only need to put up ten percent."

Roy signed a piece of paper, wrote a check for one thousand dollars. Freddy locked them in a drawer and handed him a receipt.

"Another traffic stop?" Roy said.

"Mine, this time," Freddy said. "The kid had it in the glove box, right on top. He gave permission for the search, no fuss, no muss." Freddy opened another drawer, took out a handgun. "Exhibit A," he said, "ideal for concealed carrying." He held it out, a snub-nosed black revolver with a polished wood grip. "A real lady's gun, if you ask me—feel how light."

Roy had never actually held a handgun. "No, thanks," he said.

"See where the numbers got ground off?" Freddy said. "They don't use a file—too much work." He put the gun away, rose, opened a low swinging door and led Roy around the desk, down a hall to the cells. All empty except the last one: Skippy lay on a bunk, face to the wall.

"Wakie wakie," Freddy said. Skippy groaned. "Mr. Valois here bailed you out. Again."

Skippy rolled over, sat up, rubbed his face. He shot a quick glance at Roy from between his fingers, looked away.

"Hopin' for an Oscar?" said Freddy. "On your feet."

Skippy rose. New pimple eruptions on both cheeks, forehead oily, eyes gummy. Freddy unlocked the cell door, swung it open with exaggerated courtesy. Hands in his pockets, head down, Skippy shuffled out.

They went to the parking lot, opened the truck doors. Jerry's kitchen chair still lay on the passenger seat. "I'll put that in back," Roy said.

But Skippy said, "No, um, that's . . ." and climbed in the back himself, sitting in the heaped-up snow in his light jacket, torn jeans, and sneakers, now laceless.

Roy made coffee. They sat at the kitchen counter. Skippy's right leg kept jiggling. Roy had no kids, didn't know where to start. Clichés piled up inside him. Skippy stared at the counter.

"Drink the coffee," Roy said.

Skippy took a sip.

"I thought you liked sugar." Roy slid the sugar bowl closer. Skippy stirred in three spoonfuls, took another sip, longer this time; the tips of his fingernails were blue black with dirt. "Drinking's one thing," Roy said. "This is different."

Skippy's leg jiggled.

"You agree?"

Skippy was silent.

"If you disagree, tell me why."

"It doesn't matter," Skippy said, his hair falling in his eyes. "What I say."

"Take a swing at it."

"Why? You won't believe me."

"About what?" Roy said.

"The, um, gun and stuff," Skippy said. "I didn't know it was there." Roy tried to picture a less-believable-looking person.

"Where did you think it was?" he said.

"See?" said Skippy. His leg jiggled, faster and faster. "You don't believe me." He tried drinking more coffee, but his hand was unsteady and it dripped down his chin.

"You want me to believe you didn't know the gun was in your glove box," Roy said.

"Like why would it even make sense?" Skippy said, wiping his chin on his sleeve.

"Why would what make sense?"

"Me saying that stupid cop could look in the glove box," Skippy said. "How come would I do it?"

"Maybe your judgment was off at that moment," Roy said.

"Huh?"

"From something in your system, say."

Skippy gave his head a helpless shake.

"You're saying there was nothing in your system," Roy said. "No drugs, no alcohol."

"I'd practically just wokened up," Skippy said. "It was maybe eleven in the morning. I heard the knocking."

"What knocking?"

"At the front door."

"The front door here?"

"Yeah," said Skippy. "I was sleeping in the spare bedroom, taking care of the place, like you said."

"And who was at the door?"

"The lady from the insurance."

"What insurance?"

"Said she had to take some measurements for a rebate or something."

"Measurements of what?"

"Dunno," said Skippy. "I told her to try back when you were here."

"So she didn't come in?"

"Nothing about insurance was on the list you gave me," Skippy said, glancing at the sheet of paper, still on the counter. "She was like, okay, some other time. Then I got dressed and drove down to Dunkin' Donuts. I was on my way back when I got pulled over."

"For the taillights," Roy said.

"Uh-unh," said Skippy. "I went down to Auto Zone the day before and fixed 'em."

"He stopped you for no reason?" Roy said.

"Happens all the time in this town, Mr., um . . ."

"With Freddy?"

"Who's Freddy?"

"The cop who arrested you."

"He's one of the worst," Skippy said. His eyes were livelier now; he looked a lot more believable.

"Did he ask to search the car?" Roy said.

"Yeah."

"You could've said no."

"But there was nothin' in it—that's what I'm trying to tell you," Skippy said. "I thought, you wanna waste your time, go ahead."

"Then he opened the glove box."

"And I couldn't believe it. I thought it was one of those practical jokes." Skippy's eyes met Roy's. "I hate practical jokes."

"Me too," Roy said.

"And Mr., um, Roy? I've never messed with guns and never would. What if something bad happens? You're a loser forever."

"So whose was it?" Roy said.

"No clue."

"And how did it get there?"

Skippy shrugged. His leg, which had stopped jiggling, started up again.

Fourteen

"Turk?"

"Hey, Roy. You're back? How'd it go?"

"Good." He thought about it. "Very good."

"Yeah?"

"The guy's a genius. Dr. Chu."

"What'd he do?"

"Gave me his cocktail."

"How'd it taste?"

"Turk. It's not a real cocktail. You take it from an IV."

"Oh."

"But I'm calling about Skippy."

"Skippy?"

"Murph's nephew—who I left in charge of the house."

"What about him?"

Roy told Turk Skippy's story.

"Lots of guns in the valley," Turk said.

"There are?"

"This is a well-armed corner of the country."

"I don't believe it."

"That's you, Roy. You live in a rarefied world."

"The hell I do."

Silence. "Sorry. I just meant—"

"I want you to take this case," Roy said.

"What case?"

"This gun bust, or whatever the hell it is."

"C'mon, Roy," Turk said. "It's open-and-shut."

"I admire your fighting spirit."

Another silence.

"They've got some kind of vendetta against the kid," Roy said. "He fixed his goddamn brake lights and they still pulled him over."

"With a revolver in the glove box."

"Maybe."

"Where's the maybe?" Turk said.

"Will you talk to him?"

"I'm not seeing the maybe."

"That's all I'm asking," Roy said. "On my tab."

"It's not the money," said Turk. "It's the waste of money. I hear this kind of bullshit story every day. They always turn out the exact same—"

"Yes or no?"

A sigh. "Send the little peckerhead in."

Skippy went on foot to see Turk. While he was gone, Roy brought in the chair, set it up in the corner of the big room where light flowed in from two angles. It shone on all the gluey parts—Roy had used enough to cause overflows at every joint—rendering the rest, the original chair, almost invisible. The title came to him: *Autopsy.* He gazed at it for a minute or two, feeling pleased with himself until a thought hit him: *Got to start working faster, boy.*

Silence. Where was he with that? *Silence* didn't exist yet, the blurry attenuated image in his mind and the long silver cone lying on the floor of the big room, still far apart, almost unrelated. Roy found his pad, lying on the kitchen counter, brought the tip of the soft pencil down on the blank page. At that moment, he remembered the last time he'd tried sketching ideas for *Silence* and how he'd ended up with the facade of the Hobbes Institute. A sketch that should still be there: but the top page was blank. Had he taken it with him on the trip? No.

But not a certain no. Roy dumped out his travel bag, still unpacked. No sketch. He held the pad to the window, angled it, saw faint vertical indentations from the pilasters on the top page.

"**I've got** an interview next week," Delia said.

"What kind of interview?"

"With a think tank." She flipped through her appointment book. "Called the Hobbes Institute—ever heard of it?"

Roy shook his head. "I thought you liked your job."

"I do," she said. "They came to me—a guy named Tom Parish. Very bright. It sounds like they do interesting work."

"Like what?"

"The same kind of things I'm doing now," Delia said. "But more hands-on."

"No harm in hearing what they have to say."

Roy was still sitting there, on a stool in the light-filled corner, when Skippy returned.

"How did it go?"

Skippy came over, hands red from the cold. "Okay, I guess."

"What did he say?"

"Not much. He wants you to call."

"But about the case," Roy said. "What did he tell you?"

"I could, um, go to jail."

"That's not going to happen," Roy said.

Skippy just stood there. He didn't argue, didn't disagree, but he didn't believe Roy, not for a second. If he'd ever had fight in him, there wasn't much left.

Roy picked up the sketch pad. "I had a drawing on this," he said. "The front of a building. Did you see it anywhere?"

"You think I stole it?" Skippy said, but without indignation in his voice; flat, detached, beaten.

"Of course not," Roy said. "It's not even worth anything. I'm just asking if you saw it."

Skippy shook his head. "Can I go now?"

"Go where?"

"Upstairs. Unless you want me to leave."

"Skippy," Roy said, "what's happened to you?"

"Huh?"

Roy could still see himself at Skippy's age, at least dimly. Had he ever been like this, so defeated? He'd had hockey; and his mom. "At home. At school. With your friends."

"Nothin'," Skippy said. "Can I go upstairs?"

Roy nodded. Skippy trudged out of the big room and up the stairs. Then came the muffled thump of him falling on the spare-room bed. Among other differences, some probably unknowable, they had different kinds of moms.

"Turk? What's the story?"

"The usual," Turk said.

"You told him he was going to jail?"

"No point in sugarcoating. Not with the clients—I learned that long ago."

"But he's a kid."

"Lucky for him," Turk said. "That means juvie up in Colchester and he'll be out in three years, max."

"Can't you make a deal?" Roy said.

"Only if he cooperates," Turk said.

"Cooperates how?"

"By giving up his source—where he got the gun," said Turk. "And he flat-out refuses. End of story."

"Refuses why?"

"His reason or the real reason?"

"His reason," Roy said.

"He claims ignorance of how it got in his car," Turk said.

"What if it's the truth?"

"Never is," Turk said. "I touched base with Freddy. Looks like the kid got himself caught in the middle of a turf war."

"What turf war?"

"Seems we've got two separate drug gangs in the valley, both dabbling in stolen guns," Turk said.

"The kid bought from one gang. The other gang called it in."

"Lost me," Roy said.

"With the idea of making happen precisely what did happen," Turk said.

"I still don't get it."

"An anonymous call came into the station, Roy. That's why they pulled the kid over."

"Anonymous call?"

"Five minutes before they busted him," Turk said. "A total setup, with the expectation he'd cough up his source in a plea deal, of course. Using the cops as a cat's-paw, if you get the idea, take all the business for themselves. Kind of clever for these parts."

"But if the call was anonymous," Roy said, "what makes Freddy so sure?"

"He's a smart cop, believe it or not," Turk said. "And a tough one."

Freddy was neither of those things on the ice. "I just don't see why—"

"Roy? Freddy doesn't want to screw this kid. He names a name and the whole mess goes away."

Roy went upstairs. Skippy was lying on the bed in the spare room. He sat up when Roy came in.

"You want me to split?" he said.

"No," said Roy. "I want to get to the bottom of this."

"All I know is what I said."

"So there's no name you can give up?"

"Think I wouldn't if I could?" said Skippy.

"I actually think you might not," Roy said. His legs felt tired all of a sudden, like he'd been on snowshoes the whole day; he leaned against the desk. Skippy lay back down, gazed at the ceiling.

"Sorry about the shoveling," Skippy said. "Didn't get it done."

"Hard to," said Roy, "from inside a cell."

Skippy flinched, just a little—if Roy hadn't been watching closely he'd have missed it—but the meaning was clear: the reality of Skippy's future had hit him, maybe for the first time.

"We know their theory," Roy said. "What's yours?"

"My theory? Of like what happened?"

Roy nodded.

Skippy's eyes met his. "Somebody put the thing in the glove box. Must of."

"Like who?"

Skippy shrugged.

"Do you have any enemies?" Roy said.

"Enemies?"

"Anyone you've been in a fight with, owe money to, that kind of thing."

"I got in a fight with Billy Cordero a couple months ago."

"Yeah?"

"But he beat the crap out of me," Skippy said. Long pause. Then he said, "So that's no help."

Roy laughed. After a moment or two, Skippy started laughing, too.

"I should have beaten the crap out of him instead," Skippy said. "Then we'd have a good theory."

They laughed together, long and hard, like something hilarious had just happened.

"Um, Roy?" Skippy said. "Your nose is bleeding again."

They went outside. Skippy showed Roy where his car had been parked, right in front of the garage.

"Locked?" Roy said.

Skippy shook his head. "Locks were already busted when I bought it."

They got in the truck, drove to Dunkin' Donuts and then back as far as the spot where Freddy had pulled Skippy over, just past Dee Dee's Beauty Salon.

"Wish that insurance lady had come by sooner," Skippy said.

"Why?"

" 'Cause the call came in five minutes before I got busted, right?" Skippy said. "So if the insurance lady had like woke me up even ten minutes earlier, I'd of been home safe with my doughnut."

"True," Roy said, just catching that *home safe*, "but that's not really . . ."

"Not really what?"

But Roy wasn't listening, had already started scrolling through the numbers on his phone. He came to his insurance agent.

"Hi, Mr. Valois," said the insurance agent. "How can I help you?"

"What's this rebate about?" he said.

"Rebate?"

"The one that involves taking measurements," Roy said. "A woman came out the other day."

"First I've heard of it. Can you hang on? I'll check with the underwriter." Ten or twenty seconds went by. The agent came back on the line. "Nope," he said. "Nothing like that's going on. Did you let her in?"

"No."

"Whew, thank goodness," he said. "So many scam artists nowadays, can't be too careful."

Roy clicked off, turned to Skippy. "What did this insurance lady look like?"

"I should of let her in?"

Roy got impatient, couldn't help himself. "Just what did she look like?"

Skippy bit his lip. "Um," he said, "well, she was black for one thing."

"Black?"

"Not dark black, more light-skinned—kind of like the Corderos."

"She was one of the Corderos?"

"Oh, no," Skippy said. "Nothing like the Corderos. Just that kind of skin. But she talked like you."

"Like me?"

"Educated," Skippy said. "Like from college. And she was tall, with straight hair, real shiny."

"What did you say?" Roy's voice rose.

"The part about tall and straight hair?" said Skippy. "Real shiny?"

Roy tried to bring his voice back to normal range. "Could you draw her face for me?" He had to be sure, and that meant something visual.

"Draw?" said Skippy. He looked confused, almost shocked. "I don't know how."

"Just give it a try," Roy said.

"How come?" said Skippy. "You think this has something to do with, like . . ."

They drove back to the barn. Roy handed Skippy the sketch pad and the soft pencil. Skippy, tongue between his lips, hunched over the page, made a few tentative marks. Skippy was right: he didn't know how to draw. But in the end he did the job anyway—Roy wasn't surprised—and so accurately around the high forehead and elegant neck that his attempt at glossy straight hair wasn't necessary. It was Lenore from Wine, Inc., beyond doubt; the woman who'd somehow hurt him with her grip.

Lenore? In Ethan Valley? Trying to get into his house? Trying and succeeding, even if that meant setting up a sixteen-year-old kid: What could possibly justify that?

Roy searched his house, quickly, but from top to bottom. He found no sign that anyone had been searching ahead of him, and nothing was missing except that unfinished sketch of the Hobbes Institute. A miniaturist's version of the real situation, Roy thought: the Institute itself was missing, too.

"Roy? Are you feeling okay?"

Fifteen

"I want the best defense money can buy," Roy said.
"You're talking about the kid's gun charge?"
said Turk. They sat in his office, overlooking the green;
a crow landed on the snowy top of *Neanderthal Number
Nineteen.*

"He didn't do it," Roy said.

"Someone planted the gun?"

"Yes."

"One of the gangs?" Turk said. "And the kid was
the real target, for reasons unknown? Pretty expensive
ploy—they'd be sacrificing the gun, a six-hundred-
dollar item."

"It wasn't one of the gangs," Roy said.

"No?" said Turk. "Who, then?"

Roy took out Skippy's drawing, handed it to Turk. "Her," he said.

Turk put on his reading glasses. "One of the Corderos?" he said.

"This isn't a Cordero," Roy said. "Her name's Lenore. She's supposedly a clerk or manager in a wineshop in D.C."

"I don't get it," Turk said. "What's her relationship to the kid?"

"No relationship," Roy said. "She needed uninterrupted time in the house, that's all."

"Your house?"

Roy nodded.

"She's an art thief?"

"A thief, anyway," Roy said. "Among other things."

"What did she take?"

"A sketch."

"One of yours?"

"Yes."

"How much is it worth, rough estimate?" said Turk, reaching for a pen.

"Nothing," Roy said. "Not monetarily. It's more like . . . evidence, I guess you'd say."

"Evidence of what?"

"This all goes back to Delia," Roy said.

Turk glanced at Skippy's drawing. "This woman knew her when you were in D.C.?"

"No," Roy said, but as soon as the word was out, thought: *can't be sure of that.* Lenore was probably about the same age Delia would have been now. "This is all about the Hobbes Institute."

"What's that?"

"The outfit Delia worked for."

"Yeah?" said Turk. "I always thought she worked for the government."

"You did?"

"What's so weird about that?" Turk said. "They must hire economists by the thousands."

"I didn't say it was weird."

"You're looking weird."

"I'm surprised, that's all," Roy said.

"About what?"

"That she never mentioned her work to you."

"Actually, she did," said Turk. "She told me she hated it."

Roy shook his head. "She must have been joking. Delia was dedicated to her job."

"Maybe," Turk said. "But I remember this one occasion distinctly—that night we got snowed in at the warming hut."

"Winter carnival?"

"Yeah," Turk said.

Roy remembered. One of the last winter carnivals in Ethan Valley: the selectmen commissioned a study to see whether it made economic sense for the town and canceled it soon after. He and Delia, Turk, Turk's wife at the time, and a few other people snowshoeing on the back side of the mountain got caught in a blizzard. This was before Ski America came in, before any cutting on the back side. There was just one steep and twisting path—probably going back to the Indians—that hooked up with the Appalachian Trail, and at the T stood the warming hut. They'd fired up the woodstove, shared what food they had—a surprising amount—and there'd even been a wineskin to pass around.

"We went out for wood from the pile behind the warming hut," Turk said. "All unsplit, so Delia got to work with the ax while I held the lantern."

"Delia did the splitting?" Roy said.

"I was going to at first, of course," said Turk, "but she took the ax."

"Delia never handled an ax in her life."

"Then she was awful good for a beginner," Turk said. He got a look in his eye. "In fact, I distinctly remember mentioning it to you."

"When?"

"At the rink one night. Between periods."

"I don't remember."

"No?"

But surely he would have remembered that. "I must have thought you were joking," Roy said.

"Maybe," said Turk. "The point is, the wind's howling up there, snow flying all over the place, but we're sheltered there behind the hut, in this quiet pocket, and she turns to me and says, 'I could live this way forever.' Meaning living rough, cabin in the woods, water from the stream, all that."

"That's not her at all," Roy said.

"Her exact words—they made an impression," Turk said. "And I told her she'd get bored pretty quick, start missing her job. That's when she said she hated it. I asked why, but her answer didn't make much sense."

"What was it?" Roy said.

Turk screwed up his face. "Something along the lines of 'when you see how things really happen, the fun goes out pretty quick.' "

"What things?" Roy said.

"That's what I didn't get," said Turk. "Economics is at the other end of how the world works, right? The theoretical."

"Not always," Roy said, thinking of the pineapple caper, as Paul Habib had called it—practical, hands-on. "But this kind of fits into the problem."

"Which is?"

"Delia's job," Roy said. "The Hobbes Institute seems to have disappeared."

"Disappeared like . . . ?"

Roy told his story—mistake in the obituary; Richard Gold and his cell phone; Consulate of Greece; Tom Parish; Wine, Inc.; Lenore; Sergeant Bettis.

When he finished, Turk was silent for twenty seconds or so. Outside the window, the crow perched on *Neanderthal Number Nineteen* spread its wings wide. It didn't take off, just stood there like that.

"You're saying the reporter's death is somehow connected?" Turk said.

"Not out loud till now," said Roy. He was suddenly aware of his own voice, the strain in it, the tension; was it possible he sounded afraid?

"That would be pretty extreme," Turk said. His eyes went to Skippy's drawing. "The kid drew this?"

"Yes."

"And it's the wine-store woman, for sure?"

"Lenore." Roy forced his voice back to normal. "Got to be."

Turk gazed at it for a moment or two. "One thing off the bat," he said. "We can clear up this Hobbes business." He swiveled around to his computer. "Spelling?"

Roy spelled *Hobbes*. "What are you doing?" he said.

"Heard of Google, Roy?"

"I'm an idiot," Roy said.

The crow folded its wings.

Turk tapped at the keyboard; thick fingers, misshapen from being broken so many times, but the typing was quick and agile. "Sure about that spelling?"

"Yes."

"Funny," said Turk.

"What?" Roy said.

"No hits."

"Meaning?"

Turk didn't answer, tapped a few more keys. "Rephrasing," he said. "Sometimes that . . ." He gazed at the screen, shook his head, typed some more.

"What now?" Roy said.

"Other . . . nope." He turned to Roy. "This Hobbes Institute of yours doesn't seem to be on the Web."

"So?"

Turk smiled. "Surf the Web much, Roy?"

"No."

"Ever?"

"You mean just sort of exploring around?"

"Yeah. Surfing the Web."

Roy shook his head.

"You're missing something," Turk said. "For example, let's try R-O-Y V-A-L-O-I-S." *Tap-tap.* "See?"

Roy glanced over.

"Twelve thousand four hundred twenty hits," Turk said. "Probably some other Roy Valois mixed up in there, but still, not bad. The point I'm making is that anyone who's anyone or anything that's anything gets hits on the Web."

"Try Delia," Roy said.

Turk leaned over the keyboard. "Delia Stern," he said. "Middle initial?"

"She never used it."

Tap-tap.

Roy got up, stood behind Turk, read over his shoulder.

"One hit," Turk said. He clicked on the link.

"Would have thought there'd be more," Roy said.

A long list of names in alphabetical order appeared on the screen, Delia Stern, toward the bottom, underlined in red.

"What is it?" Roy said.

Turk scrolled to the top, revealing the heading: *Former Employees, Economics Section, UNESCO.*

"UNESCO?" Roy said. "Is that the United Nations?"

Turk nodded. "United Nations Education and some-thing-or-other."

"The United Nations?" Roy said, his voice rising on its own. He read the heading again, three, four, five times. "But it's wrong." Almost unaware of what he was doing, he crowded Turk out of the way, took control of the mouse, scrolled back down.

Delia Stern.

"Why is her name underlined?"

"The search engine does that," Turk said.

"Why in red?" he said.

"Some programming thing," Turk said, on his feet now. He touched Roy's back. "Roy?"

"What?" Roy said, scrolling back to the top to see that heading again.

"Let's go for a walk."

"She didn't even like the UN—she wrote a paper about it." Roy hit the back arrow, returned to the original link. He clicked on that, landed again at the UNESCO list, unchanged in any way. He scrolled up, scrolled down, scrolled up, scrolled down, scrolled—

"Roy?"

They went for a walk, around the green. The snow from the storm lay in puffy white drifts, but slightly settled now, like day-old meringue. "Do you have a favorite?" Turk said.

"Favorite?"

"Of the *Neanderthals.*"

Roy glanced up at Number Nineteen, saw the crow was gone. "No," he said.

"This one's like an old friend to me," Turk said. "Those huge shoulders and at the same time . . ."

Turk paused, gazing up at Number Nineteen. Roy looked at him in surprise: Had Turk ever talked about his work before, outside the context of showings and money?

". . . at the same time," Turk went on, "the way he's turning, as though he's heard something, maybe there's trouble on the way, even for a giant like him." Turk saw the expression on Roy's face, misinterpreted it. "Maybe it's just supposed to be I-beam shapes and stuff—I'm no art critic, that's for sure," he said, looking a little sheepish. "But lots of people feel the same about him, kind of attached. Like he's watching over the town."

"I didn't know that," Roy said.

Their eyes met. The sunshine, bright already and brightened more by all the reflecting snow, lit up networks of tiny lines on Turk's face, lines Roy had never noticed before. He could picture how Turk would look as an old man, one of those sweet, round-faced old men with no regrets; then he thought: *something I won't see in real life.*

"I feel kind of bad," Turk said, "like all this is my fault."

"All what?" Roy said.

"The whole obituary thing was my stupid idea," Turk said. "If I'd just kept my mouth shut, you wouldn't be going through all this agitation."

"That's crazy," Roy said. "I'm not an ostrich—and I don't need protecting."

"I know that," Turk said. "But this is a time for looking out for yourself, not getting agi—not wasting your energy on some wild—some little mix-up that doesn't really matter in the end."

"Little mix-up?" Roy said. All at once, he had no air, could hardly get the next sentence out. "Mind telling me what you think's going on?" His voice, starved for air, turned thin and harsh, like a preview of how it would be, or would have been, in forty years or so.

"I don't know, Roy," Turk said. "Somebody made a mistake, wrote down the wrong thing, it all got magnified, memory plays tricks on people—does it really matter?"

"Memory plays tricks on people?" Roy said. "What's that supposed to mean?"

"It was a long time ago," Turk said.

"Delia worked for the Hobbes Institute, not the UN," Roy said. "It was real. I was inside. There was a goddamn fountain."

"Maybe it was part of the UN," said Turk.

"It was a think tank."

"Possibly funded by the UN?"

"No."

"Then who funded it?"

Had Roy ever known? "Private money," he said. But he wasn't sure.

"Like who?" said Turk.

"You mean the actual people?"

"Yeah. Private money means actual people."

"I don't know," Roy said. He'd never thought much about the funding; and the realization that specific people might have put up the money was hitting him now, for the first time.

Turk smiled, and, as though his mind had been following a parallel track, said, "You're an artist, Roy."

Roy didn't smile back. "So don't get involved with this? Is that what you're saying?"

"I'm saying there's probably nothing to get involved in," Turk said. "And if Dr. Chu pulls this—if it works out, then there'll be lots of time for your investigation. But right now it's about Roy. That's my advice as lawyer and friend." He glanced at Roy's arm. "And speaking as the goalie for the Thongs, we need you back on the ice. How's the arm?"

"Fine." In fact, it was aching in a dull way pretty much all the time. Angles changed in Roy's mind, unbending a little: if the cocktail worked, he'd have time, years and years. Where was the flaw in that? "What about Skippy?"

"He gets the best defense money can buy," Turk said. "On the house."

"What's the defense going to be?"

"No reason we can't use this robbery idea, insurance scam, getting the kid out of the house, all that," Turk said. "We'll just keep the wraps on this . . . this murky part."

So: no flaws left.

Roy went home. Skippy was in the big room, sweeping the floor. The sun shone through the windows, lighting the dust motes he was raising. They swirled around *Delia,* made it seem like she was slowly rotating, in orbit. *When you see how things really happen, the fun goes out pretty quick:* Had she ever said anything like that to him? Roy had the strange feeling that he was in motion, too. He thought of the dark side of the moon.

Sixteen

They lay in the warming hut. Delia and Roy had one of the top bunks; the air was musty, close, a little strange, maybe from so many adults—eight or nine men and women—sleeping so near each other. Roy slid his hand up under Delia's fleece, cupped her breast.

She whispered in his ear: "No craziness, buddy boy." But she encouraged his hand to stay where it was. Not by any movements or things like that: Then how? No telling. Roy just knew.

The storm sang in the trees, all high notes. The woodstove crackled. Sounds of breathing, some light, some heavy, rose all around, as though the warming hut itself had lungs. Roy slept the deepest sleep he could remember, slept in fact like a baby, a dreamless, milky sleep.

It was still snowing in the morning, but not hard. Everyone woke up looking rosy and a little confused; got their skis or snowshoes on and left without saying much. Roy and Delia were the last to leave. Delia took it all in, all three hundred and sixty degrees of a world gone white. Snow rounded everything—the cedars, the spruces, the hut. She took Roy's hand, squeezed hard.

"Meet me here, Roy," she said. "If anything ever happens, meet me here."

"Like what?" Roy said.

"Anything bad."

"Nothing bad's going to—"

"If we get separated, if you can't find me."

"That won't happen."

"Roy, I mean it," she said; a world gone white, except for Delia's dark eyes, intense and focused on him. "Meet me here."

Roy awoke. Daylight in the room, light that had lost its freshness. Quarter of ten? *Right now it's about Roy.* But he didn't like sleeping in, needed time every day with that early-morning light, light somehow untouched, if that made sense. He got up, went into the kitchen. Coffee was brewing and a note lay beside the pot.

*Hi Mr. Roy. Mr. McKenny called for me to come
see him. Back later. Also—man who said his name was
Krishna.*

Roy opened the fridge, saw not much. Was he
hungry? No. But he went outside, got in the truck,
drove down to Russo's Meat and Groceries.

"Got some nice New York strip today, Roy," said
Dickie Russo, alone in the store.

"I'll take a couple."

"How's the arm?" Dickie played for the D-Cups,
was probably the biggest guy in the league, also had
a mean streak that only showed up on the ice, would
have been pretty scary if there'd been bodychecking.

"Coming along," Roy said.

"I almost scored last night," Dickie said.

"Barhopping?" Roy said.

"Very funny."

Dickie never scored: a big guy with a weak shot. He
wrapped the steaks in butcher paper. Roy wandered
around the store, loading his cart with fattening foods.

"Those tomatoes over there actually got some taste,"
Dickie said.

Roy took some. He went on to the apples, bagged
half a dozen Macs, came to some pineapples. They
had circular stickers on their sides, showing a smiling
sun and a palm tree; the writing on the circumference

read: *Product of Venezuela*. Roy stopped right there. This was something he'd never considered: that Delia's project had ended up being successful.

"You get your pineapples from Venezuela?" he said.

"This time of year," said Dickie. "They're just as sweet as the ones from Hawaii and a lot cheaper."

"When did you start?"

"Start what?"

"Buying Venezuelan pineapples."

Dickie shrugged. "Long as I can remember."

"Ten years or so?" Roy said, trying to make calculations about how long it would take to get the plantations up and running.

"Oh, longer than that," Dickie said. "We had 'em when Dad ran the store and I just worked weekends."

"How long ago was that?"

"Hell, I don't know," said Dickie. "Twenty, twenty-five years, maybe more. Venezuela's a big-time pineapple producer, always has been. Try one—on the house."

Back in the kitchen—Skippy still gone—Roy ate double-chocolate-chocolate-chip ice cream out of the carton. It had the feel of ice cream but tasted strange, like copper. He made himself take ten spoonfuls, as though it were medicine. There was nothing to hear except eating sounds, very quiet. Time slowed down, which had to be a good thing. *Right now it's about Roy.* Hard to argue with that on a rational basis. So why didn't it feel right? Because *it's about Roy* meant being self-absorbed and passive, like . . . like what? Like an invalid. He had this disease, yes, but he was not an invalid.

That was part one. Part two: this problem of Delia didn't go away. In fact, it kept spreading, had now reached the pineapple story, the whole reason she went to Venezuela in the first place. Roy put the ice-cream carton in the freezer, moved into the big room. He gazed at those twisted helicopter blades high up on *Delia.* Thoughts he hadn't had for years came back to him, thoughts of that long spinning fall, green jungle coming up fast from below, Delia's face at the window.

Fact: Tom Parish had called with the news. Nothing could change that.

Fact: Tom Parish had also been in the hearse that brought the coffin from D.C. to the old cemetery behind the Congregational church.

Fact: Roy knew Delia, like no one else.

Fact: The guitarist by the grave played "For All We Know."

Roy went down to the storage room in the cellar, where he'd kept Delia's things—clothes, papers, all those shoes—for three or four years, finally forcing himself to get rid of everything. What seemed usable, he'd given to the Salvation Army. The papers—essays from college, backgrounders from work, financial documents—he'd burned in the fireplace in a private ceremony he'd also forced on himself. And among those financial documents: green pay stubs; he had a memory of them, browning at the edges and curling up in the flames. What he didn't remember, probably hadn't even noticed, was the printing in the payor line. But it must have read *The Hobbes Institute;* proof, if he had kept even one, that he could put before Sergeant Bettis. And did those stubs have bank routing numbers or some similar identification? *Follow the money,* as they said in so many cops-and-robbers stories. And what had Turk just told him? *Private money means actual people.*

The storage room had rough, freestanding shelves on two sides. The shelves on one side held old things of his; those on the other side were bare. What if a pay stub, even one, had slipped out of a box, fallen free?

Light flowed in from a ground-level window, high above. Roy got down on the dusty cement floor, hands and knees. He peered under the bottom shelf, saw nothing but dust balls, patted around anyway, hoping for the feel of crumpled paper. Nothing.

Roy gathered his legs under him, started to rise. For a moment, he couldn't; as though all his strength had gone at once. And in that moment, he noticed a footprint in the dust. Not his—his feet were bare right now, and besides, this print came from a woman's shoe: two separate prints, really, small square heel and larger oval toe. Lenore had been rooting around down here.

"Goddamn it," Roy said. The thought of this invasion and his own failure to stop it infuriated him. The next thing he knew he was on his feet, angrier than he had ever been in his life—angry at Lenore, who had framed Skippy and searched his house, possibly found and taken the evidence that would force Sergeant Bettis and the official world to believe him; all this while he lay in a hospital bed.

What are you going to do about it? Delia's voice again, but the effect was not as comforting as it had been in the feng shui room. "I could use some help from you," he said.

Roy heard a crunching sound in the snow outside. He looked up, through the high window, saw someone going by; just the lower half, from that angle, but the someone wore a black mink coat.

———

"Good news," said Krishna as Roy opened the front door. The limo sat idling in the driveway, exhaust rising in the cold air. "Oh dear—what happened to your arm?"

"Hockey," Roy said.

"Don't tell me you're still playing at it?"

"You don't *play at* hockey," Roy said. "You *play* it."

"A tad grumpy today?" Krishna gave him a close look. "Are you feeling all right?"

"Fine," Roy said.

"Have you lost a little weight?"

"Nothing to speak of," Roy said. "Ramping up my workouts till I get back on the ice."

Krishna nodded. "It's all of a piece," he said.

"What is?"

"This physicality of yours," Krishna said. "It informs the work."

Roy thought about that.

"Are you going to invite me in from the cold?" Krishna said.

"Oh, sure, sorry."

They went into the kitchen. "Didn't you get my message?" Krishna said. "About dropping in on the way to Stowe?"

Roy glanced at Skippy's note on the counter.

Hi Mr. Roy. Mr. McKenny called for me to come see him. Back later. Also—man who said his name was Krishna.

"What are you smiling about?" Krishna said.

"Nothing," Roy said. "Coffee?"

"With pleasure," said Krishna. "But don't you want to hear my news?"

"All ears," said Roy.

Krishna took Roy's arm, led him into the big room. He stopped in front of *Delia*. "My God," he said. "Even better than I remembered. Just breathtaking."

"Thank you."

He turned to Roy. "The news, Roy, the excellent news, is that we have a buyer. And what a buyer. And what a price. From the sight of the photos alone, he has offered—are you ready for this?"

"Probably not," Roy said.

Krishna laughed, clapped Roy on the back. Not hard—Krishna was small and soft—but for some reason it hurt. "Two hundred and fifty thousand dollars, Roy! A quarter of a million."

"Oh."

"Oh?" said Krishna. "Just oh? It's more than twice what we've gotten for anything before."

"I'm . . . stunned, that's all," said Roy; a lie—but why spoil Krishna's fun? "It's fantastic."

210 · PETER ABRAHAMS

"Fantastic, splendid, wonderful," said Krishna. He shook Roy's hand. "Congratulations. You deserve every penny. This is marvelous work—I suspect you've arrived at a whole new level."

Roy gazed up at *Delia:* he saw another flaw almost every time he looked, but that didn't make Krishna wrong about the whole new level; the very fact that he was seeing them might make him right. "Who's this buyer?" he said.

"That's the beauty part," Krishna said, "as if the money wasn't beauty enough. The buyer is Calvin Truesdale."

"Never heard of him."

"Roy! Calvin Truesdale. The Truesdale Ranch."

Roy shook his head.

"Like the King Ranch," Krishna said. "Only bigger."

"He raises cattle?" Roy said.

"Yes, I suppose," said Krishna. "Besides owning twenty percent of the oil wells in the Gulf, a couple hundred radio stations, a controlling interest in Texas Semiconductors and God knows what else. But the important thing for our purposes is that in the past ten years or so he's gotten interested in art. He's already accumulated the largest private Giacometti collection in the country, and just last April he bought

Rodin's *Seated Zola* for fourteen-point-five mil. I've tried getting in touch with his people more than once about some pieces—that Degas ballerina I had two years ago, for example—never getting anywhere. And then what happens?"

"What?" said Roy.

"Yesterday morning he just walks into the shop."

"Who?"

"Calvin Truesdale, Roy," Krishna said. "Are you following this?"

Roy nodded; those names—Giacometti, Rodin, Degas—spoken even in distant relationship, made him very uncomfortable.

"I showed him a few things—he bought that little Matisse that's been in the window on the spot, actually ended up strolling out with it under his arm, for God's sake. But I went through the catalog with him, too, and that's where he saw this." Krishna gestured toward *Delia*. "He flipped over it, Roy, just flipped."

"Like how?"

"Like how did he flip?"

"Yeah." Roy was trying to imagine some cowboy jumping for joy in Krishna's hip and sophisticated Tribeca shop, and having trouble.

Krishna shrugged. "He said amazing, incredible, had all kinds of questions—size, materials—and wanted to know about you, of course. He'd also like to come see it. 'At the artist's convenience'—he's very polite, but the offer stands in any case, personal viewing or no, bound with a check for ten percent of the total." Krishna had a huge grin on his face, one of those faces shaped for conveying happiness to begin with.

"I'll have to think about it," Roy said.

The grin faltered, went misshapen. "But why?" Krishna said. "What sort of thinking?"

"I just don't know if I want to . . ."

"To what?"

"Part with it right now."

Krishna's gaze went to Roy's cast, then back to his face. "You're not just saying that?"

"Why would I?"

"Maybe as a strategy to drive up the price?" Krishna said. "Playing hard to get?"

"Why would I strategize on you?" Roy said. "And it's already more than the thing is worth, way more."

"Hush," said Krishna.

Roy laughed. Krishna laughed a little, too.

"All right," he said. "Think about it. I understand—it's like a mother giving up her baby. But, Roy—you can make more babies. And remember Picasso's warning."

"What warning was that?"

"Don't become your own connoisseur."

Wisdom, the kind that actually shifted the mind around at one stroke, revealed what needed revealing: you didn't come across it often. Roy caught a glimpse of what separated him from Picasso, horizons beyond horizons.

They drank coffee at the kitchen counter, sitting on stools. "Does the driver want any?" Roy said.

Krishna waved the idea away. "Finished with your thinking yet, Roy?"

Roy laughed again.

Krishna sipped his coffee. "Whatever you decide," he said, "there's one thing you should know."

"What's that?"

"She would have loved it."

Roy's eyes met Krishna's. He came close to telling Krishna everything, starting with the present meaninglessness of a quarter of a million dollars and the possibility that his baby-making days were numbered. Then a thought came that helped him quell the impulse. "Do you remember Tom Parish?"

"Doesn't ring a bell," Krishna said.

"Delia's boss. He spoke at the funeral."

"I was in Rome."

Roy remembered.

"I still feel bad that I couldn't—"

"It's all right."

"What about Delia's boss?" Krishna said.

"I'd like to locate him," said Roy.

"Why?"

"Just to talk."

Krishna glanced across the kitchen, into the big room and *Delia*. Roy could see him inventing some artistic explanation. "Why don't you try what's-his-name?" Krishna said.

"What's-his-name?"

"Fellow who worked at the same place," Krishna said. "Government agency, wasn't it? Delia sent him to me."

"Delia sent who to you?"

"This coworker—he had an interest in mosaics from the Moorish period and I happened to have a Moroccan bowl, I believe it was, in his price range."

Roy was on his feet. "What was his name?"

Krishna looked alarmed. "Is it that important?"

Roy tried to control that old-man quaver in his voice, settle it down. "The name, please."

Krishna closed his eyes. "One of those combination names," he said.

"Combination names?"

"In a multicultural sense." Krishna's eyes opened. "Paul Habib," he said.

"You sold a bowl to Paul Habib?"

"A very minor piece," said Krishna. "It couldn't have brought more that fifteen hundred dollars, two thousand at the outside. A shrewd purchase, actually—this was many years ago and the market has strengthened considerably. But the point I'm making is that I'm sure to have contact information for him back at the office. Somewhat dated, no doubt, but you never know."

"Can you call now?"

"Call?"

"The office," Roy said. "Have someone look it up."

"Friday, Roy. I don't open on Friday." Krishna gave Roy another look, saw something that made him take out his phone. "Philip?" he said. "When you get this message, I want you to go to the office, open the accounts file and find contact information for Paul Habib. Paul Ha-bib. Call me when you've got it."

"Thanks," Roy said.

"You're welcome," said Krishna, finishing his coffee. "Done thinking yet?"

Seventeen

Krishna's limo backed smoothly out of the long curving lane to the street and drove away. An old woman walking her dog turned to watch it go by.

Two hundred and fifty grand: a fortune for a kid growing up in a shabby town like North Grafton, Maine, utter fantasy to dream of that kind of money coming in one fat hunk. But here it was: all he had to do was say yes.

Roy picked up the phone and called his mom.

"Roy! How nice to hear from you!"

"Everything okay, Mom?"

"Everything's super," she said. "Couldn't be better." Roy's mom wasn't one of those northerners who ended up pining for home—even in winter—after moving to Florida. She loved Florida: the little condo Roy had bought her, the Mini Cooper she'd chosen at the dealership he took her to—first brand new-car she'd ever owned—her new friends and all the card games they played and dancercise classes they took. "Guess what the temperature is this very minute," she said.

Best to aim low on that question: "Sixty-eight?" he said.

"Sixty-eight?" she said. "Brrr. It's eighty degrees, Roy—I'm looking at the thermometer as I speak. You know the thermometer I'm talking about, on the balcony?"

"Yes, Mom."

"And I can see a freighter, way way out there. It looks red."

"Sounds nice, Mom."

"My own personal million-dollar view," she said. "And how are you doing, Roy?"

"Pretty good."

"Things are still . . . selling and all?"

"Oh, yeah," he said; and smiled to himself: he knew that down deep she probably thought her Florida life could vanish like that. "No problem there."

"Good to hear." Then a pause. "Is there a problem somewheres else?"

"No, no," said Roy. "I'm just saying the business side is going particularly well."

"Wonderful," said his mom. "Any recent sales at all, if I'm not being too much of a nosey parker?"

"Now that you bring it up," Roy said, "we just got the highest offer yet."

"How much?"

"A lot."

"No fair clamming up now."

"Promise you won't repeat it."

"Cross my heart."

Roy named the figure.

"Oh, Lord," she said. "Who in their—" She stopped herself.

"Who in their right mind, Mom?" Roy said, having some fun.

"Now, Roy," she said. "You know I love your work—it's so . . . so big. I'm just wondering who has that kind of money."

"It's some rancher from Texas," Roy said.

"What's his name?"

For a moment, he couldn't recall. "Truesdale," he said. "Clifton Truesdale."

"*Calvin* Truesdale, you mean?" said his mom.

"Yeah, I guess so," Roy said. "You've heard of him?"

"Heard of him! Don't you read *People*, Roy? Just last week, I think it was, they had him hunting birds down on his ranch with the president. They're best buddies."

"What president?"

"Of the United States, for God's sake," said his mom. "What president. Didn't you meet him once, if I recall?"

"Who?"

"Who? Good grief. The president, Roy. The president of the United States."

"Sort of," Roy said.

"How can you *sort of* meet someone?"

"He was still vice president when I met him," Roy said. "And it was only a handshake."

"Listen to you. Shook hands with the president. My son—in the big time and he don't even know it."

"I'm not in the big time, Mom."

"Big enough for me," said his mom. One more pause. "How's Jen?"

"Fine."

"Still teaching skiing?"

"Yes."

Her tone changed. "You got a cold, Roy?"

"No."

"Feel okay? Your voice sounds a bit raspy."

"I'm fine, Mom," Roy said. "Got to run. Talk to you soon."

"Bye, son. Love you."

Click.

Roy cleared his throat—more accurately, went through all those sounds and peristaltic throat movements involved in throat clearing—but couldn't quite do it.

He stood before *Delia.* No rising dust motes now, but she still seemed to be turning, perhaps a kinetic illusion he'd unintentionally created. *Done thinking yet?* He didn't need the money, didn't want to sell her, not now, not ever. In fact, a strange, even repellent desire arose within him: to dig a great hole, have *Delia* buried in the ground beside him.

Then he thought of Skippy. Two hundred and fifty thousand dollars could get Skippy set up somewhere, somewhere out of town. He could take his GED, go to college, grow up safe; all of that depending on how this bogus weapons charge turned out. Roy went to the window: no Skippy. The old woman and her dog were coming back, a small dog wearing a snappy plaid vest. The old woman wore a thin coat with patches on the elbows and the acetate lining sagging out the back.

A calendar hung on the broom-closet door: hockey legends. Roy flipped through the months: Bobby Orr flying through the air; Gordie Howe holding off a defenseman with one hand, getting off a shot with the other; Guy LaFleur with his hair streaming behind him; Glenn Hall in goal without a mask; Boom Boom Geoffrion winding up for a slap shot; and on to Rocket Richard at the end of the year, with his hot, mesmerizing eyes, like there was a fire burning inside him. Roy knew he'd enjoy that December, thirty-one days of the Rocket. All he had to do was get there.

Rest, food, exercise: his responsibilities; everything else was up to Dr. Chu. Roy went upstairs, laid out his gym clothes—sneakers, sweats, jock, white cotton socks, a Thongs T-shirt with a long list printed on the back: *hooking, slashing, elbowing, boarding, spearing, tripping, holding, roughing, high-sticking, interference, fighting, unsportsmanlike conduct,* each with a little box, and a check mark in every one; and at the bottom, kings of the penalty box. Roy sat on the bed, took off his shoes.

"I hate everything about hockey," Delia said, "but you know what's worst?"

"What?"

"The way you all stink. How come no one ever washes their stuff? It comes in waves when I stand behind the bench, almost knocks me over."

"Then don't stand behind the bench."

"But that's the best place to watch the game, Roy."

He was zooming, skating so fast he barely touched the ice, reaching speeds unknown even to LaFleur or Kharmalov or Perrault on their best days, and he had the puck on an invisible string; even better, he didn't get winded at all, needed no more than a deep breath now and then, the air in his lungs almost tactile, like from a planet with a richer mixture. Then the horn sounded, game over.

Roy opened his eyes. The phone was ringing. Dark shadows slanted across his room. He lay on the bed, his gym clothes twisted and bunched around him.

Roy reached for the phone, knocked it on the floor, fumbled around. A small voice rose from the receiver, down there somewhere. "Roy? Are you there? Mr. Valois?"

Roy found the phone. "Skippy?"

"Is that you, Roy?"

He cleared his throat. "Yes—what is it, Skippy?"

"Can you come down here?" Skippy said. "Soon or like right now?" His voice was low and excited. "I found her."

"Found who?"

"The lady, Roy. You got to, like, hurry."

"What lady?"

"The lady, the lady, you know. I can see her from here."

"What lady?"

"The one, Roy. Who came to the house. Um, your house."

"The lady you drew? Who set you up?"

"Yeah! Yeah! I can still see her, just about. She's got some dude with her, a big dude and—"

"Skippy! Where are you?"

"Uh-oh. I'm gonna hafta, like . . ."

Click.

Roy checked to see if his phone had captured Skippy's number: it had. He called back.

"Yo. This is the Skipster. Leave a message or not. Up to you. Buh-bye."

"Skippy! Pick up!"

But he didn't.

Roy hurried downstairs, threw on boots, ran outside to the truck. In the driveway his right foot slipped on a glazed tire track. Roy was a fine skater and a pretty good skier, had one of those bodies that rebalanced quickly, and so hardly ever fell at the rink or on the slopes, and never hard when he did. But he fell now—landing partly on his face but mostly on his broken arm—and very hard. He heard a cry of pain, uncontrolled. It didn't sound like him.

Roy lay in the driveway. The pain in his forearm didn't want to be contained in such a small, outlying area, found some nerves and spread through his body. *Get a grip, boy. What are you?*

He reached up with his good arm, found the running board of the truck, pulled. From high above came a *whap-whap-whap* sound. It terrified him. He twisted around, looked at the sky, saw a helicopter soaring past. Just an everyday kind of helicopter—white with the words vrai transport painted in green on the side—nothing scary, or even interesting about it. *Get a grip, boy.* Roy pulled harder on the running board, got his legs under him and rose. He climbed inside and drove off, his breathing fast and light, but he was back in control, had a grip.

Where was Skippy? Roy had no idea, but he couldn't be far, not with his car still in the pound. He turned down Main Street, drove slowly along its three blocks, checking both sides. No Skippy, and daylight fading fast. Roy went around the green and back the other way on Main Street. He stopped in front of Dunkin' Donuts and went inside.

No one there but a girl—maybe fifteen or sixteen—behind the display case, sticking a "For Sale" card in a powdered doughnut.

"Excuse me," Roy said. "Do you know Skippy Bedard?"

The girl looked up. Her eyes widened.

"What is it?" Roy said. "Did something happen to him?"

"There's blood all over your face," the girl said.

Roy touched his cheek, checked his hand: red. "I'm fine," he said. "Do you know Skippy?"

She nodded vigorously, eyes still wide.

"Was he here?"

More nodding.

"When?"

She looked at the watch on her plump wrist, then up at the clock on the wall.

"When?" Roy said, his voice rising. Was he scaring her? He lowered it. "Approximately."

"Approximately," she said, speaking the word slowly, as though understanding it for the first time. "Maybe like two hours ago? He had a chocolate doughnut with sprinkles."

"Was there anyone with him?"

She shook her head.

"A light-skinned black woman? Tall, in her forties, maybe with a big guy, younger?" Just guessing on the younger part, but he described Westie for her anyway.

"No," said the girl. "Skippy was by himself. But you know what?"

"What?"

"A woman like that—tall, light-skinned black? I saw her." She pointed out the window.

"When?"

"When? I'm not sure when—but Skippy was still here. We were talking. Me and Skippy were in World Geography together, until he, you know, dropped out. The thing is, Skippy's really smart, one of the smartest kids in the whole—"

"The woman—what about her?"

She pointed out the window. "She was walking by, like maybe going to a car?"

"And?"

"And? That was it. Then she was out of sight, past where I could see. See from here, behind the counter. If I would of moved, I could of—"

"Did Skippy say anything?"

"Nooo-ooo."

"Or do anything?"

"Nothing special. He left pretty soon after that."

"How soon?"

Her eyes scrunched up. "Maybe right away." She gestured at half a chocolate doughnut with sprinkles on a table by the window. "That's his doughnut, now that I remember. I thought he might be coming back."

"Which way was the woman going?" Roy said.

She moved her hand left to right, toward the green. Roy hurried to the door, paused. "What kind of car was she heading for?"

"See, I'm not sure she was for sure doing that," the girl said. "But, thinking it over, she was kind of a cool-looking lady. And a very cool car was parked out there."

"What kind of cool car?"

"With the nice curves," said the girl. She made curves with her hands. "Porsche, I think it is. Do you say the e at the end? A silver one."

Roy threw open the door.

"Is he in trouble again?" the girl said. "Skippy's a good kid, one of the best kids in the whole stupid town."

Out on Main Street: no Skippy, no silver Porsche. Roy was getting into the pickup when across the street the doors of Normie's Burger Paradise opened and Normie Sawchuck strolled out, a fat cigar in his mouth.

Roy called out, "Normie."

"Hey, Roy." Normie waved, let the ski shuttle bus go by, walked over. "How you doin'? Heard you're on the DL."

"Temporarily," Roy said.

Normie looked more closely. "What happened to your face?"

"Nothing," Roy said, "just a little slip. Did you see a Porsche parked out here a couple hours ago?"

"Nope," Normie said. "But I was up at the mountain"—Normie, a notorious womanizer in a town full of them, gave Roy a sly glance—"for a quick meet-and-greet, just got back."

Roy slid behind the wheel, started to close the door.

"You should have the doc check those cuts," Normie said.

"Later."

Normie had a thought. "That Porsche—silver, by any chance?"

"Why?"

"I saw a silver one going up the mountain road when I was coming down."

Roy drove up the mountain road. The last rays of sunshine glowed on the upper trails, glazing the chairlifts, now still; everything else lay in deep shadow. Skiing all done for the day, but lights still shone in the bars and restaurants of the base lodge, and the parking lot was about one-quarter filled. Roy went up and down the rows, saw many different kinds of cars and trucks, but no Porsches. He tried Skippy's number again.

"Yo. This is the Skipster. Leave a message or not. Up to you. Buh-bye."

Roy drove back down, but instead of turning at the bottom, toward town, he went the other way, down valley, and stopped at Murph's yard. Murph was alone in the office, pouring Jack Daniel's into a paper cup when Roy walked in.

"Roy," he said. "Hey, what happened to you?"

"Nothing," Roy said. "Have you seen Skippy?"

"What's he done now?" said Murph.

Maybe if that arm pain hadn't picked this moment to send out one of its jolts, Roy would have reacted some other way. But it did. He lashed out with his good arm, sweeping papers off the desk, knocking the paper cup from Murph's hand, splashing whiskey everywhere. Murph rose in alarm.

"What the hell?"

"There's no time for this," Roy said. "Just answer the question."

"Jesus, Roy, I haven't seen him. Not for days. Isn't he with you now?"

Skippy's mom lived in Ethan Lower Falls, three miles farther down the valley. It wasn't exactly a shack, but close—plastic sheeting on the windows, tarp on the roof; and out front, dog turds in the snow, twenty or thirty, and rusty shapes poking up through the white. Roy scooped up a clean cold handful and washed his face.

He knocked on the door. It opened and Skippy's mom looked out. For a moment—eyes narrowing—she couldn't place him, then—eyes narrowing some more—she did. Behind her, the boyfriend with the bushy white mustache lounged on the couch, a big mongrel beside him and TV light flickering on their faces. No Skippy. The room was full of cigarette smoke.

"Have you seen Skippy?" Roy said.

"Me?" said Skippy's mom.

"In the past few hours," Roy said.

Skippy's mom scanned Roy's face. "He take a swing at you or somethin'?"

Roy came close to taking a swing at her. "Yes or no?"

"Not so easy, is it?" said Skippy's mom.

"Just answer."

"Haven't seen him," Skippy's mom said.

"Most likely out dealin' dope," said the boyfriend, eyes still on the TV. Skippy's mom nodded.

Taking a swing at the boyfriend: that was another story. Roy stepped inside. The smoke got to him right away. He started coughing, couldn't stop. Pain from his chest, right where the heart was, linked up with the pain from his arm. He backed away, coughing and coughing. The dog growled. The door closed.

Eighteen

"Thing is, Roy," said Freddy Boudreau, rocking back on the unpadded wooden chair behind his desk, "you've been in the Valley for a long time and everybody likes you, but you're not from here."

"What's that supposed to mean?" Roy said. When the cough had finally lost interest in him, Roy had driven to the station and told Freddy his story: editing it down to the insurance-scam/robbery version that Turk was basing Skippy's defense on and keeping the murky part—Hobbes Institute; Wine, Inc.; Tom Parish—to himself.

"No offense," Freddy said, holding up his hand. "Likes and respects, I maybe should have said. More than any flatlander I can think of."

"Flatlander?" said Roy. "I come from Maine. Ever hear me talk?"

"You talk like a flatlander, Roy."

"The hell I do," Roy said. "And what's any of this got to do with Skippy?"

"Everything," Freddy said, shaking a cigarette out of a pack on his desk. "Take someone like me. I was born here, went to Ethan High. So did my dad, and later on he was the gym teacher. My mom taught kindergarten, retired three years ago."

"Did she have Skippy?"

"Possible," said Freddy. "But see where I'm going with this?"

"No."

Freddy patted his pockets the way people did searching for matches.

Roy thought: *Don't smoke*. He thought it very hard, hoping the idea might jump across the desk. Freddy's hands went still.

"What I'm trying to tell you," he said, "is that I've got this town in my blood. How the folks are deep down, what really goes on, who did what to who."

"Meaning?"

"Meaning you can kiss your ten grand good-bye," Freddy said.

"What ten grand?" said Roy.

Freddy laughed. "The bail money. But I guess it's chicken feed to you, Roy."

Roy got angry. "Bullshit," he said; although the truth was, he'd forgotten about the ten grand. "What are you saying?"

Freddy's face hardened. "The kid jumped bail. He's in the wind."

"That's not what happened," Roy said. "I told you—he saw the woman who set him up. He may be in danger. We need to get out there and—"

"Whoa. Stop." Freddy rocked forward; his chair squeaked. "You really believe this woman was willing to part with an untraceable gun just to get in your house? What kind of a thief does that?"

"Some of the art's a bit valuable," Roy said.

"But it's all huge, Roy. And nothing's missing but one little sketch that you yourself said isn't worth anything. Besides, in my experience, that kind of scammer never packs a gun—raises the sentence big-time if they're caught." Freddy sat back. "One of the first things you learn in this job—when there's two stories, one simple, one complicated, pick A, ninety-nine percent of the time. The kid knows I got him cold." Freddy started patting his pockets again. This time he found matches, lit up. "What comes next," Freddy said, inhaling deeply, "one of the conditions being he stayed with you till court date, is the D.A.'ll move to revoke bail. After that we get a warrant, and before you know it someone'll bring him in." A plume of smoke curled across the desk toward Roy. "That's the way it happens, ninety-nine percent of the time. I'll do what I can about the ten grand, but don't count on nothin'."

Roy felt a cough coming on.

He went home. Late now, most of the houses on the higher slopes dark, including his. Roy went in.

"Skippy?" he called. "Skippy?" No answer.

He checked his messages. Just one: "Krishna here. Give me a call when you get a chance."

He called Skippy's number. "Yo. This is the Skipster. Leave a message or not. Up to you. Buh-bye."

Roy went to bed. Sleep moved in fast, was almost there, almost had him, when a last wakeful thought came to him: When had he last eaten? He couldn't remember. Nor was he the least bit hungry.

Roy rose, went down to the kitchen, stuffed in more ice cream. He stood by the window, gazed out. Way up on the mountain, the lights of the snowcats swept back and forth across the summit trails.

He lay in bed. Sleep was waiting, welcomed him again, so reliable, so accommodating. Sleep felt good. Our little life is folded in a sleep. Where did that line come from? Or was it rounded in a sleep? Delia would know—she had a real college education, not the hockey-player version. Folded and rounded, both so nice. An idea for *Silence*, the right idea—a kind of basket of curves— came to him at last. Even the best ideas could disappear overnight, as Roy knew well, which was why he kept a sketch pad on the bedside table. But now he was too folded and rounded in to switch on the light, to take up a pencil, even to open his eyes.

A partly eaten chocolate doughnut lay on a Formica table. Delia sat down. As she reached for the dough- nut, Skippy appeared with a dispenser of sprinkles and started sprinkling them. Mostly red sprinkles; in fact, all. He sprinkled them on Delia's head and then on his own. Not in a goofy way, like it was some prank or youthful rebellion. This was more ceremonial.

Whap-whap-whap.

Roy woke up, burning hot. Burning hot and the sheets soaked with sweat. He got up, went into the bathroom, saw his body in the mirror: red splotches all over. He took a long cold shower, cooled down. His breath came easier and easier. He felt better. Maybe all he had to do was stay in the shower.

He got out, dried himself. The body in the mirror didn't look so splotchy now. Roy realized it was day- time. He looked out the window.

The bathroom window faced the backyard. Roy owned almost three acres, most of it upsloping, but near the top it flattened into a high meadow, a wildflower extravaganza in the spring, but now all white. In the middle of the meadow sat a helicopter, white with green letters on the side: VRAI TRANSPORT.

For a minute or so nothing happened, and Roy wondered if maybe the helicopter had crashed and for some reason he just couldn't see the damage. Then he caught a movement in the cockpit, made out the form of a man, possibly two. A moment later the cabin door opened. A steel ladder swung down. A man appeared in the doorway—tall, suntanned, white-haired. He wore a cowboy hat and a long duster, maybe suede.

The man climbed down the ladder and stepped onto the snow. He sank to his knees, no surprise to Roy. But it surprised the man. He looked up, into the cabin. Another man appeared, a big man in a black suit. The man in the cowboy hat said something to him—breath clouds rising in short bursts—and made angry gestures. The man in the black suit made apologetic gestures. He extended his hand. The man in the cowboy hat smacked it away and climbed the ladder. The cabin door closed. The top rotor started turning, then the rear one. The helicopter rose, hovered, banked and flew away.

It was like a dream: a helicopter dream. He'd had helicopter dreams before, a few he remembered, many more he did not, other than the odd fragment, dark and uneasy. So close to a dream, but the tracks left in the snow by the helicopter's skids were real. Weren't they?

Roy got dressed, put on his ski jacket and hiking boots, went outside. Very cold, the kind of cold that freeze-dried the insides of your nostrils. Roy liked that feeling. His snowshoes stood by the wood box. He strapped them on, walked around the house, climbed toward the high meadow.

Roy loved being on snowshoes; that high-lifting way of walking on unfirm ground, the rhythm of it, the sounds made by different kinds of compressing snow. This snow, on the slope behind the house on this particular day, was actually kind of strange: under his feet, it made the soft thumps of light, dry snowpack, but he was only sinking in an inch or two, as though it were wetter and heavier; or the load were lighter. He climbed the slope, his breathing slow and easy—back to normal—and crossed the high meadow.

Two parallel tracks lay in the snow, each about twelve feet long and a foot wide. There was also a shallower indentation where the base of the ladder had rested, and two round holes made by the man in the cowboy hat. All real. Roy glanced up at the empty sky, that beautiful silvery blue that went with the coldest days. Not long after Delia's drugstore pregnancy test came up pink—meaning yes—Roy had looked up the scientific explanation of what made the sky blue so he'd be ready when his kid asked. But it turned out to be complicated, too hard for him to simplify; and in fact he still didn't know.

Roy followed his tracks back down to the house, breathing free and easy; he made a mental note to snowshoe every day from now to mud season. Inside, he dialed Skippy's number.

"Yo. This is the Skipster. Leave a message or—"

Roy checked the clock. Lunchtime already? He opened the fridge, saw the two steaks Dickie Russo had wrapped in butcher's paper. Menu: steak and ice cream, the two biggest treats of his childhood. He stuck one of the steaks in the broiler. The other was for Skippy. And just as he had that thought, someone knocked on the door, not loud and forceful, just a light *tap-tap*—the way Skippy would knock.

Roy hurried to the door, opened it. Not Skippy. Instead it was the man in the long duster—yes, suede— and cowboy hat. A taxi—one of two in the whole town, both owned by Dickie Russo's brother—idled in the driveway, the man in the black suit sitting in back.

"Roy Valois?" said the man in the cowboy hat.

"Yes?" said Roy.

"Sincere apologies for busting in on you like this." He held out his hand. "Cal Truesdale." He smiled a rueful smile. "What can I tell you? I just had to come see *Delia*."

Roy gazed at Calvin Truesdale, gazed up a little, Calvin Truesdale standing several inches taller. He had a prominent nose, the skin on its tip damaged by the sun, and eyes the exact silver blue of today's sky.

His hand was still extended. "I'm a fool for art," he said. "Great art, that is. And great sculpture in particular."

Roy shook his hand—a long hand with long fingers; cold, but it was cold outside. "Come in," he said.

"Much obliged," Truesdale said.

Roy stepped aside. Truesdale wiped his boots on the mat—cowboy boots, the leather glowing—and entered, taking off his hat. He had a tiny, flesh-colored hearing aid in one ear.

"My, my," he said. "So bright and airy. Must be an artist's dr—" He spotted *Delia*, went silent. Then, slowly, he crossed the kitchen and entered the big room, trailing damp cowboy-boot tracks on the hardwood floor.

Truesdale circled *Delia*, head turned up, eyes suddenly moist, unless that was a trick of the light.

"Your dealer's photos don't do her justice," he said. "Not even close."

A voice inside Roy said, *Hey, it's not that good.*

"I trust he informed you of my offer," Truesdale said.

"He did."

"Worth every penny." Truesdale moved closer to the piece. "Every detail ugly and yet a thing of beauty," he said. "May I touch?"

Roy nodded.

Truesdale reached out, touched *Delia* with the tips of his long fingers. "What is it about sculpture?" he said. He turned to Roy. "What is it?"

"I don't know," Roy said.

Truesdale's eyebrows—wild white overhangs—went up. "You must have some idea. You're the artist."

"I really don't, Mr. Truesdale," Roy said.

"Cal, please. Everyone calls me Cal. And may I call you Roy?"

"Of course."

"Then tell me, Roy—with the greatest respect—how can you create something like this and not know what makes it so powerful?"

"It's not the way I work," Roy said.

"No?" said Truesdale. "How do you work?"

"It's hard to describe," Roy said. "And not very interesting to talk about."

"Oh, but I am interested, Roy," said Truesdale. "Interested in your art. Interested in you. And as anyone who knows me would affirm, I'm a terrier when something interesting comes along. So if you'll indulge an old collector, possibly over a cup of coffee . . ." He gave Roy a big, encouraging smile; he had nice even teeth, very white, except for one of the incisors, somewhat yellower.

Nineteen

"Excellent coffee, Roy," said Cal Truesdale.

"Thanks," said Roy.

They sat on stools in the big room, steam rising from their mugs. Truesdale glanced at Roy's cast.

"Quite the hockey player in your college days, I understand," he said.

"Krishna tell you that?"

Truesdale smiled. "I'm a big fan of hockey."

"Yeah?" said Roy. Truesdale's accent somehow cast doubt on his own statement.

" 'Course I've never even had ice skates on my feet," Truesdale said. "Football was all we played when I was a boy—six-man football in the bitty little schools like mine. So I came to hockey late in life."

"In what way?" Roy said.

"Got involved with the National Hockey League," said Truesdale. "For my sins."

"How?"

"By acquiring a piece of the Stars in a moment of madness," Truesdale said. "A fifty-one percent piece."

"Who needs more?" said Roy.

Truesdale laughed, a sharp, sudden bark. "My goodness," he said. "You're one of those artists with a head for business."

"Far from it," said Roy.

"And modest to boot." Truesdale twisted around so he could see *Delia*. "But there's turning out something like that and then there's a head for business. Different magnitudes entirely—puts things in perspective."

"I don't know," Roy said; that kind of talk made him uncomfortable. "People exaggerate the differences be—"

"Think of it this way," said Truesdale, facing Roy. "No one's going to settle for fifty-one percent of *Delia*. They'll want it all."

"The thing is," Roy said, "I'm not so sure about selling it."

Truesdale shook his head. "Oh, boy," he said. "I'm in the briar patch now."

"What do you mean?"

"And how you soft-pedal that business sense," Truesdale said. "Seldom seen it done better. So I'll save us both time and effort by giving up on the spot and confessing straight out that two hundred and fifty grand was just my opening offer."

Roy laughed. "It's not the money," he said.

"You're good," said Truesdale.

"I mean it," Roy said. "This isn't a ploy."

"Anyone says that," said Truesdale, "what's my very first thought?"

"Ploy," Roy said.

Truesdale leaned across the space between them, gave Roy a friendly punch on his right arm. Not hard, and his good arm, so there should have been no pain at all.

"My kind of guy," Truesdale said. "Knew it the moment I laid eyes on you." He rose, walked around *Delia*. His voice fell, almost like he was talking to himself. "For the sake of argument," he said, "if it's not a ploy, then the obvious question comes to mind—is there a real Delia, maybe, to explain your reluctance?" He took a sip of coffee, his silver-blue eyes watching Roy over the rim of the mug.

"No," Roy said.

Truesdale nodded. "A striking name, though," he said. "What made you pick it? If I'm not being a nosey parker, to use one of my mother's favorite expressions."

"Mine, too," Roy said.

"You don't say," said Truesdale. "Is the good lady still with us?"

"Yes."

"Glad to hear it," Truesdale said. "My own mama's long gone, of course. But now let me guess—yours is named Delia."

"Edna," Roy said.

"And does mama live somewhere close by?"

"Florida."

"Whereabouts, if you don't mind my asking?"

"Sarasota," said Roy.

"Very nice," said Truesdale. "I had an aunt Edna long ago. Terrible battle-ax. Leathery old wranglers on the ranch trembled at the sight of her. Been down to Texas much, Roy?"

"A couple times."

"Ever on a working ranch?"

"No."

"Then consider this an open invitation to come visit with us." He took a notepad from an inside pocket, scribbled on it with a gold pen. "Here's my personal number." He came over, handed it to Roy. Looking down—Roy finally realizing that most of his height advantage came from his boot heels—Truesdale said, "So, what's the secret of *Delia*?"

The radiating pain from that friendly little punch began to recede. Roy felt normal again, or close. "No secret," he said. "She was my wife."

"Divorced?" said Truesdale. "Say no more. I'm on my fourth."

Divorced from Delia? That would never have happened. Could there have been a better marriage? Plus they'd been starting a family, Delia three months pregnant. "No," Roy said, "not divorced." He heard the anger in his voice, regretted it at once: how would Truesdale—this rich and powerful admirer, fan even, probably being shabbily treated right now from Krishna's point of view—know things like that?

"She died," Roy said.

"I'm sorry," said Truesdale.

Roy nodded. "It was all a long time ago."

"Still," said Truesdale. "I'm very sorry." He glanced at *Delia*. "How long ago?"

"Almost fifteen years."

"Have you remarried?"

"No."

Truesdale nodded, as though piecing things together. That annoyed Roy—a fan, but also a collector, possibly a connoisseur, making connections between the life and the work, and doing it right in front of him.

"I wouldn't read too much into that," he said. But he couldn't help remembering: *You got damaged, too— like it deadened some nerves, deep inside.*

"Oh, no, never," Truesdale said. "Just getting to know you, is all." He made a steeple with his hands, spoke quietly. "How did she die?"

"In a plane crash," Roy said.

Truesdale gazed up at those twisted blades on *Delia.* "A helicopter?" he said.

"Yes."

"Hate the goddamn things," Truesdale said. Roy waited for him to say something about his own helicopter and the high meadow, but he did not. Instead he said: "Where did it happen?"

"In Venezuela," Roy said.

"A beautiful country," Truesdale said. "I have some interests there."

"Pineapple plantations?" Roy said.

Truesdale looked surprised. "A shrimp-processing plant and some warehouses," he said. "Why pineapples?"

"It's a long story," Roy said.

"I have time."

"How well do you know the country?"

"Venezuela? I've been going there off and on for forty years."

"Travel much in the interior?"

"Some. What's this about?"

Where to begin? Roy didn't know. But here was someone rich, powerful, connected, a best buddy of the president of the United States, for God's sake, the two of them hunting together on the Truesdale Ranch: When would he have another chance like this?

"Tell me about the pineapple industry in Venezuela," Roy said.

"Don't know what to say," Truesdale said. "They grow pineapples."

"Is it traditional?" Roy said.

"How do you mean?"

"Forty years ago, for example," Roy said, "when you first started going there—did you see a lot of pineapple growing?"

"Ah, I see," Truesdale said. "Now that you mention it, I don't recall seeing a lot of pineapple growing back then, no."

"And now?"

"Now, yes. You see pineapples."

"When did the change happen?"

"Hard to pinpoint," Truesdale said. "I'm not down there that often. In the last five or ten years, if I had to say. But I wouldn't take an oath."

Roy thought about that. Delia's pineapple project made no sense if Venezuela had already been a big cultivator, as Dickie Russo said; made total sense if it hadn't been, as Truesdale said. It didn't add up: What was he missing?

"Does that help you any?" Truesdale said.

"I'm not sure," said Roy.

Truesdale leaned forward, touched Roy's knee with the tips of his long fingers. "Mind telling me the significance of these pineapples?"

Roy took a glance at those silver-blue eyes. The skin around them, darkened and creased by the southwestern sun, crinkled in a friendly, down-home way. "Delia was on a mission to get Venezuela to grow pineapples when she died," he said.

"And you want to know if the mission ended up succeeding," Truesdale said, "as a lasting tribute? A very moving sentiment, Roy."

"That's not exactly it," Roy said.

"No?" said Truesdale, sitting back, taking his fingertips off Roy's knee. "Then I'm in the dark."

"Have you ever heard of the Hobbes Institute?" Roy said.

Truesdale's eyes shifted in thought. "Can't say I have," he said. "How are you spelling that?"

Roy spelled it.

"Nope," said Truesdale. "What is it?"

"The think tank in D.C. where Delia worked," Roy said.

"Don't know that world at all," Truesdale said.

"But you know the president."

Truesdale laughed. "I like you. I really do. Know the president? Sure—known him for the best part of thirty years, back when he was VP and even before, when he was nothing but a wet-behind-the-ears congressman from the dustiest district in the state. But let me ask you something, Roy—run across many politicians in your life?"

"None."

"The truth about politicians," Truesdale said, "career-type politicians, especially after they've been around for a couple decades or so, is that you can't know 'em. Any idea why?"

"No."

" 'Cause they're unknowable—that's one of the most important things I learned in my career, helped me in ways you can't imagine." He leaned forward. "By then, Roy, twenty or thirty years into a life in politics, they got nothing left inside to know. What's not sold and bartered just got pleased away."

"Pleased away?" Roy said.

"Something an artist like you wouldn't know about," Truesdale said. "Politicians are pleasers, first, last and always. Got to be."

Was that true? "But the president—any president—has already made it to the top," Roy said. "Can't they ease up on the pleasing part?"

Truesdale laughed, a single short bark. "You're thinking Washington and Lincoln," he said. "Pretty clear that those days are long gone. We're in a late Roman phase, just scratching and clawing to hold on."

"Hold on to what?" Roy said.

"Why, global power, naturally," said Truesdale. "And the wealth and influence that comes from it."

Roy knew nothing about any of that. What would Delia say now? What wouldn't he have given to hear her opinion? But he had a rough idea. "Delia's work was all about spreading the wealth," he said.

The skin around Truesdale's eyes went crinkly again in that down-home way. "Was it really?" he said.

"That was the whole purpose of the Hobbes Institute," Roy said.

"Ah," said Truesdale. "And the Institute was sponsoring this pineapple project?"

"It was Delia's idea," Roy said. "But yes."

Truesdale twisted around again to gaze at *Delia*, almost as though she exerted gravitational force. "Can't tell you how grateful I am for your time, Roy," he said. His gaze went to those twisted blades near the top. "I understand so much better now. It all adds up."

Four months to a year: maybe Dr. Chu's cocktail would work, maybe not, but time wasn't on his side. Was he getting anywhere on this whole question of the Hobbes Institute? No. And here in the room sat the kind of man whose calls got returned, who could make things happen fast. Any negatives? Not that Roy could see. He came to a decision.

"Actually, Cal," he said, "it doesn't add up."

Truesdale's eyes stayed on *Delia*. "Oh?" he said. "How not?"

"This is going to sound strange," Roy said.

Now Truesdale turned to him. "Care to guess my age?" he said.

This was like the temperature in Florida: best to aim low. Roy went with the same number he'd picked then. "Sixty-eight."

Truesdale smiled. "All that does is show you're still a young man. The young have trouble with the big sunset numbers. I'm seventy-nine years old, Roy, be eighty come July. And when you've been around that long, nothing's really strange anymore."

"Then maybe you can figure this out," Roy said. "The Hobbes Institute seems to have disappeared."

"Gone defunct, you mean?"

"That's what I thought at first," Roy said. "But it's more like it never existed."

"How's that?"

"Take the building itself, for starters," Roy said. "I went down there a few weeks ago, hoping to find some of Delia's coworkers from back then, and—"

Truesdale held up his long index finger. "Why?" he said.

"Why?"

"Why did you do that?" Truesdale said.

Roy was silent.

"What got you interested after all these years?" Truesdale said.

Dr. Chu, mesothelioma, sarcomatous, unresectable: and all those other Latin words: did Roy want to get into any of that? No. "She's been on my mind lately," he said. He recognized the truth of that as he spoke, a truth that had its own identity, separate from the Hobbes Institute problem.

"Of course she has," said Truesdale, gesturing toward *Delia*. "Go on."

And neither was it just the work. But Roy had no time to figure it out—figure out why Delia had been stirring inside him—because now, as an honest man, he was in the kind of situation where he didn't do well. Leaving out the Dr. Chu part meant leaving out the obituary part, too: the *New York Times*, Richard Gold, Jerry, even Sergeant Bettis. But the abridged version he stumbled through still included plenty: the Consulate of Greece; Tom Parish denying he knew Roy; the vanishing room behind Wine, Inc.; Roy's belief that Lenore had entered his house; and Skippy, out there somewhere, maybe having spotted Lenore and Westie and maybe in danger. Truesdale listened without saying a word or making a sound. Nor did he move: those silver-blue eyes, on Roy the whole time, barely blinked. Even when Roy came to the end, he didn't speak for a moment or two, maybe more.

Then he took a deep breath. "I'll tell you my reaction in a minute," he said. "But what do you usually get?"

"I don't understand."

"How do people usually react when they hear this story?"

"I haven't really told anyone," Roy said; the initial lie now leading into a maze, as his mother had warned him back in early childhood. "Except for my lawyer," he added.

"A Washington lawyer?" Truesdale said.

"A local guy," Roy said. "A friend."

"And what was his advice?"

"Pretty much to forget about it," Roy said.

Truesdale shook his head. "Lawyers," he said.

It took a moment for the implications of that to sink in. "That means you disagree?" Roy said.

"Yes, sir."

"You believe there's something to it?"

"Sure as shootin'," Truesdale said. "History's a hobby of mine, Roy, and one thing I learned from history is that some of the wildest tales turn out to be true, especially the ones with a certain kind of detail. And even more specially when they come from someone with your powers of observation."

"Then what do you think's going on?" Roy said.

"Too soon to say," said Truesdale. "But I suspect there'll be financial shenanigans at the bottom of it. I sure do intend to find out."

Roy felt his spine straightening, as though he'd been bent under a burden, now lifted. "What are you going to do? Look into their funding?"

"Among other things," said Truesdale. "When did you come up with that idea?"

"It was my lawyer's," Roy said. "He says that private money means actual people."

Truesdale laughed with delight. "Private money means actual people," he repeated. "Your lawyer sounds like a smart man after all."

"He is."

"What's his name?"

"Mike McKenny," Roy said. "But everyone calls him Turk."

"That'll be hockey culture, I'm guessing," Truesdale said. "Where are you on this funding idea?"

"I wouldn't know how to begin," Roy said.

"Just as well," said Truesdale, rising; he moved like a much younger man. "More in my line. All you need is for to sit tight, let me do some digging."

"I can give you physical descriptions of these people—Tom Parish, Lenore, Westie," Roy said.

"And good ones, too, I'll wager," said Truesdale. "But not necessary."

"No?"

"Not necessary at this stage is what I mean," Truesdale said. "I'll be in touch."

"I appreciate this very—"

Truesdale held up that long index finger. "My pleasure," he said. "Practically my duty—my duty to art. Your time's too valuable to waste on all this—what should we call it—mundanity?"

"I don't really consider it—"

But Truesdale wasn't listening. "And in the end," he said, walking over to *Delia*, "when everything's all sorted out, I'm hoping you'll see your way clear to naming some mutually agreeable price. I won't ever trouble you personally about it—just let the dealer know at your convenience."

Roy didn't want to part with *Delia,* but now how could he not?

"You get on back to your work, Roy, clear your mind of all this bother," Truesdale said, his voice gentle, a little like Willie Nelson, on his Christmas album. "I'll handle everything." He reached out to touch her again, paused. "Ever thought of bringing a reporter into this?"

The answer: yes. But that meant Richard Gold, obituary, disease, so Roy said, "No."

"Probably just as well for now," Truesdale said. "But it's something we might want to consider down the road. I've got a few valuable contacts in the media." He turned to Roy and added, with a real, visible twinkle in his eye, "especially in media I own."

Roy laughed. Truesdale joined in.

Twenty

You get on back to your work.

That sounded good. The problem was that Roy no longer wanted to work on *Silence*. He didn't even want that long silvery curving tube—from a nuclear plant? was that possible?—around anymore. He bent to pick it up, found he could barely raise it off the floor. Strange: he'd carried it in, no problem. Could it have an unstable atomic weight or something like that? Roy was dragging it toward the door when the phone rang.

"Hello, Roy." Krishna.

"Sorry I didn't get back to you," Roy said. "He was just here, in fact."

"I'm afraid you lost me," Krishna said.

"Calvin Truesdale," Roy said. "Wasn't that why you called—to tell me he was on his way?"

"Calvin Truesdale was at your house?"

"Ten minutes ago. He wanted to see *Delia*."

"My God," Krishna said. "Do you know what this means? Two hundred and fifty grand is just his floor."

"He kind of indicated that," Roy said.

"What did he say? The exact words."

"The exact words?"

"Yes, yes."

"I don't know the exact words," Roy said. "Something along the lines of two hundred and fifty being just for openers."

"Truesdale came right out and said that?"

"Pretty much."

"So baldly? So black-and-white? So unambiguous?"

"He seemed to think I was a shrewd negotiator."

Krishna started laughing. "That's a good one. We're going to be rich, Roy. Rich, rich, rich."

"You *are* rich."

"I meant *rich* as a figure of speech," Krishna said. He turned serious. "But there is something very deficient in the man who can no longer get excited about—who knows?—half a million dollars, maybe more. You forget I grew up poor."

"Your parents were doctors."

"Doctors in India, Roy. It is not the same."

"You went to Exeter."

"Loomis—and on scholarship," Krishna said. "Partial. But this is about more than money, Roy—it's about taking your career to a whole new level. You're just entering your prime as a sculptor. Think of where you could be in ten years."

Roy was silent.

Krishna laughed again. "Starting to dawn on you?" he said. "The import? Don't worry—I'll handle everything. And if Mr. Truesdale gets in touch with you directly, probably best to pass him right along to me. Agreed?"

"Agreed," Roy said.

"Good, good, good," Krishna said. "Talk to you soon, then."

"Krishna?"

"Yes?"

"What did you call about?"

"Oh, right," said Krishna. "The client we were discussing, who bought the Almoravid bowl? Twelve hundred dollars was the figure, by the way—I'd forgotten certain condition issues having to do with the glaze. Nevertheless a good investment—I wouldn't be at all surprised if—"

"You're talking about Paul Habib?"

"Precisely." Paper rustled. "The shipping address was 919 Eliot Street, Cambridge, Massachusetts."

"Wait," Roy said, remembering as he hurried to the counter that Habib had been a consultant, on loan from somewhere. He wrote the address on the same sheet of paper with Skippy's message: *Back later.*

"And here's the number," Krishna said.

Roy copied that, too.

Roy tried the number.

A man answered. "Hello?"

"Paul Habib?"

"Wrong number."

Click.

Roy called it again.

"Hello?" the man said.

"Don't hang up, please," Roy said. "This is important."

"Huh?"

"Are you at 919 Eliot Street in Cambridge?"

"No. What's going on? Is this some kind of—"

"How long have you had this number?"

"I don't answer questions like that over the phone."

"But—"

Click.

Roy dialed the number again. No answer. He let it ring ten times before giving up.

Roy spent a few minutes at MapQuest. Then he packed a bag, turned the heat in the house down to fifty-five. He dragged the long silvery tube outside, the snow crunching under his boots with the extra squeak that came with real north-country biting cold, and wrestled it into the back of the truck. He dropped the thing off at Murph's on his way out of town, pushing it up against a rusted-out combine in a corner of the yard; lots of grunting and quick shallow breathing—hadn't been working out enough, not nearly. Murph watched him from a window in his office, but didn't come out, didn't wave. Roy climbed in the truck and headed south. So cold. He cranked up the blower full blast. Almost right away it was much too hot. He shut off the blower, but that didn't help. He rolled down the windows. Snow started to fall, swirled inside the cab, but it was still much too hot, like some unseen blast furnace had come to life.

"Hungry?"

"No time," Delia said.

They were in the kitchen of their little apartment; not their first little apartment, the one where Roy had started out, still living alone in Foggy Bottom, but the second, farther north. Roy stood by the stove; Delia was throwing clothes into a suitcase.

"Bacon," Roy said. "Eggs."

"I can't."

Delia loved bacon and eggs, especially the way Roy made them. He cracked open a couple of jumbo grade A's, spread bacon strips in a fry pan. Sizzling started up right away, and then came delicious smells. Roy could practically picture them wafting across the room to Delia's nose.

"No goddamn time," she said.

"Always time for bacon and eggs," Roy said, "or what's the point of life?"

She stopped what she was doing, gazed at him. The light caught the gold flecks in her eyes; like subtle clues for a prospector, Roy always thought, clues that there was a gold mine inside. "He'll be here any minute," she said.

"Who?"

"Habib. He's picking me up."

"What airport?"

"I don't even care." Delia tossed a hairbrush in the suitcase. It bounced out, landed at Roy's feet. He picked it up, handed it to her.

"What's wrong?"

"Nothing."

He put his arms around her. "Three days in the Caribbean," he said. "How bad can it be?"

"The Caribbean?"

"Isn't Venezuela on the Caribbean?"

"We're not going to that part." Her mouth opened as though she were about to say more, but she did not. That mouth: like no one else's, almost as readable as eyes. Roy kissed it.

"Stop," she said.

He lifted her up, swung her around, sat her in a chair at the table, all very gently. "Bacon," he said. "Eggs."

She looked angry for a second. Then she laughed.

They ate bacon and eggs in silence, their feet touching under the table. At first they didn't even hear the honking from the street.

Roy went to the window, looked down. Springtime in Washington. Their own cherry tree grew in a tiny plot in the sidewalk outside the building. It was in full bloom, like a frozen pink explosion. An open convertible—white with white interior—idled at the meter, Paul Habib in the driver's seat; a strange foreshortened angle: square-topped head, thick rectangle of shoulders, rounded hands on the wheel.

"He's starting to lose his hair," Roy said, turning back to the room.

"Good," said Delia. She was kneeling by her suit-case, trying to zip it closed.

"Hey," Roy said. "Did you forget your bathing suit?"

"It's not that kind of trip."

"But it's warm there, right?" Roy said, remember-ing he hadn't seen her pack any shorts either, or short-sleeve tops.

"Hot as hell," Delia said. The lightning-bolt vein throbbed in her temple; she struggled with the zipper. "Goddamn it—I broke a nail." She bit at it. Was she about to cry? Not her at all; perhaps just a reflection of the soft light—morning and spring—coming through the window. Roy zipped the suitcase closed. Their hands touched. Delia went still.

"I've had enough," she said.

"Enough of what?"

"We're having a baby." Her hand trembled against his. "That changes everything."

Roy had heard that pregnancy sometimes caused mood changes, wondered if this was an example. "How do you mean?" he said.

Habib honked again.

The lightning-bolt vein throbbed. "Let's talk when I get home."

"About what?"

Delia smiled at him. "Just good things." She withdrew her hand.

"Like?" Roy said. "He can wait five minutes."

But she just shook her head. Roy carried the suitcase down to the street.

"Hi, Paul."

"Roy. How's it going? Just toss that in back." Habib's shirt was the color of the cherry blossoms; damp patches had spread under both arms.

Roy put Delia's suitcase on the backseat. They kissed. This time she didn't say *stop*. She met his gaze for the briefest instant; then her eyes closed. Roy tasted eggs. Delia got in the car.

"See you Friday," Roy said. He patted the trunk. "Safe trip."

They drove off, Habib's squared-off head straight up, Delia's oval making an angle to the right.

Ring. A phone. Roy reached toward the bedside table. He felt nothing.

He opened his eyes. Not in bed, but slumped behind the wheel of his truck, an inch of snow on the seats, the dash, the floor.

Ring, ring.

Roy looked around, maybe a little wildly, saw he was in the corner of some big parking lot; across the lot, a McDonald's, Exxon pumps, long lines of traffic following snowplows in both directions. The Mass Pike: he was in a service area, probably the one after Exit 9.

Ring, ring.

Where was that sound coming—

He dug his cell phone from his pocket. "Hello?"

"Roy? Cal Truesdale. Didn't wake you, did I?"

"No," Roy said, checking the clock. "No, of course not."

Out on the turnpike, a truck hooted, long and loud.

"Sounds a mite noisy on your little street," Truesdale said.

"Um, I—"

Truesdale chuckled. "One beautiful valley, Roy—right out of Tom Thompson."

"Who's he?" Roy said.

"Canadian painter I collect a bit," Truesdale said. "But that's not why I'm disturbing you right now. Not quite as sharp as I once was—forgot to ask an obvious question."

"What's that?" Roy said. Cold in the cab; he switched on the motor, slid the windows up.

"This man you mentioned," Truesdale said, "Delia's former boss, who you cornered at the wine store?"

"Tom Parish."

"That's the one," Truesdale said. "What made you look for him there?"

The answer: he'd used the photo on Richard Gold's cell phone, a phone no longer around when the time came for showing it to Sergeant Bettis. That was one complication. The second: the part about Gold's cell phone couldn't be separated from the obituary, Dr. Chu, or all those other things he'd already separated from the version he'd told Truesdale.

"Roy? Still there?"

At that moment, Roy realized what lay at the root of this unwillingness of his. It had to be the same reason he'd told the truth about his diagnosis to Turk alone, and even reluctantly to him: speaking the words made them real.

"It was luck," Roy said.

"Luck?"

"I was just driving around—I used to live not far from there—and I saw him."

"I'll say that's lucky," Truesdale said. "Fortune smiling down upon you."

"Yeah." For a moment, he considered telling Truesdale about this new link to Paul Habib, to let Truesdale work on that, too. But the link was uncertain, and more than that, how could he just sit and wait? This—the whole question of the Hobbes Institute—was gnawing at him; and from another direction, he realized, the disease was gnawing at him, too: a kind of race, and therefore no waiting possible. And the stakes? The stakes were very—

At that moment, a big realization hit Roy: he wasn't the only one with a stake in this. There was another side—the side with Tom Parish, Lenore, Westie, God knew who else—a side that had gone to a lot of trouble to erase all traces of the Hobbes Institute. Why? What would happen if the existence of the Institute was public knowledge? Why all this effort? Who would be threatened? How big was their stake?

"Something on your mind, Roy?" said Truesdale.

"No," Roy said. "Just thanks for your help."

"No need for any gratitude," said Truesdale. "You take care now. Y'hear?"

Snow turned to rain east of 495, and by the time Roy parked in front of 919 Eliot Street in Cambridge there was just a light drizzle, with foggy wisps rising from the snowbanks. He knew the area slightly, a few blocks from Harvard Square, where he and his team-mates had partied after away games against Harvard, in bars that always seemed to bring out the worst in them, win or lose. Tall, skinny brick row houses lined both sides of the street, some renovated, some not. Nine-nineteen was one of the latter.

Roy climbed the steps. A sticker on the doorpost advocated impeaching the president, a bumper-sticker sentiment also seen in Ethan Valley. Did the president notice things like that, maybe discuss them with Calvin Truesdale while they waited for a covey to flush? Roy pressed the buzzer.

The door opened. A little girl, five or six, looked out. Her eyes went to his cast immediately.

"Hi," Roy said. "Is your mom or dad around?"

She nodded.

"Can I speak to one of them?"

"My mom's at work. Daddy's making stir-fry."

"Could you call him?"

"Daa-aaddyy."

A man appeared: the right age perhaps, but nothing at all like Paul Habib. He was tall, thin, with a bony, ascetic face. "Anya," he said. "You know you're not supposed to answer the door."

"I didn't," Anya said.

Anya's father glanced at Roy, took her arm, drew her behind him.

"Sorry to bother you," Roy said. "I'm looking for Paul Habib."

"No one here by that name," the man said.

"I'm pretty sure he used to live at this address."

Something changed in the man's eyes. "Habib, did you say?"

"Paul."

The man shook his head. "I don't remember any Paul," the man said, "but the woman we bought the house from was named Habib. She lived alone."

"When was this?" Roy said.

"Almost fourteen years ago," the man said.

Behind him, Anya said, "Before I was even borned."

"What was her first name?" Roy said.

"I don't recall," the man said.

"Maybe you've got it on one of the original documents," Roy said.

The man gazed at him, said nothing.

"It's important," Roy said.

"How so?"

Roy didn't have much to go on, just that sticker on the doorpost. "My wife and Paul Habib started a third-world agricultural project. The country involved wants to give him a prize." Roy was stunned at this sudden facility for lying; maybe all it took was practice.

"What country?" the man said.

That was an easy one. "Cuba," Roy said.

Two minutes later, Roy had the name: Janet. "And here's the forwarding address she left," the man said, handing him a file card. "On Cape Cod. A long time ago, but you never know. Good luck."

Twenty-One

For some reason, Roy had always thought *boy*. But it could have been a girl. They still hadn't made up their minds about how much prebirth information they wanted to know before Delia left for Venezuela. An Anya-like daughter: that made sense, especially now that he'd seen one in life: a little Delia. So it could have been either: *Isn't that part of the fun?* He'd said that to Delia. She hadn't been sure. Delia had an expression for not being sure, a quick frown, as though annoyed with herself. Now, in light traffic, with the sky clearing the closer he got to Cape Cod, Roy could picture that expression exactly, down to the finest detail, like the slight darkening of those gold flecks in her eyes. Was it the kind of look that stayed with you for life, or would she have outgrown it? He wanted to hear her

voice now, saying *fight like bastards,* or *can he do it?*
or anything.

Roy crossed the Bourne Bridge. Down below, the
sinking sun burned on the surface of the canal. A kid
on in-line skates was gliding along a bike path on the
far side, trailing a long shadow. Roy came down off
the bridge, circled a rotary and headed south. He took
out his cell phone and called Skippy's number.

"Yo. This is the Skipster. Leave a message or not.
Up to—"

A little burst of static. And then:

"Hello?"

A man's voice; not Skippy.

Roy jerked the wheel to the right, stopped by the
side of the road.

"Hello?" the man said again.

"Who is this?" said Roy. "Where's Skippy?"

"I don't know any Skippy," the man said. "This
phone's not mine—I found it about ten minutes ago."

"Where?" Roy said.

"In Ethan Valley, Vermont," the man said.

"I'm from there," Roy said. "Where did you find
the phone?"

"What's your name?" the man said. "Do I know
you?"

"Roy Valois," Roy said. "Where did—"

"Hey—you're, ah, were, um, Jen's friend, right?"

"You know Jen?"

"I'm on the ski patrol," the man said. "I'm working right now. That's how come I found the phone."

"Where?"

"How well do you know the mountain?"

"I know the mountain," Roy said.

"The back side, too?"

"Why?"

"Because that's where I found it," the man said. "Familiar with the warming hut at the end of the Appalachian Trail spur? The phone was sticking out of a snowbank near the door. Just the little antenna, but it kind of gleamed, you know?"

"The phone belongs to Skippy Bedard," Roy said.

"Doesn't ring a bell."

"He's a kid—sixteen, skinny, long hair, wears a brown-and-yellow jacket."

"Didn't see anybody like that."

"What about a light-skinned black woman, tall, midforties? Or a younger guy, maybe six-three, two-fifty?"

"Nope," said the ski patroller. "Didn't see anybody, in fact. I was doing the last sweep—just got down. The mountain's clear."

"Did you look in the hut?"

"Sure. We always do. It was empty."

Roy sat in his truck by the roadside. Should he go back? Was this news about Skippy's cell phone good or bad? Skippy was no match for people like Lenore and Westie, perhaps not much of a match for anyone. But Roy could think of ways it might be good: the other side—he had no doubt about its existence— didn't leave loose ends hanging, so the phone lying in the snow might suggest he was safe. Plus Roy was already on the Cape, close to the address he had for Janet Habib and four or five hours from Ethan Valley.

"I'm walking into the lodge as we speak," the ski patroller said. "I was gonna drop it in the lost and found."

"Don't do that," Roy said.

"No?"

"Please do me a favor," Roy said. "I'm out of town right now. Do you know Freddy Boudreau?"

"Who's he?"

"Police sergeant."

"The mean one, with the mustache?"

"He's really not mean, when you get to know him," Roy said. "Can you give him the phone?"

"I guess so."

"Now," Roy said.

"Now?"

"I'll pay you for your time."

"Hey, man." The ski patroller sounded embarrassed. "Not necessary."

"Thanks," Roy said. "Tell him where you found it. And mention me—say I'd like him to go up to the hut, look around."

"Is he going to bite my head off?"

"He'll save any head biting for me," Roy said.

"What's this about?" the ski patroller said. "Is the kid in some kind of trouble?"

Roy felt a faint twinge in his shoulder—here and gone—where Lenore had found a nerve.

He'd never been to the Cape. Roy pictured beaches, the ocean, seagulls, but ended up seeing none of that. The address he had—1 Kettle Lane, Hatchville— turned out to be deep in a piney woods, last house on a dirt road. He had to stop for directions three times, and it was almost fully dark when he found the place—a few yellow lights blinking through the trees, gold sparks rising from a chimney. A small shingled house with a brick path in disrepair: he heard wind chimes as he walked to the door.

Roy's hand was raised to knock when a woman called from the other side. "Who is it?"

"Roy Valois."

"I don't know anyone by that name."

"I'm looking for Janet Habib."

"Why?"

"My wife worked with Paul Habib. I'd like to talk to him."

Silence.

Roy had a thought. "If you're no longer together, maybe you can tell me how to get in touch."

"She worked with him at MIT?" the woman said.

"No," said Roy. "The Hobbes Institute."

More silence. Then: "What's your wife's name?"

"Delia," said Roy. "Delia Stern."

Twenty or thirty seconds passed. Then the woman said something that stunned him: "Is the bitch with you?"

"What did you say?"

No answer. Roy thought he heard footsteps leave and return. A bolt slid aside with a soft thump. Then another, heavier. Finally a chain clinked, falling loose. The door opened a foot or two, revealing a woman with wild graying hair, and a fire crackling in the background. The woman wore big hoop earrings, jeans, a colorful Scandinavian sweater: all adding up to a coherent picture, a physical type also found in the mountains of Vermont. The only thing that didn't fit was the gun in her hand, so out of place, so unexpected that Roy had to look twice. But the gun—bigger than the one found in Skippy's glove box, and different in other ways that Roy, not knowing guns, couldn't define—dominated everything, ordered all visible space around it.

Roy raised his hands, an involuntary gesture, its source in the primitive depths of the brain.

"Are you armed?" she said.

"Of course not. And point that somewhere else."

The gun didn't waver. She took a quick sweeping glance past him, taking in the truck, just inside the reach of the light from the house, and the surrounding woods. "Alone?"

"Yes," Roy said. "Were you talking about my wife just now?"

She flicked the barrel of the gun, swatting the question away. "How did you find me?" she said.

"Through the art dealer Krishna Madapan—he sold you a Moroccan bowl."

Janet Habib's eyes shifted, came back to him. "You're the sculptor?"

"Yes."

"What do you want?"

"I told you—to talk to Paul."

"You can't be serious."

"What do you mean?"

She gazed at his face for a moment or two, then lowered the gun and stepped aside. Roy went in. The first thing he saw was a charcoal sketch of Paul Habib, hanging above the fireplace. Roy moved closer: the artist had softened Habib's features, made him less interesting. He was trying to read the signature in the lower right corner when the bolts slid back into place; the chain clicked into its groove.

Roy turned. Janet's hands—bony and small—were now empty and he didn't see the gun anywhere. She wore rings on just about every finger; it made the ringless third finger on her left hand look a little forlorn.

"Is this a recent sketch?" Roy said. "He's hardly changed."

"Are you toying with me?" she said. Firelight flickered across her face, leaving her eyes in shadow. "Or drunk? Or what?"

"What are you talking about?"

"What are you talking about?" Janet said, her voice rising. "Paul died fifteen years ago. Fifteen years next spring, to be more exact."

Roy sat down, or found himself sitting, on the raised flagstone hearth, his legs weak. "He was in the helicopter?"

"Helicopter?"

"That crashed," Roy said. "In Venezuela."

Janet came forward a step; her eyes, now in the light, narrowed and angry. "A helicopter crash in Venezuela? Is that what she told you?"

"She?"

"Delia," Janet said, as though the word itself were repellent.

"Delia didn't tell me anything," Roy said. "She died in that goddamned crash."

Janet shook her head. "You're not making sense."

"Sure I am," Roy said. "I'm talking about the pineapple project."

"Never heard of it," said Janet.

"What do you mean?" Roy said. "That was the whole idea—getting the Venezuelans to grow pineapples. Your husband picked Delia up to take her to the airport. They flew to Venezuela. She died there in a helicopter crash. What I can't understand is why no one ever told me that Paul died, too."

Janet's mouth was open. "Where are you getting all this?"

"It's what happened."

"Says who?"

"Me," said Roy. "I'm saying it."

"Were you in Venezuela? Did you see the crash?"

"No."

"Then how do you know?" Janet said. "What's your source?"

His source: Did he need a source? It was a historical event, like the Chicago fire or D-day. In this case,

Delia's death, was there one actual source? Yes: "I heard the news from Tom Parish."

Janet snorted. "Oh, well then."

"What are you implying?" Roy said. "He was their boss."

Janet gave him a hard look. Then she took a Kleenex from a box on the mantel, handed it to him. "Your nose is bleeding."

Roy dabbed at his nose, checked the Kleenex: red blotches.

"Tilt your head back," she said.

But Roy didn't want to tilt his head back, didn't have time; he wanted to understand what this woman was saying, to understand now. He dabbed impatiently—even furiously—at his nose again, said, "Tom Parish brought her body back. He spoke at her funeral."

"What's your angle?" she said.

"No angle," said Roy. "Why?"

"Because what you're telling me—helicopter crash, Tom Parish bringing the body back, all that—is impossible."

"How so?"

"Because of the simple fact," Janet said, "that *she* got home safely."

"Delia?"

"Delia."

"That's insane."

"It's a lot of things, all negative, but insane isn't one of them," Janet said. "Sick, cynical, brutal—yes. Insane, no—not in the sense you mean."

Roy started to feel light-headed. A pale aura appeared, vibrating around Janet's face. "What are you telling me?" he said.

"I'm telling you this," Janet said. "Tom knocked on my door. 'There's been an accident. I'm sorry. Paul's dead.' Exact words."

"Your door in Cambridge?"

"Correct."

"This was after the trip?"

"Of course."

"That trip in springtime?"

"What other trip are we talking about?" Janet said. "And I asked, 'What kind of accident?' Tom said, 'A car crash. Delia was driving too fast. They went over a cliff.'"

Delia did drive too fast. That was the only credible part. But car crash or helicopter crash: Was there a fundamental difference? No. Roy could think of only one fundamental. "Why did you say she got home safely?"

"Tom came in a limo," Janet said. "You know, with the rear windows blacked out. But I watched from behind the curtain as he went back down to the street. When he opened the back door, there she was."

There was some mistake, huge—but didn't a mistake always mean an explanation was out there, waiting to be uncovered? "How did you know it was her?" Roy said.

Janet shrugged. "The way you'd know anybody," she said. "We'd met several times."

"Where?"

"In Cambridge, once or twice—and there was a lunch in D.C.," Janet said. "It was her, all right, in the middle seat, with some guy beside her. She had a bandage around her head, but I recognized her. A distinctive face, as I'm sure you're aware."

Janet's aura—Roy didn't believe in auras, knew this was a manifestation of things going wrong somewhere else—began to grow, spread toward him, reaching out. "A bandage around her head?" he said. His voice sounded small and far away.

"But very much alive," said Janet.

"I don't believe you," Roy said.

"Believe what you want," Janet said. "If you can believe the Venezuelan part, you can believe anything."

"What do you mean?"

"If Venezuela," Janet said, "why Paul?"

"I don't understand."

"What's so hard?" she said. "His surname wasn't Hernandez or Rodriguez—it was Habib."

"He didn't speak Spanish—is that your point?" Roy said. "Neither did Delia."

"That wasn't her role," Janet said.

Roy nodded. "They were economists."

"Paul was a historian, not an economist."

"I didn't know."

"An expert on North Africa and fluent in dialects of the Maghreb," Janet said. "Which is why they recruited him."

"By 'they' you mean Tom's section?" Roy said.

"Not Tom's," Janet said. "Why all this emphasis on Tom? It was Delia."

"Delia recruited him?"

"She was the boss," Janet said.

The aura, trembling at the edges, touched him.

Twenty-Two

Roy couldn't hear the storm, but he knew it was out there, violent and roaring. Nothing to be afraid of: he was safe and warm in his igloo. Anything to stop him from staying here forever? Not that he could think of, not one single reason. So let it blow. His mind was at ease. He listened to the fire, crackling away. He got warmer and warmer.

But: uh-oh. Igloos were built with blocks of ice. Therefore getting warmer and warmer meant . . . uh-oh. Bad things. Bad things like melting, dripping, homelessness. He opened his eyes.

Fire burned, very near. Roy squirmed away.

"Are you all right?"

He glanced around, maybe not without panic, saw a woman gazing down at him, a woman with wild graying hair and shadowy eyes: Janet Habib.

"You fainted," she said.

"No," Roy said. "Not possible." He sprang to his feet, or at least that was the signal his brain sent his body. In fact, he rose slowly and with difficulty, a little breathless. That gave him plenty of time to remember.

"Are you all right?" she said again.

"You saw her alive?" he said. The words: they sounded so strange to him; and so did his voice—like an old man's.

"Exactly the way I told you," Janet said. "You look pale."

"Delia?"

"Delia."

"But it's not possible," Roy said. "Because then why wouldn't she have . . ."

"A glass of water?"

Roy shook his head: because then why wouldn't she have come home?

Janet moved into another room, returned with a glass of water. She handed it to him: all those rings, and that naked ring finger. Roy drank, at first a sip or two, and then, as though he'd been a long time in the desert, with greed. He gulped it down. The water-life equation couldn't have been more obvious.

Janet was watching him. "Don't worry," she said. "It's safe."

"What is?" said Roy, suddenly feeling stronger, more like himself.

"The water," she said. "Pollution's spreading through the aquifer but my well tested negative just last week." She took the empty glass. "I've got something to show you."

"What?"

"It's outside."

Roy put on his jacket. Janet got a flashlight, led him outside, around to a shed behind the house. The moon had risen, just a sliver, but reflected countless times in the ripples of a nearby pond.

"This is a nice spot," she said. "If you like isolation."

Janet unlocked the shed, shone the light inside. Roy saw a white convertible, old and covered with dust and cobwebs, the top down.

"Paul's car?" he said. But he knew: white with white interior, waiting for Delia under their personal cherry-blossom tree.

"He loved it," Janet said.

Roy went over, rested his hand on the passenger-side headrest. Cold, cracked leather, but Roy, touching it, was hit by a sudden sensory memory of the exact feel of Delia's skin. If he still knew something like that, didn't it follow that he'd known everything about her?

"I had this idea of burying him in it," Janet said. "But then I started having doubts—would he have wanted that? We . . . we were young. So many things we never got around to discussing."

Roy nodded.

"The funny thing is," Janet said, "I kind of did end up burying him in it."

"I don't understand."

Janet came forward, reached into the car, opened the glove box. She took out an urn, oval-shaped with flattened ends, made of some dull silvery metal, maybe pewter.

"This came a few days later, UPS," she said. "I just didn't take the last step, burying the car. It seemed so over-the-top." She held the urn in one arm, enfolded, the way you carry a baby.

What was the expression? *Starting to show.* When would Delia have started to show? Soon, right? And then a thought struck him, struck him with physical force. If Janet Habib was telling him the truth, then it was possible Delia did end up showing. And more; an almost unimaginable chain of mores that made him lean against the car, and hold on, just in case.

"Tell me again," he said.

"Tell you what?"

"This story—of Delia coming to your house in Cambridge."

"I have no interest in persuading you," Janet said. "Believe or disbelieve, it makes no difference."

"Just tell me again," Roy said.

Outside the wind rose, banging the shed door closed. Janet flicked a wall switch, turning on a bulb that hung down from a crossbeam, the light harsh on her face. She squinted at him—what was she seeing?—and said, "You're really telling me you never saw her after the trip?"

"Tom Parish called with the news," Roy said. "And came to the funeral. She's buried in the old town graveyard."

"You saw with your own eyes?" Janet said.

"Of course—I was at the funeral."

"She wasn't cremated?"

"No. There was a coffin." White, with scrollwork highlighted in gold leaf, all paid for by the Hobbes Institute; at least, that was what Roy assumed: he'd never seen a bill.

"I don't understand," Janet said.

"That's why I'm asking you—are you sure it was Delia in the limo?"

"Beyond any doubt," Janet said.

"Did Tom Parish say where the car crash happened?"

"I didn't ask."

"Why not?"

"I didn't want to know," Janet said. Her voice grew quieter, almost as though talking to herself. "I didn't want any of the details. And I wanted Tom to know that."

"To know you didn't want to know?" said Roy.

She gazed at him. Her eyes were dark and blurred.

"Explain," he said.

"Are all artists like you?" she said. "The answer should be obvious—to make sure nothing like this ever happened."

"Nothing like what?"

"A stranger turning up with dangerous questions." Her gaze, drawn back to the urn, went far away. "Paul told me he was going to Washington, nothing more. But I knew. I knew from how nervous he was." *Habib's shirt was the color of the cherry blossoms; damp patches had spread under both arms.*

"Knew what?" Roy said.

"And from how he muttered in his sleep," she said, now meeting Roy's gaze. "Muttered in Arabic."

"About?" said Roy.

She looked away. "I don't speak a word of Arabic."

"I think you know where they went," Roy said.

She shook her head.

"Tell me."

Janet took a step back, cradling the urn. "What are you doing?" The lightbulb flickered, went out, came back on. She looked scared. "Well? What are you doing?"

What was he doing? Right now, he was trying to come up with an explanation more believable than what Janet took to be obvious—that Delia and Paul had gone to some Arabic-speaking place, not Venezuela. Did that mean Venezuela had never been in the plans, that Delia had lied to him? Or had there been some last-minute change, a message waiting at the airport?

"Why did you come here?" Janet said. "What did you want with Paul?"

"The Hobbes Institute has disappeared," Roy said. "As though it never existed."

"So?"

"What do you know about it?"

"Nothing."

"That's not possible," he said.

"Think what you want."

"What are you so afraid of?" Roy said.

"Nothing," she said. "You."

"You've got nothing to fear from me," Roy said. They were mirror images of each other. "I'd like to see his pay stubs."

"What pay stubs?"

"From whoever did the paying."

"I didn't keep anything like that," Janet said.

But here was the car, not up on blocks or preserved in any way, just retained; and the ashes, not underground, not on a mantelpiece, still unsettled. Roy didn't believe her. Much more likely that she'd held on to everything: Paul Habib was still unsettled in her mind. Roy was starting to understand that feeling very well. "Where are the pay stubs?" he said.

"Nowhere," Janet said. "I threw all that stuff out years ago. Years and years and years."

Roy shook his head. His mind grasped something important. This shed—with the car that had taken Delia away, and the ashes of the last person he'd seen her with—had to be square one. He was on the right track, if for no other reason than that here was the first face that didn't go blank at the mention of Tom Parish and the Hobbes Institute. That realization had an effect, immediate and physical. He felt pain-free and full of oxygen; strong, potent, clearheaded, felt, in fact, the way he had on any given day a year ago, six months ago, even two.

"I'm going to look for those pay stubs, Janet," he said. "I'd prefer your help, but I'm going to do it, one way or another."

"Are you threatening me?" she said.

"It doesn't have to be like that," Roy began, "but if you don't—"

With her free hand, Janet was reaching under her Scandinavian sweater, into the waistband of her jeans. A little late, Roy remembered the gun. Then—things speeding up—the gun was out in the open, the barrel rising. Roy's body, as it had done so often on the ice, took over, and flew at her, totally airborne. Not a great distance, and his legs had always been strong, but for some reason Roy fell short, swiping weakly at Janet's arm as he went down.

He landed heavily, mostly on his cast, cracking it open; he cried out in pain, lost his breath. Janet, off balance, tripped over a paint can and went down, also landing hard. The gun and the urn both sailed free, hitting the floor. The top of the urn popped off.

Roy rolled over, crawled toward the gun, fighting to get air in his lungs. He grabbed it, turned. Janet was on her knees, gazing down at a small charcoal-gray nest: the ashes.

"Oh my God," she said. She began rocking back and forth.

Roy got up, ripped broken plaster off his arm—the pain didn't get any worse, lessened if anything—and went over to her. He put the gun in his pocket, knelt beside her. She didn't seem aware of him at all.

"Oh my God," she said, "oh my God."

Roy reached for the urn, held it horizontally on the floor, the way you would a dustpan, started sweeping the ashes back in with his hand. The crematorium—perhaps some foreign crematorium—hadn't done a great job, unless it was normal to find tiny bone fragments among the ashes. And—and what was this? Something shiny?

Roy picked it out of the ashes. Beside him, Janet went still. A metal object, high-quality carbon steel—Roy knew metals—about two inches long, irregular and partly blackened at one end, sharply pointed at the other: the broken-off blade of a knife.

Janet's hands covered the lower part of her face; her eyes were wide and dark. "He was murdered?" she said.

Roy gazed at the blade. He could make out some engraved letters: *zerland*.

"Is that what this means?" Janet said. "Tell me." She dug her nails into his arm. For some reason he didn't feel that at all. "Tell me what it means."

"This is everything," Janet said. They were back in the house, in front of the fire. She dumped out cardboard boxes—three, four, more—spilling the contents onto the rug. "So much," she said.

It took hours. Roy came away with three things.

One: Among the many pay stubs, the only one not from MIT: *Verdadero Investments*, $783.56 to Paul Habib.

"What's Verdadero Investments?" he said.

"No idea," said Janet.

Two: An overhead color photograph, shot from a high-flying plane or maybe a satellite, of a large square structure with towers on each corner. Computerized printing at the bottom read: *Operation Pineapple*. But this couldn't be Venezuela. Desert lay all around, not an American-style southwestern desert, but the kind with dunes; they cast rippling black shadows.

"Where's this?"

"Couldn't tell you."

Three: Another photograph, this one black-and-white, out of focus. Paul, younger and thinner than Roy remembered him, sat on a fence rail, laughing. A man in a Stetson stood beside him, in profile. He was laughing, too. Out of focus, face in shadow beneath the Stetson brim, and hair brown, not white, but: Calvin Truesdale, almost for sure.

"Do you know him?" Roy said.

"No," Janet said. "I've never seen this picture." Her eyes were still on it. "Who is he?"

Roy could feel how intensely she waited for his answer; a little too intensely, he thought. "No idea," he said.

"But you think it's important?" She had a sudden thought—a thought that seemed to scare her. "Because of who took it?"

"Maybe."

"Who took it?"

But Roy didn't want to say. If all this was true, then: Why hadn't she come back to him? He thought again of that line Delia had once quoted, when he'd asked how work was going: the line about holding two contradictory thoughts in your mind at once. Now it scared him.

"What's going on?" Janet said. Her eyes went quickly to a window, returned to Roy.

"That's what I'm asking you," he said.

The fire had gone out; a few embers glowed faintly in the grate, and even more faintly in Janet's eyes. "I always felt uneasy," she said, "way down deep—where I could ignore it. My whole marriage." She handed him the picture. "Did you feel uneasy, too?"

"Never," Roy said.

Tears rose up in her eyes, overflowed. "I thought I was all cried out."

"That won't happen until you tell whatever it is you're hiding," Roy said. Then came a thought. "Did Paul ever mention a woman named Lenore?"

"No."

"Tall, light-skinned black, now in her midforties?"

Janet's eyes widened.

"I've seen her," Roy said. "Who is she?"

Janet backed away. "I don't know who you're talking about."

"Of course you do."

But Janet shook her head, kept doing it like a child. "Please go," she said.

"Help me," Roy said. "We can figure this out."

"Oh, sure, what a team." Her eyes found the blood spots on his sleeve, remnants of the nosebleed.

"Please," Roy said.

But she just shook her head some more. He showed himself out.

Twenty-Three

Roy drove north, back across the Cape Cod Canal, three exhibits on the seat beside him. A: Paul Habib's pay stub from Verdadero Investments. B: The overhead shot of the big structure in the desert. C: The black-and-white picture of Habib and Calvin Truesdale. Triangle ABC. He'd been no good at high school geometry—a fact that didn't make much sense in retrospect—but he'd done some thinking about triangles, especially in the middle stages of the *Neanderthal* series. Now—late at night, almost no traffic, alone in the moving yellow tunnel of his headlights—Roy turned triangle ABC over and over in his mind, an unstable form, dim and elusive, rotating not so much in space as in time, specifically time past. Whatever came next, he knew, was going to be hard: he'd spent his whole working life solving spatial problems;

temporal problems were new. *But he had them, by God.* His uncasted arm throbbed in his lap, finding a rhythm in sync with the big V-8 and the knobby snow tires on the bare pavement.

Roy switched on the radio, found a jazz station. They were playing something slow and sleepy, mostly soft bass and light brushwork. The announcer came on; he had a soft, slow voice, could probably have made more money as a hypnotist. Roy's eyelids got very heavy. He was thinking about pulling off to the side when the next song started up: "For All We Know," the Billie Holiday version.

Roy's mind came to life; he could almost feel electric circuits firing in the different parts of his brain. Delia had known the guitarist who'd played "For All We Know" by the grave site, an aging hippie who performed Friday nights at Ethan's Pub, her favorite restaurant in the valley, mostly because of the shrimp cocktail, a dish she ordered unfailingly if available. After a drink or two, she'd start making requests, requests that got more and more romantic—"Every Time We Say Goodbye," "My Romance," "I'll Be Seeing You," "Here's That Rainy Day," "It Never Entered My Mind," "Little Girl Blue." She knew all the lyrics, had a great fund of songs like those, surprising to Roy at first. The guitarist loved her requests.

He'd worn a tie to her funeral, the only time Roy had seen him in one.

Springtime—in fact, the very first day that felt like spring that year, the year Delia died: the sun shining with real warmth, the breeze bringing a softness that had been missing for months. And standing before the open grave? Roy in front, the minister beside him; Turk and his wife at the time; the guitarist; a few others, but Roy couldn't remember exactly who. Tom Parish? At the church service, yes, but in the cemetery? Roy didn't think so. All he really remembered was that soft breeze, "For All We Know," the scrollwork on the white coffin, and the thump of that first symbolic spadeful of moist springtime earth landing on the lid.

Light snow started falling as Roy crossed the Vermont line, tiny flakes that seemed to hang motionless in the headlight beams. He took out his phone; every player on the Thongs was in the directory. Roy called Freddy Boudreau.

"Roy? What the fuck? It's three in the morning."

"I know," Roy said, although the truth was he'd forgotten all about the time. "But I was wondering whether that ski-patrol guy came in with Skippy's phone."

"You couldn't have wondered a few more hours?"

"Sorry," said Roy. "But did he?"

"Yeah, he did," Freddy said. "Let's dis—"

"And did you go up there?"

"Up where?"

"The mountain hut," Roy said. "To look around."

"Telling me how to do my job?" said Freddy.

"It's not that," Roy said. "I—"

"Think there's a payoff to searchin' the woods at night?" Freddy said. "Ever in a million years?"

"Probably not," Roy said.

"Which is how come I'm waiting for daylight."

"It's just that I'm worried he—"

"Go to sleep, Roy. You're starting to piss me off."

Roy drove up to the barn. He'd left some lights on inside. Sections of *Delia* appeared in some of the long windows, like—the comparison too obvious to miss—pieces of a puzzle. He went inside. Everything normal, but he had a very weird feeling, as though the place wasn't his anymore.

When had he last eaten? Roy couldn't remember. Wasn't that his job right now, to eat, rest, get strong? More than a job—his purpose in life. What did it say about a man, forgetting his purpose in life? Roy opened the fridge, found not much: a few bottles of beer, orange juice, the steak he'd bought for Skippy, the pineapple—*Product of Venezuela*—from Dickie

Russo's. Plus a freezer full of ice cream. Roy didn't feel like ice cream. He cut the rind off the pineapple, then sliced it into a dozen disks, very precise, as though he were working on something. After that, he ate them one by one, slowly at first, then faster and faster, with a kind of desperation, almost like a starving animal, pineapple juice dripping off his chin.

Roy went into the bedroom, lay on his bed. *Worn out*—an expression a lot of people used, his mother, for example, coming home from her night job just as Roy was getting ready for school. Roy himself had felt tired many times, but never worn out. He felt it now—the difference between a battery that needed a charge and one that had to be replaced—and closed his eyes. First, a long, long sleep, and then—

But his eyes wouldn't stay closed. Some part of his mind—not the rational part that appreciated the wisdom of *think there's a payoff to searchin' the woods at night?*—refused to shut down.

Searchin' the woods: the implications of that short phrase struck him. They were very bad.

Roy went into the bathroom, had a good look at his broken arm. A little skinny, but wasn't that expected? And the throbbing just meant the healing wasn't quite done; no surprise. He turned on the tap, washed his forearm gently in warm water. Gentle warm water: it felt great. He didn't want to stop.

Roy found an Ace bandage in the medicine cabinet, wrapped his arm nice and tight. He put on long underwear, ski pants, fleece, hat, boots, took his jacket off the peg by the door. Still snowing outside; no wind. Roy checked the thermometer by the door. Nine degrees. He put his snowshoes and a pair of poles in the truck and drove to the base of the mountain.

Not as stupid as a flatlander might think, climbing the mountain at night—even a moonless, starless night like this—if you knew the terrain like Roy did. At least, that was what he told himself as he took the trails in reverse, up Banana Boat to Boo's Cruise, Boo's Cruise to Wipe Out, Wipe Out to Cross-Over. A dark night, but the trails were slightly brighter, like shadows in reverse. Soft snow kept falling; Roy couldn't see it, just felt the flakes drifting down on his face. No wind, a quiet night: except for a sound like panting that grew louder and louder. Roy was making his way up Cross-Over, toward the back side, when he realized it was him. Shameful, to make so much noise in the woods. Roy stopped, leaned against a snow gun, tried to quiet his breathing.

That took time, especially since the feeling of the lower third of his lungs being tied off had come back; maybe the lower half, to be accurate. He stretched his arms back, stuck out his chest and sucked in the deepest breaths he could, almost violently, trying to break the seal inside him. And it worked, a little. Roy took a few nice, normal breaths, knocked snow off the tops of his snowshoes with his pole tips and kept going.

Cross-Over, cut by Ski America after a long fight with state and local environmental agencies, narrowed along the curve of the mountain's shoulder, as stipulated in the final agreement. Roy felt more than saw the trees closing in, a good, safe feeling. Mostly spruce trees at this elevation: he'd chopped one down for what turned out to be Delia's last Christmas, and dragged it home.

Is that legal, Roy?

More of a gray area.

That's where the problems start.

She'd made an angel out of papier-mâché to go on top of the tree, funny-looking, more devilish than anything: she had no artistic talent at all.

The temperature fell a few degrees; the texture of the snow changed, grew rougher, crunching under his snowshoes: the back of the mountain. Now the wind started to rise. At first, Roy didn't feel it, but he could hear it whistling softly in the treetops. From somewhere up ahead came the thump of snow falling off a branch.

Roy kept going, peering into the darkness. The spur to the Appalachian Trail, only about five or six feet wide, could be hard to spot even by daylight. It split from Cross-Over at the top of a ridge the snowboarders used as a launching pad. Roy trodded on, up and up. The wind blew harder, worked its way down from the tree-tops, found him. It rose in pitch and with that came a strange wheezy sound. Roy was beginning to think he'd missed the turnoff when the trail suddenly steepened beneath him. He bent forward, pushed on his poles, climbed the ridge.

But so slow: *come on, boy.* He was almost at the top—knew that from the sudden gust blowing unimpeded into his face, when he heard a sound that might have been another branch load of snow thumping down; but, in fact, was harder, more solid than that, like the wind banging an unfastened door, for example.

Roy put his foot wrong, the heel of one shoe coming down on the toe of another. A clumsy move, not him at all; he'd been on snowshoes since boyhood. He lost his balance, fell, cartwheeled to the base of the ridge, and kept rolling—snow getting down his neck—rolling and rolling until his legs hit a tree trunk.

Roy lay faceup in the snow. It was coming down much harder now, an icy, rapid beat on his face. Easy to picture it filling his nostrils, covering him right up; wouldn't take long at all. Freezing to death was said to be fairly painless—didn't you actually feel warm at the end?

Roy made an angry grunt. That kind of thinking disgusted him. *Come on, boy.* He reached down to his straps, found they'd held. He groped around for his poles; not there. He got his feet under him, rose, started back up the ridge. Something hard struck his arm, the bad one. Didn't hurt at all. And what was it? One of his poles, sticking out of the snow. Things were looking up. He grabbed it, kept going.

Up and up, digging in with the pole, scrabbling at the snow with his free hand, down on all fours as he topped the ridge. *Not making it look easy, boy.* He knelt there for a moment, just breathing. The wind rose another notch. Roy realized he'd lost his hat. Not good.

Where was the spur? Should be to the right, unless he was totally turned around. Roy looked that way, peering in the night for a small opening, and saw a yellow light, dim and unsteady, but there.

He moved toward it, and in three or fours steps was out of the wind, and therefore on the spur, a very narrow trail, conifers packed tight on both sides. The snow was much deeper here, slow going with just one pole. He kept on, silent except for the soft thudding of his snowshoes. Then the wheezy sound began again. What the hell was that? He stopped to listen, didn't hear it. He started up, and there was the wheezy sound. After a few more steps, he realized the obvious.

The yellow light grew sharper and steadier. After a moment or two, Roy saw the bulky shape of the mountain hut, not quite as black as the night. Closer and closer. The yellow light glowed in a window; Roy could make out the division of the panes: a vision of warmth and safety. Was Skippy hiding out here? Not a bad hideout, especially in winter, with the hikers gone. Not a bad hideout. *Smart kid, even if no one else knew it.* But what about his cell phone in the snowbank outside? That didn't fit.

Then it hit Roy, an amazing possibility, like the first dawning of a religious miracle. *Meet me here, Roy. If anything ever happens, meet me here.*

Roy, absolutely silent now, holding his breath to stop the wheezing, crept toward the door of the hut. It hung open a few inches. The escaping light illuminated foot-steps—ski-boot footsteps—in the snow on the stairs; a pair of skis leaned on the wall. Roy unstrapped his snowshoes and went up, stepping silently in the foot-steps already there.

Like what?

Anything bad. If we get separated, if you can't find me.

His heart was pounding. Roy could hear it, like a drum in the night. He reached the door, put his hand on it, gave a little push. It swung open.

A woman in a ski suit was kneeling by the bunk beds on the far side of the hut, her back to him. She seemed to be looking for something underneath. A red ski suit, red hat, red ski boots. Not a miracle, but cold hard logic; all that was missing were a few facts to complete the chain.

Roy stepped inside.

"Delia?"

Twenty-Four

Her head whipped around.

Not Delia.

Not Delia in so many ways, but here were two: café au lait skin and a fringe of glossy black hair poking out from her ski hat.

Lenore. The other side: it was real.

She rose, unrushed, controlled. The look in her eyes changed. If there'd been fear, it was quickly gone, easing down through surprise to something even milder that that. Her gaze left Roy, moved to the open door behind him, to the ski pole in his hand, back to his face.

"You don't knock in these parts?" she said.

Roy said: "Where's Skippy?"

She raised her eyebrows.

"Have you hurt him?"

"I haven't hurt anyone," Lenore said. "I don't know what you're talking about."

"A sixteen-year-old kid—he spotted you near the Dunkin' Donuts," Roy said. "You and Westie." He felt cold air at his back, kicked the door shut, not taking his eyes off her. Her composure was infuriating; at the same time, some of it rubbed off on him, turned his anger icy, a feeling previously unknown to him. "Tell me about that room," he said.

"Room?" said Lenore. She backed against the bunk beds, throwing a long shadow across the floor. The only light came from an electric lantern at her feet, small and square.

"At the back of Wine, Inc.," Roy said. "The room Tom went in. What goes on in there?"

Lenore didn't answer. Roy gestured under the bunk beds with his ski pole. "What were you looking for?"

"Nothing," she said.

Roy took another step inside. Lenore backed away a little more, now right up against one of the bunk beds. "You might as well start explaining," he said. "Everything's going to come out now."

"And what would *everything* be?" said Lenore.

"Sit down," said Roy.

She stayed where she was; but not as tall as Roy, not as broad, not as strong.

"Start with the Hobbes Institute," Roy said.

"Never heard of it."

"You've been seen here in Ethan Valley, by the way. There are witnesses."

Her eyes took on an inward look. Roy was thinking, too: Could Westie still be around, maybe close by? He listened, heard nothing but the wind outside, shifted the ski pole to his good hand.

"Sit down," he said again.

She glanced at the ski pole, sat on the lower bunk.

"What were you looking for?"

"A blanket?" She met his gaze, maybe didn't like what she saw. "I got stranded up here. A blanket, in case I had to spend the night."

Roy pointed to a stack of gray army-style blankets on the top bunk. "Stranded doing what?" he said.

She didn't answer.

"Where's your lift ticket?"

She glanced down at the ticketless front of her red jacket. Therefore: she'd walked up in darkness, just like him, except in ski boots, and with skis over her shoulder, not easy.

"Or were you hiding something here?" Roy said. "Is that it?"

Lenore gazed at him, said nothing.

"Pull that bed away from the wall," he said.

"You," she said.

Roy took a step closer and pointed the ski pole at her. The wind rose higher, pelting snowflakes at the windows. "I'll do whatever I have to," he said.

He thought he saw belief in her eyes. Her tone changed. "Move it where?" she said.

Roy motioned. "So I can see under." There was enough space for a kid under the bed, especially a skinny one like Skippy.

Lenore got a grip on the two vertical supports, tugged at the bunk bed. It slid across the floor, smooth and easy. And underneath? Nothing, just dust balls on the rough pine planks, less worn than the rest of the floor. Roy looked at the bed: The same bed he and Delia had slept in that Winter Carnival night? He thought so. *If we get separated, if you can't find me.* An improbable idea—even wild—came to him; but Delia could be improbable and wild.

"Rip up those boards," he said. At that moment, he knew what Lenore was doing in the mountain hut, knew what she was looking for.

"Why?" she said.

"It'll save you time."

"You lost me," Lenore said.

"Because the hiding place won't be obvious," said Roy.

"Hiding place for what?"

Was that a little smile, flashing quickly across her face? Roy slammed the ski pole on the mattress, inches from her, very hard. The sound boomed in the hut. "The note," Roy said. His heart started up again, pounding away with excitement his chest could barely contain. "Or whatever it was she left me."

"She?" said Lenore.

"Delia," Roy said. "As you know."

"That name means nothing to me," Lenore said. But it did, all right: he could see it meaning something in her eyes, something big.

Roy went closer, peered down at the floor, saw that the plank nearest the wall fit poorly, leaving a quarter-inch gap, even more. "Start there," he said, pointing with the pole.

"Start what?"

"I told you—ripping up the floor."

Lenore didn't move. She looked him up and down, a cool, appraising sort of look. "I've got a question of my own," she said. "What's wrong with you?"

"What are you talking about?" Roy said.

"That seizure you had, coughing fit, whatever it was," she said. "Are you sick?"

"No," Roy said.

"How sick?"

"I'm not sick," Roy said. But his body trembled a little; nothing he could do about it. He pointed the ski pole in her face. "Rip up the goddamn floor," he said.

"How?" Lenore said.

The first good, honest word out of her mouth. Roy glanced around, spotted a poker by the woodstove. Couldn't let her have that, of course, but—

From the corner of his eye, he caught a sudden movement, quick and red. And then she was on him, wrenching the ski pole from his grasp and twisting him to the floor with some sort of technique he had no answer to, so fast. From above, her hands closed around his throat, started to squeeze. Nothing cool or appraising about her eyes now—they were hot. Lenore enjoyed her work. She was going to kill him. Roy writhed beneath her, squirmed, tried to roll—and at that moment felt something hard in the right-hand pocket of his jacket: Janet Habib's gun, still there, forgotten. He got his arm loose, reached down, pulled out the gun. She saw it coming free. Her eyes widened. Her grip weakened, just a little. Roy slashed the gun across her face.

Lenore cried out, fell back. Roy, still on the floor, aimed the gun at her. And her gun? In Freddy Boudreau's desk, down at the station: a pleasant realization.

"Now some answers," Roy said. "Starting with Skippy."

"Okay," she said, bleeding from her mouth. "Just let me—" And then she kicked out with her ski boot, not at Roy, but at the portable lantern. It went flying, light expiring in midair. Roy pulled the trigger. The gun went *click*. The safety? He didn't know guns. Roy fumbled in the darkness, but by that time the door of the hut was banging open and she was on her way outside.

Roy got up, saw night framed in the doorway, slightly lighter than the inside of the cabin. The wind had risen, was shrieking in the trees. He spotted Lenore, a quick dark form against the snow. Her skis clattered together. Roy ran out. She was bent over. A ski boot clicked into its binding. Her form shifted, curling over the second ski. He kicked it away from her. She made a furious noise, tried to grab the gun, missed.

Roy raised his voice over the wind, pointed the gun at her. "I want answers."

Lenore raised her voice, too. "Don't you get it?" she said. "You'll never know." Then she did the unexpected, pushing off with her free leg. Roy realized what was happening, too late. Lenore took off on one ski. He fired. The gun made a small bang, dwarfed by the storm. Lenore was out of sight almost at once, doubly lost in the night and the driving snow, leaving him standing there. Roy heard the sharp, crisp snicking sound of a turn expertly carved, not skidded. Then another. And after that, there was just the wind.

He listened, anticipating—praying for—wipeout sounds. But none came. By now, she'd be on Cross-Over. Chasing her on snowshoes? Pointless. If she knew the mountain, or had even studied a trail map for five minutes, she'd know to take the cut off to Easy Rider, a wide and bumpless cruiser all the way to the bottom. His cell phone? In the truck.

Roy went back inside the mountain hut and closed the door. He moved across the floor, bumped into the woodstove. Feeling around on top, he found matches. He lit one, and soon had two fat candles burning. Then, using the poker and the tongs, he pried off that ill-fitting floorboard, the one closest to the wall, under the bunk bed where he and Delia had slept that Winter Carnival night. There was nothing underneath. He pried up a few more boards with the same result. And then one more, just in case. But no. She was silent.

"Delia," he said. "Please."

Roy sat on the floor between the two candles, resting his back against the wall. His back had never troubled him in his life, not once; but it did now, right between the shoulder blades, where you'd put a target. He went over things in his mind, tried to form some story from all he'd seen and heard. No story came to him, no straight line of facts from *A* to *Z*. Not knowing *Z*—that was one thing. Was there even an *A* he could be sure of?

Yes: the existence of this other side. That was *A*. And therefore he probably did know some of the letters along the way. But the very biggest—Janet's insistence that she'd seen Delia in the backseat of the limo: Was that a real letter or not; true or false? *She had a bandage around her head, but I recognized her.*

He had to know.

That was all there was to it. Roy's heart—he'd never been so conscious of it—began banging again. This time it took his breath away, a greedy heart needing all available oxygen and leaving none for him. For a few moments, Roy thought he wasn't going to get it back: a few terrifying moments when he learned what drowning felt like. But slowly his breath returned, puny little puffs of air at first, then stronger, more normal; at least the way normal was now. He rose, strapped on his snowshoes, and blew out the candles.

One last thought: to leave a note of his own. *Delia—find me.* But it was too soon to know if that made any sense at all; at the moment it was like raising the question of a letter beyond *Z*. He needed some kind of proof. Roy knew where to look, also knew he had to steel himself for what might lie ahead. To steel himself: one of those expressions with metal in them, expressions that often snagged in his mind. He made himself stand straighter, seem stronger, as though sculpting his own body. Energy came, too, maybe false, but just as useful as the real thing. This new energy of Roy's was fueled by anger: anger at Lenore's escape; anger at how easily she'd overcome him in physical combat, the fact that she was a woman making it worse.

The wind had died down and the snow had stopped falling, but it was still dark when Roy parked in the lot behind the Congregational church. Snowshoes back on, a snow shovel and a spade over his shoulder and a flashlight hanging from his belt, Roy crossed the graveyard. The snow was deep; with the weight he carried, Roy sank an extra inch or two with every step. *Worn out:* he knew he must be, but his legs didn't seem to get the message. They just kept going, scissor blades alloyed from steel and anger.

The sky was dark, the woods darker, but the snow on the graveyard itself seemed to give off a faint glow and Roy didn't need the flashlight until he reached the last row, Delia's row. He'd cleared her gravestone before leaving for Dr. Chu's clinic, but it was snowed over again, the top barely breaking the surface. Gently, with the plastic snow shovel, he swept snow off the stone, then switched on the flashlight to make sure. The name on the stone was Mary Ann Little. Roy moved to the next one, tried again.

Delia Stern.

Roy turned off the light and started shoveling. He went through the top fluffy foot or so, tossing the snow to the side, into the trees. Then came firmer snowpack that slowed him down a little. He took off his jacket, rewound the Ace bandage more tightly, kept shoveling. His mind took over. His body, what he had left, obeyed.

The Hobbes Institute fountain made lovely sounds, splashing and gurgling.

"Let's have one of these."

"One of what, Roy?"

"A fountain—at the barn. Smaller than this but more fun. Maybe with big copper fish."

"That thing in your brain never stops, does it?"

"Sorry."

"It's a compliment." Delia tilted back her head, drained her champagne. Roy noticed a man watching her.

"Hey," he said. "Is that the vice president?"

"What's that toad doing here?" she said.

"An amphibian is VP?" Roy said. A stupid joke, but the kind that usually made Delia laugh. This time she didn't.

The vice president spoke to someone, looked over at Delia again.

"Do you know him?" Roy said.

"Why would I know him?"

"No idea, but I think he's coming over."

The vice president strolled toward them across the marble floor, a few men in dark suits trailing behind.

Roy lowered his voice. "What do I call him?"

"I think he likes 'Your Grace,' " Delia said, not lowering her voice at all, the opposite if anything.

"Delia Stern?" said the vice president, with a big smile. "I hear you're doing wonderful work. Congratulations." He shook her hand, using the two-handed technique Roy associated with southern pastors but had never seen in real life.

"Thank you," said Delia. "This is my husband, Roy Valois."

The vice president shook Roy's hand in the regular way. "You're a lucky young man," he said.

Roy, momentarily distracted by light reflecting off the vice president's glasses and obscuring his eyes, said something like, "Um, that's very, ah—" And then a knot of important-looking people appeared and swept the vice president away.

"Hey!" said Roy. He was impressed.

"Check your hand for warts," said Delia.

The snow shovel struck bare ground, hard enough to send a jolt of pain up Roy's bad arm. He straightened, stretched his arms back, stuck out his chest, this new position for taking proper breaths. He breathed for a minute or two. Then he traded the shovel for the spade and started digging.

Now the real work began: shoveling light snow was one thing, digging frozen earth another. But, funny thing, it wasn't. The spade sliced through the ground with hardly any resistance at all; the soil didn't seem frozen, didn't even seem tightly packed. Roy worked pretty fast, sweat coming now despite the cold, loosening up his body. Did all this motion get the microscopic warriors flowing? He thought so. Dr. Chu was a brilliant man. Still a long way to go, but Roy felt good, even tried to pick up the pace, stabbing the blade deep into the—

Thunk.

Thunk? As though he'd struck something solid, something made of wood. But he wasn't even two feet down. Surely the hole had been much deeper that that. Roy tried to call up some visual memory, some actual measurement from Delia's funeral, could not. And of course the earth never really stayed still, was always shifting things around. Roy got down on his knees, brushed away loose dirt with his hand, switched on the flashlight. He saw scrollwork on the corner of a white wooden box, the faint gleam of gold leaf.

Roy dug, but slow now, cautious, like an archaeologist, the flashlight propped on newly piled earth at the side of the hole. First he cleared the top of the coffin. Then he dug a little side cut, a place to stand. He tossed the spade onto the ground, and looking up, saw pearly light in the eastern sky, realized he hadn't needed the flashlight for some time.

Roy stepped into the side cut, bent forward, got his hands under the lid of the coffin. Then, straightening his back, pulling with his arms, he slowly raised the lid and laid it aside.

He looked down into Delia's coffin. She wasn't there. But that didn't mean the coffin was empty; letters beyond Z, oh, yes. Someone else lay inside, facedown, someone with long shaggy hair, wearing a thin jacket, much too light for winter. Roy stopped breathing, or more accurately, his breathing came to a stop, as though his lungs had suddenly been filled with cement. He barely had enough air left to step down into the coffin and turn the body over. It was Skippy.

Letters beyond Z? Yes.

Twenty-Five

Whap-whap-whap.

Oh, no. The helicopter sound. Just what he didn't need. Helicopters would be the death of him. Snow flashed by in streaks.

Hey, Bobby—you look like a snowman.

Speak for yourself, Roy.

They went crazy with the chain saws, attacking all those bags stacked away in the old cement building in the far corner of Mr. King's yard, laughing their heads off, making good money, having a blast.

Whap-whap-whap.

That's going in my nose? Down my throat? No way, my friend, no fucking way.

But there was nothing he could do about it.

Air. Ah.

Whap-whap-whap.

Everything went still. The igloo built itself around him, block by block. A little fire came to life, centered in his heart. For a while, he got anxious again about the impossibility of fire and igloo coexisting. How could that last? But the warmth felt good. He gave himself up to it. The world shrank down to air in, air out. Time stopped. It was very nice. He had the feeling he'd arrived at last.

"Roy? Are you awake?"

Roy shook his head.

Laughter, soft but pleased. Roy opened his eyes. Dr. Chu was gazing down at him. The lower part of his face was grinning; the upper part was still and watchful.

"Your mind is intact," he said. "I can tell already."

Roy tried to say *Why wouldn't it be?* but found he couldn't speak.

"Don't try to talk for now," Dr. Chu said. "You're on a ventilator, but not too much longer, I'm sure. There's been the slightest setback, no cause for alarm, everything will stabilize soon." He glanced up at a wall monitor. "Right now the best thing would be to rest."

Roy shook his head.

"Are you in pain?" said Dr. Chu.

Roy shook his head again.

"You don't want to rest?"

Roy made a noise, deep in his throat. That hurt.

"Try to stay calm," said Dr. Chu. "You're on medication—for pain, to help you sleep, to take care of all your current needs."

Roy shook his head again, harder this time. Pain spread.

Something—a hypodermic?—flashed at the periphery of Roy's vision. "Sleep is now the priority," said Dr. Chu.

And it was coming, fast. Roy raised his hand, so heavy, made writing motions.

"You want to write?"

Roy nodded, just a little nod, in case it hurt; which it did anyway. Dr. Chu gave him a pen and a prescription pad. Roy, reaching for them, found that his bad arm was back in a cast, this one plain white, thicker and heavier than the first. He held the pad and wrote in big letters: *Delia is alive.*

Dr. Chu bent closer. "Who is Delia?" he said.

Roy wrote: *My Wife.*

Dr. Chu's eyebrows rose. "You have a wife?"

Roy made a grunt of confirmation. Dr. Chu gave him a close look, then laid a hand—very gentle—on Roy's forehead.

"I don't recall that from your chart," he said.

Roy made an angry noise, tried to shake Dr. Chu's hand off his forehead. Just from the touch alone he could tell that Dr. Chu was going to live a long, long time.

"In fact, I believe the only contact in your file is an attorney—a Mr. McKenny, was it?" Dr. Chu removed his hand and reached across Roy's body, adjusting a valve on some tube.

Roy started writing on the pad: *the reason I*   He crossed that out, wrote: *what I didn't know*   So complicated. Dr. Chu's eyes—unrelenting, but so was the disease—probed down at him. All Roy could think to do was underline those words, *My Wife*. He hadn't finished when the pad slipped from his hands, and the pencil, too: it landed with a soft click and rolled for a second or two on the floor.

Roy's own eyes closed. He felt Dr. Chu's gaze for a moment or two, piercing right through his eyelids. Was Dr. Chu worried about something? At that moment, a horrible memory poked up through the fog in Roy's mind: Skippy. But too late. The igloo was already going up, block by block.

No hunger, no thirst, no pain, some drug in his system making him feel just a bit high, and air, lots and lots of it, flowing through his lungs, all the way to the bottom: What more could anyone want? Maybe not heaven, but much closer to heaven than to hell. Or: Was he dead already? Roy's eyes snapped open. Freddy Boudreau was looking down at him.

Freddy had a strange expression in his eyes, almost like he was seeing something scary, but that wasn't the important part. The important part was that just the sight of Freddy, and all those details of his rough face—like the thin high-sticking scar that divided one of his eyebrows—proved Roy was alive.

"Hey, Roy," Freddy said.

Roy tried to say hi, found he could not. Something was down his throat, up his nose, inside him. *You're on a ventilator.* Alive, but his position on the sliding scale changed, moving closer to hell.

"Doc says I can talk to you for a couple minutes," Freddy said. "If you're feelin' up to it."

Roy gave Freddy a thumbs-up.

"I guess he's been treating you for something or other," Freddy said. "Don't reveal much. But half an hour after Dr. Bronstein saw you at Valley Regional, they had you on a chopper headed down here, so I'm figuring—" He stopped, licked his lips. "You know where you are, right, Roy?"

Roy watched Freddy's face.

"Baltimore," Freddy said.

Another thumbs-up. Roy hadn't been sure until that moment.

"Been here a few days."

A few days? That couldn't be. They were gone without a trace.

Freddy came closer. "Doc says you're on some heavy-duty meds," he said. "The kind that maybe mess with your mind. I'm wondering if that's what happened."

Roy watched.

"What's been happening, I should say," said Freddy, "the last little while. Back home. This whole situation with Skippy Bedard, for example."

Roy kept watching. Freddy's face lost its shape, went blurry, as though viewed through a watery screen. But it was Roy's face that was getting wet. He tasted salt.

"Still waiting for the autopsy results," Freddy said, "but looks like he died from exposure. What we're having a little trouble figuring out are your actions. Such as why you had a gun on you, and why you were burying him in the same—why you were burying him there. And what you did with the other, uh, remains."

"No," Roy shouted, or tried to. A horrible, rending sound came out, not *no* or any other word, but very loud.

"What's going on here?" A woman in white appeared: Netty. Since Roy had last seen her, she'd developed deep furrows in her forehead and an angry voice. "Didn't Dr. Chu specifically say Mr. Valois wasn't to be upset for any reason?"

"But I—" Freddy began, and then he was out of view, and so was Netty.

Roy's eyes closed. His eyelashes, wet and gummy, started sticking together almost at once in a way that reminded him of entombment, even mummification; but there was nothing he could do.

A fountain gurgled and splashed. For a moment, Roy thought he was in the lobby of the Hobbes Institute, would finally get some answers. But there was something too quiet about these particular fountain sounds, too gentle. He opened his eyes and saw little streamlets of water flowing over honey-colored stones. The light was soft and soothing, like in a planetarium just before the show begins: he was back in the feng shui room, lying on the suede couch. The rolling IV rack stood nearby, the tube extending into his arm.

"Roy?" Netty came forward. Her face was back to normal, soft, heavy, pretty, and just the smallest bit detached. "How are you feeling?"

He watched her.

"It's okay to talk now," she said. "You're breathing on your own."

Roy took a breath. It felt good. "I need—" His voice sounded strange, thin and reedy, like an old man's. He cleared his throat. That hurt. Netty handed him a paper cup. He drank, lovely, cool water, and tried again. "I need to talk to Freddy," he said. That knocked a few years off his voice, but didn't bring it back down to normal, not close.

"Sergeant Boudreau? He's gone back to Vermont."

"But I've got—"

"Now, Roy. Your only job is to relax, stay comfortable, let the treatment do its work."

"But it's not twenty-one days," Roy said.

"More, in fact," said Netty. "But Dr. Chu had to make sure you were stabilized first."

"What day is it?"

"Wednesday," said Netty. "The twenty-sixth."

Roy glanced out the window, hoping for some clue. All he saw was a cloudy sky. "Of February?" he said.

She nodded. "Not to worry, Roy. We're only one day late—Dr. Chu doesn't believe it will make any difference at all."

Roy thought about that. "Any developments?" he said.

"What sort of developments?"

"In the study. Like how the other"—Roy almost said *guys,* as though they were a team—". . . subjects are doing."

"Nothing for you to be fretting about," Netty said.

"Are there still the four of us left?" Roy said.

"Oh, we have way more than four now," Netty said. "New referrals are coming practically every day. Just lie back, Roy. It'll be over soon." She jiggled the plastic bag on the IV rack.

Roy sank back down on the suede couch. After a moment or two, he said, "But how many are left from the original four?"

No answer. He looked around the feng shui room. Netty was gone. Roy noticed he was wearing flannel hospital pajamas instead of normal clothes. The pattern—floral, pastel—disturbed him.

But the fountain kept making its calming sounds. Roy tried to picture Dr. Chu's microscopic warriors in their millions, starving the cancer cells and turning them against each other, the way he'd done before. This time he couldn't; his mind was a visual blank.

Dr. Chu came in, rubbing his hands briskly together as though trying to ignite a spark. "Ah," he said. "This is more like it."

"What is?" Roy said.

"Seeing you up and about," said Dr. Chu.

"This is up and about?"

"Relative to how you were," Dr. Chu said. "When they brought you in."

"I want to talk to you about that," Roy said. "And I want my regular clothes. And my phone."

"Plenty of time," said Dr. Chu. He glanced up at the IV bag, almost empty.

"Is there?" Roy said.

"Certainly," said Dr. Chu. "This is only day one of round two."

He moved closer, slid the IV needle out of Roy's arm. There were drops still left in the bag, lots of them. That bothered Roy. What if the few hundred warriors in those drops made all the difference? His eyes met Dr. Chu's.

"How am I doing? I need to know."

Dr. Chu pulled up a chair. "Tell me how you feel," he said. "Start there."

"All right. A little short of breath sometimes."

"More out of breath than at your last visit? Less? The same?"

"Maybe less," Roy said. "But I meant how am I doing in terms of the study."

"Oh, superbly," said Dr. Chu. "Top of the class."

"That's a first," Roy said.

Dr. Chu laughed, and there were disconcerting traces of it lingering in his expression when he said, "And what about pain?"

"Not bad."

"More? Less? Same?"

"None right now." Not too far from the truth.

"Excellent," said Dr. Chu. "Shortness of breath. Some pain, but none at present. Anything else?"

"No."

"What about mental changes?"

"Mental changes?"

"The study has turned up several instances of hallucinatory episodes," Dr. Chu said.

"Nope," Roy said. "Nothing like that happened to me."

"Not merely imagining things that aren't there," said Dr. Chu, "although we've had some of that. But also an odd confusion—reimagining past events, even reliving revised versions to an extent."

"I don't understand," Roy said.

"These are almost surely side effects from the therapy, although the etiology is still unclear," Dr. Chu said. "For example, we had one patient who was fired many years ago from a construction crew. His next job was at a shipyard, where the asbestos exposure occurred, no doubt an essential detail. After the third round of treatment here, he went home, put on his hard hat and reported for work at the old construction site, now a long-established subdivision." Dr. Chu tilted his head slightly, as if getting a better angle on Roy. "As though to do better this time, to not get fired, to turn back the clock."

"Nothing like that's happened to me," Roy said.

"You're sure?"

"Of course."

"There would be no shame if it had," said Dr. Chu.

"What the hell—" He sounded loud in the feng shui room, like an old man again, of the angry type. Roy cleared his throat, got a grip. "I know there's no shame," he said. "But I haven't been hallucinating."

"Hallucinations can be very convincing," said Dr. Chu. "That's sometimes what makes it so challenging to—"

"Forget it," Roy said. "I haven't been hallucinating."

Dr. Chu rubbed his hands together again, not as vigorously this time. "Study is not quite the same as treatment," he said.

"I realize that."

"A study is an experimental form," Dr. Chu said. "No one should be surprised when unknowns crop up in an experiment."

"But they're not cropping up. I'm at the top of the class—you said so yourself."

Dr. Chu was gazing at the waterfall; Roy got the sudden feeling that he'd stopped listening. "We're dealing with powerful forces clashing in a very small space," he said. "The human body." He rose—his knees cracking, the sound startling Roy—and stepped over to the honey-colored rocks, where he plucked out a twist of paper, like a gum wrapper. Frowning at it, he said, "This policeman from your town—Sergeant Boudreau?—he's puzzled by recent events. I tried to explain to him what's going on but I'm not sure he really understood."

"What are you talking about?" Roy said.

"The unknowns," said Dr. Chu. "Specifically these unintended mental components." Dr. Chu turned to Roy. "In this case, strong emotions from the present seem to be mixing with strong emotions from the past."

"Lost me," Roy said.

"Resulting," said Dr. Chu, "in behaviors somewhat similar to those of the construction worker I mentioned, albeit more complex and on a grander scale."

"I still don't get it."

"Digging up your wife's remains, substituting the body of this unfortunate boy," said Dr. Chu. "That's the kind of mental confusion I'm talking about. Sergeant Boudreau seems much more concerned with the present whereabouts of the remains than in grasping the—"

Roy was on his feet, on his feet and across the room before he knew it. Dr. Chu was small and slow. He'd barely taken a step back before Roy had him by the front of his lab coat. "There are no remains. That's the whole point—they knew the space was available. They think that's being brilliant but it's diabolical." Roy's voice rose and rose, finally cracking on the last word. He went silent.

"Please," said Dr. Chu.

Roy could feel Dr. Chu's heart beating very fast. He looked frightened. For a moment, Roy felt good about that; and then very bad. He let Dr. Chu go. "Sorry," he said, his voice weaker now, the sudden eruption of strength flowing quickly out of him.

Dr. Chu's gaze fixed on some point a few inches below Roy's eyes. "There is stress," he said. "I understand. We will continue the study now?"

Netty took his pulse and blood pressure.

"Numbers okay?"

"Normal."

"What are they?"

"Pulse seventy-three. Blood pressure one twenty-five over ninety."

"And last time?"

Netty checked. "The exact same."

"That's good, right?" Had he turned the corner?

Netty gave him a little smile. *Stabilized:* it had to be good. She stuck a needle in his arm, collected three test tubes of blood—it looked richer than before, more purple—and fixed the different colored stickers in place. "If you'll just step on the scale," she said

"Take off the pajamas?" Roy said.

"You can leave them on."

"We'll deduct a pound," Roy said, "just to be fair." He stepped on the scale. Netty adjusted the weights. The bar fell, then hung, free and still. Roy weighed 144 pounds.

A lot of things sped through his mind at that moment. All that stuck was the sight of Netty slumping her shoulders. He turned to her.

"How many are left?" he said. "Of the original four."

"I really can't talk about the study," Netty said. "That's up to Dr.—"

"Three? Two?"

His chart trembled in her hand but her voice was steady. "It's just you, Roy."

Twenty-Six

D r. Chu stuck his head in Roy's room.
 "How is lunch?" he said.

Roy was eating off a three-compartment plastic tray: lasagna, corn bread, fruit salad. "Second helping," he said.

"The chef will be pleased," said Dr. Chu.

Roy laughed.

Dr. Chu made a curt bow. "A small joke," he said. "But the corn bread is very good, by reputation."

Silence. They looked at each other. The thought of the long, long life still in Dr. Chu's future occurred to Roy again, and with it came the sensation of himself as a shrinking object in a rearview mirror.

"Don't be alarmed—too alarmed—about this weight loss," said Dr. Chu. "In the final analysis, it is merely an effect."

"Of the treatment?"

"Oh, no, of the disease, certainly—that's well established. But a distant effect, not necessarily predictive. Do you see the difference?"

Roy wasn't sure, but he said yes.

"An important distinction," Dr. Chu said. "But the good news is that encouraging numbers appeared in your blood work from yesterday."

"Yeah? Like what?"

Dr. Chu went into a long explanation that Roy followed for a little while, and then not. Unfamiliar terms; complicated connections; lots of numbers: but Dr. Chu's belief in what he was saying shone through, and that was enough. Roy wanted to live, and even more than wanting, if that made sense, he needed to live. The Hobbes Institute, now gone, had sent him an empty coffin. That—and not any theory about a mix-up of past and present emotions—was his problem. Solving it was going to take time. He needed to live. Otherwise: To die unknowing?

Later, alone in his room with a shadow slowly advancing along the wall, he called out, "I'm hungry," although it was a lie. He said it again. No one came. He jumped out of bed, ran down to the street, bought a giant sub from a street vendor, gobbled it down in three bites. That last part took place only in his mind.

But the next day, Roy weighed 146 pounds. And the day after that—day three of round two—he was up to 148.

"Hey," he said to Netty. "Writing that down?"

She nodded.

"Yesterday's blood work back yet?" He was growing familiar with the routine, almost as though he worked there, one of the team.

"Just came," said Netty.

"And?"

"Excellent," said Dr. Chu. "Even better than yesterday."

"Could have told you myself," Roy said. "I'm feeling better."

Dr. Chu and Netty gazed at him.

"Way better."

"Excellent," said Dr. Chu.

"I've got some questions."

"Ask."

"Really a lot better," Roy said. "Have you seen improvement like this before?"

"Improvement?" said Dr. Chu.

"In the study," Roy explained. "I know the others all died, but before that, did they go through an improving stage?" The answer had to be no; he was different.

"Improving stage?" said Dr. Chu.

"Like I am right now," Roy said. "The blood work, putting weight back on, breathing better—did I mention that?—everything."

"Very good question," said Dr. Chu. He thought about it. Netty turned to watch him. "I would have to reexamine all the data to give you an informed answer."

"But your gut," said Roy. "What does it say?"

"That is not my method, Roy, the gut," Dr. Chu said. "I am a scientist. But when you return in twenty-one days, I will have detailed comparisons for you on this question."

"And that's another thing," Roy said. "Now that all the others are gone, how about a fourth hit?"

"Hit?"

"Of the cocktail." Or a fifth, sixth, seventh: as many hits as it would take at the rate of two pounds a day to get back up to 190.

"But you are forgetting the new arrivals," said Dr. Chu. "We are now fifteen."

Netty gave a quick shake of her head.

"Fourteen," said Dr. Chu.

"Another death?" said Roy.

Netty squeezed his arm. "You just take care of you," she said.

Roy had a thought; a thought that made him feel bad about himself, but he couldn't keep it in. "Is it possible to buy the cocktail?" he said.

"I'm sorry?" said Dr. Chu.

"I could pay you for some." Roy was prepared to go to two hundred and fifty grand, even higher. "Just a quart or two."

Dr. Chu's head tilted up very slightly, so there was just the suggestion of looking down his nose. "That would not be science," he said. "See you in twenty-one days."

Roy rented a car and drove down to D.C. He was feeling pretty good, breathing easily, hardly in any pain at all. Adding two pounds a day for any stretch of time was unrealistic, now that he thought it over, but even half a pound a day would bring him up to the one eighties by . . . Roy did the math in his head, then plotted other points on the calendar based on different weight gains. He was working out the target date for an absolutely minimal one-third of a pound per week when he turned onto Twenty-second Avenue and parked across the street from the little triptych: Starbucks; newspaper box; Wine, Inc. Everything the same, except for the display windows of Wine, Inc., now covered on the inside with brown paper, and a sign on the door that read: for rent.

The sight didn't shock Roy; he wasn't even really surprised. In fact, it calmed him in a strange way, an absence that proved to him in ways he couldn't articulate that he was on the right track. And there was a track, of that he had no doubt, going back to the empty coffin he'd buried, and before. But that didn't mean he knew the next step. Go home? Try Janet Habib again—how much was she holding back? Maybe he should do both, starting with—

His cell phone rang.

"Roy Valois? This is Jerry. You remember—Richard Gold's—"

"Of course."

"I was wondering whether you've made any progress on that obituary correction."

"Not really."

"But you're still pursuing it?"

"I am," said Roy. "Why?"

"It's about Richard's cell phone."

"You found it?"

"No," said Jerry. "But the man in the photo? The one you were interested in, fair-haired, privileged-looking? Your wife's boss?"

"Tom Parish?"

"That's not the name he's using," Jerry said. "But I've seen him."

"Where?" Roy was holding the phone very tight.

"At Tennis and Other Racquets."

"What's that?"

"A store—I do their books," Jerry said.

"I don't understand."

"I'm an accountant," Jerry said. "He came in to get a racquet strung."

"When was this?"

"Yesterday. He's supposed to pick it up today."

"Where the store?" Roy said.

"In Chevy Chase," Jerry said. "I could show you next time you're in town."

"I'm in town," Roy said.

Jerry's house, white with black shutters, still looked trim and immaculate, but now had a For Sale sign on the lawn, a match to the For Rent sign at Wine, Inc., although Roy couldn't quite say how. Jerry was watching from a downstairs window, his face a pale oval. He came outside, shivered, even though it wasn't cold, maybe in the high forties, and buttoned his trench coat up to the top.

Jerry got in the car. "Hi," he said, glancing at Roy, holding the glance an extra second or so, a puzzled look appearing in his eyes.

A look Roy understood and ignored. "Selling the house?" he said.

"Everything reminds me of him," Jerry said. "Turn left at the end of the block."

Roy turned left, drove through Rock Creek Park. "Any news from Sergeant Bettis?"

"No leads," Jerry said. "Not a single one in all this time."

"But he still thinks it was a robbery?"

Jerry nodded. "Things were taken," he said.

"Twice," said Roy.

"What do you mean?"

"They forgot about the cell phone the first time," Roy said. "And those pages from Richard's notebook."

"I don't get it," Jerry said.

"It was no robbery, Jerry," Roy said. "Richard was working on a story that someone didn't want worked on."

"What story?"

"My obituary."

Roy felt Jerry's gaze on his face. "Sergeant Bettis had a notion you might have been involved in some way," Jerry said. "But I never believed him, not for a minute."

"Why not?"

"Because of how you helped with the collage," Jerry said. "That would have taken a monster." He held his hand to the vent. "Working on the obituary—

meaning the part about where your wife worked, that institute?"

"That's just the beginning," Roy said, switching on the heat.

Jerry turned up the collar of his trench coat anyway. They were in Chevy Chase, on a street lined with fancy stores. "How so?" Jerry said.

How so? Delia was alive, for one thing. Roy knew it. But then where was she? Why hadn't she come back to him? For those questions, he had no answers at all, not even a glimmer. "There's a cover-up going on," he told Jerry. "They're willing to do anything."

"Do you mean murder?" Jerry said.

"Anything."

"Richard was murdered as part of a cover-up?"

"He wasn't the only one," Roy said. He told Jerry about Skippy.

"My God," said Jerry. "Shouldn't we tell Sergeant Bettis?"

"I tried that," Roy said.

Jerry was silent for a moment or two. Then he said, "Who is 'they'? What's being covered up?"

"The cover-up's about something called Operation Pineapple."

"That doesn't sound very menacing."

"They go in for clever touches," Roy said, realizing the truth of that as he spoke: the very name of the Institute was another. "As for the 'they' part, that's what we're doing right now."

Jerry turned, looked back. There was nothing to see but everyday suburban traffic.

Tennis and Other Racquets appeared on the right. Roy pulled over.

"Nice-looking store," said Jerry, his voice low, as though afraid of being overheard. "But they're losing five grand a month, and that's with the owner not taking any salary."

Roy glanced at Jerry. "What kind of accountant are you?" he said, his own voice at normal volume.

Jerry kept his voice low. "What kind? A CPA, if that's what you mean."

"Are you good?"

Jerry blinked. "I do my best," he said, back at normal volume, too.

"I'd like to hire you."

"To do what?"

"Find out all you can about a company called Verdadero Investments."

"Why?"

"I think they wrote the paychecks at the Hobbes Institute."

Jerry already had a notepad out. "Means 'true,' in Spanish," he said, writing it down.

"Yeah?" said Roy. He knew some French—had often heard it as a boy—but no Spanish.

"I'll get on it," Jerry said.

They sat in the car. A tall woman with a ponytail went into the store. She came out a few minutes later, a plastic-wrapped tennis racquet under her arm. Then a man—much younger than Tom Parish—walked out with a can of balls.

"Did he say when he was picking up the racquet?" Roy said.

"Not that I heard," said Jerry. "He was on the way out when I came in. He went right by me—I got a real good look." Jerry thought for a moment. "The owner said, 'See you tomorrow, Ned.' "

"Ned?"

"I'm pretty sure."

Time passed. No one went in or out.

"He's going to lose his shirt," Jerry said.

Roy opened his eyes. "What?"

Jerry was looking at him. "Are you all right?" he said.

"Fine," said Roy.

"You're a little pale."

"I'm not." Roy straightened up.

They watched the front of Tennis and Other Rac-quets. A man leaned into the display window. "Owner," Jerry said. The owner draped a tennis sweater over the shoulders of a mannequin, glanced up and down the street, withdrew.

"This is taking too goddamn long," Roy said; pretty close to a shout, and it seemed to utter itself, completely unbidden. It also seemed to open a door inside him: he banged the steering wheel. The whole cab shook.

Jerry looked at him in alarm. "I could go in," he said.

"And do what?" Roy said, lots of irritation still in his tone.

"Pretend I need to check something." Jerry smiled, very brief, but Roy saw what he must have been like before all this, and got hold of himself. "But I'd really be sleuthing around."

"Why not?" Roy said.

Jerry went into the store to sleuth around. Roy watched him talking to the owner; then they both dis-appeared behind a shoe display. Roy took an energy bar from his pocket and ate half: 145 calories. Dr. Chu's cocktail worked while he was actually having the treatment, no doubt about that. He just had to try harder during the twenty-one-day gaps.

Jerry came out of Tennis and Other Racquets, got in the car, locking the door. "Good thing I went in," he said. "He picked up his racquet this morning. Name in the order book is Ned Miller." He handed Roy a sheet of paper from his notepad. "The address." *Sweetbriar Farm, Meadville Rd., Meadville, MD.*

"Where's that?" Roy said.

"Near the West Virginia line," Jerry said. "Horse country." He lowered his voice. "Took me ten seconds—he never suspected a thing." Jerry had some thought. Roy wondered whether it was about Richard—a reporter, after all—and the fun Jerry would have had telling him this story. Jerry's eyes moistened and he turned away. A real-estate agent with a customer was waiting outside Jerry's house when Roy dropped him off.

Twenty-Seven

There were lots of farms in Roy's part of Ver-mont, but none like this. Sweetbriar Farm stood on a gentle slope near a bend in the Potomac, with bigger hills rising on the West Virginia side. Everything—house, barn, even the sheds and other outbuildings—looked grand, old and pristine at the same time, as though a set decorator with an unlimited budget had just left. Nothing moved except a flock of birds that came soaring over the river and landed in the bare branches of the orchard beyond the riding ring. Roy drove up a long lane, pea stone crunching under his tires, and parked in front of the house.

He sat in his rental car for a moment or two—the only car around—and tried to think through at least the first few steps of some plan. But he didn't get past knocking on that oversize double door—white, with a golden horseshoe knocker—and waiting to see who answered. A fat raindrop landed on the windshield, setting off a tiny dust explosion. Roy got out of the car and banged the knocker.

No one answered.

Roy knocked again, harder. He listened, heard nothing except a neighing horse, somewhere nearby. Even step one: incomplete. He had no time for this. Manners, politeness, convention: What role could they play now? Roy tried the door. Locked.

He backed away, glanced around. A single sheet of rain swept across the lawns, like a drifting curtain. It slapped silently against the side of the barn, three or four hundred yards away. Or maybe farther than that: as Roy walked toward the barn, he saw he'd underestimated its size by a lot.

He circled the barn. There was a huge roll-up door at the front, closed and unbudgeable, and another like it at the back, overlooking the river, also closed. Dark clouds now covered the hills on the West Virginia side. Somewhere in their depths, a lightning bolt flashed, very faint. The texture of the river roughened, rain on the way.

Roy went around to the side of the barn, found a normal-size door. Also locked, but it had one small, single-pane window. He peered through, into a vast, shadowy space. Some big rectangular structure stood in a distant corner. It looked like a trailer, one of those double-wides.

The horse neighed again, louder now, the sound coming from inside the barn. It startled Roy, at the same time triggering something inside him. He picked up a white-painted stone from the side of the path and smashed the window. A moment later he was inside.

Dark: and full of smells—hay, manure, saddle oil. Roy walked along a row of stalls, all empty with their gates open, except for the last. A tall black horse looked over the barrier, big liquid eyes nervous. Roy stroked its face.

"It's all right," he said.

The horse stomped back in a stiff-legged way, banging hard into the back wall.

"Easy, boy," Roy said.

The horse raised its head, snorted, then stood still, nostrils flared.

Roy moved across the wooden floor, worn soft and smooth, came to the far corner. Yes, a double-wide trailer, mounted on a low, wheeled platform; a sandy-colored trailer with no markings, and blinds in all the windows. Roy studied it from a few different angles. Then he stepped onto the platform and tried the door, a narrow door with an oval top, cut flush in the trailer body. The door opened.

Almost complete darkness in the trailer: a minute or so went by before Roy's eyes adjusted. He began to make out details: office-style cubicles with desktop computers; video monitors hanging from the ceiling; big maps on the walls, their details obscure in the dimness, no lights showing at all on any of the electronics. No workers, no sound, nothing going on, but Roy had caught a glimpse of this place before, beyond the employees-only room at Wine, Inc.: the office he'd tried and failed to show Sergeant Bettis. A portable office, a wall quickly bricked in—Tom Parish, Lenore, Westie, they'd all fooled him so easily. Why? Because he hadn't been imaginative enough, supposedly one of his strengths. He hadn't believed in the existence of— what would you call it?—a parallel world, maybe. Now he believed. What was it Delia had told Turk behind the mountain hut? *When you see how things really happen, the fun goes out pretty quick.* Why hadn't she ever said anything like that to him? Then maybe he would have— But at that moment Roy remembered: *Fuck the pineapples.* And were there other examples? He could feel them stirring, things she'd tried to tell him, deep in his mind.

Roy entered the trailer. He went into the nearest cubicle, sat at the computer, pressed a key. Nothing happened. He found the switch, on; and the power cord, plugged in. Roy opened a desk drawer. Empty.

He checked the other drawers, feeling around in the gloom, all empty.

Roy got up, went from cubicle to cubicle, pressing keys, switching switches, opening drawers and banging them shut.

"Goddamn it."

He needed answers, needed them fast. What about those wall maps? He went to the nearest one—Middle Eastern shapes barely visible in the darkness—and ran his hands over it. The map, which felt like plastic, quivered and started to slip off the wall. Roy tried to catch it, but the map, surprisingly heavy, fell to the floor and shattered; not plastic, but glass. The noise deafened him. He looked around, a little wildly—but nothing moved in the darkness. Sound returned, his heartbeat, too fast, too light, coming first.

Roy looked up at the wall where the glass map had hung. He saw that it had concealed a whiteboard, the kind for writing on with liquid markers. And this one had writing on it, maybe readable if he leaned closer. Roy leaned closer. He read the heading: *Roy Valois.*

Next came three or four lines, the writing smaller, just small enough that Roy couldn't make them out. He went back to the trailer door, found a panel of wall switches, flicked them all without result. Wouldn't there be a flashlight somewhere in the barn, a lantern, matches? He opened the trailer door. The horse neighed again. Roy paused, one foot on the raised platform, and then the small barn door Roy had broken through opened, silhouetting a man in a rectangle of outside light. Rain slanted down behind him, falling hard. A big man: he entered the barn. Roy backed into the trailer and silently closed the door.

He stood there, listening. He could hear the rain on the barn roof, like countless drumming fingers. Then came a faint clatter, maybe the horse shifting in its stall. Roy backed deeper into the trailer. He bumped into the edge of a desk. Something fell off and landed on the floor, something light—a pencil maybe—that made no sound at all; or almost none. He stepped behind a cubicle wall.

Silence; and then an almost inaudible squeaking sound that came and went, a sound Roy heard only because it was coming from so close—inside him, actually—with every breath. Not important: he was breathing easily, felt strong, still protected by Dr. Chu's cocktail. At that moment, Roy stopped being afraid of what might happen next. It took no effort at all, simply happened, a sudden ascent into courage, or at least total fearlessness, probably not the same thing. Was it a side effect of the cocktail? Roy took a small dark object off the desk. It turned out to be a stapler. He waited.

Nothing happened. Another triangle was forming, this one with two points fixed—he and the horse—and one on the move—the man at the barn door. Roy could feel it changing shape. So much silent time went by—silent except for the tiny rhythmic squeak—Roy grew sure that the moving point was back outside the barn, drawing farther and farther away. Then the trailer door opened.

A flashlight beam shone inside. It poked into corners, then began sweeping slowly back and forth. For a brief moment it must have shone on something shiny, because the man's face suddenly appeared in a weak reflected glow, a round face, shaped for looking friendly, but there was nothing friendly about it now: Westie. The beam swung toward Roy. He crouched as it passed over the cubicle wall.

Westie spoke. "Raise your hands and come out."

Roy peered over the cubicle wall. The beam had found the broken map remnants; shattered pieces glittered in its light.

"There's only one way out," Westie said. "Your situation is hopeless."

Roy didn't move. Westie entered the trailer, his footfalls soft for such a big man.

"You're one of those kids from the campground, right?" he said. "Do we really want to bring the police into this?" He whirled around, stabbed the light into a cubicle near Roy. Roy ducked, but not before he saw the gun in Westie's other hand. Then the beam sped up, zigzagging across the back wall of his cubicle in a quick clever way as though it had a mind of its own; just missing him.

"Nothing bad's going to happen," Westie said. "We can work this out." He came closer. On the other side of the wall, Roy listened to his footsteps, faint, cautious. They paused, only a foot or two away.

Was time on Roy's side? Deep down, he knew the answer to that very well. So if not now, when? Roy rose—not with the speed he'd counted on—reached over the top of the wall and brought the stapler down hard on Westie's head. He'd never done anything like that in his life—a sneak attack—but the thought of Skippy made it quite easy.

Easy to do, but that didn't mean Roy did it well. First, the stapler only glanced off Westie's head, most of the force of the blow landing on his shoulder or even upper arm. Second, the gun went off. Third, Roy lost his balance, fell against the partition wall. It toppled over, Roy above, Westie underneath. Almost at the same time came the sickening sound of a human head striking something hard.

Roy lay twisted, jammed between the floor and an edge of the fallen wall. This was a time for action but all Roy could do was lie there and breathe, shallow, panting breaths. That left Westie free to do anything he wanted. Nothing happened. Roy's breathing settled down. He rolled over, onto his knees. The flashlight lay on the floor, pointing at Westie. His chest was rising and falling but his eyes were closed. Roy took the flashlight and stood up.

The light gleamed on the gun, in a corner by the next cubicle. Smith & Wesson, short barrel, wooden grip: the same model as the one Lenore had planted in Skippy's glove box. Roy stripped off Westie's belt, rolled him over and tied his hands behind his back.

"Wake up," Roy said, picking up the gun.

No response. Westie kept breathing, nice deep breaths.

"Wake up."

Westie groaned softly, but didn't wake up. Roy stepped over the fallen partition, went closer to the whiteboard, shone the light.

Roy Valois

1. *What does RV know about Operation Pineapple?*

2. *Why his sudden interest after so long?*

3. *Connection between RV and Gold?*

4. *Mountain hut connection.*

Roy reread the four points on the whiteboard. He wet his finger, rubbed it on one of the letters. The ink smeared. Here was the parallel world, all real. His heart switched into that too-fast, too-light rhythm again. To calm it, Roy tried to get more air in his lungs, sticking his chest out and elbows back in the way that had worked before, at least a little. But not this time: instead Roy felt a sudden pain deep in his chest, a heavy pain as though he'd been kicked from inside. He staggered into a chair, lowered his head between his knees. Behind him, Westie groaned again. Roy got hold of the arms of the chair, pushed himself up; it took all his strength. He aimed the beam at Westie. Westie's eyes were open now: he squinted in the light.

"Who are you?" Westie said.

Roy shone the light on the whiteboard, let it linger there so Westie could see, then turned it back on him.

"I found Skippy," Roy said.

Westie said nothing.

"Talk," Roy said.

"What did you do to my leg?" Westie said.

"Nothing."

"I'm bleeding."

Roy shifted the beam, saw a wet patch on one of Westie's pant legs, midthigh. "You shot yourself," he said. "I'll get you to the hospital, but first, some answers."

"About what?"

"Start with the Hobbes Institute."

"Never heard of it."

Roy stood over him. "Can't you see this is over, whatever you've been doing? You killed an innocent kid."

"I don't know what you're talking about."

Roy came close to kicking him. Westie flinched, although Roy hadn't moved at all.

"I'm bleeding."

Roy glanced down at the wet patch on Westie's leg, maybe bigger than before. "Who wrote what's on the board?" he said.

Westie shook his head.

"Was it Tom Parish? Ned Miller, whatever his real name is?"

Roy caught a flicker in Westie's eye.

"What was Operation Pineapple?" he said.

"I don't feel so good."

"I'll get you to the hospital," Roy said. "What was Operation Pineapple?"

No reply.

"What's the mountain-hut connection?"

Westie shook his head.

"Is that where you killed Skippy? What were you doing up there?"

"I didn't kill anyone. It—" Westie stopped himself.

"It was Lenore? Is that what you were going to say?"

Westie was silent. There was no time for this. Roy kicked him, not as hard as he could, in the leg, the bleeding one or the other; at that moment he didn't care. But it must have been the bleeding one, because Westie cried in pain; out in the barn the horse neighed again.

In the quiet that followed, Roy said, "Was it Lenore?"

Westie raised his head, gazed down his body. The wet patch was much bigger now, and there was more wetness on the floor. Westie's face changed, seemed to grow younger: he wasn't too much past being a kid himself. "I could die," he said.

"Your choice," Roy said; which made Westie the luckier of the two of them.

"What do you mean?"

"Talk first, hospital second," Roy said. "All these secrets—are they worth dying for?"

Westie thought about that.

Roy spoke quietly. "Where is Delia?"

Westie looked at him; yes, looking younger all the time. Roy made himself ignore that. "You don't know what you're up against," Westie said.

"Tell me."

"History."

"I'm up against history?"

Westie nodded.

"How?"

"You either know or you don't."

"What's this got to do with Delia?"

A long moment. Roy thought he heard slow dripping on the floor. "I don't know anything about her," Westie said, and after a long pause, added, "not firsthand. I've only been here a few years."

"Been where?"

"Working for Lenore." A longer pause, and then: "She's head of security."

"Whose security?"

"The organization's."

"What organization?"

"It doesn't have a name."

"But it used to be the Hobbes Institute?" Roy said.

More dripping; then Westie nodded. He'd made his decision about what kind of secrets were worth dying for. Roy put down the gun, removed his jacket, ripped out the lining, used it as a tourniquet around Westie's leg. He helped Westie to his feet.

" 'Not firsthand' means you know something," Roy said, taking hold of the belt binding Westie's arms. He nudged him between the shoulder blades. They moved toward the open trailer door.

"It was a fiasco," Westie said. "That's all I know."

"What was?"

"Operation Pineapple."

"What happened?" Roy said; he slipped slightly in Westie's wet tracks.

"I don't feel so good."

"Neither did Skippy," Roy said. But he didn't give Westie another nudge, just laid a hand on his back. "What happened?"

"It went bad."

"That's why the Hobbes Institute shut down?" Roy said. "Why there's all this secrecy?"

Westie nodded. "It can't come out," he said.

"Otherwise what?"

"Disaster."

"For who?"

"The whole country."

"Why?" said Roy. "Was the Hobbes Institute part of the CIA or something like that?"

Westie laughed, soft and low.

"What's funny?"

"That was the whole point," Westie said. "So there wouldn't be any CIA-type fiascoes."

"The whole point of what?" Roy said.

"I don't feel so good," Westie said.

Roy glanced down at Westie's leg. He didn't seem to be leaving tracks anymore. "You'll be fine."

"When?"

"As soon as I get you to the hospital," Roy said. "Was the fiasco all about who stabbed Paul Habib?" Roy had a nasty thought about the answer to that question. "Is that the problem?"

Westie turned to him. "Stabbed?" he said. "No one stabbed Habib. He fell out of the chopper."

"No chopper," Roy said. "No Venezuela. I'm way past that. Try again."

"You're wrong," Westie said. "There was a chopper, all right. It's just that the venue—"

Across the barn, the huge front door rolled up, silently but very fast, letting in a rush of light, almost blinding. Lenore stepped inside, curtains of rain behind her. She saw Roy and Westie, stopped dead. She had a rifle in her hand. And Westie's Smith & Wesson? On the floor where Roy had left it, while he tied the tourniquet around Westie's leg.

Roy, one hand still on the knotted belt, stepped behind Westie. "It's over," he said, "out in the open. More violence would be pointless. I'm taking him to the hospital."

"I'm sorry," Westie said.

Lenore spoke. "What did you tell him?"

Roy misunderstood. "What did *I* tell *him*? That's hardly the—"

A flash of light, a crack of sound: like lightning and thunder on a more intimate scale, all coming from the muzzle of the rifle. Roy felt the tremendous force of the shot; it lifted Westie right up, hurled him against Roy, knocking him down, splashed with blood.

But Westie's blood, not his. Roy scrambled up on all fours. Westie, on his back, his chest wide open, was watching Roy. His lips moved. "Venue," he said, and then went still.

"Hands up," said Lenore.

Roy didn't put his hands up. Instead he dove for the nearest stall, unhooked the gate—meaning he'd picked the only occupied one—and rolled inside. Another crack of Lenore's gun: wood splintered behind Roy, very near. The horse—up close so huge—neighed that wild neigh and stomped around, jamming Roy against the side of the stall.

The horse froze like that, wouldn't budge, muscles bulging, its strength enormous, and that one eye, only a couple of feet from Roy, wide with terror. He could smell its sweat and feel it, dampening his shirt.

"Come out," Lenore said; very close now, not more than a few yards from the gate. "We need to talk. This can still have a reasonable play-out."

Roy turned his head, could see her through a narrow space between the gate and the side of the stall. Lenore had the rifle raised, the stall's exit point in her sights, play-out obvious.

Roy twisted around, fighting the weight of the horse, a massive life-form. He squeezed his arms between their two bodies, got his hands right next to one of the horse's ears. A massive life-form, but at the same time that big, pointed ear was so soft and sensitive. It twitched. Roy clapped his hands, a single, sharp sound.

The horse reared up, filling the barn with a wild equine scream, and burst from the stall. Roy's hope was that the horse might cover his escape. That didn't quite happen. Instead one great forehoof, pawing the air in panic, struck the side of Lenore's head, caving it in. She fell. The horse ran from the barn in three or four springing strides, disappearing in the rain.

Twenty-Eight

A stranger coming with dangerous questions.

Roy awoke with that phrase in his mind, and the feeling he'd been turning it over and over in his sleep. He sat up, which took a lot of effort for some reason, and found a bright light shining in his eyes—as though an interrogation was about to begin, dream leaking into life.

"Roll down that window."

Roll down the window? Where was he? Not asleep in the truck again? But yes. Shielding his eyes, Roy turned the key, slid the window down. Outside, a cop leaned closer.

"What's up, bud?"

"Nothing," Roy said.

"Been drinking?"

"No."

The cop's nostrils twitched. He shone the light around the cab; it came to rest on three objects on the seat beside Roy: Paul Habib's pay stub from Verdadero Investments; the Operation Pineapple photo; and the photo of Habib and Calvin Truesdale. "What're those pictures?" the cop said.

Evidence of a horrible crime. That response came to Roy immediately, some big truth starting to dawn in his mind. But all he said was: "Just photos."

"Yeah? Let's have a look."

Roy handed over the photos. The cop glanced at them, handed them back; he wore a D.C. Police patch on his sleeve. "Can't sleep here," he said.

"Okay," said Roy.

"You feelin' all right?"

"Yeah."

"Sweating like a pig, man."

Roy felt his forehead: dripping wet. "I'm fine," he said.

"You don't look fine," said the cop. "Using?"

"Using?"

"Drugs."

"No."

The cop shone the light around again, maybe looking for drugs. "Can't sleep here," he said.

"I don't have time anyway," Roy said.

"Huh?"

I don't have time anyway—that had just leaped free, on its own. Roy peered out, saw he was in a convenience-store parking lot, the neighborhood not good. "I'm leaving," he said.

"Do that," said the cop.

Roy drove out of the parking lot, down an ill-lit street he didn't know. A freeway appeared to his right. He headed for that. The cop followed him for a block or two, then veered off. A sudden pain burst up in Roy's chest, sharp and powerful, like a living thing in there come to hurt him. For a moment, he thought he couldn't bear it; then he found a position—chest stuck so far out his shoulder blades touched—that made things a little better. He drove onto the freeway, drops of sweat falling from his chin.

The Washington Monument rose in the distance. The sight disturbed him, although he couldn't have said why. He'd never seen anyone die, not until today. Today he'd seen violent death up close twice, even been complicit in one of them, perhaps both. His mind cleared; he remembered it all, some parts sharply defined—like everything that happened in the barn; and some not—like how he'd run away, surely not in a panic, and the details of the drive that had ended in the convenience-store parking lot—but at least now he knew where he'd been going. Roy took the next exit.

The tidy white house with the black shutters was dark, not a light showing. That gave Roy a bad feeling, like he was too late. He got out of the truck, hurried toward the front door. Hurried only about halfway: at that point he had to stop and lean against a tree, just breathing. Roy, in no way a tree hugger—he'd grown up in sawmill country—felt the great living strength of this tree, a feeling that reminded him of the feng shui room, being on the IV. But this, this leaning, this time-wasting, this softness, was no good. Delia was out there, in the world, alive. Something had gone wrong with Operation Pineapple, whatever that was, but she had survived, come back, been seen in a limo outside 919 Eliot Street in Cambridge. *She had a bandage around her head.* He needed time.

Roy sucked in a deep breath—not deep at all, air hardly reaching the tops of his lungs—and pushed away from the tree. He took a few more steps, banged the elegant silver knocker up and down.

No answer. Roy put his ear to the door, heard nothing. He knocked again, harder. "Jerry," he called. "Jerry." A light went on in a house across the street. Then came a voice from the other side of the door. "Who is it?"

"Roy. Are you okay?"

The door opened. Jerry stood there in dark pajamas, the top buttoned to the neck: undamaged. "I was sound asleep for the first time in weeks," he said.

"Sorry," Roy said. "But things are happening out there. I didn't want them happening to you."

Jerry blinked. "What things? I don't understand."

Roy stepped into the house, closed the door, slid the bolt in place. "People are dying."

"Like Richard?"

"Yes," Roy said. He moved to the nearest window, checked the street. Nothing stirred, and the house across the street was dark again.

"Did you talk to the blond guy?" Jerry said. "Tom Parish, Ned Miller, whatever his name is?"

"No," Roy said.

"Why not?" said Jerry; he sounded petulant.

"I couldn't find him," Roy said. "It went wrong."

"What did?" Jerry said. Then his expression changed. "Are you not feeling well?"

"I'm fine."

"We should sit down."

Jerry switched on lights, led Roy into the kitchen. Roy sat at the table. Jerry made tea. Roy folded his hands. He noticed they weren't the same color. The right hand was normal; the left much paler.

"Milk and sugar?" Jerry said.

"Plain," Roy said.

Jerry came to the table with two mugs, added lots of milk and sugar to his own. Roy remembered that plain wouldn't do him any good, and did the same.

"Better with milk and sugar," Jerry said.

Roy drank. The tea felt good going down, even cooling him off, which made no sense at all. *Milk and sugar from now on.*

"How does Verdadero Investments fit into all this?" Jerry said.

"Did you look into it?"

"Yes," Jerry said. "Not my kind of work, the investigative side, although I did help Richard out from time to time. There was one particular—"

"Did you find anything?" Roy's voice sharpened; he couldn't help it.

Tea slopped over the side of Jerry's mug. He set it aside. "Nothing useful," Jerry said. "Verdadero Investments no longer exists. It was a limited partnership registered in the Cayman Islands, but dissolution papers were filed almost fourteen years ago."

"What does that mean?"

"It was dissolved, closed out, terminated as a corporate entity."

"Who were the partners?"

Jerry shook his head. "They've got all these secrecy laws," he said. "I'm sorry."

"What did they do?" Roy said.

"Do?"

"Verdadero Investments—their purpose."

"Oh," said Jerry. "I can tell you that—it was a holding company."

"Holding what?"

"Various investments."

"Like?"

"Mostly shares of common stock in blue-chip firms," Jerry said. "Plus some real estate in the Caribbean— at least that was what the names suggested—and one or two other things. I made a list, if you want to see it."

Roy hesitated. Was there any point in checking lists of blue-chip firms and Caribbean resorts? The names of the partners were what he needed. *Private money means actual people.*

"It's no trouble," said Jerry. He went upstairs. Roy breathed. Jerry returned with a printout.

Roy found he was slumping in his chair. He sat up straight and took the printout. Yes, a long list of big holdings in blue chips—like Microsoft, Bank of America, Honda, Exxon, Home Depot; in property development companies in the Dominican Republic,

St. Lucia, Guadeloupe, the Grenadines; and in resorts and hotels in Barbados and Jamaica; and under Jerry's heading *Odds and Ends,* ownership of a few small companies—Leather and Suede Imports, Toys for Baby, Lone Star Office Services . . .

Roy turned to the next page to read the rest of the list, but there was no next page. Jerry glanced over. "There were only a couple more," he said. "I guess they didn't print."

Only a couple more, and Roy's legs felt suddenly and deeply weak for some reason—as though never getting up again would suit them fine—but he pushed himself erect. "Maybe I could just read them off the screen," he said.

"Sure," said Jerry. "It's the computer in the office. But I'm not exactly clear on—"

Roy went up the stairs, into Richard Gold's old office. He sat in front of the computer, rubbed his eyes and read the last items on Jerry's list of Verdadero Investments' holdings: *Bagels and Buns; Vrai Transport.*

Vrai Transport?

Whap-whap-whap.

Roy printed it out. The page shook in his hands. He went downstairs. Jerry, stirring his tea, looked up.

"What did you say *verdadero* meant in Spanish?" Roy said.

" 'True,' " said Jerry.

"It's *vrai* in French," Roy said, setting the page on the table.

Jerry read that last entry. "So Verdadero Investments owned Vrai Transport," he said, "and they both mean 'true,' but other than that—?"

"Vrai Transport still exists," Roy said. "They own helicopters. At least one, anyway—I've seen it."

"And this relates to the Hobbes Institute how?" said Jerry.

"By hooking into the present," Roy said. He remembered something Sergeant Bettis had said: *There's nowhere to hide in this country, not anymore.*

"I'm not sure I—"

Roy felt strength returning to his legs, slowly and not to their cores, but it was something. "Verdadero Investments paid the checks at the Hobbes Institute." For sure? He'd seen only one check. But Roy pushed past that. Were they in a court of law? Far from it. Everything about this was lawless: a decision that had been made long ago, and not by him, a decision made *so there wouldn't be fiascoes.* "They also owned Vrai Transport."

"So now you can work backward?" Jerry said.

"I hope so." But in fact Roy knew it, knew it because of that black-and-white photo, Exhibit C, and also because of who'd climbed down out of that helicopter and onto the snowy meadow behind his house.

Jerry licked his lips. "Is that what Richard was doing, too, working backward?"

Roy nodded.

"What did he find out?"

"Maybe nothing," Roy said. "Asking questions might have been enough."

Jerry's eyes moistened. "To kill him?" He shook his head. "I still have a hard time believing things like that can happen, Roy."

He got up, went to a window, drew the curtain aside. The street was quiet, the pavement shining black. Nothing moved except a drop of rainwater zigzagging down the windshield of a parked car.

"Did your Verdadero Investments search leave any tracks?" Roy said.

"Tracks?" said Jerry.

"Evidence of what you'd been doing."

"I don't know," Jerry said. "It's all public information of one kind or another. There must be thousands of inquiries like it every day. Who could sift through all that?"

Roy closed the curtain. "You're probably right," he said. "But maybe you should still—"

Jerry interrupted. "Frankly, Roy, that's my problem with all of this. It's so . . . so conspiratorial."

"What are you saying?" Roy said.

Jerry looked embarrassed. "It's just that so many simpler things could explain why—"

Roy's phone rang. He took it out of his pocket.

"Hello?"

"Ah, Roy. Calvin Truesdale here. How're you doing?"

"Fine," Roy said. But all at once, his lungs were tied off, almost to the top, and the edges of everything were turning yellow.

"Sounds like you're fighting a bit of a cold," said Truesdale. "Not feeling well?"

"I'm fine."

"Good to hear. I won't keep you, Roy. Just calling to let you know I looked into that Hobbes business of yours."

"You did?"

"I like to follow through, Roy," Truesdale said. "An old rancher's habit. Any event, it turns out much as I'd suspected, with one or two little twists."

"What do you mean?"

"Financial shenanigans at the bottom of it, as I thought," Truesdale said. "Mix in some mean and nasty lawsuits involving a snake pit of Asian investors, and then everything gets sealed up as per the settlement agreement—which explains why you can't find reference to the Institute."

"You're saying that Asian investors owned the Hobbes Institute?"

"As a nonprofit," Truesdale said, "in partnership with a UN agency that folded in that oil embargo scandal."

"The UN?"

"But their records are so chaotic it's not easy to see through all the layers," Truesdale said. "I'm happy to go over the details in person, if you like, at your convenience. You at home right now?"

"Why?" said Roy. "Are you in the area?"

Truesdale laughed. "I can be anywhere in a matter of hours."

"In your helicopter from Vrai Transport?" Roy said. Jerry's eyes widened.

A brief pause. "That's one way," Truesdale said.

Roy paused, too. Then he said: "What about Delia?"

And then a very long pause, so long Roy wondered if the conversation was over. But he kept his own mouth shut, and finally Truesdale said, "Delia?"

"Yes," Roy said. "Specifically the last time you saw her."

"You're losing me, friend," said Truesdale. There was a new tone in his voice; Roy heard a slight buzz underneath.

"The sculpture, Cal," Roy said. "Up at my place. I wondered whether you still wanted it."

"Well, 'course I do," said Truesdale, voice back to normal. "More than ever. Thought you knew."

"I've decided to sell," Roy said. All at once he was breathing free and easy.

"Hallelujah."

"At the offered price,"

"Deal," said Truesdale. "I've already got a spot picked out down at the ranch."

"Why don't you come up?" Roy said. "We can make shipping arrangements and you can walk me through the Hobbes business at the same time."

"How's tomorrow?" said Truesdale.

"Around four?"

"On the dot."

Roy clicked off.

"What was that?" Jerry said.

Roy smiled. He felt pretty good—that momentum-change feeling that made the blood flow: he knew it from the rink. "Got to get going, Jerry," he said. "I'm in your debt."

"But—"

"And one more thing—stay somewhere else until you hear from me."

"Somewhere else?"

"A hotel. With a friend."

Jerry glanced around his kitchen, paused on the corner where the broken chair had lain. "You really think—?"

"Promise me," Roy said.

Twenty-Nine

At first everything went well. Momentum was shifting, and taking Roy with it. Every time he checked the speedometer, he saw he was going too fast—seventy-five, eighty, even more—as though some force was pushing. He thought of that goal he'd scored against Harvard— not the physical details, although he remembered them exactly, most clearly of all how the Harvard goalie had looked back to see if the puck was in the net—but the way that goal had lifted his whole team. Which was what he felt now: that lift. The most important goal he'd scored, and much more than that, he now realized, one of the most important events of his life. If he hadn't wondered aloud to Turk about its possible inclusion in his obituary, then he would never have known—what? What he was about to learn. A plan was forming in his mind.

A few miles from Baltimore, Roy stopped for gas. He had some notion of calling Freddy Boudreau, step one in the plan, while he filled the tank, but from how he was parked that meant operating the pump with his left hand, which for some reason didn't seem to have the strength to pull the lever. Roy ended up spilling gas on both hands. He went inside and washed them in the restroom sink. That was when he saw his face in the mirror. The sight froze him for a moment or two. It might have been his portrait, painted by one of those expressionists Roy had never warmed up to, the kind who went in for asymmetry, dark outlines, and skin tones unseen in real life, like purple under the eyes, green on the cheeks, chalk white everywhere else.

When had he last eaten? Or even had something to drink? Roy couldn't remember. He felt no hunger at all, but suddenly realized how thirsty he was. Roy went into the station, bought two premade plastic-wrapped sandwiches—one labeled turkey, the other ham—and a thirty-two-ounce bottle of water. Back in the truck, he drank down the whole bottle, then took a bite of the turkey sandwich. It had no taste, didn't even seem like food. He tried the ham instead. No better. Roy re-wrapped the sandwiches, laid them on the seat beside him and called Freddy Boudreau.

"I know it's late, Freddy, but—"

"That's okay," Freddy said. "I'm at work anyways. And I wanted to talk to you, too, matter of fact."

"About what?"

"First things first—how're you doing, Roy?"

"Good," Roy said.

Freddy was silent.

"I don't know what Dr. Chu told you," Roy said. "It probably looked a lot worse than it is."

"Good to hear," said Freddy. He cleared his throat. "I owe you an apology."

"What for?"

"That theory about your meds—maybe getting your judgment warped by them and all. I was way off base."

"What changed your mind?" Roy said.

"Had a closer look at that cell phone," Freddy said.

"Skippy's?"

"Yup."

"What did you find?"

"I'd like to go over that in person," Freddy said. "Can I come over in the morning?"

Roy checked his watch. "How's ten?"

"Ten it is."

"And, Freddy?" Roy said. "Bring that equipment for"—he had to search for the term—". . . wiring me up."

"Wiring you up?"

"To make one of those secret recordings."

"Of who?" said Freddy.

"I'll explain then," Roy said.

"Looking forward to it."

Momentum, oh yes, it was shifting. The law, in the person of Freddy Boudreau—an unpopular small-town cop who often played with surprising meekness on the ice but the law nevertheless—was now on his side. Roy had never set a trap for anyone, never even considered it. Setting traps turned out to be kind of fun. Wasn't there a saying about once you'd hunted men you didn't want to do anything else? Or was it you weren't good for anything else? Roy, back on the road, remembered who he'd heard it from, and when.

She wanted to go to the fair.

"What fair?"

"The Mad River Fair, what else?"

"Where'd you hear about that?"

"It's all everybody's been talking about the whole week."

"Who's everybody?"

"Turk, Normie, all the guys."

"You'll hate it."

"I'll love it. Wait and see."

And she'd loved the Mad River Fair, everything about it. She made crazy bets on the oxen pull, ate all the food in sight, including Polish sausages, fried dough and Quebecois poutine, came third in the pan toss—beaten by two women who each outweighed her by at least one hundred pounds—and was unaware of the ketchup on her chin. She even challenged Turk at the shooting gallery. Turk had gone to some military prep school before Dartmouth, been captain of the rifle team. It was one of those old-fashioned shooting galleries—ducks going back and forth on different levels, stuffed animals for prizes. They won lots of stuffed animals. Turk only missed one duck. Delia missed none.

"Mercy," said Turk. "Where'd you learn to shoot like that?"

Delia, finally aware of the ketchup on her chin, wiped it off and said, "Beginner's luck."

"Right," said Turk. "Hey, Roy, did you know you married a great white hunter?"

"Of course," Roy said. "She bagged me."

Delia laughed and put her arm around him. That was when she quoted the saying, whatever it was, about hunting men.

But which was it? For some reason the distinction—between losing the taste for anything else and being no good for anything else—seemed very important. And more important still was the incident itself. Sharpshooting, *Fuck the pineapples,* and even, on that cherry-blossom morning, *I've had enough:* Hadn't she been trying to tell him? How had he missed all that? Was it because of a fundamental, unsuspected difference between them, that he was incapable of holding two contradictory thoughts in his mind at once, while she—

Without warning, Roy vomited up everything in his stomach. Not much: just those two undigested sandwich bites, turkey and ham, and sour liquid, but Roy couldn't stop gagging. He pulled to the side of the road—loud honking behind him—got out of the truck. There by the guardrail he stood hands on knees, his stomach heaving and heaving, but giving up nothing, now even the last few sourest splatters of liquid long gone. It went on and on, his whole body reduced to gagging then trying to breathe, gagging then trying to breathe, like some horrible two-stroke piston. Then the pain demon in his chest awoke, in a very bad mood. Roy staggered against the side of the truck. He caught the wide-eyed stare of a woman in a passing car.

Roy got himself in the truck, clung to the wheel. The gagging stopped, but he still couldn't make his lungs take in air. The pain demon, not needing air—perhaps fed on its absence—grew stronger. Roy couldn't get any air inside him at all. What did that mean? That he was drowning, drowning on dry land? He thrashed around, then remembered that strange position, elbows way back and chest stuck out, and he tried with all his might to do what no one ever thinks twice about, simply breathe, and a tiny bit of air, no more than would fill a nostril, got through. And then another, and a few more.

That seemed to enrage the demon. It squeezed things inside him, squeezed them with claws. Roy reached a whole new level of pain, and at the same time somehow knew he'd only entered the foothills. He turned the key, pulled onto the highway and started for home. Elbows back, chest out, sweat dripping off his chin, the inside of the truck all sour, a low growling sound coming from his throat, directed at the demon: he drove. Roy had to get home, no matter what. How could his plan take shape without him?

But he couldn't get enough air, just that mean trickle. Plus how he was burning up, and the demon inside him: all that hitting its highest note so far at the very moment an exit sign rose in his headlights: johns hopkins university hospital.

Roy's hands took over and turned the wheel. He tried to resist, tried at least to put up a fight, for his own pride if nothing else. But he couldn't even do that, ended up losing an important war that took two

NERVE DAMAGE • 389

seconds, maybe three. How people could surrender their rational faculties to the belief in a savior, to put themselves in the hands of a distant other: he got it at last. His was Dr. Chu.

"Roy? Roy?"

Rounded, folded in an igloo sleep. It felt good.

"Roy? Can you open your eyes, please?"

Felt good. Was there anything better than feeling just like this?

"Recognize my voice, Roy? It's Dr. Chu. If you can hear me, raise the index finger on your right hand."

Rounded and folded.

"Or make any movement, any movement you want."

He wanted to be still. Machines beeped regular beeps, very soothing.

"You can't talk right now, but that's only due to the ventilator. A temporary condition—if you continue with your improvement."

I'm improving?

"I think he moved his finger, Doctor."

"Did you, Roy? Do it again for me, please. I missed it."

Improving how? Air: for one thing, he had air, all the air he needed. A lovely planet, softly padded with miles and miles of air. He felt it, air spreading through his body, an obvious connection to the living earth, although he'd never thought of it that way before.

"Just a quick raising of the finger, Roy."

Beep. Beep. Beep.

"We have a writing pad. Surely you have some questions, Roy."

Question: Why hadn't he understood that she'd been trying to tell him something, if not consciously, then in slipups she couldn't prevent? That, out of all the possibilities, was the first question that broke through and came to mind. She'd been agonizing and he'd done nothing, not even known. Roy opened his eyes, sat up—or at least tried to—and also tried to say *Delia*.

"Easy, Roy."

Roy looked around, saw Dr. Chu, Netty, and another nurse he didn't know. Daylight flowed through the window. Oh God: the plan. He made a writing motion. Netty handed him a pen and pad. Roy wrote: *is it tomorrow?*

"Is what tomorrow?" said Dr. Chu.

Roy made an impatient motion and wrote: *today*.

"I don't understand," said Dr. Chu.

"Maybe he's asking if today is tomorrow," said Netty.

"If today is tomorrow?" said Dr. Chu. "I don't—"

"From when he came in," said Netty.

Roy made a check mark on the page.

"Ah," said Dr. Chu. He gazed down at Roy. Was there a new look in his eye? Roy thought so, and didn't like it. "You've been here for three days," Dr. Chu said. "So fortunate you came in when you did."

Roy wrote: *3 days?*

"No cause for alarm," said Dr. Chu. "We have seen much—we've seen worse. Your numbers are improving, as I mentioned. Improving practically by the hour. We'll have you up and around in no time."

Roy wrote: *Now.*

Dr. Chu laughed an embarrassed little laugh. "Soon," he said. Roy checked Netty's eyes, saw no optimism there. He glanced at the eyes of the other nurse; she was thinking about something else.

But that wasn't the main point. The main point was— He wrote the main point and underlined it twice: *3 days is no good.*

Netty leaned over, patted his hand. Hers was warm, and much more—almost like a creature of its own; Netty had life in her, and to spare.

"It must be strange," Dr. Chu said, "three days, somewhat blank. But . . ." He paused, his mouth slightly open, waiting perhaps for some hopeful phrase.

"What's passed is past," Netty said.

"Exactly," said Dr. Chu. "We must deal with the present."

Roy wrote: *I have to get home.*

"Of course," said Dr. Chu.

Today.

"Well," said Dr. Chu. He checked one of the machines. "That may not . . ."

"But if you're worried about home, Roy—don't," said Netty. "Everything's under control."

He turned to her.

"That policeman called," she said. "Sergeant Boudreau? I took the message." She fished a pink sheet of notepad paper from her pocket and handed it to Roy.

Roy read: *Sgt. Boudreau—Ethan V. Everything OK. Talk when you're back. Customer came by. Took care of it. Get well.*

Customer? His whole plan—wearing a wire, backup from Freddy—was falling apart; had fallen apart already. He had to act, this minute. Roy tried to sit up, tried and succeeded. So many tubes sticking into him: he went after the one in the crook of his elbow for starters.

"Now, Roy," said Netty, and she lowered him gently back down, Roy resisting with all his strength.

The effort wiped him out. His eyes closed. He forced them open, forced himself to pick up the pad, to write: *am I on the cocktail?*

"Not quite time for the next cycle, Roy," said Dr. Chu. "You know the procedure."

Roy wrote: *hook it up.*

Dr. Chu watched him, said nothing. Roy's eyes closed again. *Hook it up, you son of a bitch. Can't you see I need the warriors? Hook it up.*

He awoke in the night, the room dark, machines beeping softly. Something strange, but what? It took him a while to figure it out: he was feeling pretty good, pain-free, even a bit hungry. Plus he was breathing on his own. Roy let out a sigh. Ah. He took in a deep breath—maybe not that deep, but deep enough. Anyone who could breathe like that would live a long, long time. Was he back on the cocktail? Had to be. Dr. Chu had given in. Roy looked around, trying to identify which overhead plastic bag held the cocktail. At that moment the door opened.

A man stood in the doorway, silhouetted in the light from the hall. He wore a white coat, had a stethoscope around his neck.

"I'm awake," Roy said. It came out funny. He cleared his throat, tried again. It came out better this time.

The man entered, wheeling a gurney. "How are you feeling?" he said.

"Good," said Roy. "Who are you?"

"The night PA," the man said, coming to the side of the bed, looking down.

"What's PA?"

"Physician's assistant."

"Why are you wearing a mask?" Roy said.

"Just came from the OR," said the night PA.

"Oh," said Roy.

The night PA checked the tubes; actually, Roy noticed, there was now only one still connected.

"I'm a little hungry," he said.

"We can stop by the snack machine on the way down," said the night PA.

"Down where?" Roy said.

"Radiology," said the night PA. "The doctor's ordered up some tests."

"Dr. Chu?"

The night PA nodded, at the same time hooking the IV bag to a post on the gurney.

"Now?" said Roy. "In the middle of the night?"

"The machines go twenty-four/seven."

"Dr. Chu never mentioned anything," Roy said.

The night PA unhooked a clipboard from the end of the bed. "It's on the chart," he said.

"Okay," said Roy.

The PA pushed the gurney against the bed. He bent over Roy. "I'll just slide you over," he said.

"That's all right," Roy said. "I can do it myself."

A simple little thing, shifting his body a foot or two: but he'd forgotten about his left arm.

"Let me—"

"I can do it," said Roy. And he did; the only drawback being that the effort awoke the demon. Roy felt no pain, was just aware that the demon was up and around.

"Comfortable?" said the night PA. Green light from one of the beeping machines reflected in his eyes.

Roy nodded.

"Then we're off."

The gurney started moving, out the door, down a hall, into an elevator, out. Roy watched different ceilings go by: water stains all over the place, like the whole place was leaking noxious-colored stuff. The gurney came to a stop.

"Snickers, M&M's, Doritos, Twizzlers," said the night PA.

"Snickers," said Roy. "And maybe the Doritos, too."

Change clanked into the machine.

"I'll pay you back," Roy said.

"My treat."

Snacks thumped into the receptacle. The night PA handed them to Roy.

"Can I eat now?" Roy said.

"Why not?"

"I thought maybe with the tests . . ."

"Not these kind," said the night PA.

They rolled on, around a corner and into a poorly lit hall, then through a door that opened with a pneumatic hiss and into a big space, dim and cold, concrete ceiling. Kind of like a parking garage, Roy thought as he unwrapped one end of the Snickers bar and took a bite.

"Good?" said the night PA.

"Good," said Roy, taking another bite. "Want some?"

They stopped again. The night PA knocked on something. Roy raised his head, craned around to look. They were a few feet from the rear doors of an ambulance. The doors opened.

"But—" Roy said.

"PET scan's in the annex," said the night PA.

"What's a PET scan?" said Roy.

A man in the ambulance said, "On three. One, two, three."

The gurney rose, slid into the ambulance. The doors closed.

"All set," said the man in the back of the ambulance, a doctor, perhaps: he wore a nice tweed jacket.

"What's a PET scan?" Roy said again.

The ambulance started up, drove into the night. The man in the tweed jacket turned to him. For a moment, the fight went clean out of Roy, leaving him hollow.

The man said: "I believe it's a powerful scanning tool."

Roy didn't say anything at first. His insides recovered a little. He said: "Do you even have a real name?"

"Tom Parish is real enough for now."

Thirty

Roy's chart lay on the gurney. Tom Parish picked it up, gave it a quick glance, then sat in a built-in seat in the sidewall and went over the whole thing page by page. It was quiet in the ambulance, nothing to hear but pages turning and rain pitter-pattering on the roof. After a while, eyes still on the chart, Tom said, "What does *unresectable* mean?"

"Look it up," Roy said.

Tom glanced at him, an interested sort of glance, as though Roy had made a mildly unexpected remark, then went back to his reading. "You're right," he said, almost to himself. "Former classics major gets lazy. Let's see, *resect* must derive from the past participle of the Latin *resecare*, 'to cut out,' and therefore"—a proud smile flitted across his face—"*unresectable* refers to that which cannot be cut out, in layman's terms, inoperable." Now his gaze moved to Roy. "Where the heck did you come in contact with all that asbestos?"

"*Inoperable* doesn't mean nothing can be done," Roy said.

Tom waved the chart in the air; a page fell out, wafted to the floor. Tom didn't seem to notice. "I understand that," he said. The ambulance sped up. "Anything can be tried, at least."

"Pick that up," Roy said.

Tom didn't appear to hear him. He kept reading, sighing once or twice. "I'm starting to get this," he said. "Amazingly bad run of luck, all around, this sequence of events. Like serendipity in reverse."

"What are you talking about?"

"We didn't know what the hell was going on," Tom said. "There's nothing more unsettling."

"Who is we?" Roy said.

"I think you know the answer to that," Tom said.

"Let's hear it from you."

Tom went back to the chart. His eyes moved back and forth. Roy checked the IV bag—still about one-third full. No one had actually said he was on the cocktail, but Roy knew, just from how his strength was coming back. Tom, still sitting with the chart, crossed his legs, got more comfortable. That maddened Roy.

"Who stabbed Paul Habib?" he said.

Not looking up, Tom said, "Now how would you know to ask a question like that?"

Roy didn't answer. A siren sounded in the distance. It grew louder and louder. His first thought: Dr. Chu. A brilliant man, much smarter than Tom Parish: Wasn't it possible that Dr. Chu had reacted this quickly? Now the siren was blaring, right on top of them. Tom didn't seem concerned, didn't even look up from the chart. All that proved was his arrogance and stupidity. In a second or two, the ambulance would be pulled over. Roy readied his story: *You can start by arresting him for kidnapping, but there's much more. And it goes high up, all the way to—*

Then came what Roy wasn't ready for—a Doppler effect—and the siren moved on. After a minute or two, he couldn't hear it at all. There was just the rain on the roof, and maybe some faint music.

"No need to answer," Tom said. He stuck Roy's chart under his arm and rose. "The only real question is how long it will take you to die of this thing." He opened the door to the front of the ambulance. The music grew louder: *Why block the road? It's open country*—Bob Marley, *Rebel Music,* one of Roy's favorites. Tom climbed through, paused, turned his head: "When I say I understand how we got here, it doesn't mean I'm happy with you," he said. "Lenore won't be easy to replace." He closed the door. Bob Marley faded away.

Roy lay on the gurney, watching the level slowly dip in the IV bag—an almost indiscernible flow. Probably a good sign, this slowness: he pictured his body so full of Dr. Chu's microscopic warriors that reinforcements were all jammed up, couldn't get through, like a crush of fans at the turnstiles for a big ball game. But he felt better with every fraction of every lowering millimeter. How could feeling better be faked? It either was or wasn't. And feeling better, regaining strength, was his secret weapon: like Samson, with his hair growing back. He took a deep breath—yes, deep, to the bottom of his lungs—and realized that nothing was actually holding him down to the gurney.

Roy sat up. That took longer than he would have thought, and he was a bit breathless for a moment or two, but wasn't all that from being flat on his back for three days? He shifted around on the gurney, got his feet on the floor. Not just three days on his back, but three days utterly lost and gone. He couldn't let that happen again.

Roy placed his hands on the gurney, braced himself, pushed off, rose. Things went cloudy at once, and he felt much too tall. He swayed back and forth, reached out frantically for a handhold—the motion so violent and clumsy it ripped the IV out of his arm—and caught himself on the gurney. Roy clung to it. After a moment or two, his head cleared. He listened for sounds from the front of the ambulance, sounds of movement or alarm, heard nothing but the rain. Roy straightened up and stepped away from the gurney.

Down a goal in hockey, there was always that tough question of when to pull your goalie for the extra attacker. Most coaches in Roy's experience, hoping to avoid the risk of that empty net, waited until a minute or less remained, but way back in the PeeWees he'd had a coach—Mr. Blenny, of Blenny's Hardware—who sometimes made the switch with even seven or eight minutes left on the clock. Mr. Blenny would tap his big red nose. *I smell the way this is goin', boys, and it stinks.*

Roy smelled the way it was going. He looked around for some sort of weapon, but the first thing his gaze fell on was the sheet of paper that had dropped from his chart. He stooped—his body stiff, like an old man's, but whose body wouldn't be after three days supine?—and picked it up. The page was mostly blank. His name was typed at the top, along with the date of one of those lost days. Other than that there was nothing but a short handwritten notation, signed *C. G. Chu, MD.* The notation: *Re coma: if patient emerges, make aware of DNR protocol.*

DNR protocol? What was that? And: *if patient emerges? If?* Plus: *coma?* He'd been in an official coma? Roy glanced over at the IV bag, the line now dangling free, the needle just touching the floor. If he had been in an official coma—and Roy didn't really believe it— the fact that he was now on his feet, strength returning by the minute, was due to Dr. Chu's cocktail. It had the power to keep him alive, maybe not forever, but for long enough.

Roy moved silently to the back of the ambulance, peered between the slats of the blinds that covered the window, hoping to see where he was, or at least gauge the speed. He saw nothing—not night and darkness, but nothing. It took him a moment or two to realize that the glass was painted black. Blinds over a blacked- out window: that summed things up pretty well.

Two cabinets stood along one side of the ambulance. Storage cabinets, probably full of bandages, medicine, oxygen bottles: unreasonable to expect scalpels, say, but not scissors, and scissors would do. Roy turned the latch on the nearest storage cabinet, pulled it open.

The cabinet was shallow, all the shelves empty except for the top one. Three little objects lay there, all familiar, Exhibits A, B, C: Paul Habib's pay stub; the Operation Pineapple photo; and the photo of Habib with Calvin Truesdale. They'd broken into his truck: no surprise.

Roy opened the second cabinet, found just a single object, up high. A pewter urn: the remains of Paul Habib. The implications froze him for a moment or two: *Now how would you know to ask a question like that?*

"You're up."

Roy wheeled around. Tom was back, the door to the front now open. "Must have misread the chart," he said. "I didn't think this was a possibility."

"Everything all right?" called another man, up front.

"Yes," said Tom. "Just drive the goddamn thing." He closed the door. "You're not supposed to be capable of getting up."

Roy said nothing.

Tom glanced at the urn. "Know what she said when we came?"

"No."

" 'I was starting to believe this would never happen.' " Tom shook his head, as though moved. "Not her fault," he said. "I don't feel particularly good about that. But Paul was that special kind of weakling who can't keep his mouth shut. He failed to protect her. She ended up knowing too much, and, since she was smart, knowing that she knew too much, all these years."

"As opposed to me," Roy said.

"As opposed to you formerly," Tom said. "You knew nothing."

"Because Delia protected me?"

"Oh, yes," Tom said. "She was very protective of you—haven't you cottoned on to that yet? But now is different—chain of bad luck, as I mentioned."

"I don't believe she worked with you," Roy said. "Or anyone like you."

"That's a testament to her value," said Tom.

Roy still didn't believe. "I want to hear it from her."

Tom gave him a funny look. "I'm sure that would be nice," he said. "But, among other things, you're in no position to make demands of any kind."

The ambulance went around a bend. The urn bumped against the wall, then settled. "Tell me about the fiasco," Roy said.

"Fiasco?"

"Operation Pineapple."

"What would be the point?"

"Meaning you're afraid to tell me," Roy said.

"I wouldn't go that far," Tom said. A few tiny pink spots appeared on his face, as though a blush were trying to break through. "Call it a habit of caution."

"That's the way you see yourself?" Roy said. "Cautious?"

"Very much so—that's the whole point of everything we do," said Tom. "Why not climb back on the gurney?"

Instead, Roy took the Operation Pineapple photo off the shelf. "Where is this place? North Africa?"

Tom watched him.

"Is it a fort?" Roy said. "Or maybe a prison."

Tom smiled, a faint smile, not happy and quickly gone. "You're good, Roy. Maybe you missed your calling."

That annoyed Roy. He went to stick the photo in his pocket; at that moment, realizing he wore hospital pajamas. But there was a chest pocket. He slid the Operation Pineapple photo inside.

"The gurney, Roy."

Roy didn't move. "What happened at the prison?" he said.

Without turning his back, Tom tapped on the door to the front of the ambulance.

"Whatever it was involved a helicopter," Roy said.

"Oh?"

"According to Westie," Roy added. "Helicopters are big in this story."

Tom's face darkened. The door opened. A hand reached out, passed Tom a gun; like the others—short barrel, wooden grip—as though they'd bought in bulk, qualified for a discount.

"The preferred outcome," Tom said, "would be death from this . . . mesothelioma—am I pronouncing that right?"

"If it was a prison," Roy said, "were you trying to get someone out? Someone else who worked at the Institute, maybe from an earlier fiasco?"

"That's the artistic imagination at work," Tom said.

"Or . . ." Roy thought of the Mad River Fair. "Or was it the other way around?"

"The other way around?" Tom said.

Roy didn't want to voice it.

"Go on," Tom said. "You've got my attention."

And just from that, Roy knew he was on the right track: not a friend in the prison yard, but an enemy. "Was there someone down there you wanted killed?" he said.

"What kind of someone would that have been?" said Tom.

Roy didn't know. Were the North African countries considered allies or not? And the prisoners of those countries, whose side were they on?

"See how intricate this gets?" Tom said. "Let's just say he's a very bad guy."

"The helicopter flew in over the prison yard and Delia was the . . ." What was the word: shooter? assassin?

"Exactly," said Tom. "But the failure of the mission had nothing to do with her. She was, as they say, a consummate professional."

"You're lying," Roy said.

"Lenore to the power of ten," said Tom.

That brought back the icy-cold anger. "She was an economist," Roy said.

"And a fine one," Tom said. "But her role grew."

"I'll need to hear that from her."

"You believe in the afterlife?" Tom said. He gestured with the gun. "Lie back down on the gurney, Roy. I'm asking nicely."

Mr. Blenny was right. If you were going to lose, then at least lose on the attack. Roy moved toward the gurney. It stood in the middle of the ambulance, one wheel set against a rubber block. Roy put his hands on the back end of the gurney, toed the rubber block out of the way with a tiny movement of his foot. Then he gathered himself, like a weak, sick person about to try something physically taxing. That took very little acting on his part.

"Need some help?" said Tom.

"No," Roy said. He bent his knees as though to boost himself up, breathed in.

"Sure?" said Tom.

Roy nodded. He drew the gurney a few inches toward his chest. A quick glance at Tom: he had the gun down now, wrapped up in Roy's struggle to get on the gurney, a spectator's expression on his face. Roy didn't like that. He shoved the gurney forward with all the strength he had.

The gurney didn't fly across the floor, but at least it moved. Plus Roy caught a bit of luck: the ambulance braked suddenly, knocking Tom off balance just as the gurney struck him. He fell. Roy, coming as hard as he could after the gurney, fell, too, but right on top of Tom.

Tom still had the gun. Roy grabbed his wrist, tried to grab it with both hands, but his right arm was all tangled up in something—the IV tube. And his left was no good. The next thing he knew Tom had flipped him over, like he weighed nothing at all, had the strength of a child. Roy hit the floor. The impact knocked what breath he had right out of his body. Tom crouched over him, straddling Roy's chest. He raised the gun.

"It didn't have to be like this," he said. "We envisioned something more humane."

Fuck you. But Roy lacked the strength to say it, to go out the way he wanted.

Tom pointed the gun at the center of Roy's forehead. Roy felt a tiny prickle, right where the bullet was going to strike. At that moment, as the gun went off, or just before, the ambulance leaned around another bend and the urn tipped from the shelf and fell, bouncing off Tom's shoulder. The gun fell and rattled across the floor. Tom rolled toward it. Roy rolled, too, the IV tube still wrapped around his right arm; and the end of it, with the needle, now in his hand. They were both on their knees, Tom reaching for the gun, when Roy jabbed the needle toward Tom's eyes.

"Don't move," he said. "It's contagious."

"No," said Tom. But he looked terrified. He threw a punch, wild and spasmodic, grazing the side of Roy's head—only grazing, but with the way Roy was now, even that had the power to make him dizzy. Roy slumped forward. The IV needle sank into Tom's neck, all of Roy's deadweight behind it.

When Roy's head cleared—maybe just a few seconds later—there was blood all over the place, and more spurting from Tom's neck. Roy rose, picked up the gun.

"Where is she?" he said.

Tom watched him, said nothing. Or was it just that Tom's eyes were locked in his direction? Roy realized the ambulance wasn't moving. The door to the front swung open and the driver, a man Roy had never seen, looked in.

"What the hell?" he said, saw the gun and ducked back into the front, slamming the door shut. Roy heard him say, "Bus one to base. Bus one to base. Code red. Code red."

Roy didn't know what any of that meant. All he knew was that no one good would be answering the driver's call. He found the IV bag, opened the back doors of the ambulance and climbed out.

Nighttime, and the Washington Monument again in view. Roy, clutching the IV bag to his chest, found himself on a Georgetown street lined with bars and restaurants, all deserted at this hour. But around the corner, a long line of kids waited at the door of a late-night club. His pajamas attracted some attention, all favorable. Roy borrowed a phone and made a couple calls, Jerry first. He felt pretty good—he had Mr. Blenny on his side; Mr. Blenny and maybe hockey itself.

Thirty-One

ROY VALOIS, SCULPTOR, DIES AT 46
by Richard Gold and Myra Burns

R oy Valois, a sculptor whose large works are displayed in many public spaces around the United States and at several prominent museums, died yesterday at his home in Ethan Valley, Vermont. He was 46.

The cause was mesothelioma, a cancer related to asbestos exposure, according to Dr. Chan Gao Chu of the Johns Hopkins University Hospital, where Mr. Valois had been undergoing treatment.

The self-taught Mr. Valois worked almost exclusively with recovered materials, usually scrap metal, but he was "no primitive," according to Kurt Palmateer, former head of the Mass MoCA Museum in North Adams, Mass., where the first sculpture in what became Mr. Valois's *Neanderthal* series is part of the permanent collection. "There is a sense of refinement and a deep formal concern that, if anything, connects him to Henry Moore and even to neoclassicists of the nineteenth century," said Mr. Palmateer.

Roy Valois was born in the western Maine town of North Grafton. He went to local schools, where he excelled at sports, eventually entering the University of Maine on a hockey scholarship. But it was while working at a summer job that involved welding and other metalwork that Mr. Valois found his true calling. His first piece, now standing in front of the public library in North Grafton, was built in his off-hours during the summer of his junior year in college. Made from brass fixtures salvaged from a sunken freighter and titled *Finback*, the piece attracted the attention of Professor Anna Cohen of the University of Maine art department, and led eventually to a two-year fellowship at Georgetown University.

It was there that Mr. Valois began to attract the attention of collectors. Prices for several works in the *Neanderthal* series—"a tragic epic in scrap steel," in the words of the critic Hilton Kramer—have topped $100,000. It was also at Georgetown that Mr. Valois met his wife, Delia Stern, an economist later employed by the United Nations. She died in an airplane crash off Venezuela fifteen years ago. They had no children and Mr. Valois never remarried. He is survived by his mother, Edna Valois, of Sarasota, Florida.

"**Mom?**" Roy said. "Sorry to call so late."

"That's all right, Roy. I was up anyway. Something the matter? Sounds like you're still fighting that cold."

"Everything's all right, Mom." He had a printout of the obituary in his hand, still hours before the morning edition of the paper hit the streets. "I just wanted to give you a heads-up."

"Don't tell me you made another big score."

"In a different way," Roy said.

"Losing me, son."

"You'll be hearing an"—how to put this?—". . . odd story about me tomorrow. It's a kind of experiment—an artistic experiment. Don't believe it for a second. But I want you to play along."

"What kind of story?"

Roy told her.

She was silent for a moment or two. "How is this a big score?"

"Shouldn't have put it that way," Roy said.

"Is it what they call that performance art?"

"Not really. I'll explain later."

Another silence. "Maybe till then I just won't answer the phone," his mother said.

"**How did that go?**" Turk said.

They rode in Turk's Caddy—Turk driving, Freddy Boudreau up front beside him, Roy in back. "Not so good," he said. "She's worried."

"Me too," said Freddy; although he sounded like he was having a good time. He cracked open a beer, passed it back to Roy. Roy took a sip, more than he wanted, but just the feel of the cold can in his hand was nice. They crossed the Texas state line. Freddy hadn't smoked a single cigarette the whole way. Roy shifted around, lay on his side, a position the demon liked, for now. It was good to be with guys from the team. Who else could he trust? He rested his head on the IV bag.

"**I was wrong.**"

Those were the first words Freddy spoke when he arrived in D.C. with the Caddy. Turk had flown down ahead of him; in fact, been on a plane a few hours after Roy's call the night of the ambulance ride. Freddy had gone over the call records on Skippy's cell phone, printed out the three saved photos—a chocolate doughnut with sprinkles, the girl from Dunkin' Donuts, the *Delia* sculpture—dusted the phone for prints and finally gotten around to checking the record function. "Turned out to be a pretty smart kid," Freddy said, pressing a button. "This first voice is the wine-store woman?"

Just sit down on that bunk—we're not going to hurt you.

Roy nodded. "Lenore."

Yeah? Skippy: his voice not quite steady, but that might have been from the way the cold wind blew up at the mountain hut, and that light windbreaker of his. *Then why is he pointing that gun at me?*

Just sit. We'll have a little talk, that's all.

Um. I don't think so. Then a pause. *The gun. It's like that other one. Hey. It was you guys.*

What was? Westie.

Planted the gun. Got me in trouble. How come?

Nothing personal. We'll make it up to you. How does five hundred dollars sound?

Get away.

Click.

"Autopsy report came back—he was strangled," Freddy said. "A smart kid."

"And brave," said Turk.

Roy didn't speak. For the first time in his life he felt murderous.

"How're you doin', Roy?"

"Good."

"Want anything?"

"Nope."

He had everything, there in the backseat of Turk's Caddy—not the cooler full of sandwiches and drinks, no longer needed, or the bottle of seized OxyContins Freddy had borrowed from the station, pills that made him a bit stupid and that the demon shrugged aside anyway—but the mismatched pair of shin pads, lying on the floor; a "Kings of the Penalty Box" T-shirt balled up beside it; and the rumble of the road. So many hockey road trips, going way back, so many long rides: he remembered the second-string goalie at Maine, a quiet kid who, without any warning, had mooned a passing state police cruiser on the turnpike.

"What's funny?" Turk said.

"Nothing," said Roy. His eyes closed. The demon napped, too.

Roy sat up. It looked hot out there. He didn't like that, not in winter.

"Where are we?"

"Near San Antonio," Freddy said.

Roy's heart sped up, beating very fast and light. That must have been nervousness, anticipation, excitement. Roy tried to calm himself, tried to save his strength.

"Been getting some calls about the funeral," said Turk. "Including Dr. Chu."

"Dr. Chu wants to come to the funeral?"

"I told him we're thinking of a memorial service in a month or two," Turk said. "I kept it vague. He gave me all his numbers."

That was nice. They'd considered letting Dr. Chu in on the truth, but decided against—partly to protect the plan, partly to protect Dr. Chu. Freddy had called Dr. Chu, telling him that Roy must have checked himself out of the hospital and gone home, where Freddy found the body. Turk had called the *New York Times*, spoken to the reporter Myra Burns, told her about Dr. Chu in case she needed to do any fact-checking for the obit. Same MO applied to Krishna: no one would have to do any acting. It was all working perfectly, a leak-proof plan.

"Whenever it is," Roy said, "I'm not going."

Laughter from the front seat of the Caddy. Roy laughed, too, even though it was his own joke, and for a moment this could have been anytime in road trips past; except for that heartbeat, soaring to heights unknown.

Turk's phone rang. "Yeah?" he said. His voice changed. "Oh, hi." He was quiet for a moment or two. "Yes," he said. "It's terrible." He listened some more.

"Sorry," he said. "Don't know the answer to that." Roy thought he heard crying on the other end. "I'll be in touch," Turk said. "Take care of yourself." He clicked off.

"Who was that?" Roy said.

"Aw, you don't want to know."

"Who?"

"Jen."

Silence in the car.

"Hell," said Freddy. "Didn't see that one coming."

Neither had Roy. And that probably proved that Jen had been right: something in him got damaged—in a helicopter crash that hadn't taken place in Venezuela, maybe hadn't taken place at all. But Jen was wrong that some feeling part had been wiped out; instead those nerve ends were still there, but now mixed up, twisted, unreliable. A deformation that had actually improved his work? That was possible.

"What didn't you know the answer to?" Roy said.

Turk turned. Roy, lying on his side, looked up at him. "How long you knew about it," Turk said. "The diagnosis." Turk's eyes shifted away. "In terms of when the two of you split up."

"I'll—" Roy was about to say *I'll make it right with her*. But would he? And in what way? He was going to see Delia, and soon.

"Get some rest, Roy," Turk said.

Roy closed his eyes. Turned out that death didn't simplify your life. How many people had been in a position to learn that one?

He awoke in darkness. A soft breeze was blowing. Roy sat up.

"Good timin'," said Freddy, from the front seat.

They were in the Caddy, parked in the middle of some vast landscape, windows down, lights off. Roy thought he could make out a line of rounded hills in the distance.

"How're you doing?" Turk said.

"Good."

"Better eat something."

"Yeah." But he wasn't hungry.

A light appeared in the sky, faint at first, soon brighter and brighter. Ten or twenty seconds passed; then more lights flashed on, these on the ground and not far away—a yellow one that illuminated a small square building, plus two long parallel strings of glowing blue. Now Roy could hear it: first a faint buzz, then a growing drone, finally a roar overhead. The plane made a semicircle, came in low, landed at the end of the string of lights, kicking up clouds of blue dust, and rolled to a stop near the yellow-lit building, propellers motionless.

Silence. The soft breeze blew. Now it had a faint gasoline smell.

Doors opened in the building and the plane. Columns of lights spilled out; human silhouettes moved in and out of them. They got busy at the rear of the plane, in a while hoisted their long, lumpy cargo onto the blades of a big forklift truck. Motor throbbing low, the forklift drove slowly past the building, dull headlight glinting on the chain-link fence of a small compound. The silhouettes moved around some more. Then the lights started going off: forklift, blue runway strings, in the building. After a minute or two of darkness, other lights flashed on behind the building. Two big SUVs that had been blocked from view swung around the compound and headed toward the distant hills, their taillights fading, fading and gone. The moon rose, here and there adding some shine to the night.

"Okey-doke," said Freddy.

Turk switched on the parking lights; the Caddy bumped across scrubby desert, stopping by the chain-link compound. A metal plaque on the door read property of truesdale ranch—keep out. The plane, not far away, had writing on the fuselage, just visible in the moonlight: vrai transport. They stepped out of the car.

"Gotta piss," said Freddy.

They pissed against the chain-link fence, a fence about eight feet high, topped with barbed wire. Roy felt that bladder pressure meaning he had to, but hardly anything came out. Turk's and Freddy's piss made splashing sounds on the hardpacked ground.

"Ah," said Freddy.

The forklift stood only a few yards away on the other side. Its long, lumpy load lay sideways on the forks, a tarpaulin cover tied down to a plywood platform at the ends. Freddy walked around to the compound gate, rattled the padlock, shook his head. Turk opened the trunk of the Caddy, took out an aluminum ladder.

He extended the ladder until it topped the barbed wire, climbed up, pivoted around while hanging on to the highest rung and dropped down on the other side. Then Freddy, same thing. And last, Roy. He climbed up, no problem except for the breathlessness that made him take one short break halfway up. But at the top, he had some trouble with the pivoting part, mostly on account of that left arm. Roy lost his grip and fell. Turk caught him—gentle, absorbing all the shock—and lowered him to the ground.

"That wasn't necessary," Roy said.

"I know," said Turk.

They walked over to the forklift truck. Freddy untied one of the ends of the tarp. Roy reached in, felt cold steel, twisted and braided: the rotor blades that filled the broken arch on *Delia*. He turned and nodded.

"Hey," said Freddy. "This could work."

"Why not?" Turk said, his eyes full of moonlight. "It's a classic."

"How's that?" said Freddy.

"From Homer," Turk said.

Freddy shrugged. "Don't have time for TV."

Life could be sweet.

They rolled the tarp back, sat on the plywood platform. The moon rose higher. The air turned colder, as though the moon's power reversed the sun. Roy breathed a little better. Was he beginning to prefer the night?

"How're you doing?" Turk said.

"Good," said Roy.

Freddy reached into his jacket pocket. "Take this," he said. "You just press the button."

"Okay."

"Try it now," said Turk. "Just for practice."

"I know how to press a button," Roy said.

"Three-mile radius," Freddy said.

"And if you're out of range?" Roy said.

"Not gonna happen," said Freddy.

"So," said Turk, "that just leaves us with—"

"Yeah," said Freddy. "The hammer." He laughed, and so did Turk. Roy laughed a little, too: as though the three of them had cooked up a tricky play in the locker room between periods and were now going to stick it to some overweening team. Turk took out his cell phone, scrolled through some programmed numbers, dialed one.

"Myra Burns?" he said. "Who cowrote the obituary on Roy Valois?" Turk listened for a moment. "Yeah, I know it's late, but he wants to say hello."

Roy lay on the platform. Turk and Freddy tied the tarp back down.

"Doin' okay?"

"Good."

"Get some rest."

"Yup." He had to rest, had to save his strength for what lay ahead, to reach the finish line before it reached him.

"Don't forget the button."

Footsteps moved away, crunching once or twice on the dried-up vegetation. Then came a clink—the ladder knocking against the chain-link fence—and finally the Caddy, a low, throaty murmur that faded quickly away. After that it was very quiet. Roy, on his side in that comfortable position, just breathed. He felt *Delia*, hard and cold, against his back. What would he say? *Hi, baby, it's been a long, long time?* Sounded like a line from one of those old songs she liked. He shifted his body, getting closer to her. His heart took off on one of those high and rising flights it was starting to like.

Thirty-Two

"This is a disgrace."

Roy opened his eyes. For a moment he didn't know where he was, all breathless and closed in, as though buried alive. The urge to thrash around came right away, but that voice, a voice he knew, brought him back.

"An appalling disgrace," Krishna was saying. "Are you seriously asking me to believe that a work of art of this stature was left unguarded the entire night?"

"Well," said a man, "the orders didn't say nothin' about no guard."

"And," said another man, "this here is a secure area. Lookit that barbwire."

"Anyways," said a third, "no harm done."

"Oh?" said Krishna. "And how can we be sure?"

"Well," said the first man, "there it is. Just take a gander."

"I intend to," Krishna said. "Please untie that end."

"This here end?"

"If you'll be so good," said Krishna.

Roy shrank closer to *Delia,* wedged himself under a low curve of twisted rads. Then came a flapping sound and blinding daylight flooded in. Roy glimpsed, as though at the end of a tunnel, a dim yet somehow natty figure. Just as his eyes were adjusting—he made out Krishna's face, so unhappy today—the tarpaulin fell and darkness returned.

"So," said the first man. "Everything okay?"

No response from Krishna.

"Those kinda looked like rads in there," said the second man.

"Thought it was s'posed to be art," said the third. "Ain't it, Mr., ah . . ."

"Let us now load it with great care on the truck, gentlemen," said Krishna. "I will follow in the limo. Thirty miles per hour, please, and no more."

"How much is it worth, anyhow?"

"That," said Krishna, in a tone Roy had never heard from him before, "is not the point."

"What's the point?"

"Respect."

A minute or two later, the chain-link door clinked open and Roy was in motion—a short bumpy ride on the forklift; then a pause, and a scraping slide; followed by the shriek of released air brakes and they were rolling. A deep thrumming vibration rose up through the floor of the truck and the wooden platform where he lay; an easy, gentle thrumming, like a massage, but the demon didn't like it. Roy tried to find a position they could both live with. He had a crazy thought, how he was now on a secret mission, a kind of Operation Pineapple of his own—only his would make things right. Delia had had Paul Habib; he had the demon.

After a while, Roy felt the truck slowing down—pressing *Delia* against him—and then stopping. He heard voices, too faint to distinguish the words. Then someone banged on the truck body, not far from Roy, and they were rolling again. The road seemed smoother. The demon, like a resistant and colicky baby taken for a ride, finally gave in and napped. Although he'd just slept all night, Roy felt worn out. He took the IV bag from under his shirt, uncapped it and drank what was left. Then he napped, too.

"What a nice space."

Roy awoke: no longer in motion. He smelled flowers.

"So glad you like it," said Calvin Truesdale. "The roof is retractable, by the way."

Roy felt in his pocket, touched the button on Freddy's wireless transmitter; didn't press it—just made sure he knew it was there.

"Have you considered a setting for the piece?" Krishna said.

"The alcove," said Truesdale. "Knew it the moment I first laid eyes on her."

"Even before Roy made up his mind to sell?" said Krishna.

Truesdale laughed. "I never quite fell for that line. So many of these artists turn out to have a shrewd side."

"Not Roy."

"You knew him better, of course. And he must have been quite sick when I met him, surely not himself."

"I think he was very much himself toward the end."

"Oh? In what way?"

"How he handled it," Krishna said.

"Possibly," said Truesdale. He sighed. "Such a tragedy."

Krishna said nothing.

"When is the funeral?" Truesdale said.

"There's talk of a memorial service," said Krishna. "Nothing is set."

"Please keep me informed."

"You'd like to go?"

"If possible. But I'd certainly want to send flowers."

A silence.

"Interest you in something to eat or drink?" Truesdale said. "Tour of the ranch?"

"Very kind," said Krishna. "But—"

"Or even better," said Truesdale, "we're having a party tonight—that's where most everyone is right now, setting up tents by the river. Steer roast, some ropin' and ridin', fireworks off the barge—why don't you stay for that?"

"What's the occasion?" said Krishna.

Truesdale laughed. "Nothing, really," he said. "I'm just in the mood for a little shindig, is all, kick up my heels."

"I have to be in New York for dinner," Krishna said; his tone suddenly going cold, very unlike him, in Roy's experience.

"Then I'll say good-bye," Truesdale said. "Pleasure doing business with you."

"And with you as well."

"I'll walk you to your car."

"Not necessary."

"No trouble."

Footsteps moved off. When Truesdale spoke again, he was farther away, almost inaudible. "Any predictions on how the market's going to treat his work in the next five, ten years?"

A door closed on Krishna's reply.

A minute or two went by. Roy heard nothing but the distant neighing of a horse. He reached out, raised the edge of the tarp. The first thing he saw was a huge bronze seated woman by Henry Moore, familiar from his college textbooks. Beyond the sculpture stood a wall of tall windows, thirty feet high or more, all topped with stained-glass rosettes. Outside lay some gardens, green under a fine mist from the irrigation system, and on the far side of the gardens lay a corral. A horse with pinto markings—much smaller than the horse in Tom Parish's barn—was prancing through a series of figure eights, the rider a woman in a stylish Spanish hat with a flat crown and a round brim. There was no one else around.

The woman sat very still, upper body erect, hips barely moving with the rhythm of the horse, and maybe because of the intervening mist, seemed the more graceful part of the team, although the horse was beautiful. The way she carried herself, her body so trim, an intense concentration that was visible, at least to Roy, and so alive: he found that he'd somehow gotten off the platform, crossed the marble floor, almost unaware of the art around him, and had his face pressed to the window. And Roy knew: from the way she held her head, how the curving shadow of the hat brim fell across her face, and a thousand other little things, seen in all those dreams. He knew.

Roy looked around, frantic to get out there, caught his first good view of this space—a huge U-shaped gallery, all stone and glass, sculptures along both sides—and at the end, just past the tarp-covered platform, high double doors. Enormous doors made of marble, but they opened easily. Roy ran outside, really ran—no one around but it wouldn't have mattered. Nothing could have stopped him: momentum had shifted and he felt its push like the first wave of a slow-moving but powerful explosion, a wave he rode through the garden, mist cooling him—and he needed cooling, all at once realizing how hot he'd been—to the corral. He ducked under the railing, kept going. The rider came out of a turn, saw him and said, "Whoa, Angus," leaning back on the reins. The horse halted and leaned back, too. Horse and rider gazed down at Roy, ten feet away.

Not Delia. For one thing, this was not a woman of his own age, not a woman at all, but a teenage girl. For another thing—but there was no other thing. Roy moved forward, no longer running, now moving very slowly, taking in every detail of her face. His heart took off again. This was going to be a lucky day.

The rider looked uneasy, but only for a moment. Then she sat taller—a reaction to stress so familiar— and said, "Are you the new vet?"

And the voice: a slight Texas accent, but otherwise identical.

"No," Roy said, going closer. "I'm—"

She frowned, pushed back her hat. He could see her hair now, that same curly brown hair, flecked with gold. The light shone on her face, in her eyes: yes, those golden glints.

"Then—?" she said.

Roy caught himself gazing up at her, rapt, as though transfixed by a vision. "My name's Roy," he said. "Roy Valois."

She shrugged, a teenager's kind of shrug. He'd missed so much. "The name mean anything to you?" Roy said.

"No."

"I'm—" Roy took a breath, not deep; it made a funny rattling sound, maybe because of how keyed up he was. He sensed a tremendous victory, very soon, very near. Yes, a lucky day: he'd hardly dared to dream of a double triumph like this. "I'm looking for your mother," he said.

"My mother?" said the girl. "This must be some kind of mistake."

"Why?"

"I don't have a mother."

Roy opened his mouth, tried to speak. Nothing came out. He tried again. "No mother?"

Angus shied, backed away. "Easy," said the girl. The horse went still. "He doesn't like loud voices," she said.

"Sorry," said Roy. "No mother?"

"That's what I said." The girl reached into the vertical slit pocket of her Western shirt, offered Roy a sugar cube. "You could give him this."

Roy took the sugar cube. Their hands touched. A charge went up Roy's arm, down his spine. She had his hands, a softer, female version, but his: his own flesh and blood. There was no doubt. Roy held out the sugar cube. Angus took it between his rubbery lips.

"I have a stepgrandmother, sort of," the girl said. "Are you looking for her?"

"No," Roy said. "Your mother."

The girl shook her head. "She died."

"No."

"I told you—he doesn't like loud voices," the girl said, steadying Angus. "And what do you mean—no? Who'd know better than me? She died a long time ago."

"When?" Roy said, so low the word was barely audible. Angus's tail twitched.

"Like the exact date? I don't know—not long after I was born."

"Are you sure?"

"About what?"

"That she's dead."

The girl's chin went up; Roy remembered that, too. And the sharpening of her tone. "What kind of a question is that? It's the biggest thing that ever happened to me." She gave Angus a kick and he started to turn. Roy grabbed the reins.

"Please," Roy said. "I didn't mean to upset you."

"But you are," she said. "What do you want? Why are you asking all these questions?"

"It's the biggest thing that ever happened to me, too," Roy said.

She paused, wrists cocked to pull the reins away from him. "My mother dying?"

"Yes."

"But why?"

"I can explain," Roy said. "But first, are you telling me you never knew her?"

The girl nodded.

"Are you fifteen?" Roy said.

Another pause; then she nodded.

"And your birthday's in September."

"The twenty-first," she said. "How did you know that? Who are you, anyway?"

Roy met her gaze. "She was my wife."

"My mother was your wife?"

Roy took out his wallet. He had a photograph of Delia in a Velcro'd-off side pocket, a picture he'd never shown to anyone, just carried around, not quite forgotten: the two of them, actually, Roy and Delia standing on a beach, arms around each other, expressions on their faces quite solemn. He held the photograph up so the girl could see.

She saw. Then she slipped down off Angus, gave him a light whack, and he trotted away. She took the picture.

"This is my mother?"

No reply necessary: the resemblance did all the talking.

The girl studied the photo, her eyes unwavering. In a low voice, she said, "I've never seen a picture of her."

"How come?" said Roy. He glanced around: no one in sight.

"All her stuff got burned up in a fire." The girl looked at him. "Is this a trick picture or something? From the computer?"

"What would be the point of that?"

She thought; her face pinching slightly—that same annoyed look Delia had for puzzling through tough questions. "I guess none," the girl said. "So you were the husband before?"

"Before what?"

"My father."

"Tell me about him."

"He was a wrangler, just passing through." She shrugged. "I never knew him either."

"Who told you that?"

"I just grew up with it." She thought for a moment. "My grandfather, I guess."

"Your grandfather?"

She gestured at their surroundings—corral, gardens, private museum, sprawling ranch house, stables, outbuildings, and land, land in all directions.

"Calvin Truesdale is your grandfather? Where did you get that idea?"

"Not really my grandfather," she said. "More like adoptive. I think he felt responsible for my mother's accident."

"What accident?"

"The one that killed her—falling off this bronco they were training, which she shouldn't have been on in the first place. She was the cook."

Roy smiled.

"What's so funny?"

"She couldn't make toast," Roy said.

"Maybe she learned after you got divorced or—"

"Don't you see how thin this is, everything they told you?" Roy said, voice rising again but now Angus was safely out of hearing range. "How sketchy? There was no divorce. No cooking. No wrangler."

Her eyes went from Roy to the photo, back to Roy.

"What's your name?" Roy said.

"Adele," said the girl. "I'm named after her." But that statement ended on a slightly rising note.

"Her name was Delia," Roy said.

"Delia?" said Adele, eyes again drawn to the photo. "That's close, isn't it?"

"Yes," Roy said.

A moment or two went by. Then Adele shook her head and backed away. "I don't believe it."

Roy reached for her hand, held his next to it, side by side, made her see. "I'm your father," he said.

Adele tore her hand loose. "This can't be happening."

"A DNA test will prove it," Roy said. "But where's Truesdale? He can clear things up sooner than that."

"What do you mean?" Adele said.

"By filling us in on what happened after the last time I saw her."

"When was that?"

"When she was three months pregnant."

"She left you or something?" said Adele.

"She was taken," Roy said.

"Kidnapped?"

Roy started to say no, then stopped himself. "I'm still figuring it out," he said.

"You've been figuring it out for fifteen years?"

"I've been in the dark for fifteen years," Roy said. "I'm figuring it out now."

"So you never knew she was here?" Adele said. "Didn't know about the coma?"

"Coma?"

"She never came out of it—that was the worst part," Adele said. "She was in a coma for months before she had me."

"Truesdale told you that?"

"Another one of those things I always knew," Adele said. "But not just from hearing it," she added quickly. "I remember when I was a little kid there was medical stuff in the West End bunkhouse."

"What's that?"

"This old shack," Adele said. "All boarded up now."

"I'd like to see it."

"Can you ride?"

The demon reacted to that one.

"What's wrong?"

"Nothing," said Roy, straightening up. "I'm fine." And, in fact, some inner part, where no disease could reach, felt better than it ever had.

Thirty-Three

"Aren't you a bit young to drive?" Roy said.

Adele climbed behind the wheel of a pickup—same model as Roy's, but newer and equipped with shotgun rack and shotgun—that was parked behind the stables, keys in the ignition. "This is a ranch," she said.

She drove along a dirt track heading west, away from the main compound and toward the hills; a good driver, or at least a driver just like him, every touch of the wheel or the pedals exactly as he would have done. They crossed a grassy plain, with horses standing near a lone tree in the distance, splashed through a shallow, muddy stream and started up a long rise, the landscape turning brown and dry.

A big open four-wheeler appeared at the top of the rise, coming their way. "Security," said Adele.

Oh, not now. Roy went rigid. What had Turk and Freddy said to do if something like this happened? For a moment, Roy couldn't—

"Get down," Adele said.

Roy got down, squeezed himself onto the floor. He saw Adele's foot—she wore dusty cowboy boots, decorated with silver stars—move from the gas pedal to the brake, press down. They came to a stop.

A man said, "Hey, Adele, how's it going?"

"Not bad," said Adele. "You guys?"

"No complaints," said the man. "Lookin' forward to the party tonight?"

"Too much homework," Adele said.

"Hey, c'mon," the man said.

"All work and no play," said another, a little farther away, voice less distinct.

"Got to get going," Adele said. "But you could do me a favor—I left Angus in the corral."

"We'll put him back in the barn," said the first man.

"No problem," said the other.

"Have fun tonight," said Adele. Then she floored it, jamming the pedal to the floor. Roy heard the tires spin, felt the rear of the pickup start to swing out. She brought it back in line with ease. Behind them one of the men yelled, "Ooo-wee." The security guys liked Adele.

"You can get up now," she said.

Roy pulled himself up with just a little breathing problem, instantly disguised.

She gave him a quick sideways glance. "What happened to your arm?" she said.

"I—" He almost said *I used to play hockey,* stopping himself at the last moment. "Hockey," he said.

"Cool," she said.

How glad he was those words hadn't got out.

"Do you have allergies or something?" Adele said.

"No."

"City people come here and get allergies."

"I'm not city people," Roy said. "I live in a little town in Vermont."

"With snow?"

"Lots."

The track grew rougher. Adele dodged a deep pothole with a smooth turn of the wheel and said, "What do you do up there?"

"I'm a sculptor," Roy said. "Your— Calvin Truesdale just bought one of my pieces."

She was silent for a moment or two. "If everything you're saying—" She began, then stopped herself. "That's weird," she said.

"Isn't it?" said Roy. Two hundred and fifty grand and yet he'd suspected nothing: *who in their right mind,* as his own mother had said. Suspecting things was not his strength; that had to be clear by now.

The hills were much closer, not very high. In a fold at their base stood a small rectangular building, the only straight lines in sight. A big black bird circled high above.

"I take the art elective," Adele said.

Roy didn't understand.

"In school," she said. "There's something of mine in the glove box."

Roy opened it, took out a scrolled sheet of paper. He unrolled it: a watercolor still life—horseshoe, hammer, nails, all lying on a barrelhead in shadowy space. The nails seemed light, horseshoe heavier, hammer heaviest of all; and a nice, dull shine gleamed on the striking surface of the hammer.

"This is good," he said.

"I got a B," she said.

"A B?"

"From the teacher."

Roy laughed.

"What's funny?" she said; and he realized she had no idea how good it really was.

The track sloped up, rounded a pile of rocks, ended in front of the bunkhouse—wood siding weathered gray, plywood on the windows, a combination lock on the door. They got out of the truck: total silence and endless sky above, cloudless but not blue, as though a big dust storm had passed nearby. And not quite total silence—Roy heard a low, rhythmic rattle, didn't make the connection for a moment or two. The sound was his.

Adele walked to the door, spun the combination lock. It clicked open. She looked back at Roy. "I come out here sometimes."

They went in. Light flowed in through the doorway, and in shafts here and there from chinks in the walls. The bunkhouse was bare inside, long and narrow with nothing in it except a broom in one corner and a footstool sitting in the widest shaft of light. Roy had expected dust, cobwebs, spiders, maybe a lizard or two, but there was none of that, the whole place swept clean.

He walked to the far end. "What kind of medical stuff?" he said.

"I don't really remember," said Adele. "A hospital-type bed, maybe? Bandages? I was little."

Roy sat on the footstool, tried to imagine Delia lying here, possibly in a coma. All he knew was that Janet had seen her in the back of a limo, injured but conscious. Operation Pineapple, a fiasco, but she'd survived it: and then come—or been taken—here?

"What's that sound?" he said.

"Buzzard," said Adele. "Landing on the roof."

Roy rose, got that too-tall feeling again, fought it off. He saw initials carved into the rough, knotty-pine-board walls: SJW, BT, KLN; and some names: KING RICO, BUDDY, GATO. No Ds, no Delia. Wouldn't she have done that, left some imprint? Roy thought so.

He moved around the bunkhouse, scanning the walls. Nothing, except . . . Except, what was this? Roy knelt in the corner, near the broom. On the wall, about three feet above the floor, he saw a crude carved shape, very small, taking up no more space than a business card.

He ran his fingers over it: an upside-down *V*, but softened, and halfway up one arm a tiny box sticking out. Upside-down *V*, square box . . . like a mysterious glyph left on a cave wall by an unknown artist.

"Yeah," said Adele, coming up behind him. "I've seen that. Know what I think?"

"What?"

"It's a diagram of where we are, right here—the bunkhouse and the hills."

That made sense, some bored cowboy, lying in bed, scratching away at the walls.

"Although whoever it was got it wrong," she said.

"How do you mean?"

"The bunkhouse is at the base of the hill," she said, "not halfway up."

Roy nodded. "You've got a good—" And then it hit him. A little box halfway up: the mountain hut. "Oh, God."

"What?" said Adele.

Roy ran his fingertips over the image, again and again, as though through the sense of touch it could tell him something, like a message in Braille. And it was telling him: *If we get separated, if you can't find me.* Delia had carved this picture. He could even convince himself that he recognized her handiwork. She had no artistic ability at all.

He tapped at the wall, heard nothing behind the image that he didn't hear anywhere else. *The hiding place won't be obvious. Come on, Roy, even you knew that.* He tried to pry the plank loose. Nailed in tight: it wouldn't budge.

Had she simply been saying: *I was here?* Roy didn't know what else to think. He gave the plank one last tap, this one a bit harder, with the side of his hand. No hollow sound resulted this time either, but a knot in the plank below—two or three inches from the picture— fell out and landed at his feet, leaving a fist-size hole in the wall.

Meet me here.

Roy tried to reach in: fist size, but for a smaller fist. Adele knelt beside him, stuck her hand inside, felt around. Her hand reappeared, and in the palm she held a yellowed square of paper, folded small. Eyes wide, she gave it to Roy. His hands shook so badly he could barely unfold it.

Roy,

I knew you'd find me. I hope it's soon, not for my own sake—if you're reading this, I'm dead—but for your own, and the child's. Oh, Roy. Have you figured out about the Hobbes Institute yet? It's a clandestine service, a secret operation run out of the vice president's office, funded by a few rich Texans. Completely illegal, of course—would land the VP in jail if it got out, and impeach him if he ever makes it to the White House. Is he there yet? If so, you're in danger. After what happened they're probably erasing H.I. from existence now, or already have. Be careful, Roy. They don't have boundaries. Watch out for a woman named Lenore.

So, the obvious question—and one of the things I like—love—about you, Roy, is how you never ask them: What did she know and when did she know it?

Nothing at first. I swear. So gradual—like learning to walk. Maybe I wasn't curious enough about where the money came from. But all the work was so positive.

At first. There really was a Venezuelan project—conch fisheries. Then some negatives crept in. It's a dangerous world and will get more so, maybe has by the time you're reading this. But in the end I could only stomach so much. Maybe too much, you're thinking. The VP angle I didn't know till way too late. And I was young. I am young!

Operation Pineapple—stupid name, Tom's overdeveloped sense of irony—was going to be the end of it for me, even before it played out the way it did. I was so close to telling you, Roy! When Paul came to get me, remember, when you said he could wait five minutes? I had to bite the inside of my mouth till blood came. Maybe if you'd just said always time for bacon and eggs or what's the point of life? one more time.

There's a horrible prison down in the Moroccan desert. They're supposed to be on our side, but they were going to release this very bad guy—you may hear about him one day. I hope not. Anyway, it all went wrong. Dust storm, chopper down, all this screaming in different languages. I yanked Paul back inside the cockpit but too late—the way he looked at me when he knew he was dying, how something planned at a desk could end like this, my God. The fact that I'd been shot didn't dawn on me till we were airborne. In the head, Roy, but don't worry. They got it out—where I'm not even sure, that part's hazy—and brought me down here to recuperate. Did they feed you some line about being delayed in Venezuela? Way past that now, which tells me what I need to know about their plans. Problem is I said a few things in the heat of the moment—my true beliefs, but, Christ, I should have kept my mouth shut—and they don't trust me. Rightly so.

But I'm much stronger than they think now, and I've got an escape plan—for me and Baby, both. That's what I call her for now—Baby—till I get your input. You're going to love her, Roy. (She's got your hands.)

Keeping all this from you tore me up—please believe me. But I didn't want you hurt in any way, Roy, and yes—I was ashamed to tell you.

Forgive me.

Delia

Roy handed the letter to Adele. He went outside. The buzzard flew off the roof, rose into that dusty sky, spiraling up and up. Tears came, silent and not many. Even though she'd ended up dying on him twice, who had time for tears?

Adele came out, looked up at him. Her tears were streaming down her face. "So you're my dad, for sure?"

"I am," Roy said.

"What are we going to do?"

"You're going to stay right here," Roy said: his first parental decision.

Adele wiped her face with the back of her arm. "No way," she said.

They got in the pickup, Roy behind the wheel. He pressed the button that activated Freddy's wire. Then he read Delia's letter out loud, voice steady almost to the end. This time, on second reading, he could see how some people might find it a bit self-serving. But so what? As for forgiveness, he was the one who needed it: so many clues he'd missed, so many chances to find out. Roy knew he had failed her. He folded the letter with care and put it in his pocket.

"Is someone listening?" Adele said.

"Better be," said Roy.

Adele nodded. They seemed to understand each other without much effort. Wishful thinking? Was that so bad? He glanced at her, saw something very soft and childlike in the skin at the back of her neck, something that didn't remind him of Delia—or himself—at all.

"I don't really understand what's going on," Adele said, "but I never liked being around him, even though he's been so generous. That made me feel guilty."

"You can stop," Roy said. He wasn't going to fail her. He turned the key and drove back along the track, across the dry plain to the green oasis of the compound.

Roy parked behind the stables. "Stay here till I come for you."

"Why?"

"I'll explain then."

She looked annoyed for a second, then laughed, a lovely, unself-conscious sound. It followed him, at least in his mind, as he crossed the gardens. Beautiful gardens with all kinds of blooming flowers: Roy felt like his old self almost the whole way. But just as he came to the huge double doors of the gallery—now wide open—the demon sprang up and got its claws around his heart again, quick and sneaky, before his heart could soar away, out of reach. Then the demon gave a sharper squeeze than any in the past, as though squashing a frog. Roy gasped, doubled up, slumped behind one of the doors.

After a moment or two, the pain lessened slightly. Roy tried to take a breath—all his air gone in that gasp—and couldn't, as though his lungs were petrifying. At the same time, he heard Spanish voices. Men in work clothes came out of the gallery, lunch boxes in their hands, and took a path toward an outbuilding beyond the stables. None looked back, so no one saw him in that horrible emergency breathing position, chest stuck way out, elbows pulled way back. It worked, a little. Air entered his body, opened a miserly pathway, enough to keep going. Roy straightened and walked into Calvin Truesdale's private museum.

No sign of the tarpaulin-covered platform: *Delia* stood in her alcove, scaffolding on one side. The roof was open now and daylight flooded in. That strange dusty light gave *Delia* a sepia effect Roy didn't like. He entered the alcove, saw that she was looking out on a pond with a wide-spreading tree on the far shore. One of those buzzards was perched on an upper branch.

Footsteps sounded on the marble floor. Roy turned. Calvin Truesdale came into the alcove, a camera in his hand. He saw Roy, missed a step, staggered.

"Changed my mind," Roy said. "You can't have her." His own calmness surprised him.

"Roy?" Truesdale's mouth opened, closed, opened again. "I don't quite understand." His face hardened, composure quickly returning. "Didn't I see your obituary?" Roy said nothing; he could feel the rapid workings of Truesdale's mind. "Is this another case of not being able to believe what's in the papers?" he said. "Or—oh my goodness—you wouldn't be party to some sort of conspiracy, would you, Roy?" He glanced around. Fear on his face? Yes, if only for a second. That was nice.

"It's over," Roy said. A distant hum came through the open roof. "The Hobbes Institute, whatever you're doing now—everything's coming out."

"Supposing I knew what you were talking about—" Truesdale began, but Roy interrupted.

"You don't think Tom talked? Or Westie?" Truesdale's head came forward, an aggressive, reptilian thrust. "Or Delia?" Roy said.

Truesdale licked his lips. "Delia?"

"She wrote me a letter." Roy took it out of his pocket. "It's all here—the way you kept her prisoner, Operation Pineapple, the president."

Truesdale's eyes went to the letter. He laid the camera on a footstool. Roy backed up a step, bumped against the scaffold.

"Where did you get that?" Truesdale said.

Loose ends: they began tying themselves together in Roy's mind. "You've been wondering about that drawing on the wall for years, haven't you? Then, when Lenore started poking around in Ethan Valley, she found out about the mountain hut and you thought you'd matched things up."

"Where did you get it?" Truesdale said.

"You'll find out in court," Roy said. A remark the demon didn't seem to care for: claws twitched around Roy's heart.

"Court?" said Truesdale.

"There'll be trials," Roy said. "Lots of them."

Truesdale took another step. Backed against the scaffold, Roy had nowhere to go. "Things don't always work that way," Truesdale said. "We have enemies. I'm talking about our nation. Our nation has mortal enemies. They don't follow civilized rules. Think of the ammunition you'd be handing them, the damage to our institutions, to the presidency itself. Do you see the problem?"

But at that moment Roy felt on top of things, actually problem-free. "She was never going to walk out of that bunkhouse, was she?" he said. "You meant to kill her from the start."

"Certainly not," said Truesdale. "She was much too valuable."

"And I don't want to hear that she was the boss," Roy said.

"Everyone sees the world in a way that makes him look good—don't you know that?" Truesdale said. "Call her a midlevel manager if that makes you happier." The humming sound, louder now, divided into separate drones. Roy glanced up through the open roof, saw empty sky. When he looked back down, Truesdale had a gun in his hand. "I'll have that letter now."

"You're not touching it," Roy said.

A knuckle on Truesdale's trigger finger went yellow. Then came a blast from the muzzle. Roy felt a blow to his arm—but his left arm, not too useful these days anyway, and there was no pain. The only bad part was the fact that he'd had the letter in his left hand. It slipped free and glided across the alcove. They both went for it, but Truesdale got there first, a race not even close. He scooped it up with a surprisingly quick movement, and then the gun was leveled again at Roy.

"You made me do this," Truesdale said, as if Roy was already in the past.

The remark enraged him; the sight of the letter in Truesdale's leathery hand enraged him more. Roy was up on the balls of his feet, rocking forward, when a roar came from above, a roaring *whap-whap-whap*. They both gazed up: helicopters, lots of them. Helicopters would be the death of him, but not these: all of these helicopters bore the markings of news organizations.

Truesdale's mouth opened. Roy charged at him, not much of a charge, more of an uncontrolled stumble. Truesdale saw him coming, but too late. Roy fell against Truesdale's legs. They both went down. Truesdale's head struck the edge of one of those rads on the lower part of *Delia*, making a sound like splitting wood, audible even over all the noise from above. He didn't move after that.

The letter lay on the floor. Roy picked it up. He rose, dusted himself off, walked toward the double doors. A helicopter swept in low, a cameraman leaning out, focused on Roy. Roy gave him a smile and a little wave.

Yes, feeling problem-free. *Nothing to forgive, baby.* An idea for a brand-new piece came to him—something less massive than what he'd been doing, more along the lines of—

But at that point, the demon had had enough. It gave Roy's heart a special squeeze, to make clear the order of things, once and for all. Next, Roy was on his back, the smell of flowers all around. Was it snowing?

Faces gazed down at him: Turk, Freddy. And high above, all those helicopters. *Whap-whap-whap.* Victory—yes, a double triumph.

"Where's Adele?" he said.

"Right here," she said. She knelt beside him, stroked his forehead. Her hand, not quite steady, felt good just the same. "Help is on the way."

"Good news," said Roy. Had to be optimistic with your kid: Wasn't that basic? As for the work still undone, did it matter now? He'd rearranged the scraps of his own life, found coherence. The igloo closed in around him, those icy bricks going up awful fast, the speed superhuman. In the end there was this daughter of his, an unexpected bonus, even a blessing.